G000109627

Jay Bell Books

Something Like Summer © 2010 Jay Bell

ISBN: 979-8406376225

ALL RIGHTS RESERVED. This book may not be reproduced in whole or in part without permission. This book is a work of fiction and any resemblance to persons, living or dead, or events is purely coincidental.

SOMETHING LIKE® is a trademark registered with the U.S. Patent and Trademark Office and is the sole property of the author.

Cover art by Andreas Bell: www.ANDREASBELL.COM

-=Books by Jay Bell=-

The *Something Like...* series
#1 Something Like Summer
#2 Something Like Autumn
#3 Something Like Winter
#4 Something Like Spring
#5 Something Like Lightning
#6 Something Like Thunder
#7 Something Like Stories - Volume One
#8 Something Like Hail
#9 Something Like Rain
#10 Something Like Stories - Volume Two
#11 Something Like Forever
#12 Something Like Stories - Volume Three

The *Loka Legends* series
#1 The Cat in the Cradle
#2 From Darkness to Darkness

Other Novels
Kamikaze Boys
Straight Boy
Out of Time, Into you
Hell's Pawn
Switch!

Other Short Stories
Language Lessons
Like & Subscribe
The Boy at the Bottom of the Fountain
Icarus and Apollo

Acknowledgements:

A very special thanks to my editor, Linda Anderson, for being so generous with her time and her talent. And of course my friends and family for being so supportive in this endeavor.

For Andreas
My guiding star,
my happy thought,
and my dream come true.
I love you, baby!

PART ONE

HOUSTON, TEXAS
1996

CHAPTER 1

This is not a coming-out story. I put all that behind me two years ago, at the tender young age of fourteen. I'd known I was gay since I was twelve and my best friend Kevin moved away to Utah. I was heartbroken, which I suppose is considered normal behavior for most kids. After he'd been gone for two weeks I decided to take a Greyhound bus to see him. The guy at the counter wouldn't sell me a ticket so I tried passing myself off as the kid of a boarding passenger. That didn't go well. The bus driver made me get off and the station manager called my parents. Their reaction to my little plan is what tipped me off that my feelings for Kevin went way beyond the norm. Well, that and how I got a hard-on every time I thought of him.

Ben's fingers hesitated above the keyboard of his laptop as he reread what he had just written. He took a deep breath, the ozone smell of the slowly overheating machine filling his nose before he sighed. Why did it always sound so trite when he tried to write about his life? He wanted to create something different and real, but it always ended up sounding like the porn stories in his small stash of magazines.

Next time he swore to write with old-fashioned pen and paper. At least then he could enjoy crumpling the displeasing results before throwing them in a little metal trash can, like they always did on TV. The most Ben could do was to carefully save his document, close the program, and drag the file to the recycle bin. As he right-clicked to empty the bin, he wondered if the problem wasn't that he couldn't write, but that the porn stories in his magazines were just really well-crafted. He was beginning to wish he hadn't deleted it when the clock in the bottom right-hand corner caught his eye. Ten minutes until seven. Almost time for Mr. Blue Shoes to go jogging.

Ben struggled with himself for a moment. Part of him recognized just how creepy his behavior was. He wasn't sure if it qualified as stalking, but it was dangerously close. But what else was there to do? Writing hadn't worked and there was nothing on TV but summer reruns. What harm was there in an innocent stroll through the neighborhood, and if he happened to see Mr. Blue Shoes, then so be it.

Switching off his laptop, Ben tried to remember the last time he had done this. Was it yesterday? Surely it was the day before. How many times this week already? Since they appeared to be about the same age, Ben was sure that Mr. Blue Shoes would be attending his high school and he didn't want to be obvious. Being out at school led to enough taunting without the added ridicule of being criminally desperate.

Ben slipped on his shoes and quietly closed his bedroom door behind him. The sound of MTV's *Mega Summer Beach Party* or whatever they were calling it this year drifted from the direction of his sister's room. For once she wasn't hogging the bathroom. Ben rushed across the hall and flipped on the light, knowing that time was running out, that he only had a brief moment to check his appearance.

His hair was due for a cut but was still passable, he decided as he tried to smooth it into shape. His chestnut brown eyes regarded themselves momentarily, making him wish that his parents had bought him the colored contacts he had asked for last Christmas. Green, blue, purple, anything but his natural hue. At least the braces were off now. He smiled wickedly, scanning for any sign of the spinach soufflé his mother had served for dinner. If there were more time he would have brushed his teeth. Just in case life played out like one of those porn stories. If only.

He was happy to see some remnants of sun on his face from camping last weekend, and how it lent natural blond highlights to his brown hair, but he wasn't pleased to note the dopey Smashing Pumpkins T-shirt he wore, which didn't reflect his taste in music. The shirt had mysteriously turned up in a stack of fresh laundry one day. His sister's boyfriend had left it during one of his nocturnal visits, and once Ben figured that out, he wore it just to torture her. This wearable blackmail was a few sizes too large for him and draped off his ramrod-thin frame like a tent. Ben bit his lip and decided against digging through the hamper for something better. At least this shirt was clean.

Flipping the light switch, he took the stairs two at a time, landing at the bottom with a thud that was sure to trigger a yell from his mother. He paused but the only sound he heard was prerecorded studio laughter. Thank god for the hypnotizing properties of television! Ben slipped out the front door, undetected by all but Wilford, the family dog.

The August evening was still bright, but not as much as it

had been last month. Ben pondered the symbolism of the world growing darker with the approach of a new school year as he jogged down the street toward the end of the block. Behind the row of houses here were woods that connected with a large public park. He chose the yard whose owner was least likely to complain and crossed it. With the house and unfenced backyard behind him, he was faced with one of the finest forests in modern suburbia.

The mix of pine and cedar trees was disturbed only by a single dirt path that disappeared into their midst. The trail, eternally marred by the crisscrossing grooves left by countless bike riders, snaked back and forth through the trees, causing ten acres of woods to feel like a limitless wilderness.

Ben turned to the right and walked up a slope toward a more civilized path, one paved and dotted with benches and trash cans as it wound its way around a small man-made lake. He scanned the horizon for his quarry. At first he saw no one except for a middle-aged couple walking hand in hand, but then the thump, thump, thump sound of running attracted his attention.

There he was. Mr. Blue Shoes. He could more aptly be called Mr. Neon Electric Blue Shoes. Oh how Ben had searched for a pair of those shoes after seeing them for the first time! Not only did he think they looked awesome, but they would have been a potential conversation starter. *Hey, you have the same crazy shoes that I do!* Despite tagging along on all of his mother's shopping trips, he never found them. Ben wasn't even sure what brand they were. Some sort of exotic Italian label that Mr. Blue Shoes had preferred before moving here to the States, he fantasized. Not that he was necessarily from Italy, but it would explain the deeply tanned skin and jet black hair.

Ben snapped out of his reverie and realized that the object of his desire was jogging directly toward him, and all the while he had been standing there staring. Usually Ben made at least some attempt to act like he was out for exercise. His muscles froze as he tried to decide what to do. He should probably turn to the right and walk away, so as not to appear obvious. He started to do this until he realized that he wouldn't be able to get a look at Mr. Blue Shoes, and so Ben turned back to the front. Unfortunately his confused brain didn't trigger the muscles needed to actually begin walking. Ben was left standing, just as he had been before, except now he was facing Mr. Blue Shoes and unable to do anything but stare.

Lust brushed away any remaining self-consciousness. Ben looked up from the oddly colored shoes, his eyes taking in the black hairs on the finely muscled legs before darting up to check out the package bouncing away behind maroon gym shorts. Not wishing to press his luck he continued upward to the considerable pecs. The evening wasn't hot enough that he was running shirtless, but the grey tank top was minimal enough to reveal muscular arms with a sexy swirl of black hair under the armpits. Ben looked up at the handsome face, ignoring the sweaty strands of dark hair stuck to the broad forehead or the perfectly sculpted lips around the slightly ajar mouth, choosing instead to look into the silver-grey eyes that haunted his fantasies.

He noted, with a mix of relief and abhorrence, that those eyes were locked onto his T-shirt. His blatant gawking had probably gone unseen, but at the price of Mr. Blue Shoes noticing the worst thing about his appearance today. As he jogged past Ben, the silver eyes rose to meet his. Mr. Blue Shoes raised his eyebrows and nodded in a way that unmistakably said "Cool!" before flashing a smile.

And then he was gone, followed a second later by a blast of sweaty, musky air. Ben inhaled this scent and, after a dramatic moment of euphoria, found the strength to continue walking. He sauntered around the park before heading home, feeling as if he had just gotten back from a dream date. He realized that was a little pathetic, but he didn't care at this point. The hottest guy in the world had just acknowledged him and all because of some band Ben had never bothered listening to. He made a mental note to ask his sister to borrow one of their CDs that night, but not before locking himself in his room and beating off furiously while thinking about that smile.

Shopping with Allison! Was there anything better? Not only did she understand the glory of the shopping mall and share his reverence for it, but she also possessed an impressive mental map of downtown Houston's weirdest shops. He didn't know how she located such places, but he wished they could talk the owners into moving their stores north to the suburbs of The Woodlands, where Ben and Allison lived.

"Home?" Allison asked, peering into the visor's small cracked mirror. Her expressive eyes tracked the glossy coat of plum-colored lipstick as she applied it to her lips, the shade complementing her ebony skin. Then she pressed her lips together, flipped the visor up, and turned to Ben. "We can always hit more shops tomorrow. I think we did well for ourselves today."

Ben nodded. They had managed to find not one but two pairs of pants that actually hugged his waist tight instead of needing to be cinched to death with a belt. Shirts he wasn't so lucky with, but school didn't start for another two weeks, and they hadn't checked the secondhand shops yet. Ironically, thrift stores tended to have more stylish and hip clothes than retail shops.

As the Ford Escort chugged away in an effort to get them home, Ben considered just how lost he'd be without Allison—how her broad smile and the mischievous glint in her eye always kept his spirits high. He loved the jealous glances men gave him when they were out together, mistaking the tall, thin beauty on his arm as being his girl.

"Shit!" Allison shouted as the tape player sputtered and squealed.

Of course those jealous guys probably didn't realize that she could cuss like a sailor.

Allison jabbed repeatedly at the eject button with total disregard for the road until the player spit up her most recent mix tape. Spools of magnetic strip dangled from the cassette as she held it up. "I stayed up all night listening to the radio to make this stupid thing!" she cried, braking just in time to avoid running a red light.

"You need a CD player," Ben said.

"I need a new car," she countered.

As if on cue, a sports car full of teenagers pulled up to the stoplight, the music pounding from their car so loud that it shook the Escort's rearview mirror. Even though summer was almost over, the car still had "Class of '96" written all over it in white shoe polish.

"I hope we're not that lame when we graduate," Allison said when the light turned green and the car sped away, "but at least they can listen to music."

"There's still the radio," Ben suggested.

Allison pointed through the windshield at a broken stub of metal where an antenna should have been. She raised her finely arched eyebrows and bobbed her head from side to side, like she sometimes did when making a good point.

"Ah, right," Ben conceded.

Allison returned her hands to the wheel and her attention to the road before she smiled.

"Sing for me," she said sweetly.

"What do you want to hear?"

"Uhhh... What's that one called? 'Take a Chance on Me.'"

"You mean by ABBA?" Ben asked, failing to hide the disapproval from his voice.

"Yeah, the one with the comic strip video and the hot singer."

"That's 'Take On Me' by a-ha," Ben corrected, feeling relieved.

"Just make with the music, pretty boy."

Ben smiled, cleared his throat and began to sing. His voice was his favorite thing about himself. When talking it sounded as average as could be, but when he sang his voice flowed like honey. Ben loved to sing. Ever since he was a little boy, he had crooned along with his mother's country music while she cleaned and his father's oldies while he drove. When singing, everything in the world felt right to him, as if it magically placed the world in a temporary state of grace.

From the gleam in Allison's eyes, he could tell that she felt the same way. She listened to half the song, laughing when he interjected new lyrics for the ones he didn't know, before joining in with him on the next chorus. Her voice was leagues ahead of any other girl at school, the sugar to his honey. Nobody could out-sing the pair of them, which they had proven more than once in choir class last year.

Allison stopped singing and took a sharp right turn. "Oh my god, have you been down here lately?"

"No," Ben said, wishing that they could have at least finished the song.

"It's so different now, you won't believe it!"

Outside the window was a neighborhood full of newly built houses. They were just three blocks over from where Ben lived, but he hadn't paid attention to this housing development at all. He vaguely recalled his parents complaining about how these houses were just bigger and better enough to send their own real estate values down. Or up. He couldn't remember which. Either way, they did look nice even though the yards were bare, aside from the spindly new trees injected into the ground.

"This all used to be fields when we were kids, remember?" Allison sighed. "We always used to play here."

He did remember, although it was actually Allison and his sister Karen who had played together. Ben had tagged along a couple of times, but always against their will. A small age difference had ended that friendship. Once Karen was in high school, she felt being friends with a junior high kid would mean social suicide, and so Ben was automatically promoted to Allison's best friend. And now she tended to rewrite history, giving all of her memories with Karen over to him, which was flattering in a way.

"Shame about the willow tree," she said, pointing to a tennis court and a small children's playground. "Still, I wouldn't mind living here."

"It's all right," he said as he eyed three-car garages and facades with yawning windows that revealed two-story-tall entryways inside. There was something about a new subdivision that Ben found both off-putting and alluring. What he didn't like was how the houses were too new to have any character. None of them had been personalized yet by basketball nets, daring color schemes, out-of-control bushes, or curious lawn decorations. That there were only three or four architectural styles in the subdivision was all too apparent. This was the case with most neighborhoods, but the cookie-cutter uniformity was obscured over time as individual touches transformed the houses into homes.

What Ben liked came—oddly enough—from what he disliked. The generic template was similar to a blank sheet of paper. This made it easier to imagine living in any of the houses. In his mind, Ben could choose what color he would paint it, how he would decorate it inside, and even what sort of job he would have and who he would live with. The idea made him yearn to be out of school so he could finally start a life of his own.

The buzz of a lawn mower matched the unhealthy sound of the car's engine as they turned a corner. A familiar figure was pushing the machine across a yard that had barely managed to sprout grass yet.

"Pull over!" Ben shouted. "No! Not here!" he added when Allison headed for where Mr. Blue Shoes was mowing. Thankfully he wasn't facing them and didn't notice the car jerk away from the curb and back into the middle of the road.

"What the hell?" Allison complained. "I thought you were going to puke or something!"

"Sorry." Ben fidgeted in his seat and turned to glance out the back window. "Just drop me off at the end of the block."

"All right," Allison said, peering suspiciously in the rearview mirror. "You know that guy?"

"Not yet," he said with a smile as the car slowed.

Allison gave a surprised laugh. "You're feeling brave today! Come by my place later to get your things. If you aren't busy, that is."

"Shut up." Ben grinned as he hopped out of the car. He waved at her as she drove away before walking in the direction of his infatuation.

Ben was used to this little ritual taking place in the evening. Being in broad daylight was making him nervous. He worried that he would stand out too much, walking down the road without any clear purpose. Ben wished he had... What? A clipboard or something? He could at least be out walking his dog.

Ben cursed himself mentally. Wilford! He should have been walking his dog all those nights he had oh-so casually passed by Mr. Blue Shoes. Magazines always claimed that dogs were good icebreakers. Maybe Mr. Blue Shoes was an animal lover. He probably was and would have stopped to pet Wilford months ago. Was it too late to start bringing the dog with him?

The rumbling of the lawn mower was close now but Ben didn't dare look. What was he thinking? This was too obvious! He kept his eyes instead on the row of houses to the right and pretended to seek a specific address. *I belong here, I belong here,* he kept repeating in his head. *Nothing odd about me being here, pay no attention.*

The lawn mower buzzed to his left, then faded behind him as Ben kept walking. A risked glance over his shoulder revealed Mr. Blue Shoes' sweaty back as it turned to continue mowing in his direction. Ben whipped his head around, hopefully without being noticed, and increased his pace. He prayed that Allison had actually driven home and not turned the car around to watch him. Otherwise this pointless exercise would be humiliating. She expected that he was being all suave and chatting up a hot guy, when in fact, he could barely bring himself to look.

At least it was over now. Ben reached the corner of the street and heard a female voice yell something unintelligible. The sound of the lawn mower died and the voice repeated itself. "Tim! Telephone!" Ben dared another glance back and saw Mr. Blue Shoes heading for the front door as a woman held out a cordless phone for him.

Once the coast was clear, Ben took off running down the street, laughing. Not only had he learned where Mr. Blue Shoes lived, but now Ben knew his real name!

Allison was all grins as she tossed the shopping bag at him from across her waterbed where she sat. "Well? What happened?"

"His name is Tim." Ben flopped down on the bed, creating waves that sent them both bouncing up and down.

"That's a good start. So what did you say?"

"Well…"

Allison's face dropped. "You *did* talk to him, didn't you?"

"The lawn mower was running. What was I supposed to do, flag him down just to say hi? Besides, his mom came out of the house too."

"So you hung around and eavesdropped?" Allison snorted. "I'd call you pathetic if I wouldn't have done the same thing."

Ben smiled and reached across to the headboard shelf where she kept her CDs in vinyl wallets. He chose one randomly and began flipping through it. "So what do you think I should do?"

"I dunno. You'll have to invent an excuse to talk to him." Allison hoisted a sarcastic eyebrow. "Maybe go to his door and say you're selling Girl Scout cookies."

"Don't tempt me," Ben replied. "You know I would look adorable in the uniform. Hmm. I could always claim that my cat's gone missing."

"Sure, except you don't have a cat and what would it be doing inside his house anyway?"

Ben tossed the CD wallet aside and flopped onto his back with a groan. "There has to be something."

"Well, there's school in two weeks. Maybe he'll end up in one of your classes."

"Two weeks? I don't want to wait that long!"

"You'll live." Allison glanced at the digital display of her alarm clock. "Dad's home in ten minutes. Want to head back out and find those shirts?"

The two sentences weren't unrelated. Allison's father hated him. The feeling was mutual, but Ben dreaded there ever being a confrontation. The man was wound tighter than a spring, the bulging veins on his neck and temples beating out a warning every time he caught Ben visiting. He never spoke to Ben, even when greeted politely. In fact the only thing he had ever said to Ben was "cracker faggot" as he was leaving the house one day.

"Shopping it is," Ben said with an uneasy glance at the clock. "But let's go to the mall this time. There's more people around."

"Just in case?" Allison asked.

Ben smiled. "Just in case."

CHAPTER 2

There were only two days left before school started and Ben hadn't caught sight of Tim once, despite having walked by his house almost twice a day. In his recent attempts, Ben made sure to use Wilford as camouflage. He was simply walking his dog, just like any other chump in the world. This made Wilford happy but hadn't done anything for Ben except increase his sense of frustration. He blamed the ungodly hot August weather that had everyone closing their blinds and cranking up the ACs.

Narrowing down where someone might go jogging was especially difficult in The Woodlands. Countless paved bike paths ran through the entire town, most of them winding around the plentiful number of trees that hid building facades. Biking across the city without seeing anything more than woods was entirely possible. Tim might have stuck to the same path between his house and the small lake when he first moved here, but now he was probably exploring in different directions. Even so, Ben began worrying that Tim was only in Texas visiting family for the summer and had already gone back to wherever he came from.

Hoping that his luck would change, Ben passed once again through Tim's neighborhood on his way home. Thanks to a squirrel with a death wish, Wilford was straining against his leash so hard that Ben didn't even notice the commotion until a voice yelled out with enthusiasm.

"Oh wow! I can't fucking believe it! Oh. Sorry mom. It's just so fu- freaking awesome! Thank you!"

Ben gave one last desperate tug on the leash and looked up. Tim was in his driveway jumping up and down around a gleaming, black sports car. A scattering of amused people watched him. Ben noticed the balloons taped to the garage doors just as someone said, "Happy birthday." Wilford chose this moment to circle a piece of grass before squatting, bless him, allowing Ben to stand there and gawk openly.

"Thank you so much!" Tim beamed across the vehicle at a man who was the right age and build to be his father. Then he opened the car door and dived inside. A second later, the engine exploded into life with a roar. It revved a few times before the passenger window rolled down. "Wanna go for a ride?"

Ben almost said 'yes' out loud. There was muttering from the family as they debated who would go and the importance of driving safely. Ben could barely hear any of this and had run out of time anyway. Wilford was already dragging him away down the street.

He should be happy. He had finally managed to see his dream guy again, but something felt wrong in the pit of his stomach. Ben considered the feeling, which was reminiscent of having lost a game. The sports car sped by, much too quickly for a final glance, before it tore around the corner. To get a car like that for your birthday! Tim's parents must be rolling in it!

The unease in Ben's stomach increased. Then it clicked. Someone like Tim had the looks, a perfect body, and a rich family. He was probably a jock and would instantly be popular, despite being new to the area. The chances of Tim even noticing a scrawny outsider like Ben were zero to none. The fantasy had been fun, but Ben felt as though reality had barged in and crashed the party.

The first day of school was not going as planned. Allison's car had broken down the same day he witnessed Tim getting the ultimate birthday gift. Ben supposed there was some cosmic harmony in this. One vehicle had left the world as another was born into existence. Did cars reincarnate? He doubted it. He was being dramatic anyway. Allison's car wasn't dead. It just needed a new radiator line. Or was it a sparkplug filter? Ben didn't have the slightest idea what was wrong with it. He just knew that her car being out of service meant he had to share the bus with a bunch of nervous freshmen and immature sophomores. He didn't even have the comfort of Allison's company, since her father had insisted on driving her to school.

Ben worried he would be mistaken for a freshman as he disembarked from the bus. He was slender and short for his age. Five feet nine inches wasn't bad really, but it was becoming apparent that he wouldn't be growing any taller. Alone and distracted, he probably appeared to be arriving at high school for the first time in his life. A disoriented freshman confirmed this, sidling up to him and asking, "How do they expect us to find any of these classes? What's 3E2 mean anyway?"

Ben only shrugged and looked down at his own schedule, even though he knew that the '3' referred to the floor, the 'E' to the east wing of the building, and the final digit indicated the room number. His own first item was 1W0. He didn't need to read the class description to recognize what that was. P.E., or Physical Embarrassment as he preferred to call it. He swore under his breath and went toward the gymnasium where he would be miserable for an hour every morning this semester.

Ben searched for any sign of a familiar face as he pushed through the crowded hallways, but the fates were against him today. He saw people he recognized, but most of them were the jocks and snobs he despised. The bell rang as he stepped into gym, the hallways still full of baffled new kids. Ben took solace in this. The coach would have to wait until all of them found their way to the gym, the rest of the period hopefully taken up by issuing uniforms and other trivialities.

He eyed the bleachers with apprehension as he neared them and almost laughed with relief when he spotted Leon's tall stooped form sitting in the highest row, the man idly toying with one of his dreads. Ben walked directly to the one person who had made last year's P.E. classes bearable. He reached the top row of benches unscathed—even though some idiot tried to trip him along the way—and sat down next to Leon, enjoying the aromatic scent of marijuana that surrounded him like cologne.

"Hey, what's up, big guy?" Leon croaked in his all-too-typical stoner voice.

"Nothing much. I can't believe we have to do this first thing in the morning. It's child abuse."

"At least it's the final year. There's no P.E. for seniors."

"Lucky bastards," Ben muttered. "Hey, maybe the coaches will be too groggy to make us exercise."

Not to mention that Leon would probably be too stoned to exercise, relaxing on the sidelines instead of participating in whatever idiotic sport was the choice of the week. There were a few times last year when Leon's stash had run dry, leaving him sober and transforming him into an active and capable athlete. Ben hated those times, because it meant he was left alone and defenseless, when he usually would have been hiding behind Leon's magical aura that allowed him to get away with anything. Ben wasn't sure what it was exactly, but the coaches seemed to genuinely like Leon, despite him being a modern day version of the people who protested against the Vietnam War.

Ben let out a groan as one of these former servicemen came

marching into the gymnasium, a handful of nervous-looking freshmen trailing along behind like ducklings. There were four different coaches who taught P.E., but the only way to tell them apart was their hair. Each coach was stocky with limbs as thick as tree trunks. They might have been hot back in their youth, but a war and way too many beers had graced them all with tired faces and prominent guts.

This coach, the one with thinning red hair, took attendance by bellowing out each of their last names. Leon talked all through this, eagerly describing to Ben his uncle's collection of Laserdiscs that he had access to all summer. Film was Leon's topic of choice. If you knew your movies, you were his friend.

"Bendly?" the coach repeated.

Ben sighed, knowing that if he corrected the man, it would only make him a future target. "Here," he droned.

"I see Steyer managed to graduate from summer school," the coach bantered, sending a pug dog's smile Leon's way.

"Hey, Coach!" Leon answered happily. "They wanted to send me back to junior high but I told them I'd miss you too much."

The coach smiled and continued taking roll call. How did Leon do it? If Ben had tried that line he would have been called a queer and told to go run a few laps.

The rest of the period crawled by. Forms for the gym clothes were passed out for them to fill in and bring back the next day. To Ben's despair, the mint green uniforms that always smelled of body odor no matter how many times they were laundered were passed out too, but thankfully there wasn't enough time to get changed and play anything. Instead he spent the period listening to Leon talk about the Star Wars movies that he took so seriously. When stoned, he treated the events of the movies as if they were happening in the present.

"Yoda *has* to know that Luke isn't going to be able to beat Vader. He's totally just playing the emotional card and hoping to make Vader break down and cry or something, right?"

Ben didn't have time to respond before the bell rang. He practically dived off the bleachers in his eagerness to reach the hallways and look for Allison. Or Tim. Another new period meant another chance for them to be in the same class. Neither of his targets were spotted in the hallway, nor were they in his English class. The next period was his first elective, Spanish, which also failed to contain either of the people he was looking for. There was at least an amusing conflict between the teacher and a kid from Mexico who was looking to earn an easy A.

Lunch period brought relief in the form of Allison. He found her at their usual meeting spot, next to the vending machines in the large cafeteria that linked both wings of the school. They had their choice of seats since they both brought their lunches, while most of the other kids were lining up to buy hot food. As much as Ben was tired of white bread sandwiches, these tasted better than any of the culinary choices that the school offered. There were legends of neighboring school districts that allowed the fast food giants to cater for their students, but this district wasn't one of them. The "healthy" food sold at his school was soggy and flavorless. Even the soft drink machines were filled only with sugar-free lemonade and some sort of chocolate drink that didn't contain one grain of cocoa powder.

"Ronnie Adaaaams!" Allison sang as they sat down at their table.

"Who?" Ben started unpacking his lunch from the brown paper bag, wondering why the name sounded familiar.

"The fine black brother from driver's ed?" Allison prompted. "He's in my home ec class."

Ben snorted and spit the juice box straw from his mouth. "Are you telling me because you think he might be gay?"

"No!" Allison protested. "Straight guys are *always* on the prowl in home ec. Lord knows that's the only reason I'm taking it. Anyway, the nutty old teacher has us sitting alphabetically, and by some miracle he's the only A and I'm the only C with no B in the middle."

"See? It's good that I refused to take that class."

"You are forgiven," Allison said gracefully. "So how goes it with your T?"

"Technically, it would be W if we're going by last names," Ben corrected. He had long ago scoped out Tim's mailbox and discovered that his family name was Wyman, although thus far he had resisted scrawling *Ben Wyman* on any of his notebooks. "Unfortunately it isn't going anywhere. I was hoping you had seen him."

"Nope," Allison said, swapping her Cheetos for Ben's sour cream Pringles without having to ask. "Maybe he goes to a private school or something."

"Maybe," Ben said, glancing around the cafeteria. There were three different lunch breaks, so it was against the odds that Tim would have the same one. Ben was glad that he and Allison still shared a lunch period. For the third year in a row! He decided to turn his full attention to his friend and put Mr. Blue Shoes out of mind. As much as possible anyway. Like so many other things in life, maybe what he wanted wouldn't come to pass if he thought too hard about it.

Fourth-period math started out promising. There was an attractive guy in class named Craig, who looked vaguely like Zack Morris if Ben squinched his eyes up just right. Ben hadn't talked to Craig since junior high, after spending the night at his house.

What had come between them was a fairly common story in Ben's sordid history. It all began in the seventh grade, when a routine sleepover at a friend's house was transformed by a pilfered porno. Watching the video together led to trading hand jobs. This act was repeated during more sleepovers until the time his friend claimed to be too tired to mess around and insisted that they go to sleep instead. This confused Ben until, after some less-than-casual tossing and turning, it became obvious that more was expected from him. Ben happily went down on his friend that night, for the first of many times, although the favor was never returned.

Eventually, word of Ben's noble deeds began to spread around the school, and guys he barely knew were inviting him to stay over. The same routine was played out over and over again, with the hosts usually pretending to be asleep. On their backs. With their pants down. It was, needless to say, a very exciting time in Ben's life. The demand for his services came to a screeching halt when he decided to come out of the closet halfway through the school year. Suddenly none of the boys, including the friend he first started experimenting with, wanted anything to do with him. Craig was one of the last guys he had messed around with before going public, and they hadn't spoken since.

Until today that is. Instead of refusing to make eye contact,

Craig greeted him warmly and even chose a seat next to his. Hope began to burn in Ben's chest that Craig had come to terms with his own sexuality, which turned out to be true but not in the way he expected. Craig soon began ranting about the girlfriend he had found over the summer. Apparently this relationship had confirmed his heterosexuality and made it possible to deal with his experimental phase, which was now behind him. Getting laid regularly probably didn't hurt either. Ben was mildly disappointed, but happy to have a friend to make an otherwise boring class more entertaining.

Fifth-period choir meant not only being with Allison again, but being surrounded by people he had known for years. Choir was made up of either weird artistic types or religious sorts who also sang in church. Despite the two different backgrounds, everyone got along and the atmosphere was always relaxed.

Their teacher, Mrs. Hammond, had enjoyed minor success on stage earlier in her life and also taught drama. She took singing and acting seriously but was also a very disorganized person who rarely bothered to direct the class. Today she seemed as reluctant to start the school year as her students and was fine with letting the hour pass without her interference. Ben and Allison spent this time catching up with everyone they hadn't seen since spring and exchanging juicy bits of gossip that had occurred over the summer.

Science was the final class of the day. Ben walked to it slowly, feeling like Charlie from the Willy Wonka movie. This was the last possible chance to have a class with Tim, his final shot at a golden ticket and the amazing behind-the-scenes factory tour that came with it. In his mind he was pulling back that candy bar wrapper as slowly and carefully as he wanted to undress Tim. He stepped through the door just as the bell rang and stood there, waiting for his dreams to become reality.

"Hello?" complained someone who had watched way too many valley girl movies before pushing past him. "I swear!"

That left one desk for Ben. He took his seat, still looking around for any hint of silver eyes and dark hair. Nothing. Nada.

Ah well. At least he still had the chocolate to enjoy. The teacher of this class, Ms. Hughes, was the same he had last year. She was one of those rare teachers who were considered cool by her students. Some teachers tried too hard by putting up posters of trendy music bands or by ineptly interjecting slang into their lectures. Ms. Hughes wasn't like that. She was just herself—a middle-aged spinster who had a passion for science and managed to transfer her enthusiasm to those she was teaching, usually through innovative and fun experiments. The topic of the day was pheromones, which had most of the class laughing, but not Ben. His imagination kept returning to the scent of sweat hanging on the evening air as Tim ran to him, wearing a perfect smile that promised they would finally be together.

CHAPTER 3

After suffering a week of plastic green seats and hyperactive freshmen, Ben decided to give up on the bus. The mechanics were holding Allison's car hostage while parts were ordered, and Ben couldn't take the humiliation of being the only junior travelling by bus anymore. He was locking his bike up when Allison came running over from where her father had dropped her off.

"I found him!" she declared.

"Who?" Ben said as casually as possible.

"Johnny Depp," Allison retorted. "Who do you think I mean? I tried calling you last night but it just rang and rang."

Ben made a mental note to verbally abuse his sister for ignoring call waiting. "So where is he?"

"Tied up in my basement and waiting for you," Allison said, licking her lips indecently. "You wish. I just saw him in passing after sixth period yesterday, so at least we know that he goes to this school."

Allison spotting Tim must have broken the curse, because Ben saw him that very day. To be fair, the renewed hope had inspired Ben to take long detours down different hallways, but the strategy paid off. On the way to lunch he saw Tim leaning against a wall, talking to two other students.

Unfortunately they were two of the biggest assholes in school. Bryce Hunter was a beefy jock who had been the size of an ox for as long as Ben could remember. He'd always looked like he was twenty-five, even in junior high. Next to him was Darryl Briscott, who was short and bordering on fat, but he came from a very rich family, and that guaranteed his popularity.

Ben eyed them warily for a moment before turning his attention back to Tim, whose adam's apple bobbed in amusement at something Bryce was saying. There had been days when Ben questioned his recent obsession, dismissing it as temporary insanity induced by raging hormones. Crazy or not, seeing Tim again rekindled those stalker's flames. He was everything, absolutely everything, that Ben looked for in a guy. From the outside at least. His choice of company cast doubt on the rest.

"Timmy!" squealed a voice that would test even the patience of pigs. Krista Norman bounded directly in front of Ben on her way to 'Timmy.' Despite her unfortunate voice, she was one of the most popular girls and drop-dead gorgeous. She ran over to take Tim's hand in her petite little paws and beam up at him. Tim returned the million dollar smile, much to Ben's disgust.

"Hey, faggot!" These charming words were spoken by none other than Bryce Hunter himself, who had noticed Ben standing there and staring.

Any chance of resisting the oncoming blush was ruined when Krista added, "He really is, you know."

Ben risked a glare at Bryce and a sarcastic little wave to Krista as he walked away. Figuring there was nothing more to lose, he glanced at Tim one last time as he went. Tim appeared amused, returning Ben's funny little wave. The gesture was genuinely cute when he did it, which made Ben twice as angry.

Why couldn't people's insides match their outsides? The world would be such a wonderful place if the nicer someone was, the more beautiful they became. Jerks like Bryce and Darryl would be disgusting, pus-covered trolls, and everyone would see them for what they were. Tim too, if these were the sort of people he chose to hang out with. Instead of the princely appearance, he would be ugly, hunched, and so wretched-looking that Ben never would have noticed him. Or if Ben had, he would have at least known right away that Tim wasn't worth all the emotions and fantasies that had been wasted on him.

The parade of unpleasant events began in the morning. Ben was stuffing his backpack into his locker before heading to the gym when something wet splatted onto his neck. He turned around to find a spit wad almost as big as his fist lying on the ground. The hallways were still full of kids, but Bryce's massive form was easy to pick out of the crowd, a satisfied smirk painted across his face.

At least Tim wasn't with him, which was something of a miracle. Over the past two weeks Ben had run into Tim at least twice a day. Each time Ben hastily averted his eyes and cursed the flush that came over his face. He hoped his red cheeks were mistaken as angry instead of bashful. After all, he had nothing to be embarrassed about, since Tim was clueless as to Ben's former crush on him.

The fun-filled day continued in gym class. Leon was having

his wisdom teeth removed, which meant at least a week of misery without his company. Worst of all, they were playing baseball, a sport very difficult to go unnoticed in. His first time at bat, Ben cussed loudly after his third strike. This infuriated the coach, the bald one with the twisted nose, who commanded that Ben run the two-mile trail through the woods that nestled against the school. At least this was an escape of sorts. Ben slowed to a walk as soon as he was hidden behind the trees and wondered if he could get away with self-inflicting this "punishment" until Leon came back. He would rather run alone every day than play baseball.

Then there was a substitute teacher in Spanish, which of course meant the entire class was misbehaving. Ben usually enjoyed that, but one of the boys asked the teacher how to say "faggot" in Spanish. For whatever incomprehensible reason, the substitute decided to answer this question, and *"mariposa"* was happily parroted throughout the remainder of the class, with a number of pointed looks in Ben's direction.

Lunch should have brought a welcome break from the day's hardships, but Ben was greeted with Allison's announcement that she and Ronnie were now boyfriend and girlfriend. Ben callously responded to this news by saying, "That's stupid. You haven't even been on a date yet."

Allison's hurt expression made him regret these words. Ben *was* happy for her. Mostly. Ronnie was a nice guy. Dates, romance, and possibly hot kinky sex were sure to follow in due course. That's what rubbed Ben the wrong way. This was Allison's fourth boyfriend since they had been in high school. In the past three years, Ben hadn't had so much as a mildly flirtatious encounter. The ease in which she found someone stirred the green-eyed monster inside of him.

What could he do though? He wasn't old enough to get into a gay bar, and the local newspaper's personal ads were almost strictly heterosexual, except for a few placed by men older than his father. Even Ben's meager sex life had been cut off when he came out of the closet, a decision that he was beginning to regret. An unreciprocated blowjob at this point sounded as meaningful as marriage.

The rest of their meal was accompanied by awkward silence. Ben knew he would have to make amends later, but he was in too foul a mood to backpedal or smooth things over at the moment.

The remainder of the school day passed without incident, but the grumbling thunderstorm outside helped to fuel his sullenness until the last period was over.

The rain had at least stopped by the time he was buckling on his Rollerblades. Allison's car had made it out of the shop for two whole days before breaking down again. Ben had abandoned his bike and decided to start using the inline skates he had begged for and received last Christmas. He wasn't very good yet, but he managed to do everything but stop gracefully. A meandering bike path was his choice of route today. The detour would make it take longer to get home, but it would also help him avoid other students. He just wanted to get home to the comfort of mindless TV and the leftover cookie bars his mom had baked the night before.

Trees became a blur as Ben skated faster than he usually dared. He was finally getting the hang of these things! The woods gave way to a man-made channel clear of foliage. Here the ground dipped low and then high again, winding like an empty river through the woods. Ben always wondered what purpose it served, until one hurricane season when it rained nonstop for two weeks. The ditch took the excess rainwater and moved it safely away to somewhere less civilized. That was the only year he had seen the ditch full of water. Otherwise it remained a dry but green miniature valley.

Ben was beginning to feel better as he zipped down the path that ran along the ditch. That's when he saw Tim. He was further along, wearing a jogging outfit except this time with the addition of a backpack. Obviously he had decided to jog home rather than drive his Richie Rich sports car. Instead of the usual wave of hormones Ben experienced whenever he saw Tim, this time he felt only irritation. He didn't want to be reminded of the things he couldn't have. He wanted solitude.

"Get the fuck off my path," Ben muttered under his breath as he thrust with his legs and increased his velocity. He felt like a bullet shot from a gun, and right now he wanted nothing more than to barrel into Tim and knock him aside without so much as a backwards glance. Why the hell not? He was sick of being the victim of everyone else's barbs and lunacy. Maybe it was time to fight back! He wouldn't knock Tim over, but he could at least give him a scare by cutting directly in front of him, maybe jostling him a little bit in the process.

Ben grinned with wicked determination as he neared, but at the last moment he began to panic. There simply wasn't enough room on the path to pass by safely, at least not at this speed. Maybe a skilled skater could have done it, but Ben was still too green. He was more likely to veer off the path and injure himself. Tim was less than ten feet away when Ben decided to abandon this reckless course of action. He tilted his left foot to brake, before realizing that the brake was on the other skate. In his panic he tried to turn, but his left foot was still tilted, causing Ben to trip over his own leg. He was airborne for the briefest of moments before slamming into Tim, knocking the jogger off the path and into the ditch.

Impacting with Tim had mostly halted Ben's flight through the air. He landed with a thud on the grass next to the paved path, shaken but otherwise unscathed. From the gasp of pain and long string of cursing, this clearly wasn't the case for his victim. Ben pushed himself to his knees and looked over the ditch's edge. Tim was sitting up, supporting one leg in the air. He lowered it tentatively to the ground. As soon as the foot touched grass, Tim hollered and lifted it again.

"Oh god!" Ben spluttered. "I'm sorry, I'm sorry!" He stood and slid down the ravine, wanting to help.

Tim's face struggled with a mixture of confusion and anger. "What the hell happened?"

"I don't— I'm just a klutz." Ben had reached his victim's side and stretched out his arms, intending to pick Tim up, before he realized how unrealistic this was. "Is your leg broken?"

"Leg's fine," Tim answered, turning his attention back to the bloody limb that looked anything but okay. "My ankle is jacked."

Ben dropped to his knees to get a better look. The ankle seemed fine. The flesh torn away from the shin was what worried him. There wasn't any sign of exposed bone, but so much blood made it hard to be certain.

Ben tore his eyes from the injury. "We have to get you to a doctor. Can you walk?"

Tim lowered his leg a second time, managing to only hiss in pain instead of shouting. "You're going to have to help me," he said.

"Wait." Ben unsnapped the straps of his skates and started digging through his backpack for his shoes. The five most awkward minutes of his life followed as he struggled to get them on, Tim watching him silently the entire time. "Right," Ben said as the final lace was tied. "How do we do this?"

Tim craned his neck around to examine the steep slope they would need to ascend before they could get him to his feet. "You pull me up there, I guess."

"Pull you how?" Ben asked, feeling even smaller than he usually did.

"Just grab me under the arms and pull. I'll try to help as much as I can."

Ben got into position behind Tim. There was a very silly moment where he stood and stared. Both of Tim's arms were raised to his sides, as if he would start flapping them in an effort to take flight. Ben felt like asking if he really had permission to touch him, before he remembered the seriousness of the situation. He hooked his arms underneath Tim's armpits and pulled. He only managed to heave the target of his idiotic actions half a foot, but on the next attempt, Tim kicked with his good leg, bringing the movement to a little more than a foot. They proceeded in this manner until they were both on level ground again.

Ben was breathing hard from the exertion, Tim most likely from the pain. After a moment of rest, they tackled the job of getting Tim upright. They managed with minimal struggle, Tim putting pressure on the injured leg twice more out of habit. Soon enough he was stooped but standing, one arm locked around Ben's shoulders. A few experimental hopping-steps brought them to the sidewalk.

"I guess we make it to the nearest house and have them drive me home," Tim said.

"Your house is really close if we cut through the trees there," Ben said without thinking. His right arm was around Tim's torso, and he felt the muscles tense in reaction. How could he have been so stupid? Not only had he revealed himself as being an insane psychopath who physically lashed out at boys he liked, but he had followed it up with confirmation that he was a stalker to boot.

"Let's go then," Tim muttered, generously not asking how a stranger knew where he lived.

The effort of holding Tim up was a welcome distraction, both to the self-deprecating thoughts going through Ben's head and the excitement of being so intimately close to him. Now was not the time or the place to get aroused over physical contact. Ben was determined to end the day with only two strikes against his sanity instead of three.

They shuffled through the narrow width of woods until they reached a wooden privacy fence—the only thing that stood between them and the suburbs beyond. A glance left and right confirmed that any neighboring houses had the same barrier installed against the wilderness.

"Fuck," Tim swore. "How much further would it be if this fence wasn't here?"

"Half a block," Ben said, looking away to hide his embarrassment.

"Support me," Tim said after hopping one step closer to the fence and reaching out to grab the top of it.

Ben thought he intended to climb over, but grabbed on tighter to Tim's torso as he began to pull instead. He almost toppled backwards when the plank gave way to Tim's efforts and came loose, swinging to the side as it fell. This process was repeated for a second time, and then a third, creating just enough of a gap for them to squeeze through.

Tim went first, holding on to the top of the fence for support once Ben let go of him. He stumbled on his way through and landed on his ankle, bellowing as he righted himself. Ben hurried through to assist him, feeling sure that the owners of the house would hear the commotion in their backyard and come to help. As they made it halfway across the lawn, they could see through the sliding glass door that the house was empty, having not been sold yet. At least they wouldn't have to explain the vandalism.

They made it through the gate to the front yard, not encountering another living soul as they worked their way down the sidewalk. That was the funny thing about the suburbs. So much trouble went into a neighborhood looking as presentable as possible, but rarely was anyone there to appreciate it. Hire a boy to cut the grass and pull up to the mailbox before parking in the garage. Ben wondered if most of his neighbors had ever set foot on their own lawn. No, the suburbs were all prettied up and left there to sit alone, like a beauty queen awaiting an audience that would never come.

Ben tried to smooth over his earlier revelation by feigning ignorance as they reached Tim's house. "Which one is yours?" he asked.

"You tell me," Tim said smartly as they turned to hobble past his car.

"Is anyone home?" Ben asked, partly out of concern but mostly to change topics.

"No."

"Then shouldn't we drive straight to the hospital?"

"I just need to take my weight off it," Tim said irritably as they reached the front door, which was unlocked.

They stepped into air conditioned darkness. The curtains in the house were mostly closed to keep the Texas heat at bay. Tim flipped a few light switches and led them to the living room, which was tastefully decorated but not very welcoming. The room had the soulless presence of a model home. Sure, it looked nice, but it was obvious that no real living went on there.

They reached a couch with apricot fabric that Tim eased into. As he settled down on a piece of furniture that was probably being used for the first time, he sighed contentedly.

"There's a first-aid kit in the bathroom," he said. "Bring me a wet washcloth. A towel too."

"Where is it?" Ben asked.

"I'm surprised you don't know already. It's down the hall on the left."

Ben hurried out of the room, mentally chastising himself for triggering a series of events that would haunt him to his final day of high school. He found the bathroom, a simple affair reserved for guests, and collected the items that were requested.

"Are you sure we shouldn't go to the hospital?" he said as he reentered the living room. "Or a doctor at least?"

"No need." Tim took the washcloth and began patting at the crust of dried blood on his leg. "Same thing happened to me freshman year. I still have a brace upstairs and everything. It's not a big deal. A couple of days with that on and I'll be fine."

Ben had to admit that the leg was looking better now that much of the blood had been cleaned up. Once bandaged it probably wouldn't need medical attention. The ankle was a different story, swollen on each side like a chipmunk's cheeks and turning a dark unhealthy color.

"It's just—"

"Thanks for helping me get home," Tim interrupted. The finality in his voice was clear; Ben was expected to leave. He turned to do so, spluttering more clumsy apologies as he went. He stopped at the door. "Are you sure you are going to be all right? When do your parents get back?"

"In about two weeks." Tim grimaced as he wrapped the cloth bandage around his shin. "They're in Switzerland."

Ben swallowed, but it failed to flush away the guilty taste in his mouth as he left the house and began his walk home.

CHAPTER 4

Ben stood in front of Tim's door again, a book tucked under one arm. He had done nothing but worry since leaving a few hours ago. Ben returned first to the scene of the crime where he had so carelessly left his Rollerblades. They were still in the ditch, not far from a sharp blood-spattered rock that jutted out of the ground. At least the culprit for the shin injury had been discovered. That's right, blame the rock. As much as Ben wanted to shift the blame away from himself, he knew who was responsible.

Once home, he declined his mom's invitation of a snack and went instead to his room. Ben anguished over the foolishness of his actions for the better part of an hour before his self-pity gave way to a growing concern for Tim's well-being. A million nightmare scenarios played out in Ben's head, the worst being that Tim would contract some sort of infection and have his leg amputated. Or what if the infection killed him? The morbid medical fantasies piled up until Ben decided to seek out facts from his mother's family medical guide.

The gruesome book had provided Ben with hours of entertainment as a kid. Not only did it show nauseating pictures of diseases in their most advanced and repulsive stages, but it also featured self-diagnosis charts that were all too easy to navigate successfully. Ben had previously utilized their wisdom to diagnose himself with everything from vaginal yeast infections to cancerous tumors. Now, for the first time, he was turning to it with all seriousness.

What Ben learned had brought him scampering back to Tim's house. Stomach bubbling nervously and palms breaking out in sweat, Ben rang the doorbell. Someone called out in response. Thinking that Tim had fallen somewhere and was helpless, he opened the front door and gave a tentative, "Hello?"

"Hey! Come on in!"

Tim certainly sounded more cheerful. Ben rushed to the living room and found him stretched out on the same uncomfortable couch, as if he hadn't moved, which couldn't be true since an open can of Coke and a bottle of pills sat on the coffee table. The leg was now bandaged and elevated—propped up on the arm of the couch—but Tim looked pale and cold. He was still wearing his jogging shorts and tank top. With the air conditioner going full blast, it was no wonder. The ankle was just as swollen as before, but now it had graduated to a deep shade of maroon.

"Good that you're here," Tim croaked, sounding very much like Leon before he cleared his throat. "I think it might be worse than I thought."

"Yeah," Ben held the book up, brandishing it like a medical degree. "I think you have a third-degree sprain. Either that or it's broken. You really need to get to a hospital."

Tim nodded with glassy eyes. "Probably should."

"Er, I know this is a really stupid question, but are you all right?"

"Yeah. After you left I dragged my ass into the kitchen and remembered some pills from last time. They've got me feeling—" he gestured with his right arm before letting it flop onto his forehead— "Oh man," he finished.

Ben cast around for a phone. "I'll call an ambulance."

"No, fuck that," Tim muttered. "I'm not dying or anything. We'll take my car. You can drive, right?"

"Yes," Ben said a little tersely. He *could* drive, but he hated it. Since earning his license with a solid "D" in driver's ed, he had driven all of three times, each occasion forced on him by his parents.

"Well, get me up and we'll be on our way."

Tim appeared cold, but his skin was hot when Ben wrapped an arm around his back to help him up. Maybe it was a side effect of the pills, or maybe he had a fever. Either way, Ben was relieved that they were finally taking action. Getting Tim to the car was very much like all those movies Ben had seen where a drunken man hung like a limp doll on a supporting friend. Just how many of those painkillers had he taken?

There was a brief and harebrained argument where Tim insisted that no one but him could drive his car, but eventually he was safely buckled into the passenger seat and Ben was behind the wheel. He put the key in the ignition and turned it, Beck's voice exploding out of the stereo system. Ben jabbed at the controls until the voice died, leaving in its wake the noise of the engine, which sounded powerful. This wasn't the usual sports car noise that, frankly, sounded a bit unhealthy. Instead it was a constant hum that rose delicately into a growl once they were cruising down the road.

"Nice," Ben said, not knowing if it really was but feeling it was a good guess.

"Yeah, she's my girl." Tim proudly patted the dashboard.

"So this is a, uh—" Ben squinted at the steering wheel, hoping for a hint. "Firebird?" he said, once he spotted the three diamonds.

"Pfff," came the reply. "Please. This is a 3000GT!"

"Right." Ben risked a glance over to see Tim wearing an expression of mock offense.

"What kind of a guy doesn't know his cars?" Tim pushed.

"I'll give you three guesses," Ben said evenly.

Tim was silent for a moment. "So it's true?"

Ben let a slow smile play over his face. He loved this part. It always felt like revealing to a disbeliever that he had magical powers or something. "Yup."

"Hmmm."

That took Ben off guard, since it wasn't the usual response. Normally, one of two things would happen. The guy would either play it off like he wasn't surprised and name some random gay uncle or somebody else he barely knew to show that he was both worldly and accepting of such things. Or the other person would slide straight into being offensive. Tim had done neither and opted for a musing "hmmm" instead. Whatever that meant.

"You have some sort of car name, right?"

Ben chuckled. "Yeah. Bentley, but I don't know anything about Bentleys either."

"So, Benjamin Bentley, do you know my name as well as where I live?"

"It's Ben, not Benjamin," he replied, avoiding the question.

"Benjamin it is," Tim teased. "Hey! Easy on the turns! Jesus!"

"Sorry. So where are you from? I mean, I haven't seen you in school before this year."

"Kansas." Tim settled back into his seat, but was now watching the road with prepared alertness. "We moved down here so Dad could straighten out the southern division of his company. So he says. I think it's only because Mom never stopped bitching about the winters up there."

"You miss it?"

Tim sighed and looked out the passenger-side window. "I don't know. Maybe."

Ben wished he knew how it felt to leave everything behind. He had lived in The Woodlands his entire life and often fantasized about moving somewhere new. Anywhere would do, even Kansas. He just wanted to see something unfamiliar.

"Fuck!" Tim yelled.

Ben snapped out of his daydream in time to avoid hitting the car ahead of them that had slowed at a stop sign. He swung into the oncoming traffic lane and barreled through the intersection, an old pickup truck honking angrily. Ben hit the gas again to make it through before they collided with anyone and veered back into the proper lane on the other side.

"Pull over!" Tim growled. "I'm driving."

"We're almost there." Ben's hands were steady on the wheel. Such things happened every time he drove.

The car pulled up and stopped at the hospital's emergency entrance, where wheelchairs were scattered around aimlessly like shopping carts at a supermarket. Once he had Tim settled into one of these, Ben got back into the car and parked it, having to brake suddenly at one point to avoid hitting an old lady.

"It's no wonder you ran me over," Tim said as Ben pushed him toward reception. "They shouldn't let you near anything with wheels."

Clipboards and paperwork occupied the next half hour, followed by a heated debate with the receptionist as to why Tim didn't know what sort of insurance coverage he had. Eventually, everything was handed in and they were left to wait with a number of other patients with minor injuries.

Tim became withdrawn again as they waited, his head leaned back and his pale gray eyes focused on the ceiling. His jaw clenched occasionally. Ben watched, counting the seconds between each clench, like he did with thunder to measure the closeness of a storm. He noticed a hint of stubble on the line of Tim's jaw. Ben wanted to reach out and trace his finger along his skin to see what it felt like.

"I hate doctors," Tim murmured.

"Do you want me to hold your hand?" Ben asked with a straight face.

Tim was the first to laugh, Ben joining him.

"I really do," Tim insisted. "Hate doctors I mean. You have no idea!"

"I might," Ben said with a smile. "One of the few times I was in the hospital as a kid was for a couple of fillings."

"Like for your teeth?" Tim sat up and looked at Ben.

"Yeah. I screamed and bit my way through so many dentists that it was the only option left. I was terrified. Once they got me there, I ran away before the procedure began, hospital gown and all."

"How old were you?"

"This was last week."

"You're full of it," Tim chuckled.

Ben grinned back at him. "Seriously though, I must have been nine or ten. Eventually my dad came to find me and they had to put me under with a shot to the butt."

"What, did they shoot you with one of those tranquilizer guns like in Jurassic Park?"

"Something like that."

"Wyman!" a nurse called, glaring at the waiting room impatiently.

She led them down a hall to a room where, much like at a doctor's office, vitals were taken and they were left to wait again. Before long, a gray-haired doctor came in consulting a chart.

"Mr. Wyman," he said. "I'm Dr. Baker. And this is?"

"I'm the one who did this to him," Ben answered sheepishly.

"Ah, and what exactly happened?"

Red-faced, Ben recounted the accident, blaming the collision on a squirrel dashing across the sidewalk. The doctor nodded and "mm-hmed" his way through the story while examining the ankle in question.

"I see," Dr. Baker said when Ben was finished. "We'll need X-rays to be sure, but I believe the ligaments in the ankle might have torn completely."

"Yes!" Ben exclaimed victoriously. "I knew it. A class-three sprain."

"Well, well!" Dr. Baker said appraisingly. "Are you a medical student?"

"No. I did a little research, that's all."

"I think he just runs people over so he can diagnose them later," Tim said.

"Let's hope not." Dr. Baker smiled. "I'm busy enough as it is. If the X-rays check out, we'll get the swelling down and put a cast on it."

"You think it's broken?" Tim asked.

"Casts aren't just for broken bones. We need to keep the ankle protected and in position so it can heal. We'll have it off in a couple weeks, don't worry. I'll need to inform your parents about this, of course."

"They're in Switzerland," Tim said, scowling at his ankle as if it had betrayed him.

Dr. Baker adjusted his glasses. "Any other family in the area?"

"Nope."

"My family can take care of him until they are back," Ben offered. He had no idea if they would actually be willing to, but it didn't really matter. He would find some way of making it work.

"So much for parental consent," Dr. Baker said with a sigh. He consulted the clipboard. "The good news is that we managed to track down your insurance information. However, with your parents out of town, I would feel better if you stayed overnight."

Ben's stomach grumbled, prompting him to look at his watch. It was well past eight and he had promised to be back in half an hour when he had left to check on Tim. He wasn't likely to get in trouble, but he didn't want to raise suspicion that something was up. And what was up exactly? Ben felt he was on the verge of something big. In front of him was a guy who needed help, with no friends or family in the area to look out for him, except Ben. As dubious as the methods had been, he now stood a good chance of getting close to Tim. He didn't want anyone intruding on that now. If his mom found out what was going on, she would probably hire a nurse to take care of Tim, but Ben had a different plan in mind.

"I have to get home," he said. "But I can pick him up tomorrow?"

"I suppose," Dr. Baker said. "Could you please bring the number of his parents' hotel with you? Or better yet, phone it in tonight?"

"Absolutely," Ben lied.

"Wait, you're taking my car?" Tim sounded panicked.

"It's not like you can use it," Ben said, happily patting the pocket that held the keys. "See you tomorrow."

A few minutes later Ben was sitting in the something-or-other 3000GT with a big smile on his face. The next few weeks were going to be very interesting indeed.

CHAPTER 5

"Oh. My. God." Allison stood slack-jawed in the middle of her driveway.

Ben leaned over to get a better look at her out the passenger side window. The movement of a curtain caught his eye, just as he was about to say something smart. Allison's father stood in the living room window, immaculately dressed in the type of conservative business suit he always wore. Ben had never seen him wear anything different. He wondered if the man slept in a suit as well. It was hard to imagine him in anything as casual as pajamas and impossible to believe that he would sleep in his skivvies.

Mr. Cross locked eyes with him and glared.

Ben shivered. "Just get in," he said impatiently.

Once his passenger had boarded and they were a block away, he felt free to resume his jovial mood.

Allison was still fawning over the car. "When you said you were going to pick me up for school, I thought maybe you had your parents' car or something!"

Ben shrugged. He enjoyed keeping his friend in suspense. This didn't dissuade her from sniffing out the truth. She popped the glove box and pulled out the only contents—the insurance card.

"Timothy Wyman?" Once again her jaw lost the ability to hold her mouth shut. "You have got to be kidding me! Does he know you have it?"

Ben was offended. "What, you think I stole his car or something? I'm not that sick."

"Well, how then?"

"I put him in the hospital." Ben laughed. "That's how."

Allison didn't find this statement amusing until he told her the complete story.

"That's the most depraved thing I've ever heard," she said once he had finished. "You realize that you need help?"

Ben shrugged. "Say what you like, my methods get results. If things aren't so hot with Ronnie, cripple him. Guys are crazy about it, trust me."

"So what's next?" Allison asked as she reached over to gently take the wheel. She turned it slightly, just enough to stop the car from barreling into a trash can on the side of the road.

"Oh. Thanks. Next is complicated. I'm supposed to pick him up, which I figured I could do during lunch, but I don't really want to come back afterwards." Ben pulled into the school parking lot and swung into the nearest empty spot. He killed the engine and turned to his best friend. "I need you to cover for me in choir. Say I started hurling during lunch or something."

"Will do."

"I don't know how to get out of the other classes. I guess my parents will be getting a call tonight."

Allison shook her head. "You should be fine. Have you ever noticed that they only take attendance in second period?"

He hadn't until she mentioned it. The first week of school, *every* teacher did roll call, but after that only his English teacher continued to.

"The office would go mad trying to compare every attendance record," Allison continued, "so they just go by the one from second period. Mindy Scott was an office assistant last year and told me how it works."

"So as long as I'm there during English I can skip the rest? Awesome!"

"Within reason. If you don't show up for a week, a teacher will probably ask the office if you keeled over."

This was still good news and made his future plans much easier to execute. "Can you find a ride home?" Ben asked as he unbuckled his seatbelt and stepped out of the car.

"I'm sure Ronnie wouldn't mind," Allison said with a smile.

"Yeah, well, just make sure he's out of the house before your dad gets back."

"Like you need to tell me that."

Ben was resiliently happy during his morning classes. In P.E. a baseball hit him in the shoulder, giving him good cause to swear loudly and be sent on another jog around the school. He felt twice as daring as usual and made sure to stand out of sight until he heard the coach call everyone back in.

English was pleasant and the usual teacher was back in Spanish class. When Ben was called to the front for an exercise, a number of students made sure to try their new word, but *mariposa* failed to prompt a reaction in the teacher. Maybe the substitute hadn't given them the right term, or perhaps Señora Vega chose not to hear. Ben wasn't sure how aware the teachers were of his sexuality, but he guessed the faculty gossiped just as much as the students did. The name calling irritated him, but he was so close to escaping school for the day that he tried not to dwell on it.

When lunch break finally came, he had a hurried meal with Allison, his stomach bubbling with nerves the whole time. Then he made a break for it. Ben had never skipped school before, at least not like this. He had previously feigned illnesses and had his mom call in. Who hadn't? But this was different. He had imagined running into teachers or security guards on the way to the car and had a selection of excuses prepared. His best was to claim that he had forgotten some books in his car. That seemed reasonable enough. Once he was in the car he would simply drive away, or maybe he would retreat and try again between classes.

As it was, he had nothing to worry about. There were plenty of seniors who worked jobs the second half of the day, so he wasn't alone in his excursion across the parking lot. He made it to the 3000GT, cautiously pulled out of the parking lot, and then went the exact speed limit all the way to the hospital. No sense in getting pulled over at this point in the game.

Ben entered through the emergency entrance, which was impractical in retrospect since it was no longer an emergency. A different receptionist, one even less friendly than the day before, gave him a vague idea of which direction he should head. He wandered the hospital halls for what felt like an eternity, crinkling his nose at the sterile smell and trying not to stare at patients through the doors. After asking twice more and travelling three floors up, he finally reached Tim's room.

The victim of his affections was reclining in bed, an ivory-white cast now covering his foot and lower leg. Currently an attractive young nurse was taking Tim's blood pressure. At least, that's what she was supposed to be doing. The cuff was still on his arm but so was her hand as she giggled at something Tim had just said. She sat down on the edge of the bed just as Ben cleared his throat, causing her to jump back up again.

"Benjamin!" Tim exclaimed happily. "And here I thought you had stolen my car and hightailed it to Mexico."

"That's the plan—" Ben smiled "—but I thought I'd bring you along. We're checking out."

"I'll let the doctor know," the nurse said as she left.

"Feeling better?" Ben suddenly wished he had brought flowers or a teddy bear or something. Wasn't that what you were supposed to do in such situations?

"A little, yeah. Did you call my parents?"

"No. Yes! Sorry, yes," Ben backtracked once Dr. Baker's shadow filled the doorway. "They don't think they can change their flight, but they've arranged for a nurse to take care of you and everything."

"They're probably pissed, huh?"

Ben found this comment surprising. Why would they be angry at their son for getting hurt? "Not at all," he replied. "Don't worry about it."

"Do you have their number handy?" Dr. Baker interjected.

"Oh! No, sorry," Ben apologized. He had been prepared for this question. "I totally forgot it."

"Well, as long as they were informed," the doctor said meaningfully.

Ben gave him his best innocent, doe-eyed look and nodded. This seemed to satisfy the doctor, who began scribbling on his clipboard.

The nurse returned and began to help Tim dress. While she was doing this, Dr. Baker gave Ben some papers and went over instructions that were to be given to the in-home nurse. Ben tried to keep up and nod when appropriate, hoping to get through it as quickly as possible since the doctor was standing in his line of vision. By the time the droning had ended, Tim was dressed. The doctor and nurse helped Tim into a wheelchair and gave him over to Ben.

He couldn't help but be reminded of when they adopted Wilford. Ben's family had visited the animal shelter and picked him out from among his littermates. Then there was a grueling waiting period of one week, during which the dog received his shots and was neutered before Wilford could be picked up. When they finally handed Ben the leash, he had felt proud and excited. Even a little nervous! But mostly the experience had made him happy. Much like he was feeling now. He hoped that Tim would feel the same once he caught wind of his plan.

— — —

"So... No nurse?"

"No nurse," Ben repeated.

The expression on Tim's face was hard to read. He looked concerned, or maybe just confused. He leaned back on the apricot living room couch and raised an eyebrow. "And you never called my parents? They have no idea I was in the hospital overnight?"

Ben started having second thoughts. What sort of monster intentionally kept parents in the dark about their son being injured? "They have no idea," he admitted.

The worry scattered from Tim's features as a broad smile appeared. "Thanks, man! That was really cool of you!"

Ben breathed out in relief. "I'm glad you think so! I was worried that I'd done the wrong thing."

"Naw, they would have been pissed."

"Really?"

"Really. A couple of years ago I came down with the flu the day before they were flying to Japan. It totally messed with their plans. They had to reschedule everything, missed out on some group tour thing. I don't know." Tim scratched at the skin near his cast. "They were so pissy the whole week after that I wished they hadn't bothered staying.

"I'm a mistake you know," he continued. "My parents are pretty cool and all, but it's obvious that it was never on their list to have kids. I'm an only child, and my parents have done everything in their power to keep running with the lifestyle they had before me."

Ben wasn't sure what to say to this. His own parents were always supportive and loving. In a way he wished he had some dirt to dish on them so he could commiserate, but there wasn't a single bad memory that sprang to mind. "So you have two weeks to survive without them," Ben said, guiding the conversation where he wanted it to go. "I'll help you of course. That's why I didn't think we needed a nurse. I can come by a couple of times a day to cook, clean up, that sort of stuff."

"You can cook?"

"Sure," Ben lied. As much as he'd been stretching the truth in the past couple of days, it was practically instinctual.

"That's good, because I'm hungry."

"Well, let's get you comfortable, and then I'll whip something up."

"Not here," Tim insisted. "I hate this room."

With the assistance of his crutches, he stood and swung his way toward the back of the house, Ben following. He led them through the dining room, across a large, open kitchen, and down a hall that ended in a dimly lit room.

The den, as Tim introduced it, was his father's stronghold. His mother was in charge of the rest of the house, but here his father had full control. He decorated the room in typical masculine style. A big-screen TV dominated one wall with massive boxy speakers to each side. A number of bookshelves held everything but books—namely sports memorabilia, business awards, and an impressive video collection. Bar signs and beer advertisements hung on the ebony wood-paneled walls that complimented the equally dark carpet. This combined with the shuttered windows kept the room cool and comfortable.

"I figure this is a good place to make camp," Tim said, as he headed toward a brown leather couch. "There's even a fridge to keep drinks in."

Ben turned and found a wet bar in the corner. The unit was basically just a sink, shelves for glasses, and one of those tiny refrigerators that he always associated with college dorms.

"So what all do we need then? Blankets and pillows obviously... Um."

"In one of the hall closets," Tim said. "I want my pillow from upstairs. And some real clothes. Throw something in the oven too, will ya?"

"Right," Ben managed to say just before the TV blared to life. His patient had certainly taken to the idea of him playing nurse!

Ben realized with some delight that he now had free rein over the house. With Tim settled in, he was eager to explore. Ben had been tempted to last night when dropping the car off. He figured arriving home in a shiny new vehicle would be beyond suspicious, so Ben had returned it to Tim's driveway, the keys in his pocket a major temptation. With Tim in the hospital, why not snoop a little? The idea had felt too creepy. Now he was free to look around anyway.

He started with the kitchen. The refrigerator was well-stocked with frozen entrees, which meant cooking wouldn't be too hard. He chose two pizzas and fiddled with the oven for a while before he got it running. Once that was finished he went upstairs and located Tim's bedroom.

Ben entered and felt strangely intoxicated for a moment. The whole room smelled exactly like Tim, as if someone had bottled up his essence and sprayed generous puffs of teenage boy into the air. Being there felt personal. In a way, the room was an extension of Tim, everything that represented him crammed into a single solitary space. Adults had an entire house and maybe an office or workspace to spread their existence over. For their kids, a personal life was restricted to just four walls. In this small area Tim lived, slept, talked on the phone, watched TV, jacked-off, and did whatever else he wanted to do.

Ben sat on the king-sized bed and looked around. Music and baseball posters covered most of the walls. He found all sports boring, but at least some of these featured pretty hot athletes. The only exception to the generic posters was an abstract painting, a collection of cool colors that might be depicting an ocean or waves. He stared at it for a while, wondering why it had been included. Did Tim choose it, or was it his mother's idea?

Across from Ben sat a dresser that supported a medium-sized television and VCR. A closet door and bookshelves were to his right, this time actually filled with the intended content. Ben browsed the titles, hoping to get a hint of what Tim liked to read but unable to do so. They were a completely eclectic mix, some even written in Spanish. His taste in music was easier to discern, the CD rack containing nothing but popular alternative music. And the *Little Mermaid* soundtrack. Ben mentally filed that one away as potential ammunition.

He paused to gaze out the bedroom window at the long, well-manicured backyard before returning to the dressers to collect a change of clothes. Socks were easy to find, as was underwear. He didn't examine the contents of this drawer too carefully. Doing so would be cheating, like skipping to the end of a book, when he hoped to discover Tim's underwear one by one over a series of hot encounters. Ben laughed at his own presumptions and went to the closet for a shirt and jeans.

He brought these items and the pillows back downstairs to his patient. The pizza was soon done afterwards and served. They ate together while flipping back and forth between MTV and VH1 to avoid commercials, laughing at most of the videos but genuinely enjoying a handful. There were quite a few songs that Ben wanted to sing along to, but for the first time in his life he was feeling too shy to perform. Finally the Fugees' cover of "Killing Me Softly" came on, which was too perfect of an opportunity to show off.

Ben gave it all he had, belting it out along with the lead vocals and almost putting Lauryn Hill's voice to shame. Tim sat straight up, his eyes wide in amazement. He clapped and raved when the song was over and spent the next hour trying to get Ben to sing along to some of the other videos. A few, like Beck, were a hopeless cause, but for some of them Ben was able to comply.

After a while Tim switched off the TV.

"So what's it like being gay?" he asked, catching Ben off guard.

"Like anything else I guess," Ben answered. "What's it like to be whatever you are?"

"Straight," Tim assured him. "Don't you catch a lot of flak for it? I mean, everyone at school knows, right?"

Ben nodded.

"I'm surprised you don't get beaten up every day."

"I get a lot of crap," Ben said with a shrug, "but I got crap before I came out for totally different reasons. It's no different now. Not really."

"I guess that's true. If it's not one thing, it's another."

Ben rolled his eyes. "Like you would know. It must be hard being a jock with rich parents and a brand-new sports car. People must tease you unmercifully."

Tim's grin was cocky. "When you put it like that, I do have it good, but I still get crap from other people. Miss a catch or don't make it to base and your team turns on you, especially if you lose the game."

Ben made sure he didn't look convinced.

"All right, how about this then?" The smile dropped from Tim's face. "At my last school, my ex-girlfriend went around telling everyone that I raped her, just because I dumped her. I had every girl in the school coming up to me and saying the craziest shit. A few even tried to knee me. It was insane."

"What happened?"

"What do you mean? Nothing happened. It was her word against mine, but she didn't take it to the police or anything because she knew the truth. It blew over after a while, but people never treated me the same afterwards. You don't know how glad I am to have a fresh start."

"The idea sounds appealing," Ben admitted.

"Would you still come out? If you moved to the other side of the country where no one knew, would you come out again?"

"Yeah," Ben answered immediately. "Are you kidding me? What would I do otherwise? Pretend I'm into girls and start sleeping with them?"

Tim only shrugged in response.

"I'd definitely come out again. It's the only chance I have at meeting someone else who is gay. It pays to advertise. That's the theory at least."

"No luck in the romance department?" Tim asked with an amused expression.

"Not really. Not love at least."

A garish cuckoo clock came to life, the little bird popping out and returning to its little home seven times.

"Jesus, I should get home." Ben hurried to leave, pulling a shoe on the wrong foot before realizing it and reaching for the other. "Are you going to be all right? There's drinks and stuff in the fridge and leftover pizza on the counter. Should I bring it in?"

"Naw, I can manage."

"I thought I'd come by in the morning to make breakfast and check on you, and then again in the afternoon?" Ben didn't mean to phrase it as a question. He wanted to say it like it was the obvious thing to do.

"Yeah?" Tim answered with his own inquiry. "You'd do that for me?"

"That and a hell of a lot more." The words were out of his mouth before his brain could stop them. The only damage control he could muster was a nervous little laugh, which probably made him sound twice as crazy. "Uh, so see you tomorrow then," he said. Face burning red, he dashed out of the room, grinning the whole way.

The pancakes were the right shape—round and flat. They were also spongy like they should be. Only the color was off. The first few out of the pan were an albino version of the normal brown variety. The next three were almost black. Ben had no idea what he was doing wrong.

He had read and reread the simple instructions in his mom's Betty Crocker cookbook three or four times and had even written down the basics, but these didn't look right at all. He shoveled the last pancake onto the plate with the others and poured a generous amount of syrup over them to conceal their inadequacies.

If Tim noticed that they weren't quite right, he didn't let on. It probably helped that he had taken a painkiller when Ben first showed up, half an hour ago. His eyes had a certain glazed look to them when Ben presented his creation. Within five minutes the entire plate had been cleared and licked clean.

"A guy could get used to this," Tim said appreciatively as Ben carried the plate back to the kitchen.

Next up was Tim's request for a bath. This idea had already been the subject of more than one of Ben's fantasies in the past few days. In them he had to assist poor helpless Tim out of his clothes, place him in the bathtub, and sponge clean every delicious nook and cranny of his body. This, of course, would lead to an involuntary physical reaction on Tim's part, one so intense that he would beg Ben for relief.

The reality wasn't anywhere near as exciting. Ben was asked to run the bath before he left for school, Tim insisting that he could manage the rest on his own. If this was true then it was also clear that Tim could have turned the faucet on by himself, but Ben let it slide. The more indispensable he became the better.

As the tub filled and the bubble bath frothed, Ben thought of how he was supposed to be in P.E. instead. He felt deliriously happy about missing it, but he still had to make it back to school in time for roll call in English class. Even though he had risen early to have extra time, he already needed to leave if he wanted to make it.

"Bath's ready!" he yelled as he headed for the door. "See you later today!"

"Don't take my car!" Tim shouted back.

"What?" Ben responded before shutting the front door and getting in the Mitsubishi.

Ben felt conspicuous being the only person walking across the parking lot when he arrived, but he wasn't stopped and figured it wouldn't matter if he was. What were they going to do, punish him for showing up? He felt less confident when he entered the school and found the hallways empty. Having just heard the bell, he had assumed that first period just ended. Now it was clear that second period had begun. He was huffing and puffing by the time he reached his English class.

"Well?" Mrs. Carroll insisted with raised eyebrows.

Ben sighed. Some teachers were happy to wordlessly issue a tardy or not bother about it at all. Others expected explanations and apologies.

"Sorry," he panted. "Just came from P.E. and Coach made me stay behind." He doubted she would check up on this. He took his seat before she could ask any more questions. To his relief she resumed whatever lecture he had interrupted.

"Lose track of time loitering in the showers?" whispered a snide voice from next to him.

Ben looked over at the sneering freckled face of Daniel Wigmore. He didn't know how it was possible, but Daniel had ended up sitting next to Ben in at least one class every year, much to his annoyance. Daniel had become something of a ginger-headed nemesis. He was the type of student who took scholastic competition way too seriously. Daniel made sure to flash his homework when he got A's, which was always, and would speed through tests and slam his pencil down, surveying the class with a smug expression.

"Or did Coach ask you to stay behind and blow him?" Daniel pressed.

"Keep your fantasies to yourself, faggot."

That wiped the grin off Daniel's face. People never expected Ben to use a word like that. It was twice as effective coming from a gay guy, and more worrying too, thanks to the whole "takes one to know one" philosophy.

Daniel turned his attention back to his perfect-grades obsession and left Ben to mentally plan when he would skip school again. Technically he could leave after this class, but he knew it would be a bad idea. Probably.

Third period Spanish didn't help his resolve. The substitute was back and issued a test that Ben had forgotten to study for. He was lost during it, certain he had failed. A few more uses of the word *mariposa* whispered in his direction only made him more miserable.

By lunch he was anxious to leave and told Allison as much.

"Forget it!" she said vehemently. "You can't start ditching me at lunch for anyone, no matter how hot they are. Besides, your absence didn't go unnoticed in choir. You're Mrs. Hammond's star pupil. All of her hopes and dreams are being lived vicariously through you now. She practically organized a search party when you didn't show up yesterday!"

Allison might have been exaggerating, but she did have a point. Mrs. Hammond was the teacher most likely to notice his absence.

"What did you tell her yesterday?" Ben asked.

"That you were sick."

"Well, tell her I am again today. Two days in a row isn't suspicious."

Allison sighed and shook her head dramatically. "What's going on that you're so excited about? Is Tim less straight than we initially suspected?"

"No, he's straight all right, but—" Ben grasped for words but failed to find any that suited him. "I don't know. I just like him, and taking care of him is sort of like playing house. It feels real, even if it isn't."

"So in other words, you are deluding yourself."

"Maybe, but better an imaginary romance than none at all."

"I guess," Allison conceded. "I'm just worried that you're headed for a broken heart."

"Mm," Ben replied noncommittally. "What's up with your heart lately?"

"You mean Ronnie?" A sly smile crossed her face. "Things are going good. Very good. He has my class schedule memorized and keeps escorting me to each one. We still haven't been on a proper date though. Speaking of which, you and I are going to the movies on Saturday."

"We are?" Ben hadn't considered it, but this weekend he would finally be free to spend the entire day and night with Tim. He didn't want to brush Allison off for any reason, even his latest infatuation, but it might be the only opportunity to spend an extended amount of time with him.

"We are," Allison confirmed. "At least that's what I'm telling my dad. I need you to cover for me so Ronnie and I can go out. You'll do that, won't you?"

"Yes!" Ben breathed a sigh of relief. "That's perfect actually. I'll be over at Tim's until late, so my parents will think I'm out with you. If your dad calls then my parents will back up the story."

Allison took another bite of her sandwich and chewed thoughtfully before tossing the remaining crusts into the brown paper bag. "Who knows," she said with a wicked grin, "maybe we'll both be getting laid this weekend."

CHAPTER 6

The week came to an end after a series of breakneck starts and whiplash stops. Mornings and afternoons spent with Tim went by in the blink of an eye, while the truncated school hours felt twice as long as they did before. Mercifully, once Saturday finally arrived, time slowed to a meandering pace that promised a long and satisfying weekend.

Oppressive humidity forced them to crank up the air conditioning in Tim's house. Even the dark and shadowy den was affected by the thick heat outdoors as a storm of massive proportions gathered. Ben spent the morning cleaning up around the house and running the laundry machines. As fun as it was being domestic, he was glad to be done with the chores and was looking forward to spending quality time with the person in his care. Unfortunately, the painkillers had once again put Tim to sleep.

Ben wandered the house instead, absorbing the details and decorations that hinted at Tim's life. On a nightstand in the master bedroom, he found a photo of a white-haired, stern-faced man with an impressive physique. Next to him smiled a slight and beautiful Hispanic woman, the source of Tim's dark hair and tan skin. After considering them for a number of minutes, Ben set the photo back down next to the rosary beads that lay there.

As Ben continued to explore, he found a number of crucifixes hanging on the wall, as well as a small collection of Bibles in the living room. The religious items might be mere decorations to Tim's mom. Ben's own mother, who freelanced as an interior designer, had a client who loved rustic crosses despite being an atheist. The religious items he saw here didn't seem so frivolous. Ben wondered, if Tim's parents were Catholic, what they would think of him. If they ever met.

There were two kinds of spirituality, Ben felt. The first belonged to those who let their heart lead them, and who chose what fit with their worldview while disregarding what didn't. Ben's parents were like this. They rarely went to church and held a rather idealistic and loving vision of God that didn't mesh with the Old Testament's portrayal.

Then there were those who took scripture literally. Such

people unquestioningly followed each rule and obeyed every command of their spiritual leaders, no matter how nonsensical and outdated those conventions might be. These mindless extremists tended to make life difficult for everyone else. Ben certainly hoped that Tim's parents didn't fall into that category.

As for Ben, he tended not to believe in any sort of god or devil. Except when he sang. That was the only time the veil between reality and the impossible lifted for him. Singing revealed to him a million worlds made up of colors the physical eye could never see, realms populated with countless spirits and energies of all kinds. God was there too, a benevolent being of as many faces as there were religions on the Earth. Oh yes, when he sang, such things were possible, but the second he stopped it all faded away, forgotten until the next time he took up his voice again.

A snort followed by a grunt brought his attention back to the present. As did a shuffling sound followed by the crack of a Coke can opening. Tim was finally awake.

"Oh man, I slept deep," he said as Ben entered the room. Tim's hair was sticking up in all directions, which was so adorable that it took all of Ben's willpower not to reach out and muss it up further. "The house looks nice. Thanks."

"No problem. You can repay me by staying awake. I was going out of my mind with boredom."

"Sorry." Tim grinned. "I took too many of those pills. You should try them. They make you feel great."

"I might take you up on that," Ben said, remembering the mellow buzz that had followed his tonsils being removed.

Tim yawned like a lion in the savanna heat. "I feel grody. Would you mind running a bath for me?"

"Bored," Ben reminded him.

"Oh. Once I'm in the tub you can come keep me company," Tim offered.

Surely he was aware of how erotic such a situation would be for Ben. Was he offering more than it sounded like or was he just being playfully flirtatious without any real intent? Regardless, Ben rose to run the bath without revealing any interest. If Tim thought he could arouse Ben's appetite so easily... Well, he could, but Ben wasn't going to give him the satisfaction of knowing it.

Once the tub was full of steaming water and bubbles, he waited outside the door while Tim climbed in. This took much longer than it would for an uninjured person, but once he was settled, he called for Ben. The shower curtain was half-closed, obscuring everything from the waist down. It hardly mattered. Tim's impressive upper body was enough to evoke an unquenchable lust in Ben.

Ben sat on the toilet, for lack of a better place, directly across from the bathtub. Aside from being the only seat available, it allowed him a more revealing angle. There would have been nothing left to his imagination if not for Tim's injured leg. The cast was propped on the side of the tub so that it wouldn't get wet. The unfortunate side effect of this was that he couldn't see more.

"I'm guessing this isn't how you usually spend your weekends," Tim said.

"You mean watching straight guys take baths?" Ben replied innocently enough. "You'd be surprised. It's a fairly common occurrence."

Tim's laughter echoed in the small tiled room. "Well, what do you do besides that?"

Ben shrugged. "Hang out with Allison Cross. She's my best friend."

"And what do you usually do together?"

"Shop, mostly. Hit the movies sometimes or just drive around. What about you?"

"Me and my friends? Same stuff as you, I guess. We don't shop, but we drive around and try to find somewhere to hang out. There's been a couple of good parties this year too."

Ben didn't know anything about that. He was rarely invited to any parties. Such things were the mysterious domain of the popular kids. He had almost forgotten the crowd Tim ran with. How the nice person in front of him could be cronies with the biggest assholes in school was hard to comprehend.

"Haven't been on any dates yet?" Ben asked, even though he knew otherwise.

"Yeah, that too," Tim said without any great enthusiasm. "Shit. I still haven't called Krista since this happened. She's going to be pissed."

"Who's that?"

"My girlfriend. Krista Norman. Maybe you know her?"

"I think so," Ben said evenly as an image of an anorexic witch sprung to mind. "Wow, and you haven't called her for a week?"

Tim shrugged, slipping further down into the tub. "I guess I should have, but it seems pointless right now. The painkillers pretty much kill my sex drive, you know."

Ben didn't know, but now he could safely assume that Tim wasn't hoping to initiate something with his weird choice of social setting. A shame too. It would have been a scene right out of those magazine stories. The straight guy starts talking about his girlfriend and gets aroused, eventually turning to the only other warm body around…

"She never puts out anyway," Tim continued. "She's a real cockteaser."

Ben swallowed a laugh, Tim's line fitting the fantasy all too well. "That sucks, although you'll probably score major sympathy points when she sees you injured."

"Hey, yeah! You're right!" A lazy smile came over Tim's face as he considered the idea.

Ben cursed his mouth and brain for conspiring against him. Soon after he was sent upstairs to fetch a new outfit for Tim, which was fun and only helped to further the illusion that they were a young married couple. Was Tim aware of how this felt for him? Did he care, or was all this just a blur of opiate-induced numbness?

As the afternoon faded into evening, the pressure outside finally peaked and exploded. The sky opened with a grumble of thunder and a hammering of rain. They killed the air conditioner and opened the windows, enjoying the rhythmic sound of water pummeling the leaves outside.

Ben busied himself in the kitchen, attempting to make a simple dinner of spaghetti and meatballs. He had gone over the process a dozen times with his mom, who was becoming increasingly puzzled by his sudden interest in cooking.

The pasta sauce wasn't a problem, considering it came from the supermarket in a jar. The meatballs were trickier since the meat wasn't fully defrosted. Ben sculpted them into balls as best as he could, his hands stinging from the cold. Timing was something he hadn't considered before he started. The pasta was finished boiling before he had even begun frying meatballs or warming up the sauce. He took the pasta off the heat but left it in the water in the hopes of keeping it moist.

After an hour of effort, he ended up with pasta that was much too soggy and meatballs that were slightly burnt on the outside but barely cooked on the inside. Because he couldn't mess up the sauce, and as he had done with his pancakes, he used a generous amount of it paired with Parmesan cheese to help cover up his mistakes.

Ben set the dining room table, but abruptly changed his mind, feeling it revealed too blatantly his domestic fantasies. That and the result of his labors didn't seem worthy of such a formal presentation. He brought the plates into the den instead and placed them on the coffee table. MTV serenaded them in the background as they began their meal.

Tim reacted to the food like a ravenous stray dog. He tore into it at a speed that promised he wouldn't be tasting very much of anything, much to Ben's relief. They were halfway through their meal when the power went off. A vehement snarl of thunder followed the sudden silence, the storm proclaiming its role in the outage. There were a few minutes of scrambling in the dim light until matches and candles were found and lit.

"Romantic," Tim joked as they resumed eating.

"Isn't it?" Ben tried to chuckle casually.

"It's funny, like fate has some crazy plan in mind for us. You running into me that day and dragging me to the hospital. Then you took care of me, did all the stuff you're still doing. And now this." He gestured to the nearly empty plates in front of them. "Dining in candlelight. It's so close."

"What do you mean?"

"Well, you know. If you were a girl it would be perfect."

Ben raised his head to make eye contact, and for one electrical moment, Tim looked at him as if he were just that. Then the amorous expression was replaced by one of confusion followed by a few sniffs. "Is something burning?"

Ben sniffed a couple of times himself. "Shit! The garlic bread!" He darted into the kitchen or at least intended to. With the lights out, he ran into a number of walls, probably dislodging a multitude of crucifixes. Eventually he spotted a glow that revealed itself to be the smoldering remains of the bread loaf. He felt around for oven mitts, took the pan from the oven, and tossed the charred bread into the sink, running water over it for good measure.

With the emergency over, Ben leaned against the kitchen counter and took a deep breath. If only he were a girl, huh? On one hand Tim's words meant that he was the wrong gender and didn't stand a chance. On the other they also said, with a few physical differences aside, that Ben was everything Tim was looking for in a guy. Girl. Whatever.

The lawn mower sputtered and chugged, running off fumes now. Ben eyed the three remaining strips of grass yet to be mowed and hoped he could finish without having to refill the tank. He broke into a run, pushing the mower ahead of him with all his strength. A few strenuous moments later and the lawn mower gave one final protesting cough before dying just seconds after the last blades of grass had been sheared.

Ben smiled in satisfaction as he surveyed his work. The yard didn't look perfect, but then it never did. As he cast his eye over the lawn, a movement drew his attention to the house where his mother, June, stood in the window. She was peering at him intently as she had been all day, treating Ben with suspicion ever since he came home this morning. She had assigned him an unmerciful number of chores and kept checking on him as he worked, as if to catch him doing drugs or whatever else she suspected. Once the mower was put away, he entered the kitchen through the garage.

"All done then?" June asked as she handed him a glass of Kool-Aid.

"Yeah," Ben gasped after chugging the drink. "Beyond done. I'm going to take a shower now."

"Afterwards you can help me make dinner, since you've been so interested in cooking lately."

"Sure. All right."

Ben took his time in the shower, since it was apparently the only peace and quiet he would get today. So much for Sunday being a day of rest! He almost wished his parents were religious! After he relieved himself sexually, he stood tranquilly under the stream of hot water for what felt like half an hour. Then he reluctantly turned off the water and stepped out. Wiping the steam from the bathroom mirror, he eyed himself as he dried off, wondering all the while what Tim would think of his body. Was it good that Ben was so slender because it was more like a girl? Or would it be better if he had muscles that could compete with Tim's?

Once he was downstairs again, his mother switched off her usual decorating TV program and hustled him into the kitchen.

"Chili," she announced as she began pulling ingredients from the cabinets. "This is one of the easiest things to cook."

Ben helped her to reach some of the items on the higher shelves. June was so short that she actually made him feel tall. He had inherited his small build from her, as well as the blond hair. Really, he didn't resemble his father very much. "What did you eat last night at your friend's house?" she asked casually as she switched on the oven.

"I tried making spaghetti, but it didn't turn out so well."

"So you cooked for his whole family?" His mother turned her lie-detecting gaze on him.

"No, they were out of town." There was no point in lying. He never managed to get away with it. His mom saw through it every time.

"You didn't mention that when you called last night," she said. "You were supposed to be out with Allison but ended up at some guy's house. Someone we've never met."

Ben shrugged, knowing that the less he said the better.

"Did you actually know this guy, or did you meet him at a bar?" she pressed.

Ben laughed, relieved to finally understand the source of her concern.

"I wasn't at a bar, Mom. I don't even have a fake ID. I met Tim at school a few weeks ago."

June didn't respond to this. Instead she showed him the proper way to cut an onion, probably while rethinking her strategy.

"I just want you to be safe," she said as she slid the diced onion off the cutting board and into a frying pan sizzling with ground beef. "If you need something, like condoms or lube, you just have to ask."

Ben fought to hold back his laughter. His mother was imagining all sorts of illicit sex, when the most that had happened last night was a few board games. He was pretty sure that a condom wasn't required to play Scrabble or Life.

"He's not my boyfriend, Mom. He's straight."

June set down the can she was trying to open with a loud thunk. "Then why are you cooking for him? And how come you haven't been home all week? What exactly do you two do together?"

Now she was back to suspecting drugs. She would be twice as shocked to learn that he had, in reality, been doing many of the same chores that he had tackled today.

"I just really like him, that's all."

"Oh, Benjamin," she said sorrowfully. "You need to find someone who can return your feelings. Otherwise you'll end up getting hurt."

"That's what everyone keeps telling me," he responded tersely.

"You haven't met any other gay boys at your school?"

He shook his head.

"None? Maybe we *should* get you a fake ID. We could go to the bars together."

"Sure!" Ben laughed. "You can help me pick someone out."

"I would too! I just don't think that's the best place to meet a spouse."

"I'm not ready to get married!"

"You know what I mean. Have you thought about personal ads?"

"C'mon, Mom. Stop worrying about it. I'm sure I'll meet someone. I just hope it happens before I'm thirty."

"It will. It's just a matter of time before someone realizes how special my baby is."

Ben smiled as they continued making chili together. The recipe was easy. All he had to do was throw a bunch of stuff in a pot and let it cook. Even he couldn't mess this one up.

"You should have been honest though," his mother said, almost as an afterthought. "All that stuff about being out with Allison!"

Ben remained silent, wondering suddenly how she figured out that he hadn't gone to the movies at all.

"She's going to be in trouble with her father too, you know," she continued in chastising tones. "He sounded furious when he called last night."

"What? Allison's dad called?"

"Late last night. After you called and said you'd be sleeping over. He asked if I knew where you two were and, well …"

Ben didn't need her to finish. The sinking feeling in his gut told him all he needed to know.

CHAPTER 7

Lunchtime couldn't come quickly enough. Despite calling Allison at least three dozen times Sunday evening, Ben had been unable to reach her. The phone only rang and rang, not even the answering machine picking up. Unless she had entered into a six-hour conversation with Ronnie, which seemed unlikely, her phone had probably been taken away, or maybe her private line had been canceled.

Ben's apprehension increased on Monday as she failed to appear at their usual place in the cafeteria. Usually she was there waiting for him, since her third period class was much closer. Finally, ten minutes into the lunch break, she arrived looking haggard and stressed.

Ben stood and embraced her, letting loose a string of clumsy apologies.

"What are you talking about?" she demanded once he had pulled away.

"It's my fault you got into trouble." Ben confessed his guilt in greater detail, not expecting forgiveness.

Allison sat and waited until he was finished. Then she waved a hand dismissively. "I would have gotten in trouble anyway," she said as she sat down. "My dad was waiting for us in the driveway."

"No!"

"Yes! He's completely psycho. I even had Ronnie drop me off further down the street, but not far enough I guess."

Ben slid his Twinkie over to her as a gesture of peace, even though it was clear she wasn't angry with him. "So your dad spotted you getting out of Ronnie's car?"

"Yeah. He was sitting in the middle of the driveway in a foldout chair, drinking his whisky like it was going out of style. He sat there waiting for me for who knows how long."

"So what did he do?"

"Well, luckily I saw him running down the road in time to tell Ronnie to take off. He managed to get away before my dad caught up with him, but he did throw his whisky bottle at Ronnie's car. Hit it too."

Ben sat in a stunned silence, taking in this news. Allison's dad had always been a bit loony, but he seemed to be getting worse every year.

"Did it jack up Ronnie's car?"

"No. I just saw him a second ago and he said it was fine. It's the first that I've talked to him since it happened. Dad smashed the hell out of my phone in the process of grounding me."

"So…" Ben hesitated, not wanting to ask if she and Ronnie were still dating. It wouldn't be the first time her dad had managed to scare away one of her boyfriends.

"I'm not sure what he thinks." Allison sighed miserably. "He seemed okay. Concerned more than anything. He's in my last class, so I'll have a better chance to talk to him about it then."

Once again, Ben skipped sixth period to take care of Tim, so he didn't have a chance to catch up with her after school. He didn't hear anything else about it until the next day. Allison didn't show up for lunch on Tuesday, causing worst-case scenarios to fill his mind. As psychotic as her dad might be, so far he had never laid a hand on Allison. Ben worried it was only a matter of time before he did. With less than two years left before college, he hoped that she would be free before anything like that ever happened.

Ben almost cried out in joy when he saw Allison waiting for him outside fourth period choir. His relief didn't last long when he saw how panicked she appeared.

"You have to help me," she said, grabbing both his arms.

Ben's mouth went dry. "What happened?" he rasped, feeling certain that his worst fear had come true.

"Ronnie is coming over." Her eyes searched his, questioning if he understood the implications. "Tonight!"

"Wait, you invited him over? Why would you do that?"

"No I didn't invite him! Are you insane? He invited himself!"

Ben pondered this for a moment before understanding what was going on. "He's doomed." He couldn't help but laugh as he said it. Ronnie intended to introduce himself to Mr. Cross, make peace, and possibly get Allison ungrounded. The gesture was chivalrous, if not suicidal.

"It's not funny!" Allison hissed, casting an uneasy glance toward Mrs. Hammond, who had come outside the choir room to investigate.

"Is there any reason you two are so apprehensive of entering my domicile?" she asked in dramatic tones that were wholly unnecessary.

"We just have a few things to talk over," Ben said.

The look of pleasant amusement fell from Mrs. Hammond's face. Ben might be her star pupil, but her own ego came first. "What, exactly, is more important than my class?"

"The talent show," Ben said, thinking fast. This was Mrs. Hammond's favorite subject. Last year she had high hopes for them to win, until a tonsillectomy took out Ben's voice. Since then she had mentioned the next competition almost daily. "It's not more important, of course. It's just that I had a few ideas last night and—"

"Say no more!" Mrs. Hammond trilled, her mood instantly favorable again. "The talent show! Well! If you two would rather practice today, the auditorium next door is empty."

After a few comments engineered to make Mrs. Hammond feel good about herself, they were able to escape to the privacy of the auditorium. Allison flopped down in one of the chairs and aimed an expectant look at him.

"Just talk Ronnie out of it," Ben said easily. "Tell him it's a sweet but horrible idea and that'll be the end of it."

"What do you think I was doing during lunch? He kept smiling at me as if I was exaggerating things for my own amusement."

"Even after having his car pelted by a whisky bottle?"

"He acts like he didn't even notice." Allison frowned. "Now I wish it had broken one of his windows."

"I guess some lessons need to be learned the hard way."

Ben smiled sympathetically, a gesture Allison didn't reciprocate. Instead her frown increased and her forehead crinkled with concern. "I'm really worried about Ronnie," she said. "You know my dad. He gets crazier and meaner every year. I need your help."

Ben shrugged and nodded, indicating that he would do whatever she needed.

"Come over tonight," she pleaded. "When Ronnie shows up, I want you there too."

"Yeah, right." Ben's chuckle faltered when he saw that she was serious. "And this is going to keep your dad calm, how?"

"He won't be calm no matter what happens, but he's much

less likely to do something stupid with other people around."

Rubbing his face wearily, Ben paced back and forth a few times. "If you want a witness to keep the situation in check, maybe you should try the police."

Allison didn't respond, choosing instead to wait for a definitive answer.

"All right. Fine. I'll be there. When?"

"At six. Or a little earlier, so you're there before Ronnie shows up. Here…" Allison dug in her purse and pulled out her wallet. "You can bring this to me. That will be your excuse for coming by. There's one other thing."

"What's that?" he asked apprehensively.

"You totally just entered us into the talent contest a few minutes ago."

Ben rolled his eyes and smiled. "Wonderful."

Five minutes before six, Ben walked up the driveway of Allison's home with increasing trepidation about this plan. He was certain that his presence would only serve to aggravate Mr. Cross further, but he couldn't get out of it now. He had promised Allison and had no choice but to follow through.

The door swung open before he could knock. Allison put one finger to her lips to indicate that he should stay quiet and waved him into the house.

"I don't want Dad to know you're here until Ronnie shows up," she whispered.

"That makes sense," Ben muttered.

They crept into the living room and sat together on a comfortable burgundy couch. The living room, like most of the house, was warmly decorated and very inviting. Little had changed since the death of Allison's mother eight years ago. Ben had few memories of her but remembered Mrs. Cross being as expressive and friendly as her daughter. He wondered how someone like her ended up with the man she had married. He supposed Mr. Cross could have been a different man back then. Was it the death of his wife that transformed him into the domineering brute he was today?

The doorbell rang, causing both Allison and Ben to jump.

"Aren't you going to get it?" he asked her when she didn't move.

"Nope. I'm grounded."

Shivers went down Ben's spine as footsteps came tromping down the hallway behind them. There was a pause as they neared. Then they continued quicker than before.

"What the hell is he doing here?" Mr. Cross grumbled when he entered the room and saw Ben.

"He brought me my wallet." Allison nudged Ben, prompting him to dig it out of his pocket. "I left it at school today."

Mr. Cross scowled and started to say something, but the doorbell interrupted him. Shaking his head, he marched to the door and threw it open. "Yes?"

"Mr. Cross?" A figure could just barely be seen beyond Allison's father.

"Who the hell are you?"

"I'm Ronnie Adams. Your daughter's boyfriend, sir."

The door began to shut. "She's grounded!"

"I'm here to talk to you, sir. About your daughter. Please."

Mr. Cross stood there in silence, momentarily unsure how to react. Finally he stepped out of the way, allowing Ronnie to enter.

Ben hadn't seen Ronnie since biology class last year and was unaware how much he had changed. Ronnie had always been moderately attractive in a grunge sort of way, but now he had come into his own. The shoulder-length dreadlocks had been culled, revealing a handsome face with even features. The concert T-shirts and ratty jeans were gone too, replaced by trendier clothing that fit closer to his body. He had either been working out or the oversized shirts of yesteryear had disguised his nice pecs and narrow waist.

"Do you know this person, Alli?" Mr. Cross demanded as they neared the couch.

"Yes, he's the guy you threw a whisky bottle at," Allison said.

Ben held his breath, waiting for an explosion, but instead Mr. Cross reluctantly apologized to Ronnie.

"It's okay. It didn't do any damage, sir," Ronnie said politely.

He was being a bit too cordial, in Ben's opinion, but it had gotten him this far, which was more than he had expected.

"I can understand why you were angry," Ronnie continued. "I should have asked permission to take your daughter out."

"Well, that's why she's in trouble," Mr. Cross huffed, working himself up. "She won't be going out with anyone for quite some time."

"I understand, sir," Ronnie responded calmly. "I respect your position. I just felt I should come by to apologize and to introduce myself properly."

Mr. Cross eyed Ronnie suspiciously. "You can't stay. She's grounded."

"That's fair. I'll be on my way then." Ronnie held out his hand to Mr. Cross, who took it after a moment's hesitation. "Maybe once Allison is no longer grounded, you would allow me to take her out again? This time with your permission?"

Multiple expressions fought for dominance on Mr. Cross's face until it settled on perplexed consent. "That might be possible."

"Thank you, sir," Ronnie said with a final handshake. He spared a single nod and smile for Allison before he took his leave.

As soon as the front door was shut, Mr. Cross wheeled around and pointed an accusatory finger at Ben. "You think it's funny, saying my daughter is with you when she's out with a stranger?"

"No," Ben answered, trying not to make eye contact.

"You're damn right it's not!" Mr. Cross boomed.

"Dad," Allison interjected. "It wasn't his idea. It was mine!"

"But he was happy enough to go along with it!" Mr. Cross countered, still glaring at Ben. "I bet you think you're real smart, pulling the wool over my eyes, don't you?"

"No," Ben answered again, beginning to feel agitated. He handed Allison her wallet and stood. "I have to go home."

"Yeah, you go home! You won't ever be coming back here again, you hear me?"

"Fine, whatever." Big loss. It wasn't like they spent much time here with Mr. Cross being home so often.

"You won't be seeing Allison again either."

Ben stopped in his tracks. "What?"

"Your friendship with my daughter is over. You're never allowed to see her again. Or call, or anything else!"

"Dad!" Allison protested.

"Shut up, Alli!"

"You shut up!" Ben yelled, surprising even himself. "You can't tell me who I'm friends with. You can't tell me anything!"

Mr. Cross's shock only lasted a second before blind fury took control. Two long strides brought him close enough to grab Ben by the back of the neck. Mr. Cross shoved him toward the door, releasing Ben as he stumbled forward. "Get out!" he shouted. "Get out of my house!"

The second Ben opened the door, he felt himself shoved from behind. He hit the screen door, which buckled open. Sprinting to the driveway, he hopped into Tim's car, his shaking hand stabbing at the ignition until the key slid inside. Once the engine sprang to life, he put it into drive and escaped down the street. He looked in the rearview mirror to see Mr. Cross standing in the yard, huffing and puffing like a bull. Allison was behind him, her look of shock more reminiscent of a lamb. Ben only hoped she didn't get trampled beneath angry hooves.

There was, thankfully, very little that Mr. Cross could do to prevent them from seeing each other during the weekdays, short of sending Allison to a different school in another district. This possibility wasn't so far-fetched. The idea would have seemed laughable a few short years ago, but Mr. Cross's grip on reality was slipping at an exponential rate.

Seeing each other after school was too risky so soon after the fallout, but they still had the benefit of lunch breaks and choir. Mrs. Hammond enthusiastically insisted they leave class to practice, either in the auditorium or—if it was being used as it was today—outside.

The two friends were currently enjoying a sunny bench secluded by two large oak trees. Ben's head rested in Allison's lap as she played absentmindedly with his hair and he gazed at the slowly swaying leaves above.

"I asked Dad if I could go out with Ronnie this weekend."

"What did he say?"

"No, but that I could next weekend when I'm ungrounded."

"That sucks," Ben sighed. "I mean, I'm happy for you, but it seems unfair that I'm always on his shit list."

"Who knows what his deal is? The funniest part is that I'll probably have to say I'm out on a date with Ronnie the next time I want to do something with you."

"Then when you get busted I can show up and say 'sir' every other word and your dad will love me."

"Shut up!" Allison laughed.

"You know," Ben said, propping himself up on his elbows and shooting a disdainful glare toward the school, "we're going to have to start working on a song soon. It's only a matter of time before Mrs. Hammond asks us for a preview."

"For the talent show?" Allison chewed her lip thoughtfully. "I'd totally forgotten about that. So what are we going to do?"

They spent the rest of the period discussing which song to perform. Last year they were set to sing "Under Pressure" by David Bowie and Queen, but they had practiced it so much that they had grown tired of the song.

"Ronnie has a band, you know," Allison said coyly.

"I think you might have mentioned that a few million times." Ben paused to read between the lines. "Wait, you want us to sing with them or something?"

"Maybe. They aren't perfect, but they have this one song with amazing lyrics. It's about a girl, and she's watching this guy from far away that she's totally enamored with. He doesn't know she exists, but the girl knows everything about him, sees more than everyone else. It's like she knows more about him than he does."

"And I'm the girl."

"Well, yeah."

"Thanks."

"I'm not doing it justice," Allison sighed. "Just listen to it once."

When the bell rang, Ben returned inside with Allison before doubling back and heading toward the parking lot. Just as his hands were on the exit door, someone called his name. He turned around and craned his head over the crowded hallway until he spotted Ms. Hughes waving him down. Ben almost bolted in terror, but it was too late. She had seen him. His teacher for science, a class that he had been skipping for the better part of two weeks, approached him with transparent concern.

Ben's feet were glued to the floor while he tried to think of what he should do or say as she navigated the swarming students.

"I'm sorry," he blurted out when she reached him.

"Where have you been?" she asked, looking him over for signs of illness.

Ben breathed in and waited for the words to come, but they didn't. He had been so preoccupied with everything lately that he hadn't dreamed up what his excuse would be when he inevitably returned to the classes he was skipping.

"Ben?" she prompted when he failed to answer. "Is everything all right? Is something wrong at home?"

As tempting as it was to lie and say he had a problematic home life, he knew that would only lead to more trouble. "I'm really sorry that I've been skipping, Ms. Hughes," the words came finally. "It's... It's hard to explain what's going on. I'm not in trouble or anything, but there's someone who needs my help. That's why I've been leaving school early."

The school bell rang while she considered his words with an open expression of confusion. The students disappeared one by one until they were left virtually alone. He knew Ms. Hughes would stand there until she had her explanation. After all, she was often late to her own classes.

Ms. Hughes had been his teacher freshman year as well. Running late from lunch one day, Ben had seen Ms. Hughes and another female teacher standing very close together. They kissed and went their separate ways, never noticing Ben. Occasionally he had wanted to bring it up, to let her know he was gay as well, but it had always seemed such an odd subject to broach and he worried she would react defensively. Maybe now was the time to tell her.

"Level with me, Ben," Ms. Hughes said. "Do you need my help? Is there something I can do?"

Ben wanted to hug her. She was possibly the only teacher in the world who would offer to help instead of dragging him off to the principal's office.

"It's nothing too serious, but I really am needed." Ben smiled to reassure her. This only made her worry lines deepen.

"And you can't tell me why?"

"I can. But not yet." He could tell her now, but gay or not, she was still an adult and would probably insist that Tim's parents be informed and a proper nurse hired. All that mattered now was getting free of the school.

She looked into his eyes, hoping the truth would betray itself there. "When are you coming back to my class?"

"Monday," he answered truthfully. Tim's parents came back late on Sunday. That left only three more days before his domestic fantasies would come to an end.

"I'm trusting you, Ben," she said. "You owe me an explanation. And an essay since you missed the first test."

"All right." He grinned, relief washing over him. "I promise."

He glanced back as he went, Ms. Hughes still watching him, even though her classroom was full of students who were probably going wild in her absence. She still looked slightly puzzled, perhaps wondering what it was in Ben that she saw in herself.

CHAPTER 8

"Honey, I'm home!" Ben crowed happily as he struggled with a grocery bag in each hand.

Today had been the sort of Friday where even the teachers had their hearts set on the weekend. None of the classes he bothered to show up for had been difficult or involved any homework. He and Allison once again disregarded the talent show and spent the period gossiping. He related to her for the umpteenth time how much he enjoyed taking care of Tim, while she filled him in on the action she and Ronnie had been sneaking in between classes.

After school, Ben took some of the money Tim's parents had left and went grocery shopping, restocking much-needed supplies and picking up the ingredients for chili.

"Aren't you going to help carrying in?" Ben called as he deposited the bags on the kitchen counter.

"I could probably manage something," Tim said as he crutched his way into the room.

Tim had been much more active and restless the last few days. The painkillers had run out on Wednesday and he had shown no interest in a refill. Tim was wincing more often, but he seemed happy to pay this price for his sobriety.

"Seriously," he said as he followed Ben out to the driveway. "Sling a few plastic bags on my wrists."

"I've only got paper," Ben chided as he took the last one and a twelve-pack of Coke from the trunk. "Your moral support is appreciated though."

"Why'd you buy so much? My parents are coming back on Sunday."

"I know, but tomorrow I'm cooking a meal fit for a king. Well, a very poor and underprivileged king maybe."

"You're making me hungry. Why not cook it tonight?"

"My parents are on my back because I've barely been around the last few weeks and have missed almost every dinner." Ben waited while Tim opened the glass door for him. "I promised that I would actually be there tonight."

Tim rolled his eyes. "So it's frozen burritos for me?"

"That or a pot pie. I promise I'll make it up to you tomorrow."

Ben stayed long enough to put the groceries away and make sure Tim had everything he needed. He meant to leave immediately afterwards, but they started talking, first about Tim's homework that Ben had brought from school and then about some of the insane antics Tim had seen on the daytime talk shows. By the time he left, Ben was already ten minutes late for dinner.

He ran most of the way home, cursing his mom for insisting he be there tonight. What difference did it make? Couldn't they shove food down their gullets without him? He didn't see why meals were considered a social obligation. Half the time people couldn't talk anyway because their mouths were full.

Then again, he could barely wait to cook for Tim tomorrow. He supposed that preparing a meal was an expression of love and that he had been standing up his mother all week. Burdened by guilt, he burst through the door and dodged Wilford's greeting in order to reach the dining room sooner. He was in luck. The table was just now being set. Whatever June had cooked had obviously taken longer than she had intended.

Ben helped set the table as his sister and his father came into the room and took their places.

"How nice of his royal highness to grace us with an appearance," his father joked.

"Can't blame him for not showing up," his sister Karen grumped when their mom entered the room with a meatloaf.

Ben had no complaints. Meatloaf was one of his favorite meals. Lately he couldn't seem to get enough protein. His mother's meatloaf was garnished with strips of bacon on top and slathered with ketchup, which caused his mouth to water as she set it down. He was glad to be home for dinner tonight.

They went through the usual motions. His mother made them say grace, which he always mouthed to make her happy even though he didn't believe in it. Once that was over and everyone was served, Dad went into his usual rants about what had happened at work that day. Being manager of the local cable company didn't sound very intriguing, but Adam managed to bring home at least a few crazy customer stories every day.

There was a lull in conversation as the meal neared its end and they all became tired and full. The mood was meditative until Ben's sister decided to break the silence.

"Janny swears she saw you driving around in a Mitsubishi yesterday."

"A what?" Ben asked, buying for time.

Karen rolled her eyes. "A black sports car. She was next to you at a stoplight and got a good look."

Maybe he should have denied it, but Ben didn't see what he had to hide. He had earned his driver's license last year, and it wasn't criminal to drive around in someone else's car.

"Yup, that was me," he said. He didn't elaborate, enjoying being enigmatic about it.

"Whose car were you driving?" his mom asked.

"Who cares," his dad interrupted. "I'm just happy he's actually using his license. We should break out the champagne!"

"The car belongs to a friend of mine," Ben explained.

"Do we know this friend?" June asked. "Is it this Tim person?"

"Tim who?" his sister prodded.

"None of your business," Ben shot at her. "Yeah, it's him," he said to his mother. It felt good to keep Karen out of the loop. That his mom already knew and that his sister didn't irritated Karen and made Ben even happier. As it turned out, he had chosen a bad time to push her.

"I'm surprised you admit it," Karen said, a wicked gleam in her eye. "When Janny saw you school wasn't over yet."

"What are you saying?" his mother asked, keeping her attention on him.

"It was still sixth period," Karen explained joyfully. "Janny is on the work program so she leaves after fifth period. Apparently Ben does too."

"Is this true?" his father inquired.

Ben didn't need to answer. His mother saw it all on his face. Denying anything would only make it worse.

"How long has this been happening?" she demanded. "Have you and this friend of yours been skipping school every day? What's going on between you two?"

"That's not hard to guess," Karen interjected.

"Be quiet," June hissed before turning her attention back to Ben. "What's gotten into you? First you lie to us about where you are and who you're with. Now you're skipping school? I don't know who this Tim person is, but he clearly isn't good for you."

"That's not true!" Ben protested, feeling betrayed. She *knew* how much Tim meant to him. He'd told her, and now she was using it against him.

"You may not think it's true," she insisted, "but believe me it is. Anyone who asks you to lie and encourages you to skip school—" She shook her head, overcome with emotion. "Adam."

"You're grounded," his father said on cue. "Starting now."

"Grounded from what?" Ben asked incredulously.

His father looked to his mother for help. "The computer?" he suggested.

"For Christ's sake, Adam!" She glowered at her husband before redirecting her wrath to her son. "You're grounded to the house. You aren't going out with anyone until further notice. And I'll be calling your school to make sure you're there the whole day too!"

"That's not fair!" Ben managed to shout as emotion constricted his throat. "I fucking hate you!" he croaked to his sister before he ran upstairs to his room.

Things only became worse once he had slammed the door. Left alone, he had time to realize the implications of this punishment. The last few days alone with Tim—the romantic meal and whatever memories they would have made—were all gone, forever stolen away from him by his stupid sister and his treacherous mom.

Groggy and miserable, Ben pulled himself out of bed at eleven in the morning and stumbled into the shower. He had stayed up late, wrestling with the anger lurching inside and listening to music that amplified these emotions.

Before all of this he called Tim to let him know that he wouldn't be showing up after dinner or even this weekend. Tim, while sympathetic that he had gotten in trouble, didn't sound as devastated as Ben had hoped.

Once he was dressed, he stomped downstairs for some cereal. Ben was scowling at the selection when he heard the jangle of car keys. He turned to see his mother with her purse over her shoulder.

"Wanna go with me to the store?" she asked in pleasant tones as if nothing had happened.

"No thanks," Ben answered carefully. Maybe she realized how she had overreacted and would unground him.

"You sure?" she prompted. "It's your only chance to get out of the house today."

He turned his back to her, anger swelling up inside of him.

"Well," his mother sighed, "your sister and father will be back any minute."

Ben maintained his bitter silence until he heard the garage door raise and lower again. He counted to twenty before he dared move to the front windows to check that her car was gone.

"Dad?" he yelled, just to be sure that he was alone. "Karen?"

Only Wilford responded to his calls, panting happily as he trotted up to him.

"You look like you need to go potty," Ben suggested. "Don't you, boy? Don't you?"

Wilford barked and leapt in anticipation.

Ben smiled at his little victory. There was no choice but to take the poor dog out for a walk. Clearly it was an emergency. He threw on his shoes and gave himself a once-over in the mirror before leashing Wilford and escaping from the house. He ran the first block, just in case either of his parents was on the verge of returning. Once that obstacle was out of the way, he was home free.

He felt a wild sense of liberation as he approached Tim's house. So what if he got into trouble? They could ground him all they wanted. Right now he was somewhere his parents didn't know about, somewhere safe. He would have his weekend with Tim and they couldn't do anything about it.

Ben entered the house without ringing the doorbell. He realized he might catch Tim in a compromising situation by doing so, but the idea of finding him jerking off only encouraged him to make his way stealthily down the hall. It was a good thing that he did, otherwise he might not have heard the girlish voice before he entered the den.

A seductive murmur responded to a giggle as Ben tiptoed the last few steps to peek around the doorway, Wilford padding along behind him. Tim was on the couch with his leg up on the coffee table. A girl was bent over the cast, writing something on it with a pen. Her back was to him, but Ben didn't need her to turn around to know that it was Krista Norman. Tim wiggled his foot. She chastised him and giggled again. He grinned back at her in satisfaction.

Ben decided to make a silent retreat, but before he could do so, Wilford opened his mouth and starting panting loudly. Tim spotted Ben. Krista began turning to see what the noise was but Ben retreated down the hall before she could notice him.

"I'll be right back," he heard Tim say to her.

"Is someone here?" Krista sounded panicked, as if she was already being menaced by a gang of burglars.

"It's just my neighbor," Tim reassured her. "He promised to bring something by. Wait here."

Tim appeared in the hallway and brushed by Ben, barely using his crutches as he hurried away. He gestured for Ben to follow. They retreated all the way to the front door before Tim turned to speak to him.

"What are you doing here? I thought you were grounded?"

"I snuck out," Ben said.

"Jesus, man! You almost gave me a heart attack."

"Sorry. I wanted to surprise you."

"That you did." Tim squatted down to pet Wilford. "Who's this?"

Ben introduced him.

"You know, he looks oddly familiar," Tim commented.

Probably because Ben had walked him past Tim's house many times before they actually met. "He looks like Wilford Brimley," Ben explained. "You know, the old guy in the oatmeal commercials?"

"Oh yeah!" Tim laughed. "He totally does."

"That's who he's named after. He just needs a pair of glasses and the look is complete."

Tim chuckled and Ben joined him. For a moment it felt like everything was going to be okay. Tim would send Krista away, since she wasn't important to him, and they would have their day after all. These hopes were shattered when Krista's voice called from the den.

"Look, you can't stay," Tim whispered. "I'm trying to get laid. I'm playing up the injury thing like crazy, and she's eating it up."

"Sorry," Ben mumbled awkwardly. "I, uh, yeah. Good luck."

"You too!" Tim gave him an amiable punch to the arm. "I hope you sneak back in without getting caught."

"Okay. Well, see ya."

"Yeah. Wait!"

Ben turned around, a last desperate spark of hope glowing brighter.

"I need my car keys back."

"Oh yeah. Of course."

Ben handed them over and then hurried to leave. His face burned with embarrassment the whole way home. He felt humiliated and silly. How else did he think this little game of his would end? Tim was feeling better and his parents were coming home. He didn't need Ben anymore. He would be back in school soon with his ditzy girlfriend and asshole friends, and Ben would be nothing more than an amusing memory, if he was even remembered.

He didn't bother to sneak back into the house. Who cared if he was grounded now? Allison was forbidden to see him and Tim had better things to do. There was no longer a reason to leave.

Neither of his parents was home, so Ben had his bowl of cereal and numbed his mind with television. He barely noticed when they did arrive, ignoring his mother's request to help unload the car. When their attempts at communicating with him became too annoying, he turned off the TV and went upstairs to his room.

The phone rang before Ben could sit down on his bed. He picked it up irritably. It would only be one of Karen's annoying friends, but at least he could have the satisfaction of hanging up on them.

"What?" he snarled into the receiver.

"Benjamin?" came the startled response.

"Tim?" he asked, not believing his ears.

"Man, I'm glad I didn't get one of your parents. Are they still gone?"

"Don't worry about it," Ben insisted. "What's up? Are you calling to brag or something? Tell me you aren't screwing her right now!" He tittered, feeling elated that Tim would call him for any reason.

"No, almost," Tim said, his voice laced with frustration. "Came close, but she got freaked out by the European standard."

"Okay," Ben replied, not understanding what was being said or why.

"Anyway, we got into an argument and she's gone."

"Sorry?" Ben offered.

"So you want to come over?"

Of course he did, but he had missed his chance. Sure, he could still sneak out and face the same consequences that he had been willing to face an hour ago, but he didn't like the idea of playing second fiddle to Krista, of all people.

Tim picked up on his hesitation. "Maybe you and I can pick up where she left off."

Ben's mouth dropped open in shock. His brain buzzed, analyzing what he had just heard and trying to find any other interpretation of the words except what he thought they meant. "I'll be right there," he said, slamming down the phone.

Ben ran. He didn't know where his parents were, and he didn't check. He was down the stairs and out the front door in two seconds flat. Another twenty and he was in the park. Anywhere away from the road was safe from his parents. Had they ever gone for a walk or ridden a bike in their lives? His mind rejected thoughts of them and instead turned to his destination.

Was Tim really inviting him over to mess around? Jesus! Maybe there was a god! Something had scared Krista away. Maybe it was just too big for her to deal with. What was it he had said? The European standard? Did Tim measure it in metric or something? Well, whatever. He'd soon find out!

He found the door unlocked and let himself in, heart thudding in his chest as he walked to the den. Tim was waiting for him on the couch, fully dressed and looking subdued and uncertain. Was he having second thoughts? Ben hesitated in the doorway.

Tim's black hair was messy and sticking up, probably from Krista pawing at him. His silver eyes sheepishly considered Ben's own, before looking away and down at his own body. Ben followed his gaze, over the sea blue tank top to the white shorts where it was more than obvious that he was aroused. The silver eyes found his again, all hesitation in them replaced by lust.

"C'mere," he invited.

Ben went to him and sat down on the couch. As much as he had fantasized about touching Tim, he found it ironic that he now didn't know how to proceed. He concluded that there was nothing left but to do it. He reached out toward Tim's crotch, but his hand was caught by the wrist.

"What's the rush?" Tim laughed, pulling on the wrist to draw Ben closer to him.

With his other hand, Tim reached behind Ben's head and pulled him in for a kiss. Their lips met clumsily before they readjusted and found the perfect fit. Tim kissed him passionately, taking full control which was good because Ben was at a loss. This isn't how it usually went at all! Strange as it was, considering the number of guys he had blown before, this was Ben's first kiss.

He breathed in through his nose, taking in Tim's scent as he enjoyed the sensation of the tongue darting into his mouth. Ben's hand was released and so he used it to feel the chest he had spent so much time admiring. Tim moaned in approval and broke their kiss so he could take off his shirt. He leaned back and placed Ben's hand back on his pecs. Ben rubbed his hand over them and Tim smiled cockily, enjoying having his impressive physique worshiped so transparently.

Ben worked his hand downward, Tim squirming beneath his touch in anticipation of where he was going. Ben wanted to draw it out and tease him longer, but he couldn't control himself and grabbed Tim's cock through his shorts.

"Wow!" Ben gasped. He had been with a few guys slightly bigger than himself before, but Tim was significantly thicker.

He pumped his hand up and down, enjoying the look of bliss on Tim's face. His eyes were closed and his mouth was open. Ben burned the image into his mind as one of the most beautiful things he had even seen. He never wanted to forget it.

Ben reached his fingers under the elastic band of Tim's athletic shorts and pulled them back. Tim tensed and sat up with an uncomfortable expression. Ben looked down to see and was startled. It was uncut! So that's what all the fuss was about.

"The European standard?" Ben inquired.

"It's normal over there," Tim said apologetically.

"It's gorgeous," Ben said. He meant it too. He liked that it was different than his own. Tim's cock was exotic, and like the body it was attached to, breathtakingly attractive.

"You don't mind?" Tim asked, still adorably uncertain.

Ben answered by taking it into his mouth. Tim tensed up but then immediately relaxed again, letting himself enjoy the sensation. He was certainly one of the most appreciative recipients of Ben's favors. He moaned approvingly and ran his fingers through Ben's hair as he worked.

Soon Tim's hips began thrusting and his moans became louder and more insistent. He bucked wildly as he came, Ben struggling to keep him inside his mouth.

"No more, no more, stop!" Tim panted, pulling Ben off of him.

Ben unwillingly receded. This was the part that he hated most. His own cock was painfully begging for release, both from the confines of his jeans and sexually, but his mind was already troubled by the approaching awkwardness. Sometimes the guy just went back to pretending he was asleep, or if it had started when they were awake, would find a pretense to distance himself. Any second now Tim would say he had to use the restroom or feign some other important thing that he had to do. Anything to get away from the gay guy he had just used.

"Fuck, that was good," Tim said, still trying to catch his breath. "Man. I have to take a piss."

"That's cool," Ben said casually as Tim pulled his shorts back up and left the room.

He pondered leaving as he waited. It was usually less awkward that way. The toilet flushed and Tim's crutches squeaked their way back over to the couch.

"I guess I should get back," Ben said, starting to stand.

"What?" Tim laughed. "You're crazy." He shoved Ben back onto the couch and tossed his crutches aside, falling with his full weight onto Ben. He growled menacingly and wrestled Ben to his back, kissing him again.

Ben's heart swelled with happy surprise, but not as much as his cock did when Tim's hand suddenly grabbed onto it.

"Your turn," he whispered seductively into Ben's ear.

Tim slid to the side, pulled up Ben's shirt and undid his jeans, ripping them along with Ben's underwear down to his knees in a motion that was anything but gentle.

"Nice," he said appreciatively as he took hold of Ben with one strong hand and began pumping.

He pushed Ben's shirt up further and licked one of his nipples before moving upward to kiss him on the mouth. Their tongues danced together as Ben struggled to breathe. He was getting close and so opened his eyes, wanting to tell Tim what was going to happen. He found Tim's eyes locked fiercely on his own and didn't last long after that, soaking his stomach and even his chest.

Tim grinned. "I'll grab a towel," he said. "And then you're going to cook for me," he added matter-of-factly.

Ben watched him go, his head still spinning from all that

had just happened. The sex had been incredible, but what really sent his heart soaring had been the kissing. He felt certain that, after all these years of yearning and wanting, he had finally met someone who could love him back.

Nothing changed between Ben and Tim, or so it seemed from the outside. They passed the evening much as they always did. A horror movie about killer puppets entertained them while they ate chili. Tim put on a few CDs afterwards while they talked; a B-side collection of Nirvana followed by the Smashing Pumpkins. Ben barely heard the music. Instead he pondered how Tim was taking it all in stride.

The subject of what they had done together wasn't discussed. Inside, Ben felt like he was going to explode. So many emotions were stirring within him, all of them positive and excited. If Tim felt something similar, he managed to hide it well.

Sleep didn't come easy that night. Tim didn't want to struggle with the stairs, so he stayed on the couch. Ben made himself a bed of blankets, placing them as near the couch as possible, even though there were two unoccupied beds in the house. As he listened to the sound of Tim's slow rhythmic breathing, he fantasized about sharing a bed with him. He imagined they would whisper pleasantries to each other before kissing goodnight and hold each other in sleep.

The next morning Ben found himself roused by his friend and then quickly aroused. Tim pulled him forcibly onto the couch, kissing him deeply and grinding against him, leading to a replay of the day before.

"Guess we should get the place cleaned up," Tim said once they had both caught their breath.

Ben sighed wistfully. "I wish your parents were going to be gone another week."

"Yeah, me too."

Tim felt well enough by now that he was able to help with the chores. By noon the house was as tidy as could be expected when left in the hands of a teenager.

"You should probably get going. Just in case they catch an early flight or something."

Dread stirred in Ben's stomach. He had his own parents to face today, and he was sure it wouldn't be pretty.

"Look," Tim began, but it was almost a minute before he continued. "What happened between us, well…"

Ben perked up, giving him his full attention.

"It's probably best we keep it a secret," Tim said, reaching behind to scratch his head while grinning nervously. "I just don't want people to get the wrong idea."

"Wrong idea?" Ben repeated.

"There's nothing *wrong* with it," Tim backpedaled. "I just don't want people thinking I'm gay, when I'm not."

It took every ounce of Ben's willpower to keep his face straight in light of this statement. "Okay," he said. "Not a big deal."

In reality it was a big deal, but he could handle it. If having Tim meant doing everything gay with him but calling it straight, why not? He could just play it off as some sort of kinky role-playing game. Unless of course, Tim intended that this never happened again. As cliché as the question was, Ben couldn't help but ask, "So are you going to call me?"

"Yeah, totally!" Tim answered enthusiastically. "We're buds." The way he stated this was friendly, but there was a hint of a silent 'only' there in the middle.

"Cool," Ben replied. "I'm off. Good luck with your parents when they get here."

"Good luck with yours! Hope you won't be in too much trouble." Tim reached out and mussed Ben's hair as if he were sending his kid off to school.

Ben left the house with a smile on his face. His future with Tim was uncertain, he was facing the lecture of his life from his parents, and he was forbidden to see his best friend—and yet Ben couldn't remember the last time he felt happier.

CHAPTER 9

The school gymnasium, forever marred by shoe scuffs and perfumed with sweat, was lined on one side by a long hallway. This led either to the locker rooms or into the gymnasium itself by pushing open the two swinging doors set with small windows. These allowed Ben to peer through and see that volleyball was being played today. Not one of his favorite sports, but not as bad as some of the others. Still, he couldn't bring himself to enter, even though first period had started twenty minutes ago.

Ben chose to skate to school instead of taking the bus and had arrived late, despite his intention of attending all of his classes, as he had promised his mother yesterday. When he had arrived home on Sunday, he thought he would be greeted with yelling and punishments. Instead things were unsettlingly calm. His father had been the first to see him, pulling a comical "look out!" face that warned his wife wasn't too pleased with their son.

Except his mother hadn't been all that angry. She met Ben in his bedroom, sat down, and very carefully said, "You are getting to an age where we can't control you anymore. In less than two years you will be living on your own. I hope you will be going to college. If you choose to do so, we will help support you. If not, then you are on your own. Until then, you will go to *all* of your classes and you won't drink or do drugs in this household."

That was it. He wasn't even grounded anymore. His parents had set him free by giving him adult status. Ben had almost felt sad after it happened, like he was being forced to grow up. He quickly moved past those feelings though. No longer would he have to deal with curfews or tell them who he was staying with. The new arrangement was ideal for him, which was why he felt horrible that he was breaking his promise already.

He hated P.E. There was nothing redeeming about the class, and it would never contribute to his health or success later in life. If anything, facing the abuse of the coaches and his peers threatened to make him jaded and mistrustful of the human race. Why should he waste an hour every day in a class that made him feel useless and incompetent? He refused to subject himself to that, no matter the consequences.

Ben stayed in the hallway, feeling it was a safe place to hide until the bell rang. Students with flushed faces swarmed out of the locker room. He let them pass without making eye contact, waiting for someone to ask where he had been. It didn't happen until one of the very last people entered the hall.

"My man!" Leon called out. "Where have you been, Ben? Ha ha! I haven't seen you since my wisdom teeth were yanked."

"I've been skipping a lot of classes lately," Ben confided. "Have the coaches said anything about it?"

"Those clueless goons? Of course not. They're too busy reliving their glory years with the second-rate jocks who didn't make the football team."

Ben laughed in relief. "I wonder how long I can get away with this."

"I don't know man, but you've got the right idea. Tell you what, if the coaches ever notice you missing, I'll try to cover for you."

"Thanks. I owe you one."

Leon clapped Ben on the shoulder. "Hey, I hear your best friend is dating my best friend."

"Ronnie Adams?" Ben asked. "I didn't know you guys were friends."

"Yeah, Ebony and Ivory. That's our band. Ronnie's on guitar and I'm on bass. You should come by with Allison sometime, smoke a j and sing. I crooned out a few tunes with your girl already, but I'd love to hear what a real pair of singers can do."

"Yeah, all right. Sounds fun. Thanks again for covering for me."

"No problem, brother!"

Ben hurried to English class with a weight lifted from his chest. Despite the potential ramifications with his parents, he felt glad not having to worry about first period anymore. He would have to find something to do though, now that Tim wasn't accessible. He kept his eyes peeled on the way to class, uncertain if Tim would be in school today.

In English they had a test, which meant an unwilling competition with Daniel Wigmore, who finished early and spent the remaining time gawking at Ben while mentally timing how long it took him to finish.

In Spanish class a few of the kids had come up with a broken Spanish sentence that referred to him as a fat and ugly *mariposa*.

This irritated Ben more because of its stupidity rather than its offensiveness. He might be a *mariposa*, but there wasn't an ounce of fat on him and he certainly wasn't ugly when compared to the perpetually awkward idiots who were trying to get a rise out of him.

Lunch was a singularly trying experience too, since he had so much he wanted to tell Allison, but couldn't without other students overhearing. Keeping things under wraps was crucial if he wanted to have future fun with Tim, and that was one promise Ben was determined to keep. Luckily there was choir, providing them with uninterrupted free time.

Allison was the ideal audience as he spilled the details. She gasped and exclaimed at all the juicy parts and asked the right follow-up questions. Reliving the details with her triggered a longing inside of Ben. He wanted to see Tim again or at least call, but part of him was reluctant. What had happened between them had been intense, and now Ben felt it prudent to back off a little. He didn't want to scare Tim off. Plus, it would feel extra satisfying if Tim made the first move.

The transition back to sixth period wasn't the struggle that first period had been since Ben genuinely liked Ms. Hughes, even though he wasn't looking forward to explaining why he'd been skipping. He searched his mind for a believable excuse during class, and she kept her eye on him as if he would raise his hand and confess at any moment. By the end of the period, Ben considered slipping out with the rest of the students until she asked him to stay behind at the last moment.

"Well?" Ms. Hughes asked, sitting on the corner of her desk.

Ben took a deep breath. He'd already been caught by his parents, so that wasn't a worry, but he could still get in trouble with the school. Then again he didn't have a good story prepared.

"There's this guy," he began. "Tim Wyman."

Ms. Hughes nodded. "I have him in my second period class. He thinks he's Tom Cruise."

Ben laughed and nodded before all the details came pouring out of him. All of it. Even his parents didn't know about Tim's parents being out of town or the ankle injury. Ben was also open with his feelings, hesitating only when he reached the part where they slept together.

"I think I can imagine the rest," Ms. Hughes said. She was

quiet for a moment, making Ben wonder if she was doing just that. Then she said, "Sarah Niles."

"Sorry?"

"Sarah Niles," Ms. Hughes repeated. "She used to copy off my tests during freshman year. Dumb as a post, but beautiful." She paused, gauging Ben's reaction and continuing when he nodded with encouragement. "Sarah was my first love, ever since she kissed me behind my parents' rose bushes at a birthday party. I would have done anything for her, and I did. She never would have passed Physical Science if it wasn't for me. Unfortunately, like your Tom Cruise, she wasn't exactly comfortable with herself."

"So what happened?"

"She promised we could go to the dance together. I knew we couldn't go openly as a couple, but single girls go in groups all the time and end up dancing together. No one thinks anything of it. Sarah was popular and liked to keep me a secret, but still she promised. The night of the dance, I showed up on my own. We were supposed to meet there, but unbeknownst to either of us, some of Sarah's friends had decided to fix her up with a guy. She was dancing with him when I arrived. Young and brave as I was, I intended to cut in. But then Sarah shook her head."

Ben swallowed. "What happened?"

"That was it," Ms. Hughes said, straightening up. "Love isn't meant to be hidden away and life is too short for shame. I was lonely a good couple of years, but I met someone just before graduating."

Ben thought of the teacher he'd seen Ms. Hughes kiss and wondered if it was her.

"You're too bright to ruin your academic career for a guy, Ben. I hope you can bring him around to seeing things your way, but being held back a year isn't going to seduce anyone."

Ben laughed. "So what's my punishment? Cleaning the chalkboard?"

Ms. Hughes assigned him an essay and went over the details of a test he would have to make up for. She could have demanded Ben drop and do pushups, and he would have gladly complied. If only every adult in his life was as cool as she was.

After school Ben went directly home. He made sure to be a social part of the family for the entire night, helping with dinner, washing dishes and even being civil to his sister. He wanted his mom to see that she had made the right decision in cutting him some slack. Of course, staying close to home was good too, just in case Tim decided to call. By midnight, when Ben was climbing into bed, it was clear that this wasn't going to happen. As he fell asleep, Ben couldn't help picture Ms. Hughes, young and passionate, striding across the dance floor with determination but being stopped dead by the shaking of Sarah's head.

Wednesday rolled around, and even though it had only been two days, to Ben it seemed like an eternity. Waiting for any sort of signal from Tim was driving Ben crazy, so he decided to try to catch Tim in the hall where he had seen him the first time. No sign of him there, so Ben tried again the next day. His persistence paid off. Ben spotted him as he rounded the corner of the hall. Tim was much further down, surrounded by the same snobs and jocks as before. Bryce Hunter was there, repeatedly pointing at his own legs and pantomiming throwing a football and then a tackle. Tim was laughing at his story while leaning on one crutch, his other side occupied by Krista Norman who had wrapped herself around him like a python.

Ben stooped to fumble with the contents of his backpack while trying to casually keep track of them. Krista and Bryce left in the opposite direction, while Tim and Darryl Briscott headed down the hall. Ben stood, shouldered his backpack, and began walking toward them. Darryl wore his standard vacant expression, every available brain cell dedicated to keeping him upright and walking. That left Tim free to notice Ben's stare. Tim held up a hand to his face, one thumb by his ear, pinky in front of his mouth; the universal sign for "call me." Ben grinned and nodded before he broke eye contact.

Abandoning subtlety, calling was the first thing he did when he got home. The phone rang and rang, and just as he was about to hang up, it clicked and Tim's voice was on the line.

"Hey," Ben said, having no idea what to say next.

"Hey," Tim echoed. "You have to come get me. I'm totally sick of it here."

"I don't have a car," Ben reminded him.

"I think you've driven mine more than I have. Get over here."

Ben rushed to Tim's house, trying not to run. He didn't want to arrive sweaty and disheveled. Tim was waiting for him in the driveway, standing between his car and a white SUV that hadn't been there last week, meaning that at least one of his parents was home.

"Let's go," Tim said, voice tense as he handed Ben the keys.

"Everything all right?" he inquired.

"Yes!" came the impatient response. "C'mon."

Ben felt uneasy as he unlocked the black sports car and took a seat. He glanced over at Tim, who still hadn't smiled or shown any sign that he was glad to see Ben. Only after they were a few blocks from the house did the tension evaporate, allowing Tim to act like his old self again.

"Everything all right at home?" Ben asked.

"Yeah," Tim said. "I'm just sick of being there, that's all."

Ben knew there was more to it than that, but he didn't want to return Tim to his foul mood by playing twenty questions.

"Where do you want to go?"

"I don't know." Tim leaned over and checked the dashboard. "Gas station first. The tank is empty."

"Sorry about that. I didn't have any cash to fill it up last week."

"No problem." Tim pulled out his wallet and slid free a plastic card. "It's on my parents."

"Wow! That's generous of them."

Tim shrugged.

"Well, if you have all the gas in the world, I know exactly where we should go. When do you have to be home?"

"Anytime is fine. They won't even notice that I'm gone."

After refueling, Ben drove to Interstate 45 and cranked up the music as they headed south. Occasionally Tim would turn the volume down and ask where they were going, but Ben would only grin and turn the music back up. After an hour of exceeding the speed limit, they were traveling though landscape that began to give way to water and palm trees.

"Galveston?" Tim read from one of the signs.

"Yeah," Ben confessed. "Ever been there?"

"No. What's it like?"

"This is pretty much it."

They were crossing the two-mile-long causeway now that spanned the huge body of water below. They continued across to

Galveston Island, which did its best to sell itself as a hot tourist attraction, when really it was more like the trashy cousin of Miami.

"Looks pretty cool," Tim commented as they passed garishly lit restaurants that were just starting to see an influx of patronage.

They turned left onto the last stretch of the seawall boulevard. Ben kept Tim distracted and looking away from the small area where the Gulf of Mexico could be seen and continued driving until they reached the Bolivar Ferry. The stars were shining favorably on Ben that day. The ferry was docked and cars were pulling onto it. Tim sat up, looking more enthusiastic. Once the car was parked, they left it and walked to the front of the boat for a better view. To the east, water stretched out and disappeared into the horizon.

"Is that the ocean?" Tim asked excitedly. "That is, isn't it?"

"Yup," Ben said. "Well, the Gulf of Mexico anyway. My dad always calls it the poor man's Atlantic."

"It's all the same water, right? This is so cool!"

They stayed on deck during the twenty-minute ride, Ben singing sea shanties to make Tim laugh as wind blew through their hair and mist from the waves chilled their skin. When the Bolivar Peninsula came into view, they hurried back to the car and impatiently waited for the other vehicles ahead of them to disembark.

They didn't drive far before reaching a decent beach. Tourist season was starting to die down, and while it was impossible to find complete solitude, they did discover an area unpolluted by sunbathers. Tim's crutches kept sinking into the sand, so they backtracked to solid ground and settled down there to enjoy the view. The sky changed its flavor to tropical orange as the sun steadily made its descent, seagulls calling out to each other above the crashing waves.

"This is the first time I've ever seen the ocean," Tim said. "Or gulf or whatever."

"I guess there's nothing like this in Kansas," Ben replied. "I figured that you travel a lot with your parents though."

"Not really. They like to take trips on their own, but I have been to Mexico City half a dozen times. My mom's family all live there."

"What's it like?"

"Beautiful. Very different from here. That's what I like about it." A far-away look came into Tim's eyes as he remembered. "I always make them take me to the volcano, *Popocatépetl*."

"Popo-what?" Ben snorted.

"*Popocatépetl*," Tim repeated.

This sent Ben into a fit of laughter.

"That's what it's called," Tim insisted, before starting to laugh himself. "I guess it does sound kind of goofy."

"I love how you say it with the accent and everything," Ben said once he had calmed down. "Can you speak Spanish at all?"

"Fluently. I was raised bilingual."

"Yeah, it's pretty obvious at this point that you're bi," Ben teased.

"I'm not," Tim protested. "I just get really horny sometimes."

Ben tried not to laugh at this but couldn't help himself. Tim looked insulted so Ben shoved him playfully and told him to stop taking everything so seriously.

"I don't care what you are," he said bravely, reaching out to pat Tim on the back. He let his hand linger there. "I like you for who you are."

"It's not the sports car, then?" Tim asked as Ben began to run his hand up and down his back. "Or the movie star good looks?"

"Are you kidding me? I can barely stand to look at you. The car, on the other hand, is pure sex appeal."

"That she is," Tim grinned.

"*Coche bonita!*" Ben tried. He was pretty sure it meant 'beautiful car.' He suddenly wished he had paid closer attention in school. "Say something to me in Spanish."

"Like what?"

"Something nice."

Tim thought for a while before clearing his throat. He turned, looked Ben directly in the eye, and spoke. "*Enséñame a volar, mi mariposa hermosa.*"

Ben's smile faded. He didn't understand all of it, but one word had stood out. "Something nice," he complained.

"Sorry if you didn't like it," Tim responded, appearing offended.

"I know what '*mariposa*' means, and I'm sick of hearing it."

Tim scrunched up his face in confusion. "Who's been saying *mariposa* to you?"

"Everyone in my Spanish class," Ben told him. "We've got this substitute and someone asked how to say faggot in Spanish—"

"Oh man!" Tim groaned. "How could I be so stupid? *Mariposa* means butterfly."

"It does? So it's not homophobic?"

"Yeah. Well, no." Tim thought about it for a second. "It's just like the word 'fairy' in English. You can say it all day long and it doesn't mean anything bad, but call someone that in the right context and it can be offensive."

"Oh." That explained why Señora Vega hadn't reacted when the students kept using that word. In a way it was kind of cool. Basically everyone was saying 'butterfly' to him. Big deal! Knowing this would make it easier not to react in the future. "So what did you say to me then?" Ben asked.

"Forget it," Tim said dismissively. "I should have chosen my words better."

"No, tell me!"

"Maybe later."

Ben begged him to reveal what he had said a few more times, but Tim was adamant. Instead he started poking around in the sand, looking for shells that weren't broken to take as souvenirs. This led to them digging a moat, followed by the inevitable building of a sand castle. It wasn't the right kind of sand though, so all they could build was a shapeless mound. Ben made a limp flag out of some seaweed and a stick and stuck it in the top, dubbing it *Popocatépetl.*

The night had finally arrived in full, the temperature dropping. Ben was about to suggest they leave when a laugh came from further down the beach. Rowdy voices soon joined it as a group of silhouettes moved toward them. Ben hoped not to be noticed in the dark, but as the strangers passed there were puzzled murmurs before one of the voices called out. Tim answered, causing a few to scream and the others to giggle.

The group walked toward them, the distant streetlights illuminating five girls, all college age or older. Each had a beer in hand, two of them carrying half-empty twelve-pack boxes in the other. The girls were all boney clones of each other, except for one who was stocky and confident. She was the first to speak to them in a thick Bronx accent.

"What are you two doing out here? On a date or something?"

"No," Tim laughed. "What about you?"

"We're not lezzies! Ew!" mocked one of the girls to the others' amusement.

"That one is kind of cute," murmured one of the voices.

"How old are you guys?" challenged the ringleader.

"Old enough," Tim retorted to their delight.

"You guys want a beer?"

"Yeah, I need to sit," whined a girl with bleached blonde hair. "Let's drink one with them."

The girls jostled for position on the sand, ending up forming a circle like some strange council. The ringleader sat directly in front of them while the two prettiest flocked to Tim's side. Nearest Ben was a fair-haired girl with timid posture who risked a sympathetic glance in his direction before looking away.

Tim eagerly accepted the beer. Ben turned it down, as the designated driver, which caused a round of laughter. They handed him one anyway. He sipped at it moodily, not drinking more than the bare minimum.

"You guys go to college around here?" asked the brunette nearest to Tim.

"Yeah, we sure do." He turned and winked openly at Ben.

"Which one?"

Tim paused. He hadn't been in Texas long enough to bluff his way through this one.

"Texas A&M," Ben filled in for him. The college wasn't remotely local, but the girls didn't react, proving they were here on vacation. They barely acknowledged his response. All attention was focused on Tim, like dogs eyeing a juicy piece of meat. Ben hoped this wasn't how he usually appeared.

They continued grilling Tim through his first beer. By his second they were trying to outdo each other to gain his approval. Some told of their raunchy exploits back home. One tried humor and failed miserably. The girl nearest to Tim relied on physical charm, finding excuses to make bodily contact with him. So far she seemed to be in the lead. Only the bashful girl next to Ben refrained from these games. She started a cautious conversation with Ben about what life was like in Texas, which he found hard to focus on while keeping an eye on the proceedings.

When Tim stood to answer a call of nature, the brunette rose with him, wrapping an arm around his torso to help him walk.

This caused a chorus of "oooohs" from the other girls, which set Ben's teeth on edge. He tried to keep tabs on them as they left, but they were soon lost to the dark.

It was hard to judge how much time passed before they came back, but every minute was grueling. When Tim did show his face again, he was grinning.

"I'm afraid, ladies, that we must take our leave," he said.

"No way! Come and party at our hotel!" the brunette insisted.

"Tell us where you're staying and we might come by later," he suggested.

Ben couldn't wait to leave as they all clamored to give Tim the information. He didn't say anything further until they were back on the ferry, looking over the edge at the churning water below.

"That brunette sure seemed fond of you," Ben prompted, making sure to keep his voice neutral. He was certain that acting jealous wasn't going to earn him any points.

"Yeah, she was all over me when I went to pee."

"Really?" Ben asked, visualizing the girl being swept away by the tides while he pointed and laughed. "What happened?"

"Nothing much." Tim smiled coyly. "She shoved her tongue down my throat and started groping me, but I really had to piss. I barely managed to push her away so I could."

"That's it?"

"Well, I felt her up. She had a pretty nice body."

"I'm surprised she didn't go down on you then and there," Ben commented, hoping that Tim wouldn't say that she had.

"I bet she would have, yeah. But whatever."

"You don't sound very enthusiastic about the idea."

"I don't know, man." Tim turned his back to the water and leaned against the rail. "She was hot and all, but— After everything that went down in Kansas because my ex-girlfriend said I raped her, I don't want something like that to happen again. The whole school turned against me. It's just not worth it. I promised myself to only sleep with people who mean something to me."

This statement blew away Ben's foul mood. He *meant* something to Tim. Or maybe he wasn't worried about a gay guy running around school saying he'd been raped. Such a claim wouldn't be taken very seriously. Regardless, Ben chose to take this as a compliment.

Tim had a CD he wanted to listen to on the way home, giving Ben time to think while it blared from the speakers. What happened on the beach tonight had really opened his eyes. Girls found Tim just as irresistible as he did, which came as no surprise. Right now Tim was with Krista, who had a number of hang-ups, but it was only a matter of time before a girl came along who wasn't put off by the European standard. One who would be more than happy to fulfill Tim's sexual desires once she had gained his trust. When that happened, Ben would be thrown out with the weekly garbage.

If Tim was gay, or even bisexual, Ben only had so long to make him realize it before a different girl moved in on his territory. Maybe it was just wishful thinking on his part, but Tim was so affectionate, so giving when they had sex. It was totally different than the other guys. But what if he was wrong? What if Tim really was straight, and pushing the issue only ended up destroying what they had right now?

They pulled into Tim's driveway just before midnight. He didn't seem concerned about the hour. Obviously his parents kept him on a long leash as well.

"You really don't mind walking home?" Tim asked him. "I'm sure I can manage driving there and back."

"No. I'll be fine."

"All right." They stood there awkwardly for a moment. Isn't this where the goodnight kiss was supposed to take place?

"*Enséñame a volar, mi mariposa hermosa*," Tim said suddenly. "It's from a poem I— Well, it's from a poem."

"What's it mean?"

"'Teach me how to fly, my beautiful butterfly.'" He reached out and ruffled Ben's hair, his version of a parting kiss. "See you around."

Ben watched Tim enter the house before making his way down the street, no longer uncertain. He would help Tim realize who he really was. He would teach him how to fly.

CHAPTER 10

Little changed over the next six weeks, despite Ben's determination. At times he hardly saw Tim at all. An unspoken agreement kept them from interacting at school, although they would occasionally see each other in the hall, making only small gestures in acknowledgement. Often Ben would initiate these "chance" meetings during the times when Tim was more aloof than usual.

Then there were days when Tim was as hungry and affectionate as the first time they slept together. He stayed the night sometimes at Ben's house, his parents generously not making a fuss over him having a guy over. Karen argued, to no avail, that it would be like a boy staying with her. Luckily his sister had no clue who Tim was or of his status with the popular kids. To a senior, anyone younger was a scrub.

The sleepovers were usually spent doing the normal sort of things: movies, video games, and takeout pizza. Once the house was quiet it inevitably became intimate between them. Sex was now more exploratory, their prior urgency relaxed into desire. Tim was even comfortable enough to return Ben's oral favors, although the topic of sexual orientation was still completely taboo. Ben didn't mind too much. How could he complain when he was waking up next to the hottest guy in school?

There was, however, one problem that he couldn't ignore: Krista Norman. Tim was still dating her. Ben tried not to bring her up in conversation, preferring to pretend she didn't exist. When his curiosity got the better of him, it was clear from Tim's responses that their relationship wasn't going well. Ben couldn't figure out why Tim stayed with her. This became a point of contention. Even mentioning her name was enough to spark an argument.

The issue came to a head in late October, just a few days before Ben's birthday. He hadn't seen Tim the weekend before because he and Krista had been out on a double date with Bryce and his girlfriend. Ben intentionally decided not to call him afterwards, and for the next three days hadn't heard from him. While doing some early birthday shopping at the mall with his mom, Ben spotted them both. Krista, as usual, had Tim's arm in a death grip, as if he would come to his senses at any moment and try to escape.

Ben tried to steer his mother into a shop before they neared, but June had her own mind about where they were going and soon saw the couple. She started to say hello to Tim when Ben hissed for her to keep quiet. She did, mostly out of puzzlement. Tim gave a little nod as they passed by, his girlfriend oblivious as she gawked at a nearby jewelry store. As soon as Krista dragged Tim away to see it, June badgered him with a series of questions.

"I thought you two were together?"

"No, he's straight," Ben answered through gritted teeth.

"Oh come on!" she protested. "I'm not deaf, you know. I've heard what you two get up to at night."

Ben shrugged and turned away. "I'm working on it." he replied.

On the following evening, he was taking out the trash when the thumping of jogging feet attracted his attention.

"Hey," Tim said as he slowed to a stop in front of him, panting while wearing a dopey grin.

"Ankle still doing all right?" Ben asked without smiling.

"Yeah. Still a little sore but as good as can be expected." He beamed at Ben, who remained silent. "You look like you wouldn't mind spraining it again."

"Not really. I'm just not in a good mood."

"Well, maybe I can cheer you up," Tim offered. "Let's go up to your room."

His intent was clear as he stood with hands on each hip, still breathing heavily and flashing a winner's smile. He smelled of sweat and freshly cut grass. Ben wanted nothing more than to strip off those damp clothes, but his frustration prevailed.

"Why don't you call Krista if you're so horny?" Ben spat.

"Not this again," Tim groaned. "Jesus Christ! What does it matter?"

"It matters to me! Why are you even with her? You never have anything nice to say about her. She's not even the prettiest girl in school."

"Yeah, Bryce already has that one."

Ben scowled at this and considered walking away, but before he did, he gave it one last shot. He dropped the anger from his voice and asked, "Who do you like more, Krista or me?"

"You," Tim shrugged. "I like you more. When you're not pissed at me."

"Who do you sleep with? It's not Krista, is it?"

"No." Tim made sure the street was empty. "I sleep with you."

"So why do you need her when you have me?"

Tim stared off into the distance, shaking his head slowly, a frown forming on his face. He brushed the sweat from his brow and looked back at Ben, considering him for a moment before he turned away. "I'll see you around," he said as he resumed jogging down the street.

Ben waited for him to change his mind, to come back and apologize. When he didn't, Ben swore and attacked the trash cans, knocking them over and spilling their contents into the street. He kept kicking them until his anger was purged and he was exhausted. Then he began to cry.

Ben's birthday fell on the twenty-seventh, just a few days before Halloween. He wasn't robbed of any extra presents, like those poor unfortunate souls who had birthdays close to Christmas, but he could remember a few parties from his childhood where everyone dressed early in their costumes. He also tended to receive more horror-themed presents due to the unique shopping opportunities of the season.

This year his big day was on a Sunday, meaning his relatives were all free to turn an otherwise private celebration into a circus. Ben was glad for it this time. Not only did it mean more gifts, but it helped keep his spirits high. He hadn't talked to Tim since their argument. This tore at his heart, but today he was feeling better. Most of this was due to Allison, who had temporarily thwarted the ban on their friendship and was able to attend his party.

"This is supposed to be a date with Ronnie, so I expect you to put out," she teased him upon her arrival.

They needed this day together. The talent show had recently been pushed back until the end of the school year, the reasoning being that freshmen might feel too uncomfortable to enter since they were still adjusting to life in high school. Mrs. Hammond was distraught. Ben and Allison were relieved because they still hadn't chosen a song. The downside was the loss of their private time in the auditorium. Since then, they hadn't seen each other near as much as they would have liked.

Presents were top priority in the Bentley family, even taking precedence before the traditional cake and candles. So far Ben had received clothes from his parents, a wad of cash from his grandmother, and a new Discman and CDs to go with it, which his sister gave him begrudgingly, probably because she didn't have one of her own yet. Ben made sure to look at his mother when thanking his sister, since June no doubt had done the shopping.

Allison gave him a suit jacket they had discovered at a secondhand store earlier in the year. The jacket had been too expensive for him at the time and was missing most of its buttons. Not only had she sprung for it as gift, but she bought some suave new buttons and put those home ec skills to use by sewing them on. The end result was retro-chic and delightfully unique. He couldn't wait to wear it when the weather became cooler.

Ben's mother was about to light the candles on the cake when the doorbell rang. Thinking a relative had arrived late, Ben ran to answer it, happy to leave all the fuss behind for a moment. His heart lurched when the door opened to reveal Tim Wyman. Of course he had been invited, but that was before they had fought. Even prior to their falling out, he hadn't expected Tim to actually show up.

"Hey!" Ben said, not masking his surprise. "Uh, come on in!"

"That's okay. I just wanted to bring this by."

Ben looked down to see a thin present about three feet tall. Unless it was the largest book in the world, Ben guessed it might be art or a framed poster.

"Hello there!" said June as she poked her head into the entryway. "I was wondering when you'd show up! Come in and grab some cake."

Tim squirmed uncomfortably. "No really, I—"

"Come on, don't let Wilford get out the door or we'll never see him again."

Tim slunk inside, looking like a dog himself, one who knew he would get in trouble for having chewed his master's slippers. Ben's mother shut the door behind him to finalize the deal, winking at Ben on her way back to the kitchen.

"Time to meet the family," Ben chuckled. "The extended version."

"Great," Tim said, trying a sheepish smile.

They stood there, considering each other before Ben was called back to the dining room. Tim followed and was soon assaulted by a slew of greetings, handshakes, and even hugs from some of the older ladies. Introducing him to Allison was surreal, since they were the two people closest to Ben and yet their paths had never crossed. Tim seemed unsure how to behave around her, especially since Allison's knowing smile promised that she knew all of Ben's secrets.

"Wait, everyone!" June declared. "We have one more present before we light candles."

"No, you can open it later," Tim said. "Really," he added desperately when Ben took it from him.

"That's all right," Grandma Bentley crowed. "We're in no hurry."

"It's just something I—" Tim began as Ben started ripping the paper away. Whatever he had planned on saying was lost in his throat.

The wrapping paper fell away to reveal streaks of red, orange, yellow, and pink. The painting was abstract, a war of hot colors interlocking and swarming together. In their midst was something that looked very much like a heart. Two hearts, actually, overlapping so close that they appeared as one. Ben thought it was beautiful.

"Isn't that gorgeous?" June praised while clapping her hands together. "Did you paint that yourself?"

Tim opened his mouth to answer.

Karen got there first. "It looks like someone barfed up paint on a canvas," she said.

"We should have cut your tongue out at birth," Ben's father scolded.

"It's just something I found somewhere," Tim said dismissively. "You don't have to keep it."

"I love it!" Ben said.

June took the pressure off Tim by lighting the candles and coercing everyone into a chorus of *Happy Birthday*. Ben smiled, content to let others sing for a change. Allison finished this off with an extra verse sung diva-style, which sent everyone into fits of applause. Deciding what to wish for was easy. Ben knew exactly what he wanted as he blew out the candles.

No time to catch up with Tim. Ben was caught in a whirlwind of relatives who wanted to know what he had been up to, offer advice on what he *should* do, or simply hear him sing. While he was holding court with them, he tried to keep an eye on Tim, who was being cared for by Allison. Already she had heroically steered him away from Karen and their equally boorish cousin. If he wasn't mistaken, Tim was even beginning to enjoy himself.

As the party wound down, Ben suggested to Allison that she call Ronnie and they all head down to Houston to check out the haunted houses. He didn't bother asking Tim what he thought of this plan. It was his birthday after all. As the last of the relatives left, Ronnie showed up and whisked them all away in his beat up old SUV.

Tim clammed up again in Ronnie's presence, no doubt worrying about their relationship being exposed to yet another person who went to their school. This didn't last long. Ronnie found a football game on the radio and soon they were talking the indecipherable language of sports. Allison and Ben exchanged glances and rolled their eyes before laughing.

Ronnie and Tim kept the sports talk going as they stood in line at the Horror Hotel, one of Houston's newer haunted houses that Ben had never visited. Allison and Ben stood behind them, arms linked together as they pretended to be dating each other. They hoped by doing so that they would make Tim and Ronnie look like the gay couple. They even attempted to trade knowing looks with a few other people in line.

The haunted house was really good, much better than those in previous years, utilizing just the right amount of scare coupled with humor and creativity. Allison could really scream too. As the group wound their way through narrow corridors strewn with cobwebs, Ben jumped more in response to her shrill exclamations than from the monsters.

As original as the Horror Hotel was, it still had many of the same staples found in every haunted house, such as a pitch-black maze, where visitors were forced to feel their way through the corridors. These always gave Ben the shivers, especially when a hand clamped over his mouth. Then he recognized the smell of that person's skin, his fear dissipating as he leaned back and felt a muscled body against his own.

"This way," Tim murmured, pulling him into a dead end as

the voices of his friends faded away. Ben was released and then pressed up against a wall, Tim's breath tickling his ear. "I broke up with her."

"With Krista?"

"Yeah. You were right. It's you I like and it's you I want."

Before Ben could respond, Tim's mouth was on his. Sometimes those birthday wishes really did come true! They pawed at each other in the dark, Ben wishing they were somewhere more private, because the affection he felt in his heart could only be expressed in one way. He had decided to try words instead when someone bumped into them from behind and screamed.

"Boo!" Tim yelled, causing a chorus of girlish squeals to flee. Then he laughed "Let's get out of here." He took hold of Ben's hand and didn't let go until the very end, when the inevitable chainsaw-wielding cannibal sent them scrambling out the exit.

Allison and Ronnie were waiting for them, one looking clueless, the other wise to what might have delayed them. Stomachs grumbling, they found a steakhouse, the topic of sports once again dominating every conversation. Allison and Ben swore to each other to never double date again.

"I have another present for you," Tim said as the SUV drove away from Ben's house, taking Allison and Ronnie with it.

"I'm sure I can guess what that is," Ben said.

"Maybe not," Tim retorted. He pulled something from his pocket and shook it once, causing a simple necklace of metal beads to unravel, the sort that military dog tags usually hung from. Tim placed this around Ben's neck.

Ben looked down to see what was hanging from it and found a perfectly common house key. "What's this?" he asked.

"It's just in case you ever get the urge to come see me in the middle of the night."

"A key to your parents' house?" Ben asked disbelievingly. "So I can sneak in? Sounds dangerous!"

"Sounds exciting," Tim corrected. "You can try it out tonight. My parents are probably getting in bed right about now. Meet me in half an hour?"

Tim didn't wait for an answer. He just grinned seductively and headed down the street. Ben went inside and made an appearance for his parents, mentally debating whether or not to tell them he was going out again. He decided against it, just in case they tried to keep him home. Instead he said he was going to bed early and headed up to his room.

The painting Tim had given him was already hanging on the wall. Thanks, Mom! Ben sat on the edge of the bed to stare at it. He had no doubt as to who the artist was. During dinner Ben had noticed paint on Tim's fingernails that matched the colors exactly. If only stupid Karen hadn't opened her big trap. Still, it was incredibly romantic. He had never suspected that Tim had artistic impulses, but it made Ben love him even more.

Love? The word surprised him. Did he feel that way about Tim? If not, what else could it be? Ben pondered this while waiting for his parents to settle down for the night. He'd had crushes on guys before. Having feelings for them instead of just a rush of hormones was what finally made Ben realize he was different. Sexuality always seemed like the wrong term to him, because loving other guys romantically—that's what made him gay! He could have remained abstinent for his entire life, but it was feelings that came unbidden and remained uncontrolled. Like his first crush that he had tried taking a bus ride to see, but this felt different. Was it more? Only one way to find out. Ben stood, snuck down the stairs, and quietly shut the front door behind him.

Before long he was standing in front of Tim's door instead. His hand shook as he used the key, thinking that at any moment a light would turn on or an alarm would sound. At least the door was new enough not to squeak as he pushed it open. The house was dead silent, every window dark, but what if the Wymans heard him? How would he ever explain why he was there?

The air conditioner kicked on as he ascended the stairs, causing him to jump. This was *way* scarier than the haunted house had been! He took a moment to calm himself before creeping down the hallway. Ben opened the door to Tim's room as silently as possible and slid inside.

The shadows in the room were long. Ben had expected to find Tim in the bed, but he could see in the limited light that it was still made and unoccupied.

"Hey," came a voice from behind.

"Gah!" Ben exclaimed loudly. "Oh shit!" he whispered,

clamping his hand over his mouth, but Tim laughed as if there was nothing to worry about.

"Your parents!" Ben hissed.

"Business trip. They won't be back until tomorrow, but that was a good test run. I didn't hear you until you were at my door."

Ben slugged him playfully and laughed himself. He reached for the light switch, but Tim moved his hand away, pulling out a lighter instead, which he used on a handful of candles around the room.

Ben smiled from ear to ear, knowing what would happen next. He untied his shoes, kicked them off, and tossed himself into bed. "So I hear that you are officially single," he said playfully. "Does this mean that you're back on the prowl again?"

"I never stop prowling." Tim growled like a tiger, showing off two rows of teeth.

"I see, but at the ripe old age of seventeen, don't you think it's time you settle down with someone special?"

"Meaning?" Tim inquired.

"I want to be your boyfriend."

"Jesus!" Tim swore. "You don't let up do you?" He forced away a smile and shook his head. "It's not enough that you make me dump my girlfriend?"

"If she was good enough for you to date, then I am twice as qualified," Ben grinned. "Anything a girl can do, I can do better," he singsonged.

"Offhand, I can think of a few things that you can't do!" Tim taunted.

"Well, anyway. What do you think? Seriously."

"I think I want a test drive before I buy the car." Tim leapt on him, kissing his face, biting his neck, and making him laugh. They rolled and wrestled with each other until their playfulness became more serious. Tim tore at Ben's clothes as if he hadn't seen him for years. Ben followed suit, each more desperate than the other to undo the distance of the past week. Once wasn't enough tonight. After a break to raid the kitchen for food, they were back at it again, this time taking things slowly. The candles had all burnt down by the time they fell asleep, their bodies tangled comfortably together.

When the screeching of the alarm clock woke them, they moaned and griped in unison, not wanting to face the reality of another week of school. Tim got out of bed first. The sight of him standing there naked, sporting morning wood as he scratched his chest, was enough to brush away the last remnants of sleep from Ben.

"Wanna take a shower together?" he offered.

"We're going to be late," Tim countered.

"We can skip first period, you know." Ben told him how the attendance system worked, Tim listening with an intrigued expression.

"I wondered how you were able to take care of me without getting in trouble. You really know how to play things to your advantage, Benjamin. You've shaved an hour off the school day, and now you're manipulating me into being your boyfriend."

Ben beamed at him. "So we are?"

"Yeah," Tim smiled back. "Why not? But listen, I don't want anyone getting in our way. My parents can't know about this. No one at school either."

"So just like things were before?" Ben said in disappointment.

"Not like before. No Krista, no other girls, and definitely no other guys. Just me and you. I want it to stay that way."

Ben didn't think there was anything to fear from parents or school. Those were all demons he had already faced. Tim just needed time to realize these things for himself. Rather than argue the point, Ben rose and dragged his new boyfriend into the shower.

CHAPTER 11

"He hit me."

Ben stared at his best friend and waited for a mischievous smile to show that Allison was kidding. It never came. Tears formed in her eyes as he stood there holding the front door open. He had been on the verge of sneaking out to stay the night at Tim's house, as he had done so many nights in the past month, when she had thrown pebbles at his window to get his attention.

"Come upstairs," Ben whispered, not wanting to wake his parents. "Ronnie hit you?" he asked once he had closed his bedroom door.

"No! My father—" The emotional dam finally broke and she dissolved into tears.

Ben wrapped an arm around Allison, examining her as he did so, and noticed that her jaw looked red and sore. "I'm sorry," he said as he held her, letting her cry it out without badgering her with questions.

"He's such an idiot," Allison sobbed. "I had permission to go out with Ronnie and everything."

"What set him off?" Ben asked, breaking away from her to grab some tissues.

"Thanks." Allison blew her nose, her chin trembling before she continued. "He caught Ronnie kissing me goodnight. That's all. Ronnie wasn't feeling me up or anything like that. It was just a kiss! My dad flew off the handle and shoved Ronnie away, so I started screaming at him, and…" She swallowed against the pain. "That's when he punched me." Allison placed a trembling hand to her jaw.

"Bastard," Ben snarled. He clenched his teeth and tried to clamp down on his anger. "What did Ronnie do?"

"He was already gone." Allison shook her head. "I'm not telling it right."

"It's okay. Just try to calm down."

"I'm all right." She took a deep breath. "After Dad shoved Ronnie, I got in between them and told Ronnie to leave. After he was gone I started arguing with Dad, and that's when he hit me. I couldn't believe it. At first I just stood there staring at him. Then I got scared and took off running. I didn't know where else to go."

"It's good you're here," Ben said. "You should stay the night."

"Thanks." Allison sniffed and sighed. "What are we going to do about this? I feel lost. I don't even know if I have a home anymore!"

Ben chewed his lip while they considered the situation in silence. Allison didn't have any other in-state relatives, and the idea of her moving far away was unbearable. But how could she endure living with a monster? What was to stop something like this from happening again?

"I wish we were already in college," he said wistfully.

"Me too. Have you decided yet?"

That was another unhappy topic. Ben wanted to continue his vocal training at an arts college that specialized in music. Allison wanted to pursue a medical career at a more traditional university. The inevitable separation if they chose different schools was something neither of them liked to think about, and now wasn't the time to discuss it further.

"I haven't," Ben replied. "Let's not worry about that tonight. You want your PJs?"

"Yeah."

Allison used to stay the night so often that she had bought a pair of pajamas to keep in his room. It was a miracle her father had never figured out that she was actually staying the night with him and not Karen. Their former friendship had been useful camouflage in that regard. They couldn't get away with that these days. Not when Mr. Cross had gotten so much worse.

The next day presented an awkward situation, since they were supposed to go to school. Would she be safe there, or would Allison's father pull her out of class and keep hurting her? Ben needed help, so he decided to confide in his mother, who wasn't nearly as sympathetic as he would have expected. The bruise on Allison's face was twice as ugly now and left no question as to the truth of her story, but it was clear that June wasn't willing to interfere with someone else's parenting. There was no point in asking if Allison could stay with them, but his mother at least granted him permission to skip school for the day. June took off work and looked up a hotline for Allison to call, and although his friend acted grateful and interested, after they were finished eating the lunch his mother prepared, Allison confided that she had no intention to call it.

"I'm not abused!" she said incredulously.

Ben disagreed, but he kept his opinion to himself. For now.

In the afternoon they decided to go to Allison's house so she could get a change of clothes, despite the possibility that Mr. Cross might be there when they arrived. He wasn't, but the house was in more disarray than normal. Food was left out on the counter among dirty dishes. A drinking glass was shattered on the kitchen floor. Ben helped her clean up before they went to her room.

"You should go," Allison said. "There's no point in me leaving."

Ben understood how she was feeling. As they surveyed her room, it hit home how hard it would be to leave it all behind. Where would she go? She didn't have a job and wasn't finished with school. All she owned was right in front of them, but suddenly it didn't seem like much compared to what the real world demanded.

"I have to face him sooner or later, right?" Allison said. "I mean, he's my dad. We'll work it out, but you shouldn't be here when he gets back."

"Forget it," Ben said. "I'm staying and I'm going to have a word with him."

"You're sweet, but that's not a good idea. You being here is just going to upset him more."

"Yeah, yeah. I said the same thing last time you had a terrible idea, but I still went along with it," Ben reminded her. "You owe me one. In fact, I think it's best if you leave me here. Alone."

"What? You're insane."

"No, I mean it. I'll talk to your dad, then I'll meet you back at my place and I can tell you what he said."

Allison was hesitant, but Ben managed to convince her. Only after she had gone was he free to question the soundness of his idea. Who did he think he was, an ambassador? What if Mr. Cross started beating the crap out of him? He could get killed!

The sound of the front door opening caused his stomach to churn. He should have at least gone outside with Allison and returned to ring the doorbell once he saw Mr. Cross was home. Now it looked like he was a burglar.

Ben left her room and walked to the head of the stairs. Mr. Cross was already looking upward, an expression of hope on his face that turned dark when he didn't see his daughter.

"What the hell are you doing here?" he challenged.

"Allison and I came back to get her a change of clothes. She's not here," Ben added when Mr. Cross started up the stairs with a determined expression, "but she told me everything."

Mr. Cross stopped, and for the briefest moment, there was shame in his eyes. That marked the end of Ben's fear of the man. He walked down the stairs until he was face to face with Allison's father.

"She told me everything," Ben continued. "Things she would never tell the police. I would though, and I won't hesitate to if you ever lay a hand on her again."

"You little shit!" Mr. Cross's hand snatched out to grab him by the shirt.

Ben didn't even flinch.

"Go ahead and hit me," he suggested. "I'll go to the police today, and you'll never harm anyone again. Not me and not Allison."

"They'd never believe you," Mr. Cross snarled. "I'll tell them that *you* hit her. How do you like that, you little faggot?"

"Not bad," Ben shrugged. "I guess I would then tell the cops about all the times you forced me to do things for you. How you shoved me down on my knees, and how I was too scared to tell anyone, because you kept threatening me. Who do you think they'll believe then?"

Mr. Cross let go of him instantly, as if he had just learned that Ben had some horribly contagious disease.

"I never!" Mr. Cross spluttered. "You're sick!"

"It doesn't matter what you've actually done," Ben said. "The bigots and the homophobes will have a field day with it. People like that want to believe the worst about people like us, and you've got a lot more to lose, so don't try to intimidate me with lies!"

"Get out of my house, you little punk!"

"No. Not before I've had my say. Allison loves you, Mr. Cross. She would do anything to make you happy. I think you love her too, but the way you try to protect her is doing more harm than good. You need to let her go. One more year and she's going to be living on her own in a different city. You won't be able to control her then. You can't treat her like a bird in a cage.

If you do, she'll never come back to you once she's free. She'll be out of your life forever."

Much to Ben's amazement, Allison's father seemed to be listening. The anger had drained from his face and he looked like he was about to cry. Ben had hit upon the man's worst fears.

"I'm sorry you lost your wife. I can't even begin to imagine how much that must hurt, but you still have your daughter. She might be the only person left in the world who still loves you. If you destroy that, who will you be? What will be left of you then?"

Mr. Cross's face crumpled as his tears began to flow.

He didn't deserve to have his dignity spared, but Ben made his way to the front door anyway, ignoring the sobs behind him. "She'll be home in a few hours," he said. "Don't screw it up."

A block later and the adrenaline that had powered his confidence faded. Ben leaned against a tree, his hands and legs shaking. Had he really just said all that to Allison's father? And had he made things better or worse? The man had been crying when he left! What if he killed himself or something terrible? Ben second-guessed his actions all way home, sometimes feeling proud of himself, other times feeling like he should run back and apologize. But then, what difference would it make? In the end, all was said and done.

Allison wasn't in school. She had returned home the day before, calling Ben briefly in the evening to say that she was okay—that her father was upset but not at her. Ben thought everything was going to be all right, but now a number of terrifying scenarios were playing out in his mind. What if Mr. Cross had left the state with her? Even worse, maybe he had killed her before taking his own life.

As soon as he was home, Ben called but there was no answer. He kept trying every half hour until, a little past nine, Allison finally picked up the phone.

"Are you all right?" Ben stammered.

"Yeah." There was a hesitation. "Great, actually. What did you say to my dad?"

"Why?"

"He's like a different person now! He keeps apologizing to me, and today he took off work so we could have father-daughter time together."

"Really?"

"Yeah." Allison laughed. "I'm even allowed to see you again!"

Ben wanted to cry in relief. "Did he say why?"

"Something about how protective you are of me, but he didn't want to talk about it. What did you say?"

Ben considered telling her everything, but ultimately decided to give her an edited version. He didn't want her thinking that her father's actions were the result of blackmail. Ben didn't want to believe that either. He liked to think that he had appealed to Mr. Cross's heart and that everything would be fine from now on. That didn't sound very realistic though. Ben would be positive and encouraging on the surface, but inside, he knew he would never be able to let down his guard again.

CHAPTER 12

A sea of red and green wrapping paper threatened to consume the living room as Ben and his sister tore into present after present, tossing paper and ribbons away carelessly to better see what Santa had brought them. Karen squealed over some designer purse, while Ben admired his new pocket watch, which was silver with erratic maroon lines carved tastefully into its surface. He pressed the button on top and the casing swung open to reveal the time, which was already correctly set at half past six in the morning. This was their tardiest Christmas yet! Usually Ben and his sister would wake their parents and be under the tree by five.

"You can use that watch to get home at a decent time," his mother teased.

"Should have bought him a calendar so he remembers when to take out the trash," Adam said, still yawning himself awake. Ben's father was never as excited about opening presents. Not like June was.

Ben smiled and thanked her before digging around for another present with his name on it. He wasn't lacking anything. Already he had gotten new clothes, gift certificates, a couple of books, and an amp with a microphone, so he and Allison could really start belting out tunes. There was still more to be opened though. His mother always went overboard when it came to Christmas.

Weeks of shopping and preparation were over and done with in half an hour. Adam went back to bed the second he was granted permission, and Karen scooped up her booty in her arms, taking it back to her room like a rat returning to its lair. Ben played the part of the good son and stayed to help his mom clean up the mess.

"We should probably start recycling," Ben suggested as he surveyed the enormous amount of now-useless paper.

His mother didn't hear him. Her lips were pursed and her forehead was wrinkled in thought. "Think how much nicer it will be at home," she said. "We have plenty of food and I promise your father and I will stay out of your way."

Ben didn't need her to explain. This had been a constant topic between them for more than a week. Tim's parents were in the Pompanos for the holidays, leaving their son to fend for himself. Ben didn't know how they could live with themselves, but he was told this wasn't the first Christmas they were absent for.

"You know why I want to go over there," Ben said patiently. "It's going to be romantic."

"I still don't see why he can't eat Christmas dinner with us," his mom countered. "You two can go back to his place in the evening and have your naughty time."

Ben smiled and shook his head. How could he tell her that being around family was a giant mood killer? As much as he loved them, it was hard to entertain romantic thoughts when Grandpa was telling stories of his mall Santa days or while protecting Tim from Karen's constant teasing. Ben's mom might be respectful and give them their space, but the others were oblivious to such social graces.

"It's just one Christmas," Ben reassured her. "It's not going to become a tradition."

"There's only one Christmas left before you move to who knows where," his mom pointed out. "And what about your grandparents? They won't get to see you at all!"

There was no winning this battle, so in the end, Ben promised to stay for Christmas dinner, which wasn't so hard considering it took place in the early afternoon. As it turned out, he was glad he stayed. Aside from being there to receive even more presents from his relatives, he also was provided with enough leftovers to keep him and Tim fed for a week. In fact, it was too much to carry when presents were added to the equation, and Ben had to accept a ride from his dad just to make it there.

Tim was in a solemn mood when Ben arrived—no surprise considering the situation. Ben stowed away the food before kicking the house into gear. He put Christmas music on the stereo and sang to it while walking around the house and turning on all the decorative lights. He added his present to the multitude under the soulless department store tree. Not that it wasn't attractive, but like all display-floor trees, it lacked a personal touch. There weren't any homemade ornaments and it wasn't even leaning. Who ever heard of a straight Christmas tree? All the lights were the same color too, and as much as he liked blue, he missed the multicolored gaudiness that was standard at this time of year.

The holiday cheer that Ben was spreading like mad finally infected Tim, who regained his usual smile. He slow danced with Ben to the mellow parts of Bing Crosby's song, *Happy Holiday*, and laughed as Ben did a jig to the up-tempo segment in the middle. A plate of leftovers—which Tim devoured ravenously— further soothed his spirits. Watching him chow down on ham and mashed potatoes faster than even Wilford could manage was oddly endearing.

"You ready for some presents?" Ben asked once he had finished.

"Oh yeah!" Tim answered enthusiastically.

They adjourned to the living room where they started pulling out package after package. All of them were for Tim, which was shocking. Ben had assumed that they were for the whole family. Obviously the Wymans were trying to compensate for leaving their son alone.

"The haul was huge last time too," Tim explained as he unwrapped a new stereo. "At least it shows they feel guilty."

The better part of an hour passed before all of his gifts were opened, leaving only two presents under the tree: the one from Ben and another small box wrapped in snowflake-themed paper. Tim handed this to Ben somewhat shyly.

"You shouldn't have," Ben lied, accepting the present with curiosity. As he unwrapped it, a wonderful scent reached his nose. He knew it was designer cologne before he could read the label.

"I almost bought that for myself," Tim explained. "The scent drives me wild, but you can never really smell it once you spray it on yourself. It's kind of cool having a boyfriend. This way I can smell it all the time."

"I like it!" Ben said as he sprayed some on.

Tim leaned over and inhaled, growling with pleasure. He attacked Ben, play-biting his neck before kissing him.

"Hey, cut it out!" Ben laughed. "You have to open yours now!"

"Later," Tim insisted.

"No, now!" Ben pushed him away with a smile. "We have the whole night to snuggle up and stay warm."

"Yeah right," Tim said as he backed off and reached for his gift. "We could practically go for a walk in shorts and flip-flops.

Texas winters are crazy. Don't you ever miss the snow?"

"Sometimes," Ben admitted. "We visited my uncle in Minnesota once and—" He trailed off as the paper fell away from Tim's gift, nervous about what he had chosen.

Two topics were forbidden with Tim. Sexual orientation was one. The most Ben could get him to admit was that he was bisexual, but he had only said it once to appease Ben and put an end to a heated argument. The other taboo subject was his painting. Tim had never openly admitted that hobby of his and met any inquiries about it with dead silence. This made Ben's choice of present this year somewhat risky.

Tim examined the wooden box full of paintbrushes. They were expensive, the best that Ben could afford. Tim's face was guarded, but his eyes were impressed. Next he looked at the four tubes of paint: red, green, white, and ice blue.

"Christmas colors," Ben explained.

Tim looked up at him, expression questioning.

"You don't have to say anything," Ben assured him. "I just want you to know that I love the painting you gave me and I think you are exceptionally talented."

He swallowed, waiting for some reaction from Tim, who remained still. Ben was on the verge of apologizing when the silence broke.

"These are *really* good," Tim said, holding up the brushes. "I'll do my best with them."

Ben gave an exaggerated sigh of relief.

"You are a very persistent person, Benjamin Bentley," Tim said. "Pretty soon I won't have any secrets left."

"You mean there's more?"

"Maybe. Hey, do you want a glass of wine?"

"Um, okay." Ben had never actually drunk wine before. Aside from some cheap booze that tasted like spiked Kool-Aid, he hadn't done much drinking at all.

They left the giant mess behind and went into the den, where Tim chose the bottle that he felt most certain his parents wouldn't want him opening. He poured two glasses, handed one to Ben, and held up the other.

"Merry fucking Christmas," he toasted with a toothy grin.

"Merry Christmas," Ben responded, taking a sip gingerly. The taste was bitter, but it wasn't too bad. "What?" he asked when the grin failed to diminish on Tim's face. "Am I holding the glass wrong or something?"

"No, no. I was just thinking about something you said on your birthday."

"What's that?"

"How did you put it?" Tim feigned deep thought. "I think you said that there was, quote, 'nothing you couldn't do that a girl could,' unquote."

"Yeah, so?" Ben didn't see where this was leading.

"I thought we could put that theory to the test tonight."

Ben's second sip of wine almost went through his nose. He had given some thought to anal sex before, but it honestly wasn't something that he ever fantasized about. Even when he had experimented by himself, it really hadn't done anything for him. And now Tim was suggesting they try it? For the first time Ben wasn't leading the bull by the horns. That wouldn't do at all.

"All right," Ben said. "I'll fuck you. Bend over."

"What? That's not what I meant!"

"Sure it is! Don't be shy," Ben taunted. "I promise not to hurt you!"

"We'll see who gets fucked," Tim threatened. He set his wine glass down and launched himself at Ben, who almost spilled his drink all over the carpet.

"Wait! Wait!" he giggled, making a show of carefully setting his glass down before sprinting out of the room. This earned him a two second lead, Tim in close pursuit.

They chased each other around the hall, laughing and hollering, and finally kissing once Tim caught Ben around the waist. The joking subsided as it became clear that Tim intended to carry through with his idea. Their heat was broken momentarily by a puzzled conversation over what they should use for lubrication. They knew there was supposed to be something, but their knowledge on the subject stemmed mostly from gay jokes. Ben shot down Tim's suggestion of Crisco, and a raid on Mrs. Wyman's bathroom failed to manifest any Vaseline. In the end they found some fancy facial cream and decided to make do with it.

"Do you want to go up to your room?" Ben asked uncertainly.

"Nope. It's Christmas." Tim took him by the hand and led him to the living room, which was dark except for the tree's lights.

"Here?" Ben was bemused as he was pulled down onto a bed of wrapping paper.

They began kissing each other while trying to undress, twisting into odd positions in order to remove clothes without their lips breaking contact. Ben went to work on pleasing Tim, part of him hoping to satisfy him before things escalated to the next level, but he only succeeded in bringing the moment closer. Once worked up there was no stopping Tim, who rolled over on top of Ben while fumbling with the cream in one hand.

Tim pulled back to ask, "You ready?"

"Yeah," he replied, even though he was anything but.

The first attempt resulted in pain like Ben had never known, as if someone was twisting a knife deep within his gut. Tim apologized, but didn't hesitate to try again. This time he managed to get it all the way in, but Ben forbade him to move in the slightest as he tried to grow accustomed to the feeling. He knew Tim was hung, but now it felt three times as big as it looked.

Eventually Tim started to move slowly. Just a tiny fraction of an inch at first, and then more as the physical sensation overtook him. Ben gritted his teeth and wondered how he would survive this experience as Tim's thrusting intensified. He had no choice. Ben would have to ask him to stop.

He opened his eyes to do so and saw his lover above him, body bathed in the eerie blue light of the tree. Tim's face was lost in passion and more handsome than ever. Ben was so taken by this ethereal vision that he forgot his discomfort and relaxed. The pain disappeared, replaced by something akin to pleasure. Ben reached down to touch himself and the pleasure multiplied. Soon the chorus of Tim's moans was joined by his own.

He reached up with his free hand to pull Tim in for a kiss, bringing their bodies closer together in the process. Their movements became one, increasing in need and intensity until they exploded together. Tim collapsed onto Ben, his heavy bulk warm and comforting. They lay there several minutes, catching their breath before they both started laughing with mad joy at what they had discovered.

— — —

Streams of purple, green, and blue rushed from three sides of the canvas, gathering together wild and free before attempting to continue their journey eastwards. The colors were halted by a dull grey barrier that couldn't be broken, even though all three streams had joined forces against it. Was that how Tim felt? Was that why this painting hung on his wall, surrounded by superficial car and sports posters?

"Wanna see more?" Tim asked from behind.

Ben flinched, not having noticed that the shower water had stopped running. "See more what?"

Tim regarded him cautiously while toweling his hair dry. "More of my paintings. In my studio."

"Of course I do!"

"Good. We can grab breakfast afterwards."

Ben expected the studio to be somewhere in the house, but instead they drove to an office park on the edge of the city. Tim unlocked a nondescript door in an equally dull building and disarmed an alarm system by punching a code into the keypad.

"This is one of my dad's offices," he explained as he ushered Ben inside.

"What does he do exactly?" Ben asked as he peered into a shadowy sea of cubicles.

"Provides medical supplies. It's boring, but he makes a lot of money doing it. Over here."

At the end of a hall filled with doors was one with its window obscured by paper. Tim used another key on this door and flipped on a light switch. The room was small but well lit, thanks to the large window occupying one wall. Ben could see the backs of two easels that faced this window. Before them was a small desk topped by large pieces of paper that drooped over the edges, each decorated with charcoal sketches. Ben looked to Tim, tacitly seeking permission to proceed. He nodded, but stayed by the door.

Ben moved first to the desk to examine the sketches. Each featured the exteriors of buildings. Some were more technical than others, but all of them experimented playfully with shape and form.

"Sometimes I think about becoming an architect," Tim explained.

"They're really good. This one is really great!" Ben held up what looked like a skyscraper that gradually widened the further up it went.

"That's supposed to be a water tower." Tim frowned in dissatisfaction. "I don't know."

"You should be proud!" Ben said as he set it down and moved to the easels.

Work had just begun on the canvas he went to. The style was much different than Ben's birthday present or the art in Tim's room. This painting was realistic rather than abstract, and portrayed a man covering his face with both hands.

"Self-portrait." Tim chuckled nervously. "I've been working on that one forever. Hands are really hard to do."

"I bet. Why your hands and not your face?"

"Don't read into it. It's just a part of me I can easily see. Maybe I should get a big mirror in here or something."

"Or maybe I could model for you," Ben joked.

"Why not? That would be cool! Of course I would insist on painting you nude."

"In that case you should probably opt for the mirror." Ben smiled. "It's cool that your dad lets you use this space."

"Mom insisted. Some of my paintings get pretty messy. C'mon. Let's get out of here."

Once he was away from the studio, Tim felt free to talk more openly about his art, his hand clasped tightly to Ben's the entire ride home. Ben felt he had been through a rite of passage, allowed to see a side of Tim that was even more intimate than sex. No small feat considering what they had done yesterday.

The realization came then, in a quiet moment when Tim was parking the car, when it should have been accompanied by confetti and the swelling of music. Ben had lusted after Tim's body, yearned to belong to him, and later simply enjoyed whiling away the hours in his presence. And now that had evolved into something much more meaningful. Ben wished the current situation was appropriately romantic so he could speak the words, but it wasn't. Not only that, but he still felt the need to be cautious. He would wait until the right time, when Tim had hopefully reached the same conclusion. This was love.

CHAPTER 13

With the coming of a new year, Ben felt himself reinvented. He enjoyed more freedom than ever, maintained an increasingly serious relationship, and he had even found employment. Ben had taken a part-time job at a local supermarket, handling menial tasks such as bagging groceries or stocking the shelves. This earned him enough that he no longer had to beg his parents for pocket money, even though they now found excuses to reward him for being responsible. All in all, he felt very much like an adult.

The world even seemed a little less lonely for an out-of-the-closet teenager. Evan, one of Ben's coworkers, was a year older than him and went to school in the neighboring city of Conroe. Evan quickly became like a long-lost brother. They even looked alike, but Evan had a wicked sense of humor that was all his own. He was still in the closet but wasted no time in coming out to Ben, once he figured things out.

Evan's experiences at his school were even more limited than Ben's own. He'd only had one sexual encounter after loitering outside a gay bar one night, but hadn't enjoyed the experience and hoped to find something more meaningful. He was cute and transparently interested in Ben, but he couldn't hold a candle to Tim. Ben made it known that he was dating someone, but kept the details a secret, an attitude closeted Evan could appreciate.

Ben's adult life reverted unwillingly to childhood for the five periods he suffered at school every day. He still skipped first period, but he did so now with full confidence. His report card from the previous semester had the standard "C" that he always received in P.E. and showed no indication that he hadn't been present for months. His name was simply one among the many that the coaches ignored in favor of more talented athletes and would likely remain so.

In an effort to find a class that he actually enjoyed, Ben enrolled in a new elective. He chose journalism in the hopes that it would fuel his occasional interest in writing. If only that's what they spent their time doing. Journalism started slow, with tedious textbook studies of what constituted a good story and the formula for creating one. By the second month this gave way to preparing articles and photos for the school newspaper. The first few Ben submitted received good grades but didn't get published. Feeling particularly sappy in the spring weather, he then submitted a love poem that the teacher, Mrs. Jones, immediately suggested should be printed in the next issue.

Ben was thrilled, not only because his work was appreciated, but because it had been a very progressive decision on Mrs. Jones's part. His poem played the pronoun game and remained fairly neutral until the last couple of lines which were blatantly homosexual:

He looks into my eyes, mine mirrored in his,
and we each see a boy, lost in paupers' bliss.

Mrs. Jones was no spring chicken and didn't seem the type who would publish something so potentially controversial in a high school paper, but her enthusiasm suggested she was determined to go through with it. Perhaps literary types were simply more open-minded.

Two weeks later and his poem was in print. Ben grabbed a copy of the paper on his way to second period, only having time before class to check that it had actually been printed. The poem was there, right along with his name and everything! As class started, Craig whispered that his girlfriend had really liked it, although he was surprised to discover who the author was. Ben decided to take that as a compliment. He received more praise in journalism class and a few jeers on the way to lunch, but he didn't pay much attention. He was more eager to hear what Allison thought.

"Did you read it?" he asked as she sat down next to him, the paper in one hand.

"Not yet. It's been a crazy day. I will now though."

She dug through her lunch bag and slowly nibbled on carrot sticks as she read. Her eyes were wide and interested as they worked their way over the lines. Until the end, that is, when her face scrunched up in puzzlement.

"What?" Ben prompted, his stomach sinking.

"It's good," Allison answered. Her face was still confused. "I'm just surprised, that's all."

Exactly what Craig had said. "I don't get what's so

surprising," Ben retorted, starting to feel defensive. "Straight people aren't the only ones capable of romantic feelings."

"That's just it," Allison said, thumping the paper. "You wrote about a guy and a girl."

"What?" Ben grabbed the paper from her, hands clenching as he read the final lines:

She looks into my eyes, mine mirrored in hers,
and we each see a soulmate, lost in paupers' bliss.

"The bitch changed it," Ben snarled. "This isn't what I wrote!"

"Who?"

"Mrs. Jones," he explained. "My version was gay, but she changed it to this!" He shoved the paper away from him, not wanting to look at it any longer.

"And she didn't even talk to you about it first?"

"No! I would rather it was never published than for her to ruin it this way." He thought of Tim, the source of his inspiration. Had he read it? Would he think that Ben was more closeted than he had previously claimed? Or did it make him think of Krista Norman and miss what they had together?

"You have to go talk to her," Allison said. "Tell her that she just can't change what other people write. That's worse than censorship! She owes you an apology."

"There's no point," Ben complained. "The stupid thing is already published."

Allison was right though. He wasn't going to stand aside and silently take this abuse. After school he would confront Mrs. Jones and tell her exactly how he felt.

After sixth period, Ben stood in front of the journalism door, trying to compose himself. To freak out or not freak out, that was the question. He would try to stay calm during the confrontation, but he didn't know if he could maintain his cool or even if he should. He opened the door; the room inside dark and empty. After a moment's hesitation, he flipped on the lights and stepped inside.

Of course journalism wasn't taught six times a day like other courses were. He had never considered it before, but it was obvious now. He wondered what other classes Mrs. Jones taught.

Perhaps history, drawing from her own childhood memories from hundreds of years ago, changing truths as she pleased like she had done with his poem.

Ben went to her desk and began riffling through the papers on it. He wanted the original copy of his poem back. He wanted to see. Had she dared to cross out his words with red ink and replace them with her own? Ten minutes later and his search was fruitless. He would simply have to ask for it back when he saw her again tomorrow.

He returned to the now-abandoned hallway and spotted another student passing by. He began to duck guiltily back inside the classroom room when he realized it was Tim.

"Hey!" he whispered.

Tim saw him and looked around nervously.

Ben beckoned him silently as he stepped back through the doorway. Tim followed, eyes searching the room for anyone else as he entered.

"There's no one else here, you dork!" Ben said once the door was closed.

Tim laughed. "What are you doing?"

"Did you see the paper today?"

"Yeah, nice poem. You lost me with 'pauper's love' though."

Ben sighed. "When two people are so poor that they have nothing, they still have each other. That is their happiness."

"Ah, but neither of us are poor," Tim winked.

"We aren't a guy and a girl either!"

Tim understood immediately. "Someone screwed with your poem, huh?"

"Yeah, my douchebag of a teacher changed it." Ben shook his head irritably. "I came here to tell her off, but there's nobody home."

"Why don't you leave a message?" Tim glanced around, spotted the hat rack Mrs. Jones kept by the door, and knocked it over with a roundhouse kick. It landed noisily on the floor with a crack that suggested it was no longer in one piece.

"Don't!" Ben scolded before smiling with satisfaction.

"You should try it," Tim suggested. "It'll make you feel better."

"She does deserve it," Ben conceded. He looked around for inspiration. He grabbed the nearest student desk and tipped it over. Considering that the surface had been empty, this wasn't very impressive.

"C'mon, you can do better than that. How about *her* desk?"

Ben matched Tim's wicked grin, the anger at his mistreatment rising. He marched over to Mrs. Jones's desk, and with swipe of his arm, sent all of the desktop contents flying to the floor.

"Yeah!" Tim laughed manically as he grabbed the drawers and pulled, papers swooping everywhere. "What's next?"

"Wanna see the darkroom?" Ben asked with sudden inspiration.

"Sure." Tim followed him through the revolving door to a small cramped room glowing with red light.

"What'd you have in mind here?" Tim asked, pressing up against Ben from behind and breathing on his neck.

He didn't answer. Ben was distracted by the developed photos that had been pinned up to dry. Some were of sports scenes or grinning faces in drama club, but a handful were of couples hugging and leaning on each other. These photos would never be censored. They would be put in the paper without anyone ever questioning them or insisting they be altered. The people in those photos would always have their relationships accepted at the most basic level. They would never have to fear ridicule for something as innocent as holding hands in public.

Ben's eyes flickered over to a small fire extinguisher clamped to the wall. He shrugged Tim off and took it down, struggling to pull the safety pin free before aiming the nozzle at the photos.

"I hate this fucking school," Ben swore before white foam exploded over the photos, soaked the hanging strips of negatives, and seeped into the delicate developing equipment.

Soon it became difficult to breathe, so they fled through the spinning doorway and back into the main room where Ben began spraying everything he saw with artificial snow.

"Let me try," Tim said.

He took the extinguisher and walked around the room, spraying a bookshelf until it dripped with foam. Tim's jaw clenched. Ben was fascinated by the rage in his eyes. What did Tim have to feel so angry about? Was it his parents? His inability to be open about who he really was? Did he hate the very society that he fit into so perfectly?

The fire extinguisher began to sputter. Having exhausted its supply, Tim threw it at the marker board on the far wall, putting a nasty dent in its center. They left the room without trying to be stealthy. For the first time, they walked side by side down the school corridors. Once they were out of the building, they broke into a run, laughter making their sides ache as they tried to put as much distance as possible between themselves and the school.

They reached the bike paths and followed them into the sanctuary of the woods. There they fell onto the pine needle carpet, laughing and gasping for breath until they were exhausted.

"Hey," Ben said as something occurred to him. "Did you like it?"

"Like what?"

"My poem."

"I don't know," Tim said soberly. "I haven't heard the true ending yet."

Ben recited the censored lines for him, his face flushing with embarrassment.

Tim grinned, and proving he had known all along who the poem had been written for, he said, "Come look into my eyes, my little pauper." Then he pulled Ben close for a kiss.

The adrenaline rush that followed the afternoon's destruction had worn off by night, leaving Ben tossing and turning in his bed. He was certain that they would be caught, that someone had seen him standing outside the journalism room while he had gathered his thoughts. By the time he awoke from a meager three hours sleep, he had already accepted that he would be in the principal's office—possibly even in police custody—before lunchtime.

He considered attending P.E. for the first time in the year, worried that someone would be there looking for him. In the end, he decided that trouble was trouble. It was much too late to play innocent now. Ben arrived in second period English, his nerves on edge the entire time as he waited for some sign of his impending doom. He snapped at Daniel Wigmore for glancing over at his notes, which were pitifully sparse as he watched the door.

The bell rang. The next class was journalism. Ben found himself eager to revisit the scene of the crime, to discover what had happened. Mrs. Jones was standing outside the door, surrounded by a half moon of students.

"No one may enter," she announced. "There has been an incident. We'll be using room 2E6 in the meantime."

Ben nervously waited for her to acknowledge him. Her eyes met his momentarily as she counted under her breath to see if every student was present. No moment of recognition or even suspicion. She was clueless! The weight left his chest so suddenly that he almost laughed out loud. They had gotten away with it!

Once settled in the replacement classroom, Mrs. Jones emotionally described the crime. A few of the students seemed upset that their work had been ruined. Others snickered. Ben did his best to appear concerned as Mrs. Jones repeated the same information over and over, which basically boiled down to her knowing nothing.

"When will we be able to use the darkroom again?" asked a girl who was particularly keen on photography.

"Tomorrow," Mrs. Jones answered, "or perhaps the next day. The police don't want anything disturbed until they can dust for prints."

The weight returned, knocking the smugness out of Ben like the oxygen from his lungs. He imagined Tim grabbing the desk drawers and yanking them out, the prints left on the handles visible to the naked eye, like a signed confession. His own would be on the fire extinguisher. But did it really matter? It's not like either of them had a criminal history. The police wouldn't have his prints on record, would they?

A blurry childhood memory came rushing back. His mom had taken him to the public library, where his prints and a mug shot had been taken. He remembered playing cops and robbers with Karen afterwards. This had been for a missing child database, so he and his sister could be identified under dire circumstances. His fingerprints had been much smaller then, but Ben knew the pattern never changed.

Tim's prints might be on file for a similar reason. They hadn't gotten away with it at all. They just hadn't been caught yet! For the next half hour, Ben thought long and hard about what to do. Short of burning the school down and destroying all the evidence, he felt there was only one option left to him.

"I did it," he croaked, interrupting Mrs. Jones as she tried to dole out an assignment.

"What did you say?" prompted a guy next to him.

"I did it," Ben said louder, attracting the attention of the entire class. "There's no sense in wasting the time of the police because it was me who trashed your room."

He looked up to see a condescending look on Mrs. Jones's face, one that scolded him for making a tasteless joke. She didn't believe him!

"I'm not fucking kidding!"

Now he had her attention. He was out in the hall in seconds, an explanation demanded of him.

"You shouldn't have changed my poem," he said extra loud in the hopes that the other students would hear. He wanted the whole school to know why he had done it.

Talons fastened around his arm as Mrs. Jones escorted him to the principal's office, yammering the whole way, her disbelief ramping up to anger. He tuned her out, focusing instead on his plan. It was very important that he never slip up—that he never mention Tim or even another unnamed person. He was only turning himself in to protect Tim and didn't want that to go to waste.

His parents were called. Ben was interrogated by both the principal and Mrs. Jones until they arrived. By the time they did, his story was flawless. He parroted the details again and again, not expressing any remorse. The police were sent for and he gave a statement, repeating the story once more, making sure this time to emphasize that he felt discriminated against. The principal looked only slightly concerned at this new twist. Had it been a matter of race or religion, the issue might have been taken more seriously. Instead they asked him if he was responsible for the recent rash of fires, because somehow being a disgruntled gay guy also meant he might be an arsonist.

Ben was suspended for three days, which made him laugh. How was taking three days off a punishment? There were damages to be paid. That wasn't so funny. Ben vowed on the car ride home that he would handle it and not a dime would come out of his parents' pockets. This did little to calm them. They lectured him repeatedly, telling him what he already knew: He should have fought with words, used his mind instead of violence.

Ben knew it was true, and he might have felt ashamed had he done it alone. Instead he cherished the Bonnie and Clyde moment that he and Tim had shared together. He enjoyed playing the martyr. He had made a sacrifice, taken a bullet for his lover. In his mind it was the perfect expression of how he felt about Tim.

CHAPTER 14

"I owe you."

Tim's voice rumbled into the ear that Ben had pressed against his chest, startling him just as he was dozing off.

"Hm?"

"I owe you," Tim repeated, shifting so Ben was forced to raise his head and look up at him. "Big time. I'll pay for the damages, how does that sound?"

Ben yawned and propped himself up on an elbow. "There *is* something I've been thinking of."

"Name it. My parents would have killed me if we'd been caught. Whatever you want, it's yours."

"It's your parents I had in mind," Ben said hesitantly. "I want to meet them."

Tim snorted, but the amused expression disappeared when Ben failed to smile. "No way."

"Fine. Your car then." Ben rolled over onto his back. "Sign it over to me. Or dinner with your parents. You decide."

"Why do you want to meet them?" Tim asked. "They're just as old and boring as anyone else's parents."

"They're a part of your life, that's why."

"No they aren't."

"They are!" Ben insisted. "You may not always get along with them, but they raised you, and they know you better than anyone else in the world."

"You have no idea what you're talking about. My parents aren't the same as yours."

"How many times do I sneak over a week?" Ben asked, changing his tactic.

"I don't know. Three times?"

"It's inevitable that one night I am going to run into your mom checking to make sure the door is locked, or your dad getting a glass of water. It would be nice if they recognized me so they don't shoot me on sight."

Tim was silent, so Ben let him think. "Okay," he said eventually. "Come over this weekend. You can say 'hi' to them before we head out."

"Dinner," Ben persisted.

"How am I supposed to manage that?"

Ben smiled, already enjoying his victory. "You'll think of something."

Weeks went by before the dinner took place. Tim complained that parents usually insisted on meeting friends, and that reversing the request was weird. Eventually, Mrs. Wyman cooked something large enough that Tim hurriedly called Ben so he could show up "unexpectedly." Everything went according to plan. Tim answered the door and then asked his parents, as casually as possible, if Ben could join them. The Wymans agreed, even though they didn't look particularly pleased with the idea.

Ben, dressed as snazzy as possible without appearing too formal, took his seat across from Tim at the narrow dining room table. His feet accidentally brushed against Tim's leg, which recoiled defensively. Ben gave him the most positive and reassuring look possible, before turning his attention to Tim's parents. Mrs. Wyman was even more beautiful than he remembered. She was spry and energetic as she busied herself about the table, earnestly fulfilling her role as hostess.

Mr. Wyman sat rigid in his chair as he watched his wife work. Much of Tim's handsomeness came from him, but the stoic demeanor was thankfully not something he had inherited. His white hair and lack of movement made him seem made of stone.

A plate of *chile rellenos*—battered peppers stuffed with meat and cheese—was placed before Ben. He "oohed" and "aahed" over the meal and thanked Tim's mother graciously. Her mouth relaxed into attractive lips that smiled in appreciation. Mr. Wyman remained unimpressed, studying Ben evenly before folding his hands. He led his family in prayer before they ate. Ben was prepared for this. Tim had tutored him multiple times on the ritual and what to say. Ben seamlessly intoned grace along with the Wymans as if he had long since been a member of their family.

There was no lull in conversation. Ben had done too much research for there to be. He started with Mexico City, Mrs. Wyman's birthplace. After poring through encyclopedias for hours, he had learned it was nicknamed the City of Palaces, that it was built by the Aztecs in 1325, and boasted more museums than any other city in the world. He worked through these topics, claiming to have recently written a paper about the city for history class. Mrs. Wyman became animated, adding to his knowledge with great enthusiasm. Occasionally the topic of religion came up, ninety percent of Mexico City being Catholic, but Ben gently steered the conversation away every time it did.

Next he turned his charms on Mr. Wyman. This was much more difficult since the topic Ben had chosen to use was football, something he knew little about. Tim had coached him there too, teaching him the basics of the game before moving on to specifics involving Mr. Wyman's favorite team, the Kansas City Chiefs. It would have been too blatant for Ben to claim to like the same team, so he chose instead to playfully attack a few of their players and games while defending the Dallas Cowboys. Ben felt fake during his conversation with Mr. Wyman, since he had absolutely no interest in sports, but Tim's father didn't seem to pick up on his insincerity.

"It is so nice to finally meet one of Tim's friends," Mrs. Wyman said in perfect but exotically accented English. "He's been so protective of his social life since Kansas."

"Not protective," Tim contradicted. "I just like going out instead of staying home. I'm too old for sleepovers you know."

If only they knew, Ben thought merrily.

"Do you know his other friends?" Mrs. Wyman asked. "His girlfriend?"

Ben quickly wiped his mouth with his napkin in order to cover the frown. Girlfriend? Her name had better be a codename for him, like Benita, Benjamina, or something along those lines.

"Of course he knows Krista," Tim said, staring a hole into Ben's head.

Krista Norman. Of course. "She's really pretty," Ben forced himself to say. "Popular too." He wasn't happy with this deception, but he wasn't about to let it ruin the evening.

"And what about you?" Mrs. Wyman inquired with a smile. "A fair-haired boy like you must also have a pretty girl."

"Well actually," Ben began before his leg was kicked from under the table. He didn't spare a glance for Tim as he kicked him back. If he wanted to stay in the closet then that was his problem, but Ben wasn't going back in for anyone. "I have a boyfriend."

Mrs. Wyman smiled and shook her head as if she had misheard, while Mr. Wyman cleared his throat nervously.

"He's really great," Ben continued, filling in the silence. "Goes to the same school as us." He knew what to do next. He had to make it a nonissue. If he tried to explain who he was, or even defend his sexuality, they would instantly perceive it as weakness. He wanted to be as casual as if he had just declared his own eye color or favorite song. Time for the next topic.

"If I could find a restaurant around here that served authentic Mexican food like this," Ben said, gesturing to his nearly empty plate, "I would eat there every day. Everyone else would too. Such a place would make a fortune! Maybe you should open one."

Mrs. Wyman accepted this compliment, but it was clear that she was still confused. Ben distracted her by asking about her own career. Within minutes, the cloud formed by the revelation of his orientation had blown out the window like so much smoke. At the end of the meal, Ben was sure he had both of Tim's parents eating out of his hand. Not literally, but close!

When they left for the movies as planned, there was a marked change in Tim's behavior. He was more optimistic than ever before, having seen that the gay issue hadn't caused his parents' heads to explode. He even held Ben's hand in the theater, something he was usually too nervous to do.

This was, Ben felt, the beginning of something grand. Once home, he enjoyed fantasies of both families being present and accepting at the wedding. He wanted nothing more than to share these hopeful visions with Tim, but they had decided to spend the night apart. It wouldn't do to be caught sleeping together and destroy the delicate bridge that had been built.

Early the next morning, before Ben had even poured his ritual bowl of cereal, Tim was at his front door. Ben greeted him with a victorious smile, but the gesture wasn't mirrored.

"They don't want me to see you anymore," Tim stated bluntly.

"What?" Ben made him repeat the sentence, not believing what he had heard. "What happened? I thought they liked me?"

"They did, Benjamin, but they're Catholic!" Tim's voice was rising, threatening to attract attention, so Ben stepped outside and closed the door. "They aren't going to ignore their religion just because you can bullshit about sports or geography!"

"Maybe they just need some time to—"

"To what? Call the Pope and ask him to change the rules for you?" Tim scowled at the concrete walkway. "I knew this would happen. I told you they would get in the way. How could I have been so stupid?"

"Nothing is in our way!" Ben said, trying to keep him calm, but he was beginning to feel panicked himself. "So they aren't going to invite me to dinner again. Big deal! We just go about things like we did before."

"Do we?" Tim demanded angrily. "We just keep screwing around until the day they find us together? Jesus!"

"I think we can definitely leave him out of this," Ben joked.

"This isn't funny! My parents are going to be looking at me differently now. Questioning why their son is hanging around with someone like you!" If Tim noticed Ben's startled reaction, it didn't stop him. "Gee, honey," he said, mimicking Mr. Wyman's voice, "how come our son brought a gay guy to dinner and not his girlfriend? Hmm. I fucking wonder!"

"Stop it," Ben said, desperately suppressing his own anger.

"That's exactly what we should do!" Tim spat before storming away.

Ben wanted to chase after him, but not to comfort. He wanted to knock Tim to the ground and beat some sense into him. Instead he yelled, "Don't ever come back!" and stormed back into the house and up to his room, where his anger turned to tears.

Late that night, when the moon was high and the lawn mowers and luxury cars had all fallen silent, Ben crept through the streets and into Tim's room. Wordlessly, he took off his clothes and slipped between the sheets. They made love, violently at first, expressing their frustration with each other and the world before they slowed and their touches became gentle and apologetic. They would get through this. They had to.

Normally, with only four weeks left in the school year, Ben would be counting the days, but he and his friends were too preoccupied. For Ben it was preparing for the talent show. Allison had dragged Ben to Ronnie's garage one day, where Ebony and Ivory played their song. The music was perfect, but Leon's stoner voice didn't do it justice. Ben and Allison were soon sharing the mic. They had found their duet.

Tim's attention was focused mostly on his baseball. The next two games could bring the school's team to the state finals. Ben had managed to attend some of these events, watching Tim from the bleachers while pretending to be the wife of a famous Major League player. Or maybe the mistress of one, considering that their relationship was still shrouded in secrecy.

A week had sped by since they last saw each other. Saturday night, after one of Tim's games and a practice session with Allison, they agreed to meet halfway between their homes. The Wymans were hosting a dinner party and there was never much privacy at the Bentleys, so Ben and Tim decided to enjoy the warm night together. The air was electric with energy as spring slowly morphed into summer, the cicadas buzzing their hypnotic song in the woods where Ben waited.

They had an anniversary coming up, Ben realized. Almost a year ago, he had first seen Tim jogging along the path that circled the small lake. They had come so far since then. Tim had gone from being a hopeless fantasy to the most important person in Ben's life. He couldn't help but wonder how much further they would go together. Prom in two weeks? College? An apartment, marriage, kids?

The sound of thumping feet echoed out of the past and into reality. He turned to see Tim running toward him. For one brief moment, Ben felt as if the past year had been nothing but a dream. Tim broke the spell by grabbing and kissing him.

"Damn, I'm horny!" Tim said with a grin.

"Good game?" Ben asked.

"The best!" Tim filled him in on the details as they strolled together. Ben nodded and gave the appropriate responses, even though he still didn't fully understand the logistics of the game.

"Want to sit down here?" Ben asked rhetorically, kicking at pile of charred wood that had previously been a bench. There had been a number of small arson incidents recently. So far nothing as serious as a house burning down, but the recurring fires were enough to make most of the area's homeowners nervous.

"I think the playground is still intact," Tim suggested. "Are you a swinger?"

"You know it, baby!"

They were heading for the swings when Tim grabbed him by the arm and spun him around. He moved in close, pressing himself against Ben. The hardness in his pants made his intentions crystal clear.

"Not here!" Ben protested. "Think of the children!"

"We're the only ones around," Tim murmured. "All the kiddies are at home with their parents, glued to their idiot boxes."

It was a fair point. Ben could spend hours walking the suburbs at night without seeing another living being. A citizen venturing off the safely lit streets into the tamer territories of Mother Nature was even less likely. People always imagined that muggers and rapists lurked in these abandoned parks, which was silly since they would be waiting an eternity for any potential victims.

He let Tim press him up against one of the playground's wooden structures, lips mashing together as they fumbled at each other's pants. Ben succeeded first, switching places with Tim before going down on his knees. He listened to the soft sound of Tim's moans drifting away on the night air as he worked, feeling an odd mix of urgent lust and inner tranquility.

"Police!"

"Hold it right there!"

Ben's eyes shot open at the unexpected voices. He winced against the bright light. He felt Tim push him away as he struggled to see past the two flashlights that were bobbing toward them.

"Run!" Tim said.

Events finally caught up with Ben as Tim hastily buttoned his shorts and took off into the night. A policeman shouted in protest as Ben raced to follow. The sound of his heart pounded in his ears, the dark sliced sporadically by flashlight beams. Ben caught up with Tim just as the path forked in two different directions.

"Split up!" Tim hissed, heading to the left.

Ben took the right path and considered diving into the woods and lying low. That's when he slammed into something that grunted. The collision knocked Ben to the ground, a noise skittering across the pavement, but he didn't have time to identify it. He was more concerned with getting away, since the flashlights were already catching up.

More shouts came as he was spotted by the police again, prompting Ben to leap to his feet. He spared one glance down at the illuminated path and looked into the confused eyes of Daniel Wigmore, who was still splayed out on the sidewalk. Ben's stomach sank as they both stared at each other with shocked recognition.

Then Ben was running again, this time through the woods, branches slapping against the hands he raised in defense. Eventually he spilled out into a backyard that he recognized. He allowed himself to stop and gulp down air before running toward home. When he finally made it there, he forced himself to calmly enter and walk up the stairs as if nothing had happened. His lungs were aching as he willed normal short breaths until he reached his bedroom.

He left the lights off and looked out his window, but for what? Squad cars? A helicopter equipped with searchlights? He wondered if it was too soon to call Tim's house to see if he had made it safely. What if the police were there right now, talking to his parents? Ben calling at that moment would be the most damning of evidence.

He swore at their stupidity as he paced his room, trying to decide on a course of action. How much had the police really seen? Had they found Daniel? Maybe they would put the blame on him. That would be a nice twist. Of course, Daniel wouldn't hesitate to rat out Ben. He probably already had.

Ben looked out the window for the twentieth time and saw a patrol car pulling into his neighborhood. He cussed and quietly descended the stairs to the front door and peeped out the window. The police cruiser had already pulled into his driveway. Indecision gave way to desperation. He slipped through the house, slid open the glass door that led to the backyard, and ran.

Going through the woods was too risky since cops could still be there, so he crossed into another neighborhood, making a wide arc to where Tim lived. Ben wanted nothing more than to ring the bell or use his key, but he knew what a bad idea that would be. He could see a number of adults through the windows, drinking wine and laughing, oblivious to the drama unfolding around them. The backyard was mercifully empty, the party contained indoors, and there was a light in Tim's window. Ben threw coins from his pocket up at it until the light turned off. Then he waited.

Tim's eyes were wild with panic when he stepped into the backyard. Wordlessly, he grabbed Ben's arm and led him to the side of the house.

"Did they catch you?"

"No. Well, yeah. I don't know. They're at my house."

"Shit!" Tim craned to see his own driveway.

"Don't worry, they only—"

"Don't worry?" Tim repeated incredulously. "The fucking cops caught us screwing!"

Ben sighed, trying to find the right words to defuse the situation. "They don't know about you! They only know about me because I ran into Daniel Wigmore."

"Who?"

"A guy in our school."

Tim's eyes widened even more. "Someone was watching us?"

"No!"

"How do you know?"

"He was too far away. I don't know!"

"No, you don't know," Tim snarled. "You don't know what your parents are saying to the police right now either. Who do they think you are out with tonight?"

Ben refused to answer, choosing instead to return Tim's glare. "Look, I'll tell them I was blowing Daniel," he suggested at last. "Problem solved."

"*They saw me,*" Tim stressed, his voice cracking. "We're fucked!"

"No we aren't!" Ben reached out, wanting to touch Tim, to comfort him and close the gulf he felt opening between them.

"Yes we are," Tim said, pushing his hand away. "Everything's fucked up. Jesus, what did I let you do to me?"

"Do to you? I didn't 'do' anything. This isn't a choice, you know. It's who we are!"

"Get away from me." Tim shoved him and tried to walk away before Ben caught his arm and swung him back around.

"This isn't something you can control!" Ben said, hanging onto him with all his strength. "You can't just push me away and expect to stop feeling—"

"I can't do this anymore!" Tim bellowed, pulling his arm away and shoving Ben again when he tried to get close. His face was a twisted mask of rage, but tears were flowing from his eyes. "It's over. Go home."

Ben tried moving toward him once more, but this time Tim pushed him so hard that Ben fell to the ground. Tim towered over him, his silver eyes wet, angry, reluctant, and scared, before they closed and he turned away. Ben watched the best thing that had ever happened to him fade into the shadows and disappear around the corner. As he lay in the grass, listening to the muffled sound of laughter and clinking glasses, he marveled at how quickly his world had fallen apart.

CHAPTER 15

The next week was spent waiting. Ben tried to tell himself this was just another fight. Tim would calm down, feel safe again, and would eventually return to him. All he needed was space. That was what Ben's brain was telling him. His heart, on the other hand, felt something very different.

During the second week, when his calls still weren't returned, Ben decided to write Tim a letter. He stressed that there wouldn't be any trouble with the cops. Ben's father had covered for him, claiming that Ben was out with his sister that night. Adam was no fool. He understood that it would be inconvenient and possibly expensive if he let the police take his son. Ben's parents hadn't been happy, of course, but they preferred to administer their own justice. Ben explained as much of this as he could. That's all the letter was meant to be, but his overwhelming emotions spilled out onto the page. Ben begged for Tim to come back to him. Then, before he could second-guess himself, he left the note in Tim's locker.

They would be okay. If only he could make Tim see that! Gossip wasn't likely to spread around the school. Daniel Wigmore was uncharacteristically tight-lipped about the events of that evening. He had undoubtedly given Ben's name to the police, but for some reason, had no intention of informing his peers at school. Probably because he was afraid they would put two and two together. The police were out that night looking for an arsonist. Ben and Tim were innocent, but what had Daniel been doing there? In retrospect, Ben could've sworn that the sound he had heard clattering on the pavement was a plastic lighter. That, added to Daniel's silence, was a sure sign of his guilt.

By the end of the second week, it was clear that Tim had no intention of responding. He could try what had worked last time—sneaking into the Wyman residence at night and slipping into bed with him. Ben rebelled against the idea. He was sick of feeling like he had done something wrong. Any other couple would laugh over being caught by the police, or at the very least, stand together in times of trouble. Why did Ben feel like he had to apologize? Why should he have to talk Tim into being with him? That wasn't how love worked. Was it?

"Ronnie changed the lyrics." Allison shoved a piece of paper into Ben's hand.

"What? The talent show is tomorrow!"

"I know, but he only changed a few lines. Just read it."

Ben browsed the new text, eyes growing wider by the second.

"I hope you're not mad," Allison said. "I told him everything, and it just fell into place. What do you think?"

Ben features set with determination. "If they're willing to play it, I'll sing."

They spent the evening practicing the new lines, Ben's emotions growing with every word he sang. They carried him through to the next day, when his nerves started playing up at the idea of performing in front of the entire school. The gymnasium, usually separated by a folding wall between the girls and boys sides, had been opened. The bleachers were moved to the far wall, opposite the stage on the other end. Students were stuffed into every available inch, the bleachers groaning under their weight, the floor lost beneath a mass of bodies.

Ben felt like he was going to pass out. Luckily they weren't the first act. Cheerleaders performed coordinated dance moves to the latest and most dreadful pop songs. Band kids played different instruments, some more successfully than others, and a handful of choir students attempted to sing against the constant chattering of students.

Then there were the drama class kids performing small scenes and skits. The most notable of these was two guys dressed as Mario and Luigi who squatted repeatedly while making farting noises to the video game theme song, taking breaks only to hit each other with large inflatable mallets. This was particularly popular with everyone.

Finally it was their turn. As Ebony and Ivory set up their instruments on stage, Ben's bravery returned. No matter what the school thought of him and what he was about to sing, he was among friends. Allison, of course, but Ronnie too, who had been so sympathetic with his song writing. Leon had always been a comforting presence to Ben, and even the drummer was someone he knew. Craig smiled at Ben and showed off by twirling a drumstick.

Ben turned back to the audience—to a room full of strangers and enemies—but he felt strong. Ronnie struck the first chord and the music began. The instruments were loud enough to drown out the audience's voices. Every single person in the room was forced to listen. Just before the first line, Ben saw him. Five rows back and surrounded by his false friends was Tim Wyman. The timing couldn't have been better as Ben and Allison started to sing.

> *"I spotted you, cresting wave upon a distant sea,*
> *a moon of perfect splendor set high above the trees."*

Tim's eyes grew wide, as if Ben were about to single him out, but Ben and Allison began to dance around each other to enact the next line and Tim was lost to his sight.

> *"Hopeless I pursued, hungry shadow chasing light,*
> *You ran, I stumbled, until somehow we took flight."*

Ben and Allison turned to face each other, and he could see that she had spotted Tim as well. Her eyes asked Ben if he was okay and he nodded before they sang the next verse.

> *"So proud to be near you, I found warmth beneath your wing,*
> *But you only covered me so they couldn't see a thing."*

Allison and Ben retreated to the back of the stage as Ronnie and Leon stepped forward, tearing up the stage with the instrumental bridge and chorus. They seemed to have most of the audience hooked. Ben scanned the crowd until he found Tim again.

"Sing the rest of it to him," Allison shouted in his ear. "Sing it *at* him!"

Why not? As they returned to the front of the stage, Ben fixed his gaze on one person alone and opened the floodgates.

> *"All those traits I dreamed were you, I found inside of me,*
> *The bravery and beauty, that you're too blind to see."*

Tim squirmed under Ben's stare, and for a moment it looked as though he was going to turn away, but he couldn't. Maybe he didn't want to appear too obvious or maybe he simply needed to hear what Ben had to say. Either way, he couldn't leave yet.

"The wave I once knew has crashed, wet thunder come undone,
The hollow light of your moon, glitter stolen from the sun."

Ben felt Allison's hand on his shoulder, and he understood. The last verse was his. She was letting him sing it alone. In that moment, Ben convinced himself that he and Tim were alone, that they were the last two souls on Earth. Ben still loved him, but more than that, he was angry and hurt.

"There's a coward and a fool, and both of them are you,
My heart is cracked and broken, but yours is frozen through."

As the song ended, judgment was cast simultaneously in thousands of minds. Some applauded while others were just glad to be able to socialize again, but there was enough clapping that Allison rushed back to Ben's side, took his hand and raised it. Tim was momentarily forgotten as they bowed together and made their exit.

Ben didn't look back. He was through chasing someone who lived a lie. Off to the side of the stage, a group of teachers took notes, acting as judges. Ms. Hughes was one of them, and when her eyes met Ben's, there was understanding there. Love isn't meant to be hidden away. Life is too short for shame.

They took second place in the talent show. First place was swept up by the cheerleaders. The male students made sure they got the audience vote, and most of the teachers bought into their school spirit. Ben and Allison were happy they had at least beaten the Super Fartio Brothers. They graciously accepted their $50 gift certificates to a local mall and used them that weekend to buy summer clothes.

Prom followed a week later. Allison went with Ronnie. Ben didn't go. He wasn't the least bit surprised when she told him that Tim was Krista Norman's date. He tried not to let it get to him. After all, he had his own date that night. While he didn't go to the actual prom, Evan from work invited him out to dinner. It wasn't until Evan dropped him off at home and clumsily kissed

Ben that it officially became a date. In his mind, anyway.

Ben had mixed feelings about this. Evan was attractive and fun to be around. Had they met a year ago, Ben probably would have pursued Evan with unbridled enthusiasm. Now it was difficult to be around him without making unfair comparisons. He tried anyway, even going on a second date. When they held hands at the movies, Ben couldn't help but miss the calluses on Tim's palm, or the telltale flakes of paint on his fingernails which he would sometimes scratch at—or once, Ben had brought Tim's fingers to his mouth and pretended he would chew the paint off. Little dumb moments like those now seemed irreplaceable.

Even if he did manage to move on and start focusing on Evan, was he really a healthier choice? Evan was still in the closet, both at school and to his parents. The only difference was that he accepted who he was. This still wasn't enough for Ben, but as the school year ended, the summer days seemed twice as empty without Tim, so Ben found himself seeing Evan outside of work more often.

They slept together for the first time, a stark contrast to what Ben had known with Tim. Evan was passive and inexperienced. This wasn't a problem, but the absence of emotion left Ben feeling he was only going through the motions. Sex still felt good, but without love it was little more than assisted masturbation. Ben broke up with him the next day. Evan took it well, saying that he knew he was just a rebound. Ben couldn't have disagreed more. He hadn't rebounded from anything. In fact, he now felt he would never get over Tim.

Ben soon quit his job at the grocery store and left without saying goodbye to Evan. A few weeks later he found a new job at a little frozen yogurt store in the same strip mall. The tediously simple work left him free to think, for better or worse. On good days, Allison came to keep him company. The worst days were when it rained and the demand for a cool treat was minimal. On such occasions, Ben would often leave work, closing up shop hours earlier than he was supposed to.

On one such day, the rain ceased just as he was locking the door. He decided to leave anyway and began walking home along the winding bike paths. He enjoyed catching glimpses of various backyards, imagining the lives that ran their courses inside the homes and creating different family histories in his mind. He was in the midst of one such daydream when he was rudely awakened by a familiar voice.

"Well, well. If it isn't the local faggot!"

Ben looked up at the approaching figure of Bryce Hunter. He was flanked by two others. One was a spiky-haired guy Ben had never seen before. His heart sank when he saw the other was Tim.

"What are you doing out here?" Bryce taunted, blocking his way as Ben tried to pass. "Looking for some cock to suck?"

"You'll have to pull your skanky girlfriend off the football team if you want that," Ben retorted. "I'm definitely not interested."

Bryce grabbed Ben by the embarrassing green polo shirt that he was required to wear to work. "What did you say?" He yanked Ben closer with an audible tearing noise.

"Leave him alone," Tim said, pushing past the other guy.

"He called Stacy a slut!" Bryce said, not taking his attention off his soon-to-be victim.

And since Ben was dead anyway... "Technically I said she was skanky," he corrected, furious at being exposed to such an ignorant primate when he wasn't in school. "She's also a brain-dead snob, but I guess that's your common bond, isn't it?"

Bryce released Ben and cocked his arm back, the fat slab of his fist ready to make contact with Ben's face. Before it could, Tim was between them, pushing Bryce away and trying to restrain him.

"What the fuck?" Bryce demanded.

"Forget him," Tim said. "Let's just go."

Tim was strong, but Bryce was built like an ox. He had no trouble pushing Tim away, his frustration at being denied making him twice as dangerous. Yeah, these were definitely Ben's final moments. All he could do was pray for a quick death. He watched Bryce's fist swing toward him, and before he could react, it cracked across his face, sending Ben tumbling to the ground like a rag doll.

Lights flashed before his eyes as he reeled from the blow, instincts begging him to escape any that followed. Ben managed to prop himself up on his elbows before dizziness caused him to slump back down. He took a couple of deep breaths, surprised that he wasn't being kicked while he was down, and managed to roll over and push himself up onto his knees.

The sound of a struggle erupted behind him. He glanced

backward. Tim and Bryce were fighting each other! Tim's nose was dripping blood, but he was holding up well against the mammoth he was facing. Tim took a couple of punches to his right eye before felling Bryce with a swinging blow to the temple. As the giant groaned and hit the ground, Tim pounced on him like a panther.

"Get off my cousin!" yelled the spiky-haired guy as he rushed forward to help. Tim's back was to him. He would never see it coming.

Ben's mind focused, his entire body tensing for one purpose alone. He was on his feet within seconds and running toward Bryce's cousin. Ben ploughed into his side, making the cousin trip, but he recovered and, with surprising speed, turned to elbow Ben in the face, knocking him down again.

Ben wasn't as dazed this time. He looked up to find shorts directly in front of him. One man's crotch is another man's target! Ben punched, managing to strike twice before the other guy stumbled backwards with a shriek. Ben capitalized on this temporary advantage and got to his feet, punching, kicking, and screaming—all in a wild violent blur until his adrenaline receded. He found himself and Tim standing over two groaning, balled-up forms.

"Run," Tim said when it became clear that Bryce intended to get up again.

They took off down the path, sprinting instinctively toward their homes. Ben's house, to be precise. They reached it and stood in the driveway, panting to catch their breath between bursts of crazed laughter. Both of them looked terrible, faces covered in blood with swollen red blotches that promised of bruises to come.

"Thanks," Ben gasped when he could talk again.

"You and your big mouth," Tim said with a grin, shaking his head.

For a sliver of time, everything was good again, as if nothing had gone wrong between them. "Do you want to come inside?" Ben asked.

Tim started to nod, smiling in agreement before something clicked. Then his face became somber, the light in his eyes disappearing. "Goodbye, Benjamin."

As Ben watched him go, he knew there was no longer any point in trying to stop him.

— — —

There remained one possibility, one iota of hope in the form of a key. The idea kept Ben awake at night, tormenting him with promises he knew were impossible, but still it whispered to him, urging him to try. Where words fail, only action can succeed.

On a humid July night, Ben decided that he'd had enough. He had been staring at the red LED light of the clock, unable to sleep. Tired of temptation, he threw off the sheets, got dressed, and grabbed the key. Once outside, he walked the familiar path he had followed so many nights before. He could have walked it with his eyes closed.

He tried to brush aside the fear welling up inside him as he used the key. Two months had passed. Would it still work? Was there an alarm system now? The small click only worsened his feelings of anxiety. It might have been better if the key hadn't fit. Now there was so much more to face.

Moonlight poured through the window in Tim's room, allowing Ben to see that little had changed. He ignored the slumbering shape in bed and walked instead to the window. Ben looked up at the moon and said a silent prayer to it that he might be strong enough. Then he stared down at the empty backyard where everything had fallen apart. Ben listened to the sound of Tim's breathing until he could resist no longer and went to him, sitting on the corner of his bed.

He studied the curve of Tim's shoulder, following the line down to a tan arm resting against white sheets. Ben's heart ached. He wanted nothing more than to reach out and touch that skin, to slip beneath the sheets and wrap his arms around Tim. Together they would lie there for all eternity, the world crumbling to dust around them so that nothing could ever stand in their way again.

Ben stood and Tim stirred in his sleep, rolling over onto his back. His face was cast in shadow, but Ben could see enough to make him want to weep. He was so handsome, so beautiful. Inside and out. Ben leaned forward, bringing his lips as close to Tim's as possible without actually kissing him.

Then Ben pulled away. As he left he hung the key that Tim had given him on the doorknob. He glanced back one final time and saw light reflecting off Tim's open eyes. Ben didn't hesitate or linger. The moon had granted his request. He was strong as he shut the door and walked out into a long lonely night.

PART TWO

CHICAGO, ILLINOIS
1999

CHAPTER 16

Snow. Freezing, eye-stinging, finger-numbing snow. Had he ever really wished for such weather in Texas? The bottom five inches of Ben's jeans were soaking wet as he tromped through the damnable substance. TV had given him a false impression of snow. Sure, it was beautiful when it first started falling, the blanketed mounds inspiring warm Christmassy thoughts, but that was just the beginning. The honeymoon stage. It didn't take long for Chicago's infamous traffic to turn it all into ugly gray slush.

A warm glow from a coffee shop window beckoned, promising warmth and dryness. Ben hadn't yet developed a taste for coffee, but surely there would be something else in there he could drink. One of those weird Italian sodas where you could choose the flavor, or maybe a hot cocoa. He paused on the sidewalk a moment before forcing himself onward to his apartment. He had a date with Mason.

Of course it was his boyfriend's fault that Ben was running late. Last-minute Christmas shopping on a shoestring budget had taken up most of the day. To even worry about being timely was silly. Mason suffered from Chronic Late Syndrome, always an hour overdue if not more. That was Ben's inspiration for his choice of gift; a pocket watch. This same idea had failed Ben's mother three years ago, but he had found the gesture charming. The watch was sterling silver, suited his own tastes, and hadn't been engraved. Even with Christmas just around the corner, Ben knew there was a fair chance that he and Mason would no longer be an item.

In the twenty days they had been together, Mason had burned through three different jobs. When Ben first met him, Mason had been the punky bartender at Mertyl's, an out-of-the-way lesbian bar. Ben had instantly fallen for his bad boy appeal. The colored hair, piercings, and poorly realized tattoos were in complete contrast to the preppy pretty boys and delicate artistic types on campus. Most students had at least one of these rebellious body decorations, but there was something genuinely trashy about Mason.

The job at the bar had ended abruptly among rumors of money missing from the register. Next there was the construction job at an outlet mall, something Mason's ripcord muscles might be suited to, but this only lasted two days. Ben was never sure what had happened, although he suspected a marathon drug binge had gotten in the way. Mason was currently working retail at a record store. At least he had been a few days ago when Ben had seen him last.

With a prayer of gratitude to any god listening, Ben hurried into the minimal amount of warmth offered by his apartment building. "Apartment" was a laughable term, as the tiny living quarters barely qualified as dorms. The slumlord owner knew it too. Aside from a few senior citizens and weirdos, all ten stories of the building were inhabited by students who didn't want to live on campus. The concept had sounded so mature to Ben at the time, but the reality was far from glamorous.

He bit the tips of his gloved fingers and pulled his hand free. Ben struggled with numb digits to find the keys and unlock the door to his apartment. The smell of cigarette smoke greeted him as he entered. Mason was here. Ben called out, puzzled by the darkness of the apartment. Was Mason sleeping?

Ben entered a living room that was barely big enough for a couch and flipped on the light. After a two-second delay, the exposed bulb above came on, revealing a blank spot in one corner. After a moment, Ben realized that the twenty-two inch TV was missing. Fear tiptoed up his spine. He'd been robbed! That wasn't the most frightening thought either, because the robber might still be lurking in the apartment!

He went next to the closet-sized kitchen to fetch the biggest—and only—cutting knife he owned. Wielding it like a thief detector, he made a sweep of each room. Considering the apartment's size, this didn't take long. Whoever had been there was gone and had taken Ben's TV and boombox. The six-pack of beer that Ben had begged a friend to buy earlier in the day was also missing from the fridge.

Ben didn't need to play Sherlock Holmes and examine the sole cigarette butt in the ashtray, but he did anyway. The familiar generic brand underlined Mason's name in triplicate, which was overkill since it was already highlighted and accompanied by a row of exclamation points.

Oh well. One less present to wrap.

He threw himself on the couch, too despondent to take off his winter jacket. The worst part was yet to come. Ben could deal with the loss of his crappy TV or the beat-up old boombox, but being single for the holidays would leave him free to entertain old ghosts that he would rather forget. Still, there were a few days left. Maybe that was enough time to fall in love with someone new.

Ben finally looked to the blinking red light that had been clamoring for his attention. At least Mason hadn't stolen the answering machine. Hell, maybe he called to leave a drunken apology. Ben wouldn't put it past him. He rose and jabbed at the machine, which beeped in protest before playing its message.

"Ben?" The voice was strained. "It's me."

Allison? She sounded so different. Something was wrong.

"My dad. He's—" There was sobbing, in the midst of which sounded like the words heart attack. "Please call me back. I love you."

The machine beeped again, signaling the end of the message. Ben grabbed the phone and dialed Allison's dorm room in Austin before gut instinct made him hang up the phone and dial a number he knew by heart. The same one he had always called when they were growing up. After two rings, the line clicked and Allison answered, her voice sounding strained, even though she only spoke a single word.

"Hello?"

"Allison? What happened?"

"He's dead, Ben." Allison broke down, Ben trying to console her while she regained her composure. "My father," she managed at last. "He's dead."

Convincing his parents to send him a plane ticket wasn't difficult. They had been begging him to come home for Christmas for months, but Ben loved the idea of being alone in Chicago, celebrating the holidays alone with his boyfriend.

Ex-boyfriend.

Ben's parents managed to get him a ticket on Christmas Eve and had probably paid through the nose to do so. The only available flight was a midnight express. The plane boarded in record time due to having so few passengers. Ben's seat was in the front of coach in the emergency exit row, and while still not first class, it did have more leg room than all the rows behind him. With the seats next to him free, Ben was soon stretched out and sleeping, but not before looking down on the city that had been his home for the last year and a half.

Ben stirred when the air pressure changed, indicating that the plane had begun its descent. He shifted uncomfortably, the pocket watch pressing painfully against his hip. He regretted keeping it. So far it had been a constant reminder of his losing streak with love. Only his own poor taste was to blame. Since starting college, he had found plenty of legitimate guys who had taken an interest in him. These relationships never lasted more than a few weeks, while Ben's appetite for unavailable straight guys continued to thrive. Once he'd even broken up with someone after developing a crush on his straight brother.

All of this left a bad taste in Ben's mouth, reminding him too much of high school. He had waited so long to be free of that environment, where every guy he wanted was straight or closeted. The number of openly gay students in college appeared limitless, but still Ben was attracted to those he couldn't have and he didn't understand why. Was it a fear of commitment or a fetish for forbidden meat? Probably neither. He wanted nothing more than a serious long-term relationship. Perhaps his particular tastes couldn't be satisfied by anyone, straight or gay.

Or maybe he was still yearning for Tim. Ben looked out the window at the orange city lights and wondered for the thousandth time what had become of him. Since the summer they had broken up, Tim had disappeared. He still lived in the same house, since his car was often in the driveway, but Ben never saw Tim out jogging or at school the next year. He must have gone to a school in the next district, maybe a private one.

"Funeral, huh?"

Ben came out of his repose to see a flight attendant sitting next to the emergency exit in one of those fold-down chairs they used during takeoff and landing. The man was in his mid-twenties and thin, with the sort of high cheek bones that guaranteed models their job security. His dirty blonde hair was short on the sides and medium length on top, with just enough styling product to make it playfully messy. Overall he was attractive and looking rather dapper in his airline uniform.

"Sorry?" Ben inquired.

"You're flying because of a funeral," the man stated in a pleasantly deep voice.

Ben was taken aback. "Well, yeah. How did you know?"

The flight attendant rested a hand on his chin, a long index finger on his cheek. "Your face was too sad. People never look sad when they fly, unless there is a funeral involved."

Ben felt a pang of guilt. He had been reminiscing about failed relationships when he should have been thinking of Allison and what she was going through.

"Of course," the flight attendant mused further, "we also get sad faces when people have to leave their partners behind, although passengers usually recover from that by the time we land."

"Well, if you must know," Ben began testily. He was irritated that this stranger felt free to pry into his personal affairs. "Not only is there a funeral, but my boyfriend robbed me yesterday, thus becoming my ex."

"That would explain it. A double whammy. Here. On the house."

The flight attendant reached into a pocket and took out two mini bottles of vodka. "My name's Jace, by the way," he said as he tossed them to Ben.

"Your name tag says Jason," Ben pointed out.

"I know." Jace took hold of the tag and angled it to see better. "Isn't that mean? I told them I wanted one that says Jace, but that's not my legal name. Where do they get these things, anyway? Is there a store that sells them somewhere? That would be cool. Then I could buy my own."

Ben laughed and introduced himself.

"That can't be your legal name either," Jace replied. "It must be Benjamin."

"Just Ben," he replied tersely. He didn't like anyone to call him by his full name. Not anymore.

"Very economical. Only three letters. I approve."

Ben looked down at the two tiny bottles of booze. "Care to join me?" he asked, offering one.

"Nope. Not allowed to drink on duty," Jace explained. "I don't drink vodka anyway. I only take them because they make such nice stocking stuffers."

"Are there flights on Christmas?" Ben asked, wanting to keep the conversation going.

"God yes," Jace replied with an exasperated look. "There isn't a day of the year that the airlines don't serve."

"That must suck."

"It can, but this year I finagled it so I have Christmas off." Jace paused and stared wistfully out the window. "It'll be nice to be home again."

"So you live in Houston?"

"Sure do. You?"

Ben shook his head. "Chicago."

"Too bad." Jace said this casually enough, but the words hit Ben like a lightning bolt.

"I'll probably be in town a few weeks," Ben amended hurriedly.

Jace raised an eyebrow and smiled. He didn't reply. Instead he looked expectant. "You know," he said eventually, "there is a strict company policy against asking passengers out on dates."

"Oh."

"That's not to say that you can't ask me."

Jace's grin matched Ben's own. Looks like he wouldn't be single during the holidays after all.

Christmas came and went, but Ben barely noticed. The entire day was spent trying to console Allison, who was now alone in the world except for an aunt and a few cousins who had decided not to leave Colorado for the funeral.

Details of what had happened unfolded during the lulls of Allison's crying spells. A neighbor had seen Mr. Cross collapse in the driveway and had called the police instead of an ambulance. Allison's father had been found passed out in the street a month before, so the neighbor thought he was simply drunk again. By the time the police arrived, Mr. Cross was in critical condition from a heart attack. He died on the way to the hospital.

"He never really got better," Allison confided as they sat together in the living room of her childhood home. "He always drank too much, and it only got worse once I went to college."

"At least his temper mellowed," Ben said.

Allison shook her head once.

Ben sat up on the couch. "You mean it didn't?"

"No," Allison confirmed. "Well, it did. In a way. I was able to date boys and also hang out with you again, but my dad still flew into rages and acted really paranoid. Especially when drunk. He even claimed that you were blackmailing him."

"I kind of was," Ben admitted. "I threatened to tell people that he was molesting me if he ever hit you again. He didn't, did he?"

Allison shook her head, but looked away as she did so. Ben wondered if she was being honest, but he might not ever know. Not now. People had a funny way of forgiving the dead.

The following day, Ben tackled the long list of affairs to be set in order, starting with the funeral home. Allison decided to have the body cremated and to not hold a memorial service. She and Ben were the only ones likely to attend anyway, since there were so few relatives and Mr. Cross never socialized.

Next they dug through piles of paperwork in Mr. Cross's office, searching for a will. They found a mortgage that was almost paid off, and a life insurance policy that would cover the rest while leaving Allison with cash to spare. They still weren't sure how much money was in the bank or if he left any credit card debt, but Ben planned on searching the computer for this information the next day. What little they had accomplished had already taken them well into the evening. The process was especially tiring for Allison.

Ben waited until she was asleep before pulling Jace's number from his wallet. He felt slightly guilty about dating in the midst of Allison's loss, but those feelings were soon replaced by nervousness as he punched in the number. A woman answered the phone.

"Hello?"

"Uh, hi. Is Jace there?"

The woman paused before sternly asking, "Who is this?"

Not another married guy! Ben came close to hanging up when a rustling sound preceded the woman's laughter.

"Idiot!" Jace's muffled voice said, probably through a hand on the receiver. "Sorry, this is Jace," he said in a much clearer tone.

"Hey, it's Ben. Look, did I call at a bad time?"

"Ben! Hey! No, not a bad time at all. That was just my sister. She enjoys destroying my social life."

"I know what you mean," Ben said sympathetically. "I have one of those too."

"Yeah, they're a pain. She was just leaving anyway," he added pointedly. "Hold on."

Ben listened to a hurried goodbye between the siblings, wondering what in the world he was going to say when Jace was free again. *How about that flight? Did everything go okay with handing out the peanuts? Any trouble with the overhead bins?* Usually he met guys in person. Over the phone it felt much more awkward.

"So what did Santa bring you for Christmas?" Jace asked suddenly.

Ben laughed. "What?"

"For Christmas. What did you get?"

"Oh. I haven't opened any presents yet. I've been with my friend the whole time since landing. My parents are probably dying to see me."

"They'll have to wait," Jace said. "Do you want to meet tonight?"

"It's almost midnight!"

"Is it already?" He sounded genuinely puzzled. "You see what flying so much does to you? I have no concept of time anymore."

"Tomorrow would be good," Ben suggested.

"Can you ice skate?" Jace asked.

"No."

"Excellent! Why don't we meet at the Galleria Ice Rink? Do you know where that is?"

"Of course," Ben answered, his head spinning. This was all going too fast!

"Next to the skate rental booth. Around dinner time?"

Ben didn't answer right away.

"I'm not a serial killer or anything," Jace said, noticing Ben's hesitance. "It's just that I would prefer to stare into those lovely brown eyes of yours when we talk."

"My eyes are green," Ben lied, trying to throw him for a loop.

"No they aren't. I'll prove it to you tomorrow. Seven o'clock?"

"I don't even know your last name."

"It's Holden," Jace said instantly. "Feel free to call the police. My record is clean. So are we good? Seven o'clock tomorrow?"

"Yeah, okay." Ben smiled into the receiver. "Central Time Zone. Don't forget."

"I won't. Promise. Go see your parents tomorrow!"

"All right, all right!" Ben said in mock irritation. "Geez. You'd think we're married already."

"Now who's rushing things? Goodnight, Ben."

"Goodnight."

Ben hung up the phone, chuckling to himself. The man was a complete stranger! This was a bad idea. Then again, Jace couldn't be any worse than Mason, and if it turned out he was, at least his television had already been stolen. Silver linings!

CHAPTER 17

Houston's Galleria might be one of the largest malls in America, but the three million square feet could have easily fit inside the pit in Ben's stomach. The amount of butterflies there contended with those of his first day in kindergarten. Dates never made him nervous, but usually Ben would meet a guy at a party or on campus, where conversation would flow naturally until they reached some level of comfort. Instead there had been a brief and groggy flight, from which he retained only a fuzzy impression of a handsome flight attendant. Hopefully his memory didn't cheat, because his evening was now committed to this mystery date.

The mall's layout was fairly typical — rows of stores on each floor separated by an empty gap that allowed a shopper to see the floors above or below. Ben peered over one of the railings to the lowest floor, which was an ice rink. People of all ages glided by below, comfortable on their ice skates. Some were even graceful. He wouldn't be. This would end in disaster.

There was no sign of Jace, but then they were supposed to meet by the skate rentals. Gathering his courage, Ben pushed his way through the swarms of people. Two days after Christmas meant the mall was a nightmare of after-holiday sales and gift returns. Once the elevator that Ben squeezed into dinged open, he spotted Jace immediately.

Ben's date was handsome, which did little to dispel his anxiety. Jace was dressed sharply in a black knee-length winter coat. The sort a classy New Yorker might wear. This was tempered with a casual pair of jeans and a well-worn pair of tennis shoes. His hair was styled to perfection, which made Ben wish for a mirror to check his own, but Jace had already seen him.

They greeted each other clumsily, unsure whether to shake hands or hug. Waiting in line for their skates was awkward, Jace attempting to make small talk while Ben tried to find a part of himself that wasn't feeling bashful. Now he was eager to get out on the rink, just so they would have an activity to distract themselves with.

"Are you any good at this?" Ben asked as they were pulling on their skates.

"I do all right." Jace finished tying his laces and looked to

Ben's. "Wait. You missed a rung and the tongue is stuffed in. Here."

Like a father helping his child, he stooped, untied Ben's skates, and then laced them up correctly. When finished, he smiled and offered his hand. Ben accepted it and hobbled with him to the edge of the rink.

"I really can't ice skate at all," he said. "I did once when I was eight, and all I remember is falling on my ass until I finally gave up."

"You didn't have me then."

Jace's eyes twinkled as he led them out onto the ice. Ben started slow, keeping a white-knuckled grip on Jace's elbow, and wished he hadn't stopped rollerblading so many years ago. A minute later and his legs slipped out from under him. Jace caught the back of Ben's jacket before he could fall and allowed Ben to steady himself on the wall of the rink.

"You have to move your legs like this," Jace explained, showing him the odd diagonal movement needed to propel forward.

Over the next twenty minutes, Jace patiently coached him. Ben began to get the hang of it. The method wasn't so different from his old inline skates, really. Another twenty minutes and he was really enjoying himself. He still wasn't confident enough to let go of Jace, but then he didn't want to. Ben released his death grip on Jace's elbow and took his hand instead. He noticed that while Jace was slender, there was a lot more muscle than it appeared. His hands weren't boney and cold. They were strong and warm.

"This is nice," Ben said as they made their way around, hand in hand. "Anywhere else and people would be staring at us, but here we have a reason to hold on to each other."

Jace smiled at him. "I'll admit that was part of the plan," he confessed, "but I don't need a pretense to hold another guy's hand in public. Let people stare if they want."

Ben sighed. "Where were you when I was in high school?"

"I was wondering that myself. You look much younger now that you aren't suffering through a late flight."

"Oh." Ben wasn't sure if this was good or bad. "I just turned twenty. You?"

Jace exhaled dramatically. "I'm a little older than that."

"Thirty?" Ben asked in shock.

"Hey!" Jace let go of Ben, his expression offended. Ben's arms pinwheeled for a second before Jace came back to stabilize him with an arm around his waist. "I'm only twenty-six!"

"You were the one acting dramatic about it," Ben teased. "What do you like better anyway? Younger or older?"

"Doesn't matter. It's the personality that counts. Mind if I do a couple of rounds on my own?"

"Sure."

Jace parked Ben somewhere safe before gliding away. He moved skillfully, navigating past slower skaters and travelling in sweeping arcs. Ben watched him, admiring his skill while taking the chance to check out Jace's body. His frame was tall and his shoulders broad, but it was hard to tell more with the thick winter clothing. Despite this, more than Ben's curiosity was becoming aroused.

Ben struck out bravely on his own, determined to do at least one round under his own power. Jace nodded approvingly as he swept by, showing off by skating backwards for a few strokes. When they met back at the entrance to the rink, their stomachs grumbled in unison. Carpooling in Jace's practical silver coupe, they drove to a seafood place not far away.

"My legs are really starting to hurt," Ben winced as they sat down at the table.

"Wait until tomorrow," Jace informed him. "You'll be walking bowlegged all day."

"Because of the skating?"

"Of course," Jace replied innocently.

Their order was taken by a disgruntled waitress who rightly felt it was much too soon to be returning to work after Christmas. They sipped the drinks she brought them, making eyes at each other and often smiling without reason.

"So I take it you're still in school?" Jace asked.

"Yeah, up at Columbia College in Chicago."

"How do you like it?"

Ben shrugged. "It's all right."

"I couldn't wait to get out," Jace said. "The only good thing about college was having four extra years to figure out what I wanted to do."

"I didn't know flight attendants went to college," Ben said, considering too late how that might sound, but Jace didn't appear offended.

"It's not a requirement. It's just that— Well, what do you want to be when you grow up? What's your major?"

"I have no idea." Ben chuckled. "It changes on a daily basis."

"There you go. Paying tuition is just an expensive way of buying time."

"So I take it you didn't always want to be a stewardess?" Ben taunted.

Jace smiled. "Originally I wanted to be a nurse."

"That's cool. What changed your mind?"

"I started to doubt that I'd be able to handle the emotional strain of the job. In the long term it either depresses you or you become numb. I didn't like the idea of either happening."

"Hmm." Ben eyed the plates of the other diners, impatient for his own to arrive. "Can I ask you a very direct question without you getting mad at me?"

Jace cocked an eyebrow. "Sure."

"How come flight attendants always act so pissy?"

"Was I so terrible to you?" Jace laughed. "No, I know what you mean. The reason we act a little, uh, irritable sometimes is because people misunderstand our job. Everyone thinks that we're the waiters and waitresses of the sky, when we're not."

"You're not?"

"Not at all. Our primary duty is to ensure the well-being of the passengers. There are a number of safety checks and procedures that we are responsible for, and I don't just mean the pre-flight demonstration that everyone ignores. Ensuring the health and safety of every passenger is a flight attendant's primary function. It's much more than just food service, and there are a great number of unsung heroes who have saved lives because of the skills required for the position."

"Wow." Ben had to respect Jace's passion for his job. "I didn't know that."

"The first-ever stewardess was a nurse," Jace continued. "Ellen Church. Before her there were only stewards, and they really were just errand boys. Ellen Church realized that a nurse had a number of skills useful in an emergency, and the rest is history. Reading her story is what made me want to become a flight attendant. That, and the travel."

Plates appeared on the table, barely noticed through the conversation. Jace spoke more about his job and the long hours involved before asking about Ben's life and discussing the different options available to him. Ben had never dated someone as old as Jace and already found his stability appealing. Guys his own age were just as confused as him about the future. Jace already had it figured out, something Ben admired greatly.

They talked for hours, even after the food had disappeared. Ben noticed the time and announced that he should make his way home. Jace grabbed the check, claiming that it was a crime to expect a college student to pay for anything, and drove Ben back to his parents' car. They stood beside the vehicle, making small talk as they both wondered how the goodbye would work.

"This is no place for a first kiss," Jace said, gesturing to the grey landscape of the parking lot. "You could come home with me, meet the cat."

Ben smiled. "Not on the first date."

"Nothing has to happen," Jace said easily.

"Trust me," Ben said with a grin, "if I get you somewhere private, something *will* happen."

"Well, well! I guess this means I get to see you again?"

"How about Thursday?" Ben offered. Sooner would have been fine, but he felt it best to play a little hard to get.

"It's a deal," Jace agreed. "Look, I'm kissing you tonight, but I refuse to do it here. Just follow me in your car for a minute and I promise I'll let you go home afterwards."

"Okay."

Jace led him out of the parking garage and two blocks down the road before pulling over at a park. It wasn't the sort with trees and charming pathways; rather it was flat and cleared for different sporting events.

"Are you sure about this?" Ben asked as he exited the car.

"No," Jace responded looking around. "I'm improvising. Over there."

Jace took him by the hand and led him across the grass to a baseball diamond. Ben thought they were heading for the bleachers, but Jace brought him instead to one of the bases.

"First base?" Ben asked. "You've got to be kidding."

"I assure you," Jace said dramatically, pulling Ben close, "I'm quite serious."

Jace kissed him, his warm body chasing away the winter chill. His lips were soft but commanding, and Ben responded instantly, catching fire and wanting more.

"Second base is just over there," Ben suggested.

"Not on the first date," Jace said with a smile, gently detaching himself and walking them back to the cars. Ben watched Jace in the rearview mirror as he pulled away, already knowing that he wouldn't be able to wait three days to see him again.

Jace Holden's answering machine dutifully took Ben's call the following afternoon. Ben loitered around his parents' house afterwards, waiting for the phone to ring. Why had he played so hard to get? He was only in town a few weeks. He didn't have time to be coy.

In the evening Ben left to have dinner with Allison, leaving her number with his parents and asking them to give it to Jace if he called. Ben found his best friend in surprisingly high spirits. He knew she still had a great amount of sorrow beneath the surface, but he was proud of her for putting on a brave face. Ben filled her in on all his news while enjoying her homemade lasagna.

The phone rang shortly after eleven. Allison answered it, smiled broadly, and handed the receiver to Ben.

"Hope I didn't call too late," Jace said, sounding tired.

"Not at all," Ben replied, worrying that the other man's enthusiasm for him had waned.

"I'm afraid I have to cancel our date," Jace continued. "I was called in to work today."

"I thought you were on vacation?"

"I was supposed to be. A number of 'mysterious' holiday-inspired illnesses means we're understaffed, and I have to pick up the slack. I'm calling from Boston right now."

"That sucks. When will you be home again?"

"Friday afternoon. Do you have any plans for New Year's?"

"Uh, I don't know." Ben looked at Allison. He didn't want to leave her alone on a holiday considering the situation. Then again, would she really feel like partying so soon? "New Year's?" he repeated, asking both Jace and Allison at the same time.

Allison rolled her eyes, smiled, and waved her consent. Ben knew her well enough to tell that she honestly didn't mind. He confirmed plans with Jace and talked to him a while longer before hanging up. He had thought waiting an extra few days would be hard. Now it would be even longer.

As it turned out, the time went quickly. He still had a lot of catching up to do with his family and much to take care of with Allison. They retrieved her father's ashes together and drove down to Corpus Christi, the city where Mr. Cross was raised and had met Allison's mother. They scattered his ashes out into the Gulf and cried together—Allison because she wasn't ready to say goodbye to her father, Ben because it hurt him to see his friend in so much pain.

"He was a bastard," Allison said, shocking Ben. "You know I found a box of love letters the other day? A whole shoebox full, hidden in his closet. Some of them were from my mother, but most were from him."

Ben couldn't imagine Mr. Cross doing something as emotional as writing sappy prose, and the surprise must have shown because Allison responded to it.

"I didn't know either," she said. "He must have loved her so much that it broke his heart when she died, but it pisses me off. Mom might have been gone, but I wasn't, and I could have used that love. Instead he bottled up his feelings, but the worst part is that now I understand why. Losing him makes me hurt so bad that I want to do the same." Allison began crying again.

Ben put an arm around her. "You won't though," he said. "You're better than that. What did you always tell me when I broke up with Tim and was so miserable?"

"Lean into it." Allison managed a laugh.

"That's right. Lean into those feelings and let them wash over you. As wretched as they might make us feel, they're a part of us, and we shouldn't ignore them. It only hurts worse if we do."

"I'm so glad you're here," Allison said, resting her head on his shoulder.

"Me too."

They sat together in silence, watching the sea gulls dive and soar on the horizon. The skies were winter gray but the weather was warm enough to be comfortable. Ben couldn't deny how much more he felt at home here than in Chicago.

"Don't go back," Allison said, sitting upright and hanging her legs over the dock's edge.

"What?" Ben asked, taken aback.

"I'm tired of you being so far away." Her best doe eyes were focused on him. "I need you close. Especially now."

"That's not fair," Ben countered, but his heart wasn't in the argument. As soon as he had stepped out of the airport into mild weather he had once considered cold, he knew he was home again. Chicago felt like a distant dream, but a part of him was still reluctant to return to the world he had grown up in.

"Austin is much more liberal," Allison said. "It's nothing but weirdoes. Being gay is about as risqué as white bread there."

Austin could work. Sure it was Texas, but also an unexplored city. Home, yet somewhere new. The idea sounded good, but he intended to show some resistance. That way he would score twice as many brownie points. "Why don't you go to school in Chicago?"

"And switch schools mid-semester? Only an idiot would do that!"

"Thanks!"

"Well, an idiot or a very committed best friend." Allison blinked seductively. "Please?"

"I'll think about it," he promised, even though his mind was already made up. The idea of not having to muck through the snow, of not having to worry about Mason breaking in again, was too tempting. As much as Ben enjoyed the idea of living far away from everything he knew, he had tired of homesickness. Not to mention that he'd never had a friend like Allison before or since.

"All right. Done thinking about it," he said. "We'll have to get our own place. I'm not moving into your dorm!"

The first authentic grin on Allison's face since her father's death was worth the hassle of switching schools. The big hug she gave Ben only sweetened the deal.

CHAPTER 18

The better part of New Year's Eve was spent in front of the mirror, where Ben tried on every possible combination of clothing, even dipping into the closet for items he hadn't worn in years. Jace had invited him to a party, but Ben didn't know if this was a casual shindig or formal affair. Considering it was New Year's Eve, everyone there might be decked out in tuxedos. Ben tried to find an outfit suitable for all possible scenarios, but in the end he could only hope his navy blue dress shirt and jeans were passable. Next came an endless battle with his hair, which needed to be cut, followed by cologne that had to be washed off in favor of another scent. Once he felt presentable, Ben drove into downtown Houston and scouted for the address that Jace had given him.

An attractive and transparently drunk woman answered the door, waving him in without even looking at him properly. The party was in full swing, loud music pumping and people swaying to the beat, although instead of dancing, most of them were merely trying to keep their balance. T-shirts mingled with tuxes, assuring Ben that he wasn't the only one uncertain of the dress code. He made his way through the apartment twice, excusing himself more than once for squeezing between conversations and stepping on toes, before he spotted Jace. His date was seated on a couch and had his arm around a woman who looked quite a bit like the person who had answered the door. In fact, almost everyone here was of an indeterminate age and thin, with a certain vibe that suggested they were all flight attendants. For a moment Ben felt like he had stepped into some secret underground culture known only to those inside the airline industry.

Jace jumped to his feet when he saw Ben and wasted no time in kissing him deeply, causing a couple of bystanders to "woooo!" in appreciation.

"Well, hello to you too!" Ben said with a flush.

"I'm glad you made it!" Jace grinned. "Did you have trouble finding the place?"

"A little, but—"

"Who's this, then?" a woman exclaimed, taking a hold of Jace's arm and ogling Ben.

Jace made the introductions, the first in a seemingly infinite series. Each interruption was the same—a courteous amount of interest was shown to Ben, then Jace and his friends would talk about people and places he had no knowledge of. Jace's popularity signaled good things about his personality, but Ben's frustration was rising. He wanted to be alone with Jace and get to know him better, not listen to meaningless gossip. The frequent mention of someone named Sam, who was purportedly very cute, didn't help either. Was this an ex-boyfriend?

"All right, see you later," Jace said cordially to the latest visitor, his smile dropping once they were out of sight. "We have to get out of here," he muttered from the corner of his mouth. "Let's make a run for it."

Ben didn't need encouraging and made a beeline for the door. Jace was further behind, choosing a less direct path to avoid other potentially social situations.

"Sorry about that," Jace said as they spilled out onto the street. "A party full of nosey coworkers wasn't the best date idea. Where to now? A bar? Or something to eat?"

"Somewhere private."

Jace forced back a smile. "There's only one place that I know of. Are you sure?"

"Don't read into it too much," Ben said demurely. "I just need some quiet."

Jace walked him to his car and Ben waited inside it while Jace fetched his own. From there they drove to an increasingly unpleasant area of town. The neighborhood beyond the freshly locked car doors was run-down and poorly lit. Several rough-looking people drank and loitered on the sidewalks, some of them setting off fireworks. Ben hoped that this was some bizarre shortcut, but they parked only a few blocks later.

Jace gave him a funny look when Ben stepped out of the car. "You all right?"

"Yeah," Ben said, trying to look cool, and then casual, and failing at both.

"Hmm. Where did you say you were from again?"

"The Woodlands. Why?"

Jace nodded as if that explained everything. "It might not be the prettiest neighborhood, but I've never had any trouble here."

"It's fine," Ben insisted. "You should see my place in Chicago."

A passage through one of the buildings led to a courtyard. Jace opened a door to a stairwell and an old-fashioned caged elevator, the sort that Ben had only seen in movies. It rattled loudly as they rode it to the top floor.

"Home sweet home!" Jace unlocked the only door in the tiny corridor. He flipped on a light switch and stepped aside so Ben could enter first.

Lights flickered into life, illuminating a sprawling studio apartment. The floors were hardwood, the walls raw brick. The décor was a mismatch of old furniture and antiques. Vintage advertisements hung on the wall, stewardesses from days gone by beaming above slogans or art deco airplanes. Ben noticed a pinball machine in one corner and a ladder leading up to a loft bed before a grey streak of fur sped across the room.

"Samson!" Jace declared happily as he reached down to pick the cat up. "We have a visitor."

The cat rubbed its face against Jace's chin before turning its head to regard Ben with large orange eyes.

So this was Sam! That so many people knew of Jace's cat meant he was one of those crazy cat people who talked about their pets like they were children, but that was preferable to Sam being a hot ex-boyfriend. Ben reached out to pet Samson. The cat's head dodged and came back around to smell his hand.

"Security scan initiated," Jace said in a robotic voice. "Mm-hm. I think you've passed. Let's see about getting you something to eat."

Samson hopped to the floor and followed Jace to the large kitchen. Ben watched the cat being served a plate of canned food while taking in as many of the other details as possible. There was an inordinate number of paper fortunes lying around, implying that Jace liked Chinese takeout. He also enjoyed cooking, judging from the well-equipped kitchen.

Ben strolled back into the living area and headed for the bookshelf. The selection was almost exclusively biographies without any common theme. Jumbled together were politicians, comedians, historical figures, famous serial killers, and celebrities. The Dalai Lama was neighbors with Hitler, Ben noted with some amusement.

"I love reading about people's lives," Jace said from behind. "Do you read?"

"Yeah, but mostly fiction."

"That's what some of these are," Jace said. "If you were writing an autobiography, would you really be able to resist the temptation to doctor the past? Who wants to write about crapping their pants in grade school when it's more fun to exaggerate success and talk trash on old flames?"

"Good point," Ben chuckled.

"Biographies are even worse since they're mostly speculation written by adoring fans, or spoon-fed lies from the celebrity's agent. Regardless, I can't help but read them. It's a guilty pleasure of mine."

Ben pulled his attention away from the books and noticed that Jace was holding two glasses of champagne. "Oh wow! I didn't hear the bottle pop!"

"It didn't," Jace confessed. "More freebies from the airline. They only have the single-serving bottles with the screw top."

"It's cool that you get stuff like that for free."

"Not exactly free." Jace grimaced. "At least, it's not supposed to be, but who doesn't pilfer from their job?"

"Just promise me you have something better in bed than those dinky airline pillows," Ben said as he accepted his drink.

"Wait and see." Jace raised his glass. "Here's to new millenniums and new friendships. Assuming the Y2K bug doesn't destroy us all, that is."

Ben clinked glasses and took a sip. For his first champagne, it tasted great. "How much longer until the New Year?"

"About an hour."

They moved to the couch, which faced a large window. City lights sparkled, the neighborhood Ben had found sinister now tranquil from above. Once Jace was seated, Samson claimed his lap, closing his eyes and purring as Jace scratched his ears. Ben set his glass on the coffee table, pushing paper fortunes out of the way to do so.

"You sure like Chinese food!"

"Not really." Jace looked embarrassed. "I just *really* like fortune cookies. There's a restaurant down the road that sells me full shipping boxes. I know it sounds insane, but they're my absolute favorite treat."

Ben laughed and shook his head. Every time Jace opened his mouth, another eccentricity was revealed. Maybe it was this strangeness that scared potential boyfriends away. After all, Jace was attractive, intelligent, and funny, and he had a steady job. What else could anyone want in an eligible bachelor?

"So explain to me how it is that you're still single?" Ben pried.

"I could ask you the same question."

"Well, I wasn't until a week ago." Ben took a good swig from his champagne.

"Right, right. The burgling boyfriend. Have you heard from him since?"

"Nope, and don't change the subject. Are you the kind of guy who can't settle down?"

Jace looked pained. "Quite the opposite. I've had my share of boyfriends. It's just the job that gets in the way."

"What do you mean?"

"The hours suck. I'm gone for days at a time, and until I have more seniority, my schedule is constantly shifting. So I can't promise anyone when I'll be home, or if I'll even be there at all. Something about sleeping in a hotel every night gives people ideas, so if it isn't the hours, it's the jealousy."

Ben chewed his lip thoughtfully. "I don't know. It doesn't sound all that bad to me. Being apart and not seeing each other every day would keep things fresh. I think I could deal with that."

"That's what they all say at the beginning. Not that I'm trying to discourage you. I'd love for you to prove me wrong. Speaking of which, I fly to Chicago all the time."

Ben smiled. "What are you suggesting?"

"That I like you and that I want more than to just sleep together." Jace studied Ben's face as he spoke. "I know we're moving fast, that we don't know each other very well, but what I've seen so far is a charming, considerate, and surprisingly mature college student who is on his way to becoming someone great."

"Thanks." Ben grinned. "I think you're the bee's knees too."

Jace laughed. "What I'd like to know is how serious you and your prince of thieves were. Are you coming out of a relationship of years? How long before things turned sour?"

"Just a few weeks. He was nothing. Really." Ben paused. None of them had been. Not a single guy had made his heart beat to a funky fresh rhythm, not since his junior year of high school, but Ben thought Jace was the first to have that potential. "What about you? Any emotional baggage I need to know about?"

"There was," Jace said, "but the airline lost it all. Typical really."

The silence that followed was heavy. Both of them were done with talking, and Ben couldn't help but look to the loft bed above, causing Jace to chuckle.

Samson leapt instinctively to the floor before Jace stood. Before Ben knew what was happening, Jace had slid an arm under his back and another under his legs. He scooped Ben up effortlessly and carried him toward the ladder leading up to the bed. Jace paused in puzzlement once he reached it, before tossing Ben over his shoulders in a fireman's carry.

"Put me down!" Ben said, but Jace had already begun to climb.

"This is like a hot gay version of King Kong," Jace gasped as they reached the top. He leaned over, allowing Ben to fall into bed first before climbing the rest of the way up.

"Airline pillows!" Ben complained when he saw the pile of them. He tossed a couple at Jace in protest.

"You won't be sleeping much tonight," Jace promised as he climbed on top of him.

Ben fumbled at the buttons of Jace's shirt, but his hands were moved away and Jace kissed him instead. Ben wanted to tear his clothes off, but each time he tried, Jace restrained him. Only after enough kissing was Ben allowed to proceed.

So far, Ben had only seen Jace in his work uniform and in winter clothes, never gleaning a clear impression of his physique. As he peeled back the dress shirt, a lean but toned torso was revealed. Ben ran his hand along the lightly haired chest and followed the happy trail down to the waist of his pants.

"Nuh-uh," Jace said, taking control again. He pulled Ben's shirt off next. Then he started kissing his neck and touching his nipples. Jace stroked his fingertips over Ben's skin, moving tantalizingly south before pulling his hand away again. Ben felt like he was about to explode and they hadn't even begun yet!

Jace teased and taunted, but eventually Ben was allowed to seek out his prize. His amusement at Jace's skimpy Speedos faded when he realized what was making them so tight. He wasn't as thick as Tim had been, but he was definitely longer.

Jace finally set him loose to do as he pleased. Ben went wild, but Jace kept his cool. Somehow he managed to control his desire, to rein it in, but Ben could tell he was just as fired up by how hard he was. They took turns, both equally eager to pleasure each other as they were to receive. Several times Jace brought Ben to the brink with little effort, and sensing he had done so, backed down just before the point of no return. Ben thought he might go insane from the euphoria.

Jace's urgency increased as he finally lost control and brought them both to a climax at the same time. The sensations were so powerful that Ben felt as if his entire body was coming and not just his cock. He saw stars and heard fireworks. The stars cleared, but the sound of explosions didn't. Flashing lights from the window caught his eye.

"Happy New Year," Jace said, pulling him in for a kiss.

"Happy New Year," Ben murmured. Past the groggy contentment that was slowly overtaking him, he wondered if he had rushed in too fast. Maybe. Maybe not. Either way, Ben knew he would stick around to find out.

The morning light cut through the air like a blade, transforming dust particles into tiny glowing suns. Ben stretched and looked over the rail of the loft bed at the apartment below. The unfinished game of Trivial Pursuit still lay on the table, a half-eaten cheesecake in the center of the board like the ultimate playing piece. Ben rolled over to find Jace's back to him, just like the previous two mornings. He knew what he would find if he looked over him but peeked just to be certain. Sure enough, Jace's arms were curled into a basket for Samson to sleep in.

Ben idly drew a picture on Jace's back with the tip of his finger. Tomorrow was the day that Ben was supposed to fly back to Chicago. It was also the day that Jace was returning to work and had to bid for his schedule. The process was complicated, but Jace had explained that when and where a flight attendant flew was suggested by each individual and then rewarded by seniority. Ben barely understood the chaotic system, but he hoped it meant that Jace could fly to Austin.

Not that Jace knew he was switching schools. Ben was too scared that Austin would be impossible for Jace, forcing him to choose between going to school with Allison in Texas or heading back to Chicago to be accessible to Jace. Now time had run out, and Ben had to confess. Otherwise Jace would bid for the wrong schedule.

Jace stirred, smacked his lips, and stretched. Samson meowed in protest, insisting that Jace stop moving.

"Good morning," Ben said, not wanting his boyfriend to fall back to sleep. He needed to tell him now, while still feeling determined. He slid out of bed and climbed down the ladder to fetch a glass of orange juice from the refrigerator. Jace accepted it gratefully when he returned, sitting up and sipping it.

"Do you ever fly to Austin?" Ben asked out of the blue.

"Austin?" Jace shook his head. "No. Why?"

"I'm thinking about changing schools. Well, not really thinking. I am."

Ben explained everything to him while searching Jace's impassive face for reaction.

"It would be strange," Jace said when Ben had finished. "Arranging my schedule to overnight in Chicago makes sense, but getting a hotel an hour away from my apartment?"

"It's farther than that," Ben corrected.

"Not by plane it isn't."

"So you don't want to?" Ben asked, trying not to sound as defensive as he was beginning to feel.

"It's not that," Jace said, rubbing his eyes sleepily. "I just think the airline will find the hotel expense superfluous."

"You won't need a hotel," he pointed out.

"Look," Jace said, reaching out to take Ben's hand, "no matter what, I'll find a way to see you. I can fly for free and Austin is only an hour away. You go wherever you feel like you need to be. We'll work something out."

"Really?"

"Really," Jace laughed. "Now, is it going to be breakfast or are you getting in the shower with me?"

Ben chose the shower.

CHAPTER 19

"Our duplex, is a very, very, very fine duplex. With a hmmm-hmm-hmm yard. And a hmm-hmm-hmm-hmmm-hm."

Allison glowered at Ben over her bowl of cereal. He grinned cheerfully back, forcing her to move the jumbo box of cereal until it blocked him from view. Ben didn't let this bother him. She was probably still hungover from another night out with Ken. Her boyfriend was drop-dead gorgeous but he drank like a fish.

Ben was tempted to sing another line, but decided he better not risk it, especially since he didn't know the lyrics. Regardless, it really was a very, very, very fine duplex. Living here with Allison was a dream. He originally feared that being together so often would strain their friendship, but instead it had been strengthened. They were even closer now than they had been in high school.

Ben considered making an omelet before opting for much less complicated instant oatmeal. He would probably be eating proper food for dinner when Jace got into town tonight anyway. There was a new Indian restaurant down on Sixth Street that Ben was eager to try.

Living in Austin was an easy adjustment. The city had its own skyline, waterfront, and culture centers, so it was in effect a smaller, warmer version of Chicago. Well, not exactly, but Ben found it much more vibrant than Houston had ever been. He had also settled nicely into the university. Allison had been there to guide him around all of the usual newbie pitfalls, and after eight weeks, Ben never got lost around campus anymore. Well, hardly ever.

The phone rang, making Allison wince and Ben jump to his feet. He knew it would be Jace calling with his flight times. He waited until he was out of the kitchen before allowing himself to shout with excitement.

"Hello?" Ben gasped once he had finally found the phone.

"Hey, bucko," Jace said in forced jovial tones that Ben had already learned to interpret.

"You aren't coming."

Jace sighed into the receiver. "I wanted to call you yesterday but it was the night from hell. I didn't get in until three in the morning."

Ben frowned and plopped down on the sofa. "Do you have to work this weekend?"

"No," Jace answered cautiously, "but my sister is out of town and someone has to take care of Samson."

"Oh come on! This is the third time you've canceled! I haven't seen you once this month."

"The other two times were because of work," Jace replied calmly. "This is the first time because of Samson."

"He's a cat! Load up his food bowl and he'll be fine overnight."

"I haven't been home for over a week," Jace countered. "He needs to see me *sometime*. Anyway, I can get you on an afternoon flight and we can—"

"Forget it."

"What?" Jace asked, sounding startled.

"Forget it," Ben repeated. "You have fun with your cat. I'm going to do my own thing."

"Ben, I'm not trying to—"

"I need my space," Ben interrupted. "I'll see you next weekend."

Ben hung up the phone, feeling instantly ashamed. He wasn't being fair to Jace, he knew that. Part of him also knew that he could get away with acting like this. As difficult as Ben could be, he never managed to ruffle Jace's feathers. Not once. Ben supposed this skill came from dealing with annoying passengers every day.

The phone rang again. Ben wanted to pick it up and be civil, but he also didn't want to appear insane by letting his mood shift too suddenly. He should probably pretend to really be angry, at least for a little while. He picked up the phone.

"Just let me—"

"I'll call you later," Ben said before hanging up again.

All right. So maybe he was being psychotic.

He didn't really mind that Jace was so crazy about Samson. That proved that he was capable of long-term love and dedication. Sure, he was a little possessive with his cat, but then, Samson was overprotective of Jace. They were cute together, and Ben had ruined his chance to be curled up in bed with both of them. And for what? Because the plan had changed? Jace had managed to visit Austin five times in two months. Just because schedules were tight the last three weeks was no reason to punish him. Ben was being childish.

Time to admit he was being an idiot. He didn't know why love made him act so irrational, but he was pretty sure he wasn't alone in this emotionally induced insanity. Every time he saw Jace the feelings intensified. They got along so well and their relationship had been so harmonious that it was hard not to selfishly want as much as he could get. Instead, his behavior had cheated him out of more of that time. Ben reached for the phone so he could call and apologize. It rang before he could pick it up.

"Hello?" he said tentatively.

"Italy," Jace said as quickly as possible.

Ben furrowed his brow in confusion. "What?"

"I'm taking you to Italy, you spoiled shit!"

"You are?" Ben asked, feeling like a fool, but a very happy one.

"Yes. I wanted to tell you in person, but—"

"I was being a dick, I know," Ben said apologetically. "Are you serious?"

"Spring break," Jace confirmed, sounding friendlier. "You up for it?"

"If you still want me," Ben chuckled nervously.

"God knows why, but I do." Jace's voice took on a seductive tone. "Now get your ass to the airport and come apologize to me properly."

The world was a very big place. An obvious statement, but Ben had never known exactly how large until now. Time crawled by during the flight, and even at five hundred miles per hour, the ocean below refused to give way to land. The sun set unnaturally soon, obscuring with its departure any sign of progress or time. Ben tossed and turned in his tiny seat, immensely uncomfortable, but unable to do anything about it.

Jace dozed peacefully beside him, as much at home here as anywhere else. When Ben's attempts to "accidentally" wake him failed, he turned his attention to the in-flight movies. The individual monitors on the back of each seat were okay, but the program selection was dreadful. Already Ben had drudged through multiple films that he never would have watched on the ground, and that he wished he could purge from his mind.

Eventually he did manage a sort of fitful sleep until the flight crew began serving breakfast with pursed lips and raised eyebrows. Except when it came to Jace. They were all smiles and courtesy with him, even though he insisted he didn't know any of them personally. Maybe they sensed he was cut from the same cloth.

Ben wanted to weep with joy when the plane finally began its descent, which turned out to be extremely gradual because it took another hour before the airplane was on the runway, and what felt like three eternities before it taxied to a gate and they were allowed to disembark.

"We're never doing that again," Ben swore while they stood waiting at the baggage carousel. "We'll start new lives here in Rome. Anything but another flight like that."

"I liked it." Jace stretched contentedly. "It was really relaxing. Back home you barely get in the air before landing again. I'm thinking about applying for international routes. The pay is certainly better."

"Wouldn't you be gone more often?" Ben asked. He already couldn't get enough of Jace. Any less time spent with him and he would start developing withdrawal symptoms. He could just see himself clinging desperately to a framed photo of Jace while trembling with the shakes.

"I don't think it would be so different really," Jace answered. "We'll see."

Local time was three in the morning. Some careful math in Ben's head told him it was around dinner time back home.

"Hopefully we can still take a shuttle bus to the main terminal," Jace said, checking his watch. "After that it's just a few train connections to the hotel."

"All right," Ben said, snatching their luggage off the conveyer belt as it came by. "Let's do it!"

Jace looked surprised. "Really?"

"Of course," Ben replied, trumping his puzzled look. "Why not?"

"I was sort of counting on you not being up for it."

"Public transportation you mean? Hey, I used to live in Chicago, don't forget."

Jace sighed. "Well if you aren't going to insist that we take a taxi, then it's up to me."

"Big baby," Ben laughed.

They walked out of the relatively small airport and were assaulted with offers as soon as they stepped into the night air. A dozen taxi drivers were competing for their attention, making offers in English and a slew of other languages. Feeling completely overwhelmed, Ben pressed past them to where the actual vehicles were. He was vaguely aware of Jace asking him to wait, but he was eager to get into the solitude and comfort of a car. Not wanting to be in cramped quarters again, he headed for the biggest vehicle, a white minivan.

The driver appeared, happily taking his luggage from him. Ben allowed himself this luxury and crawled into the backseat. Jace was soon next to him, tutting something about not choosing so quickly. Then the driver was behind the wheel, but before they pulled out, another man took the passenger seat.

"My brother," the driver explained with a smile. "Where you go?"

Jace gave him the address. The man nodded wordlessly and guided the vehicle away from the airport. Ben looked out the window, eager for his first glimpse of a European city. So far, Rome didn't look all that different from Houston.

"Are you sure we actually left Texas?" he asked Jace.

"Hm? Oh, I see what you mean. All highways look pretty much the same. Wait until we're in the center of Rome. You won't believe the difference."

Ben checked the meter to see if cabs here were as notoriously expensive as they had been in Chicago. Except there wasn't a meter. That couldn't be right. He shifted in his seat, scanning the dashboard as casually as possible. He was certain now that there wasn't a meter. Nor was there any sign of a taxi license or the driver's ID. Surely such things were required, even in a different country. How did people know if they were getting ripped off? Were they supposed to haggle the price before they got in the vehicle? He looked worriedly to Jace who met his gaze and nodded knowingly.

"Told you we picked too soon," he said in hushed tones. "This little trip is probably going to cost us an arm and a leg. It's all right," he added when Ben's face crumpled with guilt. "We'll be fine."

The all-too-familiar sight of the highway receded into the distance as they barreled down one of the exits. There was good reason for the universal stereotype of taxi drivers being demons behind the wheel. They zipped past a small village in the blink of an eye and entered farmland, the road dark and empty except for the illumination from their headlights. The two men in the front seat, who had up to now been chatting rapidly in their native tongue, grew silent. Jace tensed up as the van pulled over to the side of the road. Ben reached over, his hand crawling along the seat in hopes of finding Jace's.

The driver's brother turned to face them, his brow furrowed. "How much money you have? We need more money to go."

Jace said something in Italian, causing the other man to look surprised, but he recovered quickly. "You give us money, you have no problem." He raised a hand and wagged a flat metal object at them. A knife! It was still folded shut, but his meaning was clear enough.

Ben felt cold panic. Had he traveled all this way just to die in some remote Italian field? If all these guys wanted was money, that was fine with him. He shifted to reach for his wallet, but Jace's left hand stilled him. His right hand was already holding a wallet out. The man took it eagerly and turned forward again to examine its contents. Ben wanted to say something to Jace, comfort him or discuss some sort of cunning plan that would get them both out of this mess, but the driver's eyes in the rearview mirror were locked onto them both.

"This all?" the brother demanded.

"That's two-hundred thousand lira!" Jace replied.

"That nothing!" the brother spat back.

"Well it's all we have," Jace said. "Everyone uses credit cards these days."

The man looked skeptically at Ben, who shook his head in what he hoped was a convincing manner. He did have money on him, and he was more than willing to give it up, but he didn't want to prove Jace a liar. Who knew how the men would react?

"Get out," the driver said.

"Fine." Jace nodded to him that they should exit, but Ben faltered.

He didn't like the idea of being abandoned in the middle of nowhere any more than he liked being robbed. The audacity of the suggestion incensed him, causing his panic to recede as he slowly saw red. "You can't leave us here!"

"Your hotel not far," the brother said in friendly tones, as if he was performing a public service. "You walk that way. Half hour, you there."

"You just took all our money," Ben retorted. "You can at least drive us the rest of the way!"

"Ben—" Jace tried.

"No! I'm not getting out of the car. Go ahead and cut us up! Stain your upholstery with our blood and go through the hassle of hiding our bodies. I don't care. Or you can take us to the hotel. You decide!"

Ben could barely breathe by the time he was finished. The two brothers yammered at each other in Italian for a few moments before finally reaching a conclusion.

"We take you," the brother said moodily.

Ben wished he felt relief, but at this point he could only suspect the worst. Maybe they were being driven to some mafia hideout where the professional cleaners would make short work of them. His muscles remained tense and his pulse throbbed until the neon hotel sign finally came into view. The taxi pulled over before reaching the U-shaped driveway.

"Get out," the driver ordered a second time.

Ben wanted to, he really *really* wanted to, but another thought had occurred to him. The second they stepped out of the vehicle, it would drive away, taking their luggage with it. There was something he had worked very hard on in his bag, and he wasn't willing to give it up.

"Take our luggage out," he insisted. He wanted to look at Jace, but he didn't dare take his attention off the two men up front.

The driver's brother appeared ready to snap and carve his initials all over their bodies. His jaw clenched as his eyes bored into Ben's, but the unblinking gaze that he received in return wore him down. He stepped out of the van, slamming the door loudly behind him. Then he opened the rear hatch and took their luggage, tossing it carelessly to the side of the street. As soon as it was out, both Ben and Jace followed suit.

"Crazy Americans!" the brother spat, literally this time, at Ben's feet before reentering the taxi and speeding away.

A cool breeze blew across them as they watched it disappear around a corner.

"You were amazing!" Jace said, grinning and picking Ben up

in a hug. "Jesus! You should be a hostage negotiator!"

"That was horrible," Ben said, his voice trembling. His braveness had fled along with his adrenaline, returning the fear he had been ignoring. His legs were feeling shaky too. "Come on. Let's go." He removed himself from Jace's embrace and picked up his luggage. He just wanted to get into the hotel where they were safe before the thugs came back to gun them down or something.

Check-in went by in a blur. Ben repeatedly looked out the lobby windows for any sign of trouble. The receptionist barely blinked an eye when Jace explained how his credit cards had been stolen. A couple of calls had to be made to cancel them and to secure the reservation. Jace switched to Italian again and must have found some way to work it out because they got their room.

Ben sat down on the bed and tried unsuccessfully to hide his trembling hands. Jace noticed and kneeled before Ben, taking them in his own. "It's okay," he soothed. "We're safe now. We just got into the wrong taxi. I should have known better and been more careful."

"It's my fault," Ben said, refusing to let him take the blame. "No, screw that. It was theirs. That was really fucked up."

"It was," Jace agreed. "But you shouldn't let it ruin our trip."

How could it not? All of Jace's money had been taken, and relaxing in a country where you could get robbed just by getting inside a taxi didn't sound feasible. "I want to go home," Ben blurted out.

Jace smiled sympathetically and sat next to Ben, wrapping an arm around him. "I know you're shaken up. You have every right to be, but that was just bad luck. Italy is a wonderful country. The people are fantastic here. We just ran into a couple of bad seeds, something that could happen anywhere. I can't let you leave now. I won't let you go home with a bad impression of this place."

Ben sighed and leaned against him. The idea of the long flight home was almost worse than being robbed. "Okay," he agreed. He was starting to calm down. Being near Jace always made him feel safe.

"You did great with the luggage."

"Well, I didn't want to lose your present."

"My present?" Jace asked. "Sounds good, but look what else you saved."

Jace unzipped his bag and dug around until he found a cheap

figure of a plastic cat. The toy split in half like a Russian doll revealing a wad of cash inside. "Never put all your eggs in one basket."

"How much is that?"

"Pretty much the whole vacation budget," Jace laughed. "I only had enough in my wallet for the taxi and a meal out."

Ben smiled with relief. He thought he had only been saving their clothes, but now he was especially proud of his actions. Feeling more like himself again, he dug into his own bag and brought out a small cellophane-covered basket. He handed it over to Jace and waited nervously for his reaction.

"*Cestino*," Jace said warmly.

"Huh?"

"It means basket. I could teach you some Italian. If you want."

"Just open it," Ben said, leg bouncing in anticipation.

"Okay, okay." Jace pulled away the plastic to reveal a basket full of fortune cookies. They were a little misshapen but came in a variety of colors.

"Wow! These look amazing," Jace exclaimed. "I love the colors. Look, a blue one! Where did you get them?"

"They're homemade," Ben explained. They were a pain to make, but the expression on Jace's face was worth the effort.

"No way! What about the fortunes?"

"Check it out." Ben bit his bottom lip as Jace broke one open and tossed half into his mouth.

"Mmmm, good. What's in my future?" He examined the scrawl on the little strip of paper and raised an eyebrow. "*A thousand kisses will soon cover your body.*" He turned to look at Ben, a smile on his lips. "Let's see if we can make this one come true."

Before leaving for Italy, four nights had seemed too short a visit. By the third day, Ben's leg muscles were shredded and his feet felt on the verge of falling off. He couldn't imagine his condition had they stayed for a week or longer. There were simply too many sights to see. Ben found it impossible to rest for very long before the urge to continue exploring overtook him again.

Rome was a fascinating mix of old and new. They visited the obligatory sites: the Colosseum, the Vatican, the Pantheon, and the Circus Maximus. Ben's favorite was the ancient ruins of the

Forum. While there he imagined travelling thousands of years into the past, the crumbling buildings restored and proud again, the streets teeming with Roman people going about their daily business. Being in the midst of the ruins brought home the reality of this bygone era.

Modern Rome had much to offer as well, especially for a shopaholic like Ben. They ducked into designer fashion stores where the price for a pair of jeans was more than what Ben paid for rent, but they also found some smaller shops where he picked up a couple of shirts he was certain never to see back home. The grocery stores were more humble, full of variations of familiar Italian staples but new items as well.

The quality of Italian restaurants varied wildly. For the first couple of meals, Jace took them to back streets where the menus weren't even in English. The food here was exquisite and gave credence to Italian's reputation as one of the best cuisines in the world. Ben was impatiently hungry once and allowed a pushy proprietor to pull them into a restaurant near a tourist attraction, where Ben's pizza was flavorless cardboard and Jace's pasta microwaved.

Having learned his lesson, Ben let Jace choose from then on. Today he had managed to find a lunch café that looked like a tourist trap, but was visited almost exclusively by locals. Jace ordered for them in Italian, loving the opportunity to show off his language skills. Ben was more than happy to allow him, enjoying the helpless feeling that came with not being able to read or speak the local tongue.

"To the bravest boyfriend I've ever had," Jace toasted once their wine had been served.

Ben blushed. "You're not still going on about that?"

"I don't just mean the way you handled the taxi drivers," Jace said. He considered his wine as he swirled it around the glass. "How old were you when you first came out?"

"Fourteen," Ben said after a moment's calculation.

"I'd say that's pretty damn brave."

"Yeah, maybe in the nineties," Ben countered, "but kids are coming out younger and younger these days."

"All right. What about that time at the Greek restaurant where the waiter disappeared for half an hour and you marched into the kitchen—"

"Only to find him smoking a joint with the chef," Ben finished wryly.

"At least you got us our food. How about that guy you punched in the chest after we saw him kick his dog?"

"Fat lot of good it did. His dog turned on me like I was the jerk."

"It was still brave," Jace insisted.

"Look, I'm not trying to go overboard with humility," Ben said, "but I think you misunderstand. Sometimes I get angry and do crazy things without thinking. That doesn't count as bravery. Recklessness would be a better description."

"Call it whatever you like, but there's something there." Jace shook a breadstick at him. "Usually you're adorably sweet and sympathetic, but I've seen glimpses of something else. There's something stronger than titanium inside of you."

"Like the Terminator?"

"Exactly like that." Jace laughed. "That bravery, recklessness, whatever you want to call it, is one of the many things I love about you."

They both went silent at the mention of the "L" word. Funny that they could dive headlong into sex, a relationship, even a trip across the ocean, but saying those three little words was something they still balked at.

"So what's next?" Ben asked, leaving the question open for interpretation.

"It's our final day here, but don't be too sad because I've saved the best for last."

Ben didn't have to wait long to find out what this meant. A few blocks from the restaurant, in the midst of clothing stores and newspaper kiosks, was another set of ruins. Archeologists had dug down so that an entire city block was below street level. Jace led Ben by the hand down the cracked and ancient stairs and into the excavated ruins where a familiar smell greeted their noses.

"Cats?" Ben asked, but an answer wasn't necessary as there were already half a dozen in sight.

"They're using this area as a sanctuary," Jace said, stooping down to pet a three-legged cat that was rubbing against his leg. "We have to hurry. I think the tour is about to start."

As it turned out, direct access to the ruins, known as the *Torre Argentina*, was only possible via one of these guided tours.

Otherwise, the land that had once belonged to Roman gods and their temples was now the exclusive home of felines who behaved as if they were equally divine. Every site their guide led them to was occupied by a cat, sunbathing on ancient steps or stalking through broken columns in search of mice.

"And it was here, in 44 B.C., that Julius Caesar was stabbed to death by his fellow senators," their tour guide informed them, causing a frenzy of picture taking.

"*Et tu*, Kitty?" Ben joked. When Jace didn't respond, he looked back to find his boyfriend some yards behind the tour group. He was sitting in the dirt, two cats on his lap, another on his shoulders.

Ben had a great respect for animals. So much so that he usually left them alone, figuring that they didn't care for people constantly trying to pet them. His experiences backed this up, and so he kept his distance. Jace was different. He loved cats so much that it flowed out of him and somehow changed the world. Even the most troubled cat willingly gave into his affections. He was like a gay version of Snow White with all the forest creatures flocking around him.

"I love you," Ben said. He'd meant only to think it to himself, but it felt good to finally say it aloud. Jace didn't react, too far away to hear, so he said it again, this time yelling. "I love you!"

Jace looked up, surprised, before a wild grin broke out on his face. He stood, sending the poor cats flying, and strode over to Ben. "About time you admitted it," he said before picking him up and kissing him. Behind them came a few shocked gasps, a couple of titters, and at least one burst of applause. "I love you too," Jace murmured into his ear.

The rest of the tour was embarrassing; most of the group keeping an eye on them and waiting for a repeat performance. Ben was relieved when the tour ended, craving private time with Jace so they could explore this new confession.

"Hotel?" Ben asked as he stuffed money into the donation box.

"No time," Jace responded. "I told you I saved the best for last."

"This wasn't it?"

"No. Well, for me it was. Especially now." They grinned at each other before remembering they were in the middle of a conversation. "No, I had something special in mind for you."

The exterior of the *Teatro dell'Opera* couldn't compete with the rest of the city's architecture, but the interior didn't disappoint. Opera had never been an interest of his, but he understood why Jace might think he would enjoy it. Ben felt severely underdressed as they entered the theater. He had felt that way almost the entire trip due to the fashion-conscious Romans. Ben felt a little better when he spotted other couples in T-shirts and shorts—cameras around their necks, hats and sunglasses still on in some cases. His fellow Americans, most likely.

Once the performance started, Ben found himself enthralled by the vocal talents of the singers. Each voice had so much raw power that he found it difficult to believe they weren't boosted electronically. He sat in rapt fascination for the first hour, soaking up as much as he could. During the second hour he began to squirm, eager to leave the theater so he could attempt to imitate what he was hearing.

While the music had won him over completely, the plot left much to be desired. From what he could understand it was simply a string of rocky relationships, passionate betrayals, and untimely deaths. Perhaps that's all real life was, he mused. He'd had his share of dysfunctional love, but he hoped to avoid betraying anyone he cared for. Death was inevitable, but he expected it to be a long time coming.

He looked over at Jace, who was lost in his own thoughts. Ben wondered if they would be together on that final day. If so, would they go at the same time, or would one of them be left behind to struggle with grief? These thoughts were too abstract to be frightening and were quickly forgotten by Ben, who chose instead to dwell on the warm feelings of love and desire that always came from being near his boyfriend. The future was always uncertain, but at least now it wouldn't be lonely.

CHAPTER 20

Time became a blur that swept Ben along, often leaving him breathless and disorientated. Not all of his academic credits had transferred seamlessly, meaning he had extra work to catch up on. His classes were much more demanding than those of his old school. Often he would spend his every waking hour trying to balance his projects and studies, barely finishing one before more work was added to the pile. And then Jace Holden would arrive like an angel, pulling Ben free from his frenzy and forcing him to slow down and relax, if only for one night. Ben began to appreciate rather than resent the demanding schedule of Jace's job, since he had so little time of his own to give.

Finals battered Ben like a hurricane, testing his determination and will. Just when he thought he couldn't take anymore, the clouds pulled away to reveal the empty bliss of summer. Ben flew home, intending only to stay a week, but ended up staying the entire summer break. After the first few days, he moved his luggage from his parents' house to Jace's loft apartment.

Ben took a job as a waiter at a vegetarian restaurant downtown. He didn't enjoy the work, but it helped keep him occupied on the frequent nights that Jace was away. He also felt proud being able to take his boyfriend out instead of expecting him to pay for everything.

With Jace absent so often, Samson slowly warmed up to Ben. At first he was only willing to occupy the same mattress to guard Jace's side of the bed. Eventually he moved over to cuddle against Ben's leg. By the end of the summer, Ben would often wake up with the cat sprawled on top of him, something Jace insisted he had never seen the cat do with anyone but himself.

The days when Jace *was* in town were bliss, and he often suggested using his airline connections to take short trips. Ben declined, preferring to have as much privacy together as possible. His appetite for Jace was insatiable. Sometimes they would venture out and explore Houston, searching for nooks of the city that neither of them had yet seen. Mostly they would stay home, taking turns cooking. Jace was even able to save the meals that Ben messed up with a little intervention and help from the spice rack. Other times they would simply lounge around, talking the hours away.

Jace met the family and performed stunningly, charming Ben's mother and managing to talk shop with his father. Karen insisted on being present, which had Ben nervous, but her typically rude comments were parried by Jace's subtle wit, leaving her puzzled and everyone else laughing.

Life couldn't have been better.

When summer break ended and Ben had to return to Austin, his heart ached as he packed the possessions scattered around Jace's apartment. He wanted to continue staying there, so much so that he considered transferring to the University of Houston. Jace dismissed the idea, reminding him of the complications that came with transferring credits, and that the connections Ben had made in his current school would be crucial in the final year.

These points made sense, but Ben couldn't help wondering if Jace was slowly tiring of him. He supposed that his constant presence might have been too much. They spent plenty of time apart when Jace was working, and when he was home again, Jace never got any privacy. Who wouldn't find that tiresome? Then again, Ben had been invited to stay, and wouldn't their relationship lead to living together eventually? Maybe it was too soon for Jace, but Ben had no reservations and was willing to give all of himself to the other man.

His fears seemed confirmed once he had returned to Austin. Jace's calls became less frequent, and when they did come his boyfriend sounded distracted. Distant. Ben became convinced that Jace was hiding something, no longer forthcoming about what he did with his free time. During the third week Jace cancelled a planned visit, and by the fourth he didn't call at all.

Ben could no longer deny it. Their relationship was falling apart, and he had no idea how to fix it. How could he when he didn't understand what was wrong? He was playing Monopoly with Allison one night—both of them doing shots of tequila every time they landed on each other's property—when he decided to take action. The outcome wasn't pretty. He called Jace and left an angry voicemail, one that ended with him sobbing into the phone.

Allison tried to console him by breaking out two tubs of Ben & Jerry's ice cream and pigging out with him. Ben was scraping the bottom of the carton when the doorbell rang. He looked to Allison moodily, silently asking her to answer it. Good friend that she was, she complied.

Murmured voices came from the entryway. Ben was straining to hear when Jace walked into the kitchen with an armful of roses. Ben wiped the ice cream from his mouth and reached up to check his hair, before giving up and blushing.

"I'm sorry," Jace said, proffering the roses. He set them on the kitchen table when Ben didn't take them. "Look, I've been an idiot, but I think you'll forgive me if you come for a short drive."

"I don't know," Ben said, his head spinning. He wished that he hadn't done all those shots and was beginning to regret scarfing down all the ice cream too. "I just don't understand what I did wrong."

"You didn't do anything wrong." Jace sighed. "I was trying to be romantic and surprise you, but I overdid it."

"Overdid what? Why haven't you called?"

"Just come with me, okay?" Jace held out his hand. "There's something I want to show you."

Ben's heart melted quicker than the ice cream had. He reached out and took Jace's hand, and he swore he felt electricity as they touched. His treacherous heart insisted that his brain forget everything and forgive Jace. He would still demand answers, eventually, but right now all he wanted was a kiss.

Jace laughed once their lips had parted. "What have you been drinking?"

"Tequila," Allison said from the doorway. "Sorry."

"It's all right." Jace guided Ben toward the front door. "I'll try to have him back soon."

Allison smiled knowingly. "No you won't."

Once in the passenger seat, Ben focused on sobering up. He had always believed this an issue of mind over matter, but the streetlights refused to stop swaying.

"Wait a minute," Ben said abruptly. "This is your car! Did you drive out here?"

"Yup," Jace confirmed.

"Why?"

"You'll find out in about two blocks."

The car turned down a side street, pulled into an apartment complex, and parked. Jace considered Ben, the engine clicking as it cooled.

"What do you think?"

"That depends. What are we doing here?"

"You'll find out soon enough. Come on."

Ben stumbled out of the car, wondering what was in store. Did Jace have kids or something? A secret heterosexual life? Or maybe he was being brought to some underground swingers club. Oh god! Was he being sold into sex slavery?

"Are you all right?" Jace said, putting an arm around him. "You don't look so good."

"I just drank too much," Ben replied, realizing it was true. Sex slavery indeed, although he wouldn't mind knowing what his value would be on the black market. Maybe it would help pay off his student loans.

Jace led them up two flights of stairs, pulled out his keys, and unlocked a door.

"You're staying here?" Ben asked, starting to feel excited.

"You could say that." He opened the door and a familiar ball of grey fur appeared in the entryway.

"Samson!" Ben said in disbelief, reaching down to let the cat smell his hand. He looked up to see more that was familiar. Along with the cardboard boxes stacked in the hallway were souvenirs from Jace's travels hanging on the wall and the old-fashioned coat rack with the jacket that Jace had worn on their first date.

"No!" Ben said, finally catching on. "No freaking way! You live here now?"

"Since last week," Jace said in apologetic tones. "I wanted to have everything set up to surprise you, but then I was called away for work and—"

"You're so dumb!" Ben said affectionately. "I can't believe you moved here!"

"After all our time together during the summer, I realized it would be too hard to live so far apart," Jace confessed, pulling Ben toward him. "I hope this doesn't freak you out."

"What about your work?"

"With my job, it doesn't really matter where I live."

"It does if you want to fly overseas," Ben said. Austin's airport was international, but didn't have near as many connections as Houston.

Jace shrugged. "I'll figure something out."

"I love you," Ben said, meaning it now more than ever.

"I love you too. Sorry about being so dense."

"It's all right. Show me the apartment!"

Jace gave him the grand tour, or rather Samson did. The cat marched from room to room, head and tail held high. The apartment was the standard two-bedroom affair, but already personal touches were evident: fortune cookie wrappers, toy mice, the smell of Jace's aftershave in the bathroom along with the endless supply of hotel shampoos and soaps he always brought home.

"This is the best part," Jace said, tugging open the sliding door that led out to the balcony. "Samson loves this. I couldn't get him to come in the first night."

"Not bad," Ben said, leaning over the railing to look at the uninspiring courtyard below.

Jace wrapped his arms around him from behind. "So how's school?"

"I finally chose my major."

"And?"

"English Lit."

Jace barked laughter, and when Ben turned around he saw a smirk.

"What?"

"It just so happens that I have a degree in English Lit."

"Really?" Ben was surprised that he had never asked before.

"Yup." Jace nodded. "What do you plan on doing with it?"

Ben grasped for any of the ideas he'd had over the last few weeks, but all avoided his intoxicated mind.

Jace winked. "Exactly."

"Oh no!" Ben said in mock horror. "Am I going to end up a stewardess too?"

"Ha ha," Jace deadpanned. "I don't think you have the temperament for it."

"Seriously though, do you think I should change my major? I figured it was a nice general degree. I could write for a newspaper, teach, edit... things. Who am I kidding? I don't have a clue!"

"It's okay," Jace said reassuringly. "Most people have a degree that doesn't match their eventual profession. A degree is mostly just a piece of paper proving that you've made it through boot camp. Your employer will glance at it and never give it a second thought, if they even ask to see it."

Ben sighed. "I still feel like I should know what I want to do."

"What do you like best?"

"Singing, but we've been over that before." The problem was, Ben didn't see how he could make a career out of singing. He had no illusions of becoming a pop star. He didn't enjoy composing or performing in a choir. What did that leave, singing telegrams?

"It will all fall into place," Jace said confidently. "You'll see."

For now he still had time. And a boyfriend who lived just minutes away. Before this news, Ben had liked Austin. Now he loved it!

With Jace now living in Austin, Ben was home so infrequently that Allison threatened to get a new roommate. Eventually he invited her over to house-sit during one of Jace's absences. This helped appease her. Soon afterwards, academic insanity swept up both of them again. Allison's major was in psychology, since she now planned on being a counselor. Her workload made Ben's look light in comparison. He began to spend more time at home again, helping to clean and also cooking for her since she rarely ate well otherwise.

Ben and Jace celebrated their one year anniversary on Christmas Eve and recreated their first date as best they could a few days later. Ben took on a teacher's assistant position in the second semester, feeling it would look good on his resume. After a couple of nervous lectures he fell into the routine and began to actually enjoy it, but it was a constant challenge, especially since the professor would sometimes leave the class in Ben's not-so-capable hands.

Spring break was once again met with a surprise trip from Jace, this time to Berlin. His boyfriend had a limit to his talents, because he didn't speak a lick of German. This meant they were often lost and found themselves in embarrassing situations that left them clutching their stomachs with laughter.

Jace promised that these trips would become a yearly tradition. Ben requested Paris next, but Jace shook his head, insisting that Paris would have to be a special occasion. The gleam in his eye suggested that he intended to propose to Ben there. From then on, whenever the subject of marriage came up, they simply referred to it as "visiting Paris."

The following year, Jace took Ben to London. Of the three trips so far, this was his favorite. Big Ben (his namesake!) was haunting at night, Buckingham Palace was unlike anything the United States had to offer, and Madam Tussaud's was creepy in the best way possible. Despite the impressive sights, the shopping was what really made the trip for him. From the Portobello flea market to the big retail stores along Oxford Street, Ben couldn't get enough!

These vacations held special significance for them. With all of life's little distractions stripped away, they were able to focus solely on each other. That could be disastrous in the wrong relationship, but more and more, Ben felt certain that he wanted to "visit Paris" with Jace.

The return from London was accompanied by a somber mood. Spring break was over, leaving only a small stretch of time before he and Allison graduated. Dreams of the future gave way to the more pressing matter of the present. The biggest question was: Where next?

Cut free from the university, they could seek out work in any city or state they desired. Their choices were overwhelming. Jace was an important part of the equation, but his work was so flexible that it had little influence on Ben's decision. He almost wished that Jace's job would force them to stay in one particular city so that the choice was no longer his to make.

"I think I've decided," Allison announced.

"What?" Ben snapped. She wasn't supposed to decide! He wasn't ready for that yet. Their frequent brainstorming sessions in coffee shops weren't meant to deliver results. They were supposed to delay the making of actual decisions with circular conversations that never went anywhere.

"I've decided," Allison repeated. She sipped her cappuccino and gazed out the café window as if she could already see her future. "There's nothing left for me in Houston. No family, obviously, and I've lost touch with all my high school friends. Except you. No, there's no point in me going back."

"Yeah, fine," Ben said, "but that still doesn't eliminate any of the other places we've talked about. Not returning to Houston is one thing, but what about the band we were going to start in Seattle? Or the hippie commune in Santa Fe? I was going to grow out my hair!"

Allison rolled her eyes and tried not to smile. "Seriously though, think about it. Finding a job and starting new careers will be hard enough without the added hassle of relocating."

Easy for her to say. Ben still didn't know what he wanted to do after graduation. He shoved his vanilla cappuccino away. No point in suffering the taste if it wasn't going to allow him to procrastinate. "I thought we agreed that Austin is overrun with fresh graduates looking for jobs. That's a lot of competition."

Allison didn't seem to hear him. She was staring over his shoulder. Her eyes widened and flicked back to Ben, then over his shoulder, before once again focusing on him.

"What's up?" Ben said, starting to turn around.

"No!" Allison said quickly. "It's nothing. Just— What were you saying?"

Ben didn't answer, choosing instead to scrutinize his friend who was suddenly acting crazy.

"Don't turn around," Allison pleaded. "You'll regret it if you do. Oh god! Never mind."

"Benjamin?"

His skin tingled at the sound of that voice, shivers running up his spine to the base of his skull. Ben turned around and saw him, Tim Wyman, an impossible dream moving past the café chairs and tables. He looked the same, and yet completely different. His teenage body had given way to manhood, the muscles defined and straining against an artificially-aged T-shirt. The last vestiges of baby fat had gone from Tim's face, leaving it even handsomer than before, and the short-cropped hair—styled spiky on top— was doing him all sorts of favors. In other words, he looked like he had stepped right out of a fashion catalog. Or maybe a porn magazine. Those irresistible silver eyes were already smiling at Ben.

"It's really you, isn't it?" Tim had reached the table and put his hand on Ben's shoulder.

At his touch, Ben was seventeen again, clutching the grass while watching Tim walk away from him, certain the damage was irreparable. That, no matter how much he begged or pleaded, or how badly he wanted to feel Tim's arms around him, he never would. Their time together was over. Except, here he was.

"Yeah," Ben responded, not even remembering the question. His breath was so short that he could barely speak a single word. He shrugged Tim's hand away, an act that probably seemed cold, but his only other option was to start sobbing.

The light in Tim's eyes flickered with uncertainty. "Man. So are you just visiting or what?"

"I'm enrolled here," Ben answered, heart thudding in his ears.

"Since when? I thought you were in Chicago?"

As one, Ben and Tim both looked to Allison. She gave Tim a blank expression before turning to Ben. Her eyes said "Don't be mad at me." He understood. She had previously run into Tim and had told him that Ben was in Chicago. Maybe he actually had been at the time, but she had never mentioned the encounter to him, which could only mean one thing.

"I'm guessing we go to the same school?" Ben asked, his focus still on his best friend.

"Yeah," she confirmed.

"Jesus," Tim said, sitting down at the table.

This was too much. "I have to go." Ben stood clumsily, the chair almost tipping over behind him. He was out the door before anyone could say anything to stop him.

"You should have told me!" he heard Tim scold Allison before the door of the coffee shop closed.

Ben hurried down the street at a pace desperate to become a run. He was heading toward Jace's apartment until remembering that he was out of town for another three days. Home was in the opposite direction, which would mean having to walk by the coffee shop again. Ben turned and saw Tim sprinting down the sidewalk toward him.

"Wait," Tim called out. "Please."

Ben looked down at himself, half-expecting to see the same dopey Smashing Pumpkins T-shirt he was wearing the night that Tim had jogged past him.

"Hey," Tim panted as he came to a stop. It sounded so casual, as if they were two friends who regularly saw each other.

"What do you want?" Ben shook his head, unable to imagine the answer.

"I don't know," Tim said. "I just want to talk to you, I guess."

Ben breathed in heavily, the scent of Tim filling his nose and making him want to cry. This wasn't happening. "I can't."

"I know you're mad at me," Tim said, stooping an attempt to make eye contact. He failed. "Look, take this."

A cell phone was pressed into Ben's hand.

"I'll call tonight, okay? We're both in shock right now and

need time to think, but I still want to talk to you. Cool?"

Ben nodded. Why the hell not? He could always dump the phone somewhere if he changed his mind.

"All right. I'm going now," Tim started to walk away, but hesitated. "You were right, Benjamin."

Ben finally raised his head. "About what?"

"A lot of things. See you around." Tim flashed his winner's smile and left.

Ben watched him walk down the street, expecting Tim to disappear at any moment like a phantom.

CHAPTER 21

There was no good cop, bad cop in this interrogation. Only bad cop, and Ben wanted answers. If need be he would deny his prisoner food and water. Or refuse to pay his share of the rent.

"Sophomore year," Allison reported from the couch, while Ben stood over her, arms crossed like an angry parent. "We would pass each other in the hall on campus. I noticed him right away, but it took Tim ages to see me."

"But one day he did and stopped to talk to you?"

"Mm-hm. The first thing out of his mouth was a question about you. He wanted to know where you were and how you were doing."

"And?"

"I didn't tell him anything. Well, I said you were in Chicago, but that was it."

"Was I still?"

"No. I lied and would have again today if you hadn't been there." Allison crossed her own arms. "I did it to protect you."

"You could have told me! I wouldn't have run off to meet him."

"No, but you would have ended up in that hallway one day, just out of curiosity."

Ben's shoulders sagged. He knew she was right.

"Anything else?"

"Not really. Eventually he gave up trying to pump me for information and we didn't see each other after that year."

Ben sat down on the couch and leaned against her for support. "Do you think I should answer when he calls?"

"No. Think about Jace."

"Why? Talking on the phone isn't cheating. It's not like I'm going to have phone sex with him or something."

Allison didn't respond right away. Ben could tell that she was holding information back, maybe trying to decide whether it would help or hurt her case. Ben waited. If she decided not to tell him, he would force it out of her somehow.

"I've heard things," Allison said at last.

"Go on."

"Tim has a sugar daddy."

"What do you mean?" Ben asked, his stomach clenching.

"Some old guy. I don't know details, but he's supposed to be rolling in it. You really think someone as pretty as Tim is hanging around a rich old guy for fun?"

Ben was quiet. He didn't want to imagine his high school sweetheart grunting over some old bag of bones for cash. Maybe he shouldn't take Tim's call. Why tarnish his memories even further with lurid details?

"Why don't you call Jace instead?" Allison suggested.

She was right, of course. That's just what he would do.

Summer burned with a vengeance, as if it had something to prove. Ben tossed and turned in bed, the sheets tangled up around his legs. The window air conditioning unit couldn't cope with more than mild warmth, so he had shut it off and opened the other window. Cicadas buzzed outside, invigorated by the heat as they sang their strange song.

Ben had stripped down to his underwear but was still sweaty as he drifted in and out of sleep. He hadn't called anyone, not even Jace. After thinking it over, Ben decided it wasn't worth worrying him about, especially since he still wasn't sure he would answer if Tim called. That's something he debated as he fiddled with Tim's phone, looking at the stored numbers and wondering what sort of people were on the other end. Each male name listed was a leering old man in Ben's mind, clutching a wad of hundred dollar bills in one hand while gesturing to the bulge in his plaid trousers with the other. Then there was the number listed as "Home." Where did that lead? A place of Tim's own, or to his parents back in The Woodlands? Eventually Ben grew tired of wondering and longed for the blissful limbo of sleep. He left the phone on the pillow beside him, and it was still there when it began to buzz like a bee.

Ben groped around until he found the vibrating phone. He answered blearily, forgetting that it wasn't his own. "Hello?"

"Hey! Were you sleeping?"

Ben jolted awake. "No! I mean, yeah."

"It's only eleven p.m.," Tim chided. "What sort of college boy are you?"

Ben hesitated. Should he enter into casual banter, or should he start shooting off questions? He didn't want to pretend nothing had happened and that they had always been on good terms.

"Where were you?" he tried.

"Oh. I had a study group and we went out for—"

"No. I mean, *where were you*?"

"What? You mean the last five years?" Now it was Tim's turn to lapse into silence. "All right, uh, high school. Fuck. Senior year I went to Conroe High instead."

"Just to get away from me?"

"To get away from myself," Tim corrected. "Man, you aren't going to make this easy, are you?"

"No."

"Maybe doing this over the phone was a bad idea."

Or a good idea. Being unable to see how handsome Tim was made it easy to stay angry. Ben switched on the bedside lamp and reached for the photos from London. He flipped through them until he found one of the London Eye. While riding the massive Ferris wheel, Jace had held the camera out at arm's length and snapped a photo of him and Ben kissing. That memory was like a cold shower right now.

"Can't we meet up? Talk face to face?" Tim tried.

Ben almost laughed. "No, I don't think so."

"Why? Are you indecent? Lying in your bed with nothing but your boxers on?"

Ben paused, having heard a strange echo over the phone.

"You're still so damn scrawny!" Tim chuckled from the window, snapping his phone shut. "But it suits you."

"What the hell?" Ben swore. "What are you doing here?"

"Let me in before somebody calls the cops," Tim said, pressing his face against the screen.

"I should call them myself! How did you find me?"

"Looked up Allison in the phone book. C'mon, let me in."

Ben shook his head ruefully and grabbed a shirt. He headed to the front door, but stopped to check himself in the bathroom mirror. He wanted to look good so Tim knew exactly what he was missing. Ben decided to make him wait even longer and went for a glass of iced tea before opening the front door.

Tim stumbled inside, ignoring Ben's personal space. He smelled like cologne and beer, an enticing combination.

"You know what?" Ben placed a hand on Tim's chest to stop him, not the best move considering how impressive it felt. "This isn't a good idea. Wait outside. I'll get dressed and we can go for a walk."

Tim looked disappointed but shrugged and stepped back into the night. Score one for the home team! Ben was in charge of the situation, not Tim. He hurried to get dressed, a sense of excitement welling up within him that he mentally chastised before giving into. Why not be excited? He would finally get all the puzzle pieces he had been missing over the years. Tim would answer his questions, Ben might even flirt, but at the end of the evening there would only be blue balls. For them both probably, but at least Ben could call Jace and talk dirty for some release.

Ben was about to turn off the bedroom light when he noticed the London photo and pocketed it to use as a talisman, should his body stop listening to his heart. When he left the duplex he found Tim leaning against a sports car in his best James Bond pose. Ben wondered if Tim's sugar daddy had bought it for him as the image of a leering old man returned to his mind. He made sure to ignore the car, no matter how impressively shiny and new it was. He walked past Tim, gesturing that he should follow.

"Same old Benjamin," Tim remarked as he pushed away from the car. "Always knowing what you want and getting it."

"Yeah, well, not everything's the same," Ben retorted, not having a clue what he meant. All he knew was that he needed to sound more mysterious than he actually was. "So how did Conroe High treat you?"

"Same shit, different school," Tim replied. "Well, not completely the same. There was no you."

"What about girls?" Ben asked.

"Tried to avoid them. Just had a prom date senior year."

"Krista Norman again?" Ben spat, feeling surprised at how much he still despised her all these years later.

"No. Not Krista. I stopped seeing her about the same time that we beat the crap out of Bryce."

Ben smiled at the memory.

"That was another good reason to switch schools," Tim added. "I'm sure Bryce was aching for a rematch. They give you any more trouble?"

"Not really." The usual name calling but nothing more, although Ben had carried pepper spray until graduation.

Ben led them to a tiny park squeezed between two parking

lots. There was only space for a few benches, a tangle of untended plants, and the occasional drunk. They pushed past the bushes to a large flat rock that offered a view of the river and the city's skyline.

"Nice," Tim commented.

The tranquil sound of burbling water combined with the reflected city lights made this one of Ben's favorite places for solitary thinking. Occasionally he brought Jace along. They once had frenzied sex here, wondering all the while if they were going to get caught. Tim being here wasn't a betrayal. Ben was using the memories of Jace to reinforce his willpower.

Tim let Ben sit first before plopping down himself. With both of them cross-legged, the little rock didn't afford enough room for them to sit without their knees brushing against each other. Ben readjusted, pulling his legs up and holding them against his chest.

"What about you?" Tim asked. "Drag any lucky guys to the prom?"

"So you went straight from high school to Austin?" Ben asked, ignoring the question.

"Yeah, pretty much. My dad graduated from here and insisted that I do the same. I didn't know what I wanted to do, so I agreed. It's worked out pretty well so far. People are so liberal in Austin. It's easy to be gay here."

Ben almost toppled over. "You came out?"

"Yeah." Tim beamed at him. "Got kicked out of a fraternity because of it too."

"Seriously?" Ben asked, grudgingly impressed.

"Yeah. It was stupid, since I'd slept with half of them before coming out. Well, not *half*, but you know."

Ben didn't know, but he couldn't help imagining. He thought such things only took place in porn movies.

"A lot of the frat boys were the same way I used to be," Tim said. "Some just liked to mess around, which was all right, but others were so closeted they couldn't even admit it to themselves. I got a good taste of what I put you through."

Ben was silent. He hadn't expected Tim to ever come out. That he had was incredible. How had his life changed since then? Did he have boyfriends? Did he take them home to meet his family? How did his parents feel?

"So tell me about your life," Tim pressed. "Was Chicago just a lie to keep me away from you?"

"No, I was there for almost two years."

"Did you like it?"

"I loved it. Everything but the weather. The museums were amazing, the shopping—just the city itself. There was always something going on. Culture thrives there. It didn't feel like a dead city, like Houston."

"Yeah." Tim nodded, remembering. "Austin must seem boring in comparison."

"Not really. It's taken me a little while, but it's starting to feel like home."

"You know," Tim leaned toward him, "they say home is where the heart is."

"They also say you can never go home again," Ben pointed out.

"Touché!" Tim shrugged. "So what about guys? I guess you've probably dated a lot?"

Now it was Ben's turn to shrug. Part of him wanted to keep Tim in the dark about his love life, to reinforce that Tim had forfeited his right to be a part of his life. Then again, bragging about Jace would be satisfying. Inspiration struck. Ben took the photo of him and Jace out of his pocket and handed it to Tim.

"His name is Jace. We've been together for over two years. Someday he's going to take me to Paris."

Tim took the photo and examined it wordlessly. He swallowed roughly. He was holding back tears! Ben instantly regretted his decision and cursed himself.

"I guess I deserve this." Tim's chin was trembling.

"I'm sorry," Ben said, wanting to reach out and comfort him in ways that he no longer could.

"Don't be," Tim said, pulling himself together. "I missed my chance, right? A guy like you doesn't stay single."

"You either," Ben smiled sympathetically.

Tim shook his head. "Nope. Not since you."

"But you said— The frat boys?"

"That was just sex." Tim snorted. "All the guys I've been with were nothing more than a one-night stand or fuck buddies. None of them meant anything."

In Ben's darker moments, he had hoped that Tim would

never find anyone else and would always regret leaving him. Now that he was face to face with that reality, Ben wished the opposite. They should be sitting here while boasting about their boyfriends and exchanging stories of their romantic escapades. The idea of Tim being alone all these years was tragic. A bit unlikely too!

"You can't tell me that none of those guys fell for you," Ben challenged. "If not a frat boy, then someone."

Tim grinned, having fully recovered. "There were a few, yeah, but they weren't—" He shot a glance at Ben and let the sentence hang before he stood and stretched. "I tracked you down tonight in the hopes of seducing you, but instead the evening was a complete embarrassment."

"No, it wasn't."

"You aren't the one who almost cried. I think I'm going to cash in my chips and call it a night. Hey, you still have my phone?"

"Yeah." Ben stood to dig it out.

"Good. Here, trade me. You can have this one," Tim handed him one that was nearly identical. "I bought it to stalk you tonight, but I obviously don't need it anymore. It's all paid up."

"I can't," Ben protested.

"You can. Besides, I like the idea of being able to get a hold of you whenever I want."

"Oh. Well, thanks."

They walked back to Tim's car in silence. Ben struggled for something to say. So much of his life revolved around Jace that making conversation without bringing him up was difficult. He didn't want to upset Tim further. As they approached the car, the sugar daddy issue came to mind, but there were some things Ben would rather not know about.

"I'm happy for you, Benjamin," Tim said. "I'm glad that someone recognized how special you are and held on tight."

"Thanks," Ben said awkwardly. "I'm sure there's someone out there for you too."

"Oh, there is." Tim winked.

Ben didn't know quite what to make of that as Tim slipped into his car and was gone. Then he looked down at the new cell phone in his hand and sighed. What had he gotten himself into?

CHAPTER 22

Ben didn't know what Tim's major was, but it wasn't in subtlety. He didn't hesitate to make use of the cell phone he had given Ben. Tim called the next morning to "test the line" and to ask about Ben's class schedule. Then he called again in the afternoon to invite him go-kart racing. Ben gave a flimsy excuse and declined. In the evening, Tim called to say that he was picking him up anyway.

Ben gave in, despite Allison's disapproval. On the go-kart track that night, an epic race of tiny proportions took place. Ben stole the lead, the symbolism of being chased by Tim not at all lost on him. He half expected a go-kart version of an airplane, piloted by Jace naturally, to descend from the sky. Like a miniature Red Baron, Jace would rain twin trails of bullets down the track until Tim's car exploded into flames. Of course this never happened. Instead Tim announced that Ben had earned a round of beers for winning the race and chauffeured him off to a bar.

Ben carefully nursed two beers, determined not to do anything stupid. As flattering as it was being the center of Tim's attention, he wasn't about to ruin things with Jace. His heart knew to whom it belonged. Regardless, Ben was careful not to hurt Tim's feelings again by mentioning Jace, and Tim never brought up his sugar daddy.

Ben was dragged to lunch the next day and invited out to dinner, before Allison launched a defensive maneuver and made him promise to take her to the movies. Ben fulfilled his social obligations, but he couldn't help checking out the other cinema seats before the lights went down, almost expecting to see Tim lurking there.

Tim's counterattack came the next morning. Ben had finished showering and just barely managed to get his Calvins on when a rapping on his window made him jump. He tried not to dwell on how long he'd had an audience. Instead he got dressed and went outside. Tim hustled him into the car, which was stocked with a dozen donuts and a couple of Cokes. By the time the sugar rush kicked in, they were well on their way to San Antonio.

"It's Saturday!" Tim howled, rolling down the windows and sending Ben's hair flying.

Tim didn't share the same problem due to his new hairstyle,

the dark spikes matching the black sunglasses he wore. He looked good. As always. Tim caught him staring and grinned in approval when Ben didn't look away.

Their secret destination turned out to be Six Flags Fiesta, a massive amusement park filled with rollercoasters and other fear-inducing rides. Ben had attempted to visit Six Flags with Jace, but the park had been closed for maintenance, so they had spent the day shopping instead. And now he was about to carry on with that missed opportunity, except with Tim. The idea made him uncomfortable. Any unease he felt disappeared on the first exhilarating ride.

Like all amusement parks, Six Flags had long lines. As they waited, they spent most of their time talking and laughing. During this, the years of distance between them dissolved as if they had woken up in their junior year of high school looking five years older. So many of their conversations began with...

"Do you remember," Tim said, nudging him, "the time you let me paint you."

"Valentine's Day," Ben said, sighing wistfully. "That was one of our better days together."

"They were all good!" Tim said as the line shuffled forward. "Admit it!"

"Some were better than others," Ben replied. "Do you remember when I made us stay in bed the entire day?"

Tim shook his head. "Remind me."

"Your parents went out of town, and I made you promise—no, I think you lost a bet. Or maybe I did—"

"That's right! *You* lost the bet. I wanted you in bed all day, and you made it happen by packing meals for us to eat. Drinks too. I definitely remember that, because when we had to pee—"

Ben laughed. "We had to make a trail of pillow and blankets to the bathroom, so *technically* we were still in bed. Even when we weren't."

"I remember trying to reach the hall closet just so we could get more sheets to build a path with."

And so it went. By late afternoon, Ben could feel sunburn on his neck and his stomach grumbled with a serious hunger the park's junk food couldn't satisfy. All he had to do was mention his appetite, and Tim offered to take them to dinner. He had been paying for so much the last few days that Ben was starting to feel like he had a sugar daddy of his own.

A display of plush animals caught Ben's eye on the way out. One of them, a black stuffed cat, would have looked familiar had it been a different color.

"Samson!"

Tim looked confused.

"Jace's cat," Ben explained. "I totally forgot to feed him today. I haven't been over there since yesterday morning."

"We'll swing by after dinner," Tim offered.

"I kind of need to go now," Ben said apologetically. "Maybe we can get something to eat on the road?"

"Yeah, all right."

They navigated the horizonless parking lot until they found the car, Ben worrying about his oversight. How long could a cat go without food? His concern was more than just that. Samson needed regular company, something he had been neglecting the last couple of days.

"I hope he's okay," Ben said as they pulled onto the highway. "Usually I stay over there when Jace is out of town."

"So why haven't you been?"

Yeah, Ben, why haven't you stayed at Jace's place lately? Once he put the question to himself it was obvious. That first evening he had felt uneasy about waiting for a call from Tim while at Jace's apartment. And last night, well, he supposed part of him he liked the idea of Tim being able to find him. And look how that had paid off. He had gotten a date out of it.

Perhaps this little nostalgia kick had gone too far. Time to make Jace a part of regular conversation. Tim might be hurt at first, but surely giving him false hope would do even more harm. "I'll crash there tonight," Ben said. "Gotta make sure the apartment looks nice before Jace comes home."

"When's that?"

"Tomorrow night."

"So I have you to myself until then. We can still do dinner tonight. We'll feed the cat and then head out. My treat."

"You don't need to pay for everything," Ben said. "I have money too, you know."

Tim shrugged. "I can afford it."

"How?"

Tim's brow furrowed, as if the question was complicated. It might be, but Ben needed an answer.

"I inherited some money," Tim said. "A lot, actually."

Ben's stomach sank, his fears backed by one more detail. "From who?"

"No one you would know," Tim answered.

Ben didn't press any further, but he didn't offer another topic of conversation. His short-lived vow of silence paid off.

"His name was Eric. He was a friend of mine. He died late last year."

"I'm sorry," Ben said. "Still," he added after a moment, "it's a little unusual. Inheriting money from a friend, I mean."

"Is it?"

"Yeah. Unless he was your sugar daddy or something." Ben gave an artificial laugh that didn't convince either of them.

"Allison has filled you in on the rumors then?" Tim's jaw clenched. "I guess there's no point in telling you what you already know. Eric was rich, old, and gay. What else could it have been, right?"

"I don't know," Ben replied weakly, surprised at the sudden anger in Tim's voice.

"Well it's bullshit! People think the whole world revolves around sex and money, but they're wrong. Eric was a good person and one of the best friends I ever had. That's *all* he wanted. Friendship."

Ben didn't know what to say, but he was afraid he fit into the category of the small-minded. Some rich old guy wanted Tim around for company and nothing more? Had Eric been blind? Add money to the equation and the whole thing stank.

"I didn't mean to pry."

"Yeah, you did, but it's okay." Tim's posture relaxed a little. "I just get tired of what people say. They don't know me. They take a couple of facts and warp them into something they can feel superior about."

"Yeah, that does suck. So what's the truth?"

"He was like a father to me. The way I always wish things had been with my real dad. He knew everything about anything, was funny, and had the craziest ideas. Talking to him was the greatest. That's all we'd ever do. He was already pretty sick when I met him, so he couldn't get out more. We'd just sit there and talk for hours. Hell, I practically became his nurse. It was the best time of my life. Well, second-best."

Ben knew he shouldn't ask, but he wanted to be sure. "So there was never sex involved?"

"No! Christ! Can't gay people just be friends?"

"Sorry," Ben apologized. "It's just the money thing—"

"What else was he supposed to do with it? He didn't have any kids. Just a sister. She got most of the money. I got a small part, which really was still a tremendous amount. And the house. She didn't want it anyway."

Ben exhaled, trying to imagine what he would do if he were suddenly wealthy. Tim seemed lost in thought the rest of the drive home. Ben also had much to think about. Neglecting Samson and then hearing about Tim's strange relationship with Eric had taken the shine off their fairytale day. He found himself missing Jace and the simple life they shared. If only he were coming home tonight.

The afternoon's surrealism only increased when he walked into Jace's apartment with Tim. His ex-boyfriend silently took in the apartment, examining the walls and making his own judgments. Was he sizing up Jace and mentally knocking him down? Did he feel intimidated or insecure? Did he ever?

"Should I make us something to eat?" Ben asked after tending to Samson.

"No, let's go out. It'll be fun."

Ben agreed, eager to get Tim away from the apartment.

"Tell you what," Tim said once they were back in his car. "Why don't we avoid the crowds? We'll go back to my place and I'll cook for you."

"Eh, I don't know." Ben saw the ruse to get him somewhere private.

"It'll be cool," Tim said, switching lanes. "You'll like it there."

"Said the spider to the fly," Ben muttered.

Tim lived out in West Lake Hills. The area was notoriously expensive. Tim's house was modern with rustic elements. The main part of the home was a jumble of minimalistic cubes, but the covered entrance was hewn from rough-cut wood and supported by twisted iron columns. The window shutters were warped with age and reinforced with crisscrossing wire, as if the architect had created them with recycled chicken coops. Even more out of place was the separate garage, as unremarkably middle class as possible. Maybe that was the architect's intention. One touch of normality to put the rest of the building's eccentricities into context. The result felt like a tornado had swept up a cabin, a suburban home, and a museum of modern art and dropped them again all jumbled together.

Tim parked his car in the driveway and led the way to the door. The interior was just as eclectic as the exterior, although with much more warmth. Thick colorful carpets were strewn across polished wooden floors. Oversized couches and chairs in earthy colors filled the spaces they walked through. In the living room, practical bookshelves built low into the wall doubled as benches and were set in front of tall windows on either side of the fireplace. The massive kitchen, their final destination, had all the trappings of a professional restaurant, including two ranges and an indoor grill. Ben sat at one of the bar stools at the kitchen's island and stared.

"I gotta hit the john," Tim said, slipping off his sneakers. "There's anything you could ever want to drink in here. Feel free to poke around."

"Thanks," Ben said.

Wherever the bathroom was, he worried Tim might need half an hour to navigate the sprawling floor plan. Ben opened the refrigerator and grabbed a can of cola. The noise it made when he popped it open sounded deafening in the silence. Despite its cozy appearance, the house felt lonely, the humming appliances too loud in the stillness. A home without a family was a haunted place. Here it was easy to imagine why Eric was desperate for company, and how Tim's proud speech and laughter could chase away the emptiness. But it wasn't Eric who was now left here alone.

"It's a huge house," Tim said, causing Ben to jump. "Too big for me. I plan on selling it and finding a place in Allandale, so don't go getting used to it."

Ben rolled his eyes at the flirtation but smiled. "Allandale is a nice neighborhood, but I don't know if you're enough of a hippie to fit in there. Eric really lived here alone?"

"Yeah, when I first met him. It wasn't long before he asked me to move in. Don't give me that look! I can see what you're thinking."

"What would you think if anyone told you the same story?"

Ben said. "You have to admit that it sounds fishy."

"I guess so," Tim conceded. "You believe me though, right?"

"Why not? The world's a crazy place."

"I would have though."

"What?"

"Slept with Eric." Tim nodded to himself. "If it would have made him happy, but he never even hinted at that."

"Did you want to?"

"I don't know." Tim started to pull ingredients out of the cupboards. "Sometimes you can't tell your friends from your lovers, you know what I mean? The line gets kind of blurry. That's how it was with me and Eric. Maybe if he wasn't on so many meds he would have wanted something more physical. Or maybe not."

"What was wrong with him?"

"Cancer. Multiple kinds, multiple places."

"Geez."

"Yeah." Tim paused, staring blindly at the items in front of him. "He toughed it out until the end. Eric never complained, never felt sorry for himself. He had so much spirit. That's why I can't sell the place yet. It feels like he's still here."

Ben watched him with curiosity. The Tim he knew of old never would have expressed his emotions so openly and without shame. If only he had been this way five years ago.

"Anyway," Tim forced an upbeat tone, "What did you have in mind for dinner?"

Ben took stock of the ingredients gathered on the counter. There was pasta, a can of pineapple, a box of rice, a bag of flour and some brown sugar.

"You don't know how to cook, do you?"

"Busted!" Tim laughed. "But I had to get you here somehow. We could do delivery. Or we could get nostalgic and you could cook for me. I'll even lay myself out on the couch and pretend my ankle is jacked up."

"Tim—" Ben's warning tone matched his expression.

"Too far? Sorry. I just wanted you to see my home, since it's so connected to my past. You being here really livens the place up. I wouldn't mind you visiting more often. Bring Jace along. I'd love to meet him."

Ben eyed him, trying to weigh his sincerity. "All right.

I'll cook, but you have to help. I don't care how rich you are, everyone should know how to make at least one meal."

Even without many fresh ingredients in the house, they managed to put together a decent sauce made from canned tomatoes and spices they found in the cupboard. Some aged cheese grated over the top, along with a blend of pastas for variety, completed the dish. They ate straight from the pot, laughing about old memories and arguing over misremembered details.

The makeshift meal was, unfortunately, very endearing. As much comfort as Ben took in Jace's experience and the security that provided, he was aware of something equally gratifying in how much Tim needed from him. Ben began to wish that Tim was an annoyingly talented cook, had acquired his wealth by illicit means, and was still emotionally stunted. Instead he was doing everything right to reawaken Ben's old feelings.

"I really need to get back to Jace's," Ben said while Tim was digging through the freezer for ice cream.

"Aw, you can't leave. You haven't even done the dishes yet!" Tim winced at Ben's glare. "Only kidding. Geez! There is a pool here, you know. We could go for a swim, have a couple of beers. You can even crash here."

Ben scoffed. "I don't think so!"

"Your virtue will remain unchallenged, princess, you have my word. There are two guest rooms. Take your pick. I'll even sleep in the car."

Ben's trust in Tim wasn't the issue. Rather he didn't trust himself. Ben needed very badly to go home, relieve some sexual tension, and reexamine everything from a healthy distance. After resisting a few more onslaughts of charm, he won and was driven back to Jace's apartment. Tim killed the ignition after parking, the resulting silence creating pressure in the car. Why was it suddenly so hard to reach over and open the door?

"Thanks for the last couple of days," Tim said. "I know I went a little overboard, but it's been a long time since I've had someone like you around."

"I enjoyed it too," Ben said, "but I'm also looking forward to Jace being back tomorrow."

"Hint taken," Tim said with good humor. "I'm serious about meeting him. The man behind the legend and all that."

"Yeah?
"Yeah."
"Okay."

Maybe it would be fun. The two greatest loves of his life together in one place. What could possibly go wrong, aside from everything. The scientists who split the atom had probably felt the same way. They knew their actions might be dangerous, but like Ben, they were too damn curious to stop themselves.

CHAPTER 23

The airport buzzed with conversation as people wove around each other with the precision of worker bees tending a hive. Outside the security checkpoint, a group of people waited, each fidgeting with anticipation, their minds focused on the arriving passengers. All but Ben, who couldn't stop thinking of the cell phone turned off and stowed away in a kitchen drawer. Instinct had driven him to hide it. Only later did he consider how incriminating this behavior appeared.

Hugs burst out around him as reunions took place, but he couldn't stop thinking of that phone. Had he the time, Ben would have driven home and set it out on the counter in plain view or even brought it with him. Anything was better than it being hidden.

"Ben?"

Luggage in tow, Jace was dressed in uniform, wearing only a vest over his dress shirt and tie due to the warm season. His smile was amused, as if Ben was being silly by staring at him so dumbly. Then those long arms enveloped him in a hug. The scent of Jace's aftershave and the murmured words against his neck were like a tonic. With a single kiss, Jace broke Tim's spell and woke Cinderella up from the strange dream of the last few days. Or perhaps he should call himself Benderella instead. Or better yet, he could focus on the wonderful man standing before him.

"I'm so glad you're back!" Ben nearly broke down into tears as he said this, which would have been even stranger than hiding a cell phone.

Once they were home, Ben expressed his desperation in the bedroom. Jace might not have understood why he was behaving this way, but he was happy to comply. Only afterwards, securely nestled in Jace's arms, did Ben feel safe enough to speak the truth.

"I ran into Tim the other day."

"Ah," Jace said, the puzzle pieces falling into place. No need for an explanation. There was only ever one Tim, and Jace knew Ben's history well enough to understand how monumental an impact this would have on him. "I don't suppose he's horribly overweight? Probably bald and missing a few teeth too, I imagine."

Ben wanted to laugh, but instead the details poured out, everything except his fear that he still had feelings for Tim. Jace would share the same worry, so there was little point in voicing it. There were no arguments or accusations, not from Jace, but he did frown about the cell phone, and sighed at the mention of the theme park visit. For once Jace had little advice to offer. Instead he held Ben tightly, as if knowing this was the more effective strategy.

As they dozed off, Ben's mind drifted to the distant teenage world he had once inhabited. All of it seemed so far away. This new version of Tim, with his money and strange connection to an older man, didn't fit into that time and place. If not for all the reminiscing about the past they had done, Tim wouldn't have felt like the same person at all. Jace was reassuringly familiar, a solid part of the last two years that Ben intended to hold onto like flotsam in a storm-ravaged sea.

The cell phone came out of its drawer, but only two days later did Ben consider turning it on. His finger hovered over the power button, as if pressing it would summon a genie from its lamp. Not the big blue friendly variety, but the sort who twisted the meaning of a wish before granting it. Ben hated that Tim was all alone inside his silent mansion, but at least there he didn't pose a threat to his happily-ever-after with Jace. And so the genie bottle stayed plugged. They were just friends, after all. Friends could go days without speaking. Weeks even!

Or about four days as it turned out. After class, Ben made a token appearance at home for Allison's sake before rushing over to Jace's apartment, stopping along the way to pick up their favorite Thai food. He took the steps two at a time and rapped on the door instead of struggling with his keys. The door swung open, but where someone tall and debonair should have stood was someone brawny and completely unexpected.

"For a pizza boy, you're pretty hot," Tim said.

Mouth agape, Ben stared until Jace arrived on the scene. He gave a helpless little shrug from behind Tim before speaking. "Look who dropped by. Says he has a surprise for us."

"It's nothing really," Tim said, gesturing for Ben to come in as if it were his apartment.

This was getting a little creepy. Then again, Tim had been

on the receiving end of such behavior back in high school. Ben hadn't been near as transparent, although as stalkers went, he could do a lot worse. He kissed Jace hello, which felt strangely like cheating, before heading to the living room to tackle his food. Let them do the talking. He planned to keep his head down and his mouth full until the entire incident was over.

The doorbell rang, causing Tim to jump out of his seat just seconds after he had sat.

"*That* must be the pizza," he said.

"Or another ex-boyfriend, who knows," Jace murmured as he watched him leave the room. "So, that's the famous Tim?"

Ben nodded, following it up with a sympathetic sigh. "How long has he been here?"

"Half an hour or so," Jace answered, poking around in the Thai bag for any sign of a fortune cookie. "He's a little different than I expected. You didn't tell me that he looked so— Uh…"

"Abercrombie and Fitch?"

"Exactly."

"Well, maybe he's here for a threesome," Ben said in just the right tone to pass it off as a joke.

"You're more than enough for me," Jace replied smoothly. "Anyone else in the bedroom would be an unwelcome distraction."

Ben smiled, surprised by the feeling of relief. At least he could count on Jace not to develop any unwanted feelings for Tim.

"Look, Ben—" Whatever else Jace was going to say was cut short by Tim's reappearance in the room, pizza balanced on one palm.

Ben bartered for a few slices by offering some of his Thai food, and soon they were all eating a mix of both meals. The combination was strange and never meant to intermingle, but the same could be said about those dining together. Ben watched while Tim focused on developing a rapport with Jace. Was he interested in who Ben had chosen to be with or was he sizing up the competition, gaining his trust and collecting data that he could later use?

Once the mashup meal was finished, Tim finally revealed the purpose of his visit.

"I have a friend, well, the friend of a friend really, who is throwing a big birthday party at Splashtown in San Antonio."

Ben didn't know San Antonio had a Splashtown, but he
assumed it was the same as the one in Houston: a massive water
park full of pools and slides.

"Marcello has the whole place booked for his party," Tim
continued. "He just so happens to owe me a favor, and I asked
if I could bring you guys along."

The pretense for dropping by was weak, but Ben's interest
was piqued. Crowds and lines always limited the fun at theme
parks, but there would only be so many guests at a birthday
party. As a kid he'd always fantasized about never having to get
off the rollercoaster, and this was the next best thing.

One look at Jace brought these fantasies to a screeching halt,
the smile on his face *slightly* too tight. His boyfriend was being
polite, but he wasn't interested.

"We don't have to go," Ben told him when Tim slipped away
to the restroom.

"But you want to," Jace said.

"Well, yeah, it would be fun, but we could always go together
some other time."

"Do you plan on staying friends with Tim?" Jace asked. "He's
going to be in your life from now on?"

Ben cast a nervous glance toward the bathroom. He knew the
risks, but he also didn't like the idea of abandoning Tim to his
lonely life. Tim must have other friends too, like this Marcello
person, but he seemed so happy to be around Ben, so grateful.
"I guess so," he answered.

"Then it's a good idea for Tim to see us together as a couple."
Jace's vibe wasn't at all resentful, causing Ben to feel a sudden
surge of love for him. Any other guy would be jealous and
possessive, but Jace's solution was to welcome Tim into their
lives.

Ben didn't celebrate yet. This trip could turn awkward,
and fast! Tim brought out the impulsive teenager in him, while
being around Jace encouraged Ben to be smart and responsible.
Situations like these always made him feel like he had multiple
personalities and left him unsure of how to act. No, their trip to
Splashtown would be a disaster. Only a miracle could save the
day. Or his own personal superhero…

— — —

"Double date!" Allison sang as they piled into the car.

Ben beamed at his secret weapon. Allison was the ultimate

solution to his problems. She would interact with whichever guy Ben wasn't talking to. That way he could be himself around either one. Already she had outperformed his expectations, calling shotgun and sitting up front with Tim to keep him occupied. That left Ben free to snuggle up with Jace in the backseat, although this only worked for so long. Tim started craning his neck to talk to Ben, the car swerving dangerously as the road was ignored.

At the next gas station they thanked various gods that they were still alive and decided to switch plans. Allison hopped into the backseat with Ben, making Jace sit up front. Whenever either of the guys tried to talk to them, Allison and Ben would break into song or pretend to be deep in conversation. Eventually the two men were forced to keep each other company instead.

Once they arrived and a guard checked their names against a list, they were allowed into Splashtown. The restaurant nearest the gate was set up as birthday headquarters. Marcello turned out to be a toadish man of fifty—according to the banners at least—whose fingers, wrists, and neck all sparkled with jewelry.

"Bling bling," Ben murmured to Allison as they watched Tim greet the man and give him a hug.

"Why are all his friends old men with money?" Allison whispered back.

"I don't know," Ben said, trying not to judge. "How come all of ours are young and poor?"

She snorted in response. "You're right. Maybe it's time we mingle with high society. Allison Cross," she said louder, stepping in front of Tim to offer her hand.

"Charmed," Marcello replied. "On a day when I am facing the second half of my life, it's nice to be reminded of the effortless beauty of youth. Speaking of which, who do we have here?"

Tim gestured at them. "This is Benjamin Bentley. Oh, and Jace Holden."

"Ah! Guests of honor!" Marcello gripped Ben's hand first, but quickly turned his attention on Jace. Not only did they shake hands, but Marcello placed a palm on Jace's forearm and left it there while staring into his eyes. "My goodness! I could be mistaken, but I believe the temperature just went up a few degrees."

Jace responded with good humor. "My hand is definitely feeling the heat."

"My apologies," Marcello said, releasing him, but not right

away. "Why don't you all strip down to your swimsuits and cool down, either by taking a dip in the pool or—better yet—by joining me in the air conditioning? Yes! I insist!"

"Why would we need our swimsuits then?" Ben countered.

Marcello barely spared him a glance. "Or leave them off entirely. I don't mind. That would expedite the cooling down process, although I would imagine it having the opposite effect on me."

"Swimming sounds good," Tim said, suddenly eager to guide them away. Once they were at a respectable distance he added, "Marcello has a strange sense of humor."

And his ex-boyfriend kept strange company. This wasn't the only mystery to distract Ben. They went to the nearest locker room to change. Jace stayed close to him, which made it easy not to peek, but once they were outside again, there was no avoiding it. He hadn't seen Tim shirtless since high school. Of course Ben was curious. Tim's physique was a strange mix of the familiar and the unknown. The curves and lines of his muscles were mostly the same, just bigger, and he now had a scar running down his shoulder. Ben wondered about the story behind it. Where had Tim been the past five years? Would his body feel different to the touch?

Some hurried mental exertion was necessary to avoid embarrassment. Turning his attention on Jace didn't help, since the playful swim trunks with a pink flamingo theme only put Ben more in the mood. He loved how Jace was confident enough to be goofy. Allison was the only safe person to look at, an ironic truth considering how stunning she looked in her bikini.

Music pumped from the park's loudspeakers as they walked the park. Occasionally they would pass another group of birthday guests, but there were no crowds, and most waterslides were without lines. The lifeguards on duty yawned in the sun, many only perking up when Allison came around. At the third set of slides—blue covered tubes that twisted in all directions—Ben's secret weapon defected.

"You can't leave me," Ben complained. "You're supposed to be my chaperone!"

"Just look at him!" Allison nodded in the direction of a lifeguard who was openly flexing his ebony muscles. "And what do you mean 'chaperone'? I thought I was just running interference. Don't tell me you're tempted!"

"I'm not," Ben said, tearing his eyes away from the lifeguard. "Are you sure you want to hang around here when there's a whole park to explore?"

"As tempting as it is to spend the entire day with gay men, I'll take my chances with tall, dark, and interested over there."

Down to three now, their little party hit the wave pool next, followed by tubing around the winding river before they returned to the restaurant for some food. Afterwards they debated whether the "wait thirty minutes after eating" rule was an urban legend or not. In the end they compromised by lounging in the artificial lagoon.

Unlike the rest of the park, the water here was dark, the bottom lined with sand. Half the lagoon was ringed by a beach, the rest by a jumble of rocks coursing with waterfalls. Together they waded into the water, engaging in the usual antics of splashing and dunking each other. Jace eventually retreated to the beach to catch some sun while Tim went to explore the rocks. Ben floated on his back, idly watching the clouds drift across the azure sky. He was in danger of dozing off when Tim called out to him.

"Check it out! There's a cave behind this one."

Ben chuckled to himself. This was sure to make the evening news. *Tim Wyman, budding archeologist, discovered a previously unknown cave in Splashtown today.*

"You coming?" Ben asked, turning to look toward the shore.

Jace didn't respond or move from his deck chair, meaning that he was probably sleeping behind those sunglasses. Ben made a mental note to turn him over later before he burned. Then he went exploring.

The central waterfall was the strongest, and it was here that Tim stood, the water coursing over him. He waited until Ben was near before holding an arm out, redirecting the water and creating a makeshift entrance. Ben bowed through, ending up in a small cave with an even smaller pool, the water only reaching his waist.

"You know this is where everyone goes to pee," Ben said.

Tim grinned, joining him in the water. "Or to do other things."

"They should put a hot tub in here," Ben replied, doing his

best to ignore the come-on. "That would be way cooler."

"I liked hearing you sing today," Tim said. "In the car. It was nice."

Blood rushed to his cheeks. "Thanks."

"Sometimes at night, on the very edge of sleep, I swear I can hear you singing." Tim paused and laughed. "That sounds cheesy, but it's true. Never in a million years did I think you'd be in my life again, that I really would be able to hear the sound of your voice."

Ben looked to the ceiling, hoping to find some random detail to turn the conversation toward. This was where he was supposed to recognize Tim's intentions and shoot him down, heading back out into the open where his boyfriend was waiting. His brain knew this was the best course of action. His body disagreed. His heart was just confused.

"Do you still paint?" Ben managed at last.

Tim remained silent until Ben looked at him. Then he sloshed through the water toward him. Ben started to say something, but Tim shook his head warningly, white tiger eyes locked onto their prey.

Ben remained frozen in place, his heart thudding furiously as Tim closed the gap between them. He stopped, just inches away, near enough that Ben could feel the heat of his skin. Tim reached up and touched a lock of hair above Ben's right ear. Then his fingers slid to the back of his head, gently taking hold before pulling Ben in for a kiss.

At first Ben didn't respond. The last part of him that still resisted wouldn't allow his lips to move. But it was too late. The rules had been broken, trust had been betrayed. All that was left now was to enjoy it. He kissed back, their bodies pressing together, Ben's hands eagerly discovering all that had changed, and rejoicing in what remained the same. He moaned against Tim's lips when he felt their increasingly hard cocks rub together through their swimsuits.

Then the breaking of the waterfall's steady rhythm stopped them both.

"About done?" Jace asked evenly.

Ben shoved Tim away so hard he fell backward in the water. This left his bulge exposed, but it was clear from Jace's expression that he had seen enough anyway.

"I'm sorry," Ben apologized as Tim stood back up.

Jace didn't look away from Ben. Already his anger had faded to disappointment.

"Maybe you should wait for us outside, Tim," Jace suggested.

"I'm so sorry," Ben sputtered once they were alone. "It just sort of happened. I don't know—"

"It's all right."

Ben couldn't believe his ears. "What?"

"I said it's all right," Jace repeated, sitting on the rocky shelf next to the entrance. "I knew something like this would happen eventually, if it hadn't already."

"I didn't do anything with him before!" Ben said. "Just now, I promise."

Jace shrugged, seemingly unconcerned.

"Aren't you angry?"

"Not really. Old feelings don't just disappear overnight. It's normal that you and Tim still find each other attractive."

"That's it?" Maybe it was the hormones still coursing through his system, but Ben was starting to feel angry enough for the both of them. He would have been furious if he had caught Jace making out with someone. Ben wanted Jace to tell him off. He had it coming! Ben had done something wrong and now it was time for him to pay the price. Or were Jace's feelings for him so flimsy that he honestly didn't mind?

"I wish you *were* pissed," Ben blurted out. "At least then I could tell that you care."

Jace looked confused. "I care," he said, his irritation rising as he stood. "I just thought I'd give you the benefit of the doubt."

"What's there to doubt?" Ben demanded. "You saw everything. I did something stupid, and you should hate me for it!"

"I'd never hate you," Jace said solemnly.

Ben bit back tears. A furious Jace would have been so much easier to deal with. Instead he was hurt, and it was all Ben's fault. Normally when Jace was unhappy, Ben would kiss away his pain. He couldn't do that now, especially considering where his lips had been. Jace might not hate him, but Ben was starting to hate himself.

A shadow moved behind the waterfall before Tim pushed through again.

"Hey," he said to Jace. "It's my fault. I grabbed Benjamin and started kissing him. He wasn't even kissing back. Really. Please don't blame him." The apology might have been effective if Tim wasn't grinning while delivering it.

Jace punched Tim. One moment he was standing there in perfect stillness, the next he had swung with the lightning fast reflexes of a cobra and slugged Tim right in the jaw. The smacking noise was still echoing throughout the cave when Tim fell back into the water. Jace grabbed him after his head submerged and leaned him against a wall until he recovered enough to stand on his own.

"How's that for angry?" Jace said to Ben. "Come on, we're going home."

Ben risked only the smallest glance at Tim as he followed Jace out of the cave. He expected to see shame, humiliation, maybe even anger. Instead he noticed that Tim's jaw—as sore as it might be—was now set with determination.

Considering how drastically hormones could impair judgment, sometimes even more potently than drugs or alcohol, they should be classified as a controlled substance. Ben felt he was living proof of this. One act of impulse that had lasted seconds now threatened to destroy years' worth of love with Jace. He had never imagined that a single kiss could come at such a high cost.

The car they were cruising along in wasn't free either, but Ben felt lucky to be a passenger in it. Jace had insisted on walking to the rental company alone, which was only down the road from Splashtown, but as he began his hike, Ben feared that would be the last they saw of each other. Alone in a near empty parking lot, he had little else to do but replay the mistake he'd made over and over again. When the rental car had actually pulled up he nearly wept with relief.

"I'm sorry," he mumbled for what felt like the thousandth time. For once Jace didn't respond with his standard "It's all right." Maybe he had finally decided that it wasn't.

Jace shifted in his seat and sighed. "I had a close call once."

"Close call?"

"About six months ago. On a flight to Boston. We had a real nervous flyer, a younger guy. I'm not sure he was even eighteen, but he was attractive. Very attractive." Jace glanced over at Ben without malice. "Anyway, he was one of those rare people who have a genuine phobia of flying. He had never flown before and had no idea of his own fear until we were in the air. I had to sit with him the entire flight and talk him through it while holding his hand."

"That's not quite the same," Ben pointed out.

"Let me finish. Once we landed he suggested we have a drink together. I suspected he only wanted someone old enough to buy him alcohol from the bar, but I figured he had earned it and I was off work for the day, so—"

"Did something happen?" Ben asked, wanting to hear the end of the story. The anticipation was torture.

"Almost," Jace continued. "My personal life became a topic, and even though I mentioned you during the course of the evening, he still tried to kiss me when we were saying goodbye. He was hot, and I won't lie and say that I didn't want to, but I made my choice when I decided to be with you."

"So you didn't?"

"No. I didn't."

Ben sighed, feeling relieved but also twice as guilty. The mere idea of Jace cheating hurt. How much pain then had Ben's actual infidelity caused?

"There's a difference though," Jace continued. "You were once in love with Tim. You probably still are to some extent. You two have a history, and that complicates matters."

"I still shouldn't have kissed him."

"Get over it," Jace snapped. "What's more important to me is what you're going to do now. You're stuck with an old-fashioned guy. I like monogamy. I don't want to have a threesome or share you with anyone. So now you need to decide if you can handle that or not."

"I think I can," Ben said.

"Good." Jace nodded. "The next thing you have to figure out is what you're going to do about Tim. I'm not going to forbid you to see him. I'm not going to say you can't be his friend. I'm going to trust you now as much as I did before. There's no point in going on otherwise. But I want you to ask yourself if you can resist doing something like this again."

The question weighed on his mind the rest of the drive home. Was it possible to love two people at the same time? Jace seemed to think so and Ben's heart was in agreement. Couldn't Jace and Tim hit it off? They could all be in love and pile into bed at night. Then again, the jealousy Ben felt while Jace talked about his own close call made him wonder if he could really handle such a scenario.

No sense in dwelling on that fantasy, since Jace wasn't willing. What mattered now was whether Ben could get himself under control enough to be friends with Tim and nothing else. He wasn't the only one who needed convincing. Their attraction to each other was mutual. They could never only be friends, because every time Ben looked at Tim, all he saw was his high school sweetheart. Much in the same way that he couldn't picture Jace as being anything but his boyfriend.

Choosing between them wasn't easy. Jace was kind, worldly, and loving. Tim was aloof, artistic, and passionate. But only one man had never given up on Ben, even though he now had good reason to. Jace had stuck by him over the years. Tim had not.

"I've made my choice," Ben said, reaching over to take Jace's hand.

"Good." Jace flipped the turn signal and took the exit ramp for Austin. "Now there's one final obstacle we both have to face."

"What's that?"

"How to apologize to Allison. We left her at the park."

Ben groaned. With all that had transpired, she had slipped his mind. Earning back Jace's trust and saying goodbye to Tim no longer seemed such a daunting task compared to the hurricane of anger he'd face when Allison finally found her way home again.

CHAPTER 24

How did someone go about deliberately ending a friendship? Television dramas were full of breakups, but those usually involved moments of high passion. Breaking up with a friend was more subtle and calculated. Were there any guidelines to be followed? Was breaking up in person required? Or did one friend simply stop calling the other and let the bond gradually deteriorate into nothing?

Ben had already called Tim to tell him that they needed to talk. In retrospect, he probably should have been more specific. What if Tim was getting his hopes up? Ben had considered meeting him in public, but worried that one of them might cry, which would be embarrassing. Instead he was on his way to Tim's house. He debated stopping to grab some booze. Getting drunk with Tim wasn't advisable, but a beer could help make this talk easier on them both. Even better, Ben could have an alcohol-free beer and leave a six-pack for Tim to nurse his wounds with.

He pulled into a strip mall and parked in front of one of the small liquor stores that were often found near major grocery chains. An unexpected sight attracted his attention on his way into the store. In the parking lot, a large blue van had both its rear doors open. A baby gate stretched across the gap, rattling occasionally as something tried to escape. A disheveled woman adjusted the gate before replacing a fallen sign that read *Free Puppies*. Memories of Wilford prompted Ben to investigate.

"Looking for a pet?" the woman asked as he approached.

"Not really," Ben answered, "but I sure miss having one." He looked over the gate to see only one puppy left, its tiny body a fat sausage decked out in a fur coat one size too large. The dog stopped romping around to consider him with a smooshed face. "Is it supposed to look that way?"

The woman tittered. "Totally normal for a bulldog. They only get uglier when they're older, but you'll have fallen in love by then."

"He is sort of cute," Ben admitted as he watched the puppy attempt to scale the gate. When this failed it crouched and barked instead.

"She, actually. This one's a girl. Do you have a home big enough for a dog?"

"Well no, but—" Everything clicked into place. "My friend has a huge house and he lives there all alone. I think a dog would be perfect for him."

The woman clapped her hands together, her eyes filled with desperate relief before they became shrewd. "Now, the dog is free, but I'm asking for a thirty dollar donation. Completely optional, but all proceeds go toward getting mama-dog spayed."

The woman took Ben's money, as well as any contact information she could shake out of him. She was obviously concerned about the puppy's welfare, but Ben was sure they were both making the right decision. After she handed the puppy over to him, its surprisingly powerful legs treaded air as it strained to lick his face. Then it peed down the front of his shirt. Ben laughed and brought it to his car.

Driving the rest of the way to Tim's house was a small nightmare, the animal bouncing around the interior like a rubber ball. Tim met him in the driveway, his jaw dropping when a puppy jumped out of the car.

"You got a dog?" he asked.

"No, *you* got a dog," Ben corrected.

It took a few moments of explaining, but Tim quickly took to the idea. "I don't have anything a dog needs. We've got to go shopping. Ready?"

"What, now?"

This wasn't exactly what Ben had planned, but what could he do? Was he really supposed to drop off the puppy and say a quick goodbye? So after borrowing a clean shirt, he was dragged off to a pet store with Tim and the puppy, who had been christened Chinchilla. Tim filled a shopping cart to the brim with more food and toys than a single animal could need. He ordered a doghouse that would be delivered the next day and signed up for training classes too. Chinchilla was going to have a good life.

Once they were back at Tim's home, Ben almost forgot the real reason he was there. They sat on the floor together, trying out different toys and laughing as Chinchilla made a fool of herself. She tore around the room, barking and making messes. Already the house felt more alive.

"This was a nice surprise," Tim said eventually. "I thought you were coming over to tell me that Jace wants my head on a platter."

"No." Ben's smile faded. "He was very understanding about everything, but there is something we need to talk about."

"Oh yeah?"

"I can't handle this," Ben blurted out. "My feelings for you, I mean. They never went away—"

"That's a good thing," Tim interrupted.

"No, it's not. I love Jace. I've been with him for over two years, and I plan on staying with him."

Tim reached out and grabbed his arm, as if he was afraid that Ben would try to flee. "I can give you everything he can. More even."

Ben knew arguing would be fruitless. "I'm with Jace," he said. "And that's how it's going to stay."

"Okay," Tim said, releasing him. "But that doesn't mean we can't be friends."

"Yeah, it does, because that's not how I see you."

"That's not how I see you either, so why fight it?"

"Because I love Jace, and I've already hurt him more than I ever should have."

"And you don't love me?" Tim challenged. "I know you do, because I feel the same way."

Ben struggled to remember if Tim had ever said "I love you" when they were younger. Was he even saying it now, or just implying that he did?

Ben stood. "I have to go. I don't think we should see each other. For a while at least."

"Benjamin, wait!" Tim called after him.

He couldn't. Ben didn't dare stay a second longer. He ran for the car, and as he pulled out and drove away, he saw Tim holding Chinchilla back so she wouldn't run into the street. The hurt on his face matched the ache in Ben's heart, but at least he knew that Tim would no longer be alone.

Whatever academic gods were out there received multiple daily prayers from Ben, mostly as pleas to help him complete his finals and put formal education behind him forever. Other times he thanked them for providing limitless distraction during a difficult situation. The first time he had said goodbye to Tim had been against his will. Now it was his own doing, but he still couldn't claim that this was what he wanted.

Scholarly pressure accelerated time until two months had gone by, and even though Ben thought of Tim every single day, his relationship with Jace was back on track. Some weeks they barely managed to see each other, but when they did their relationship was just as loving and intimate as before. If Jace harbored a grudge, he didn't show it.

After a late study session in the library one evening, Ben had decided to go home, a term that now referred to Jace's apartment. He had barely stayed a night at his duplex in the previous month. Allison wouldn't normally tolerate such a thing, but she was busy with her own finals.

Ben was leaping up the stairs to the apartment when he saw someone tacking a note to the door.

The stranger turned when he heard Ben approaching, eyes and mouth wide in surprise. The eyeliner, base, and powder on his young face meant he was only a microphone away from being in a boy band. Surprise became disinterest before the stranger turned away, evidently feeling Ben's presence was of no consequence.

The boy band reject had already reached the far set of stairs when Ben saw that the note was addressed to Jace. His name was surrounded by hand-drawn hearts. Underneath these was a long series of X's and O's followed by the name Aaron.

"Hey!" Ben called after him.

"Oh," Aaron said when he turned around. "Are you Jace's roommate or something?"

"I'm his boyfriend," Ben challenged.

"Yeah, right," Aaron laughed. "'fraid I beat you to that one! Make sure he gets that note, 'kay?"

Aaron turned and walked down the stairs toward the parking lot. Ben felt like grabbing him by his over-styled hair and dragging him back for some answers, but he figured the note would tell him all he needed to know. He tore it off the door and went inside, ignoring Samson's purrs of greeting.

The note was written in purple ink in handwriting that was annoyingly loopy. It read:

Surprise! Bet you didn't expect to see me so soon, huh? My parents sprung for a ticket. Guess I should have called ahead to tell you I was cumming. At least I hope I will be. How about a rerun of what we did in your hotel? Then again, maybe not. I'm still sore! Just in case you forgot my number-

Ben glanced at the number to confirm that it was a cell phone from a different area code. Blood boiling, he let the note fall to the ground and ran outside to chase after Aaron. He circled the block to no avail. When he came back, Jace was struggling to get the key into the door, arms loaded with bags of groceries.

"Hey!" he said happily when he saw Ben. "You ready for dinner?"

"A note just came for you," Ben said, trying to keep his face impassive.

"A note?"

Ben gestured for him to enter. Once they were in the apartment, he swiped the note off the floor and handed it to Jace. Ben searched his face as he read it. Jace looked puzzled, as if he didn't understand, but Ben knew he had a good poker face—a necessary flight attendant skill.

"Is this some sort of joke?" Jace asked.

"Come on. Where were you last week?"

"A lot of places," Jace replied.

"Including Boston?"

"Yeah. So?" Recognition dawned. "You think— No, this isn't from that kid. I haven't talked to him since."

"Since what exactly?" Ben demanded, wondering how many boy-toys Jace had scattered across the U.S. Like a sailor pulling into port, he probably had one waiting for him in every state.

"You know the story. Nothing happened. This is—" Jace gestured with the note. "I don't know what this is."

"It's perfectly clear what it is," Ben shouted. "Or is there another gay guy next door named Jace, and Aaron just happened to pick the wrong door?"

Jace set down the note, took a deep breath, and looked Ben in the eye. "I've never cheated on you."

"Then how do you explain it?"

Jace shrugged and considered the question for a moment. "If I had to guess, I expect Tim thought this might—"

"Tim? Get a grip, Jace! He's not Moriarty! I saw the guy who put this on the door, and it sure as hell wasn't Tim."

Jace's jaw clenched, his patience finally nearing its end. "I don't know what's going on, but if anyone deserves to be under suspicion, it's you!"

That was enough to send Ben over the edge. Their words became more heated and ugly with every sentence. Blinded by rage, one of them shouted that it was over. Afterwards it was difficult to remember who.

Ben ended up back at the duplex after driving recklessly through town. What he needed was to talk to Allison. Unfortunately she wasn't home. He waited for two hours, pacing the house and trying to make sense of his thoughts when the painting caught his eye. Two hearts, overlapping in a swarm of fiery colors.

Why the hell not? He would go see Tim. Ben could confront him, because maybe Jace was right. Maybe this was some crackpot scheme to get them to split up. If so, it had apparently worked. Some of the anger ebbed away, replaced by sorrow. They hadn't really broken up, had they?

Tim's car was in the driveway of his house, but so was another he didn't recognize. Ben thought of Aaron, certain that he was here and conspiring with Tim over their next move. He pounded on the door. Tim answered almost immediately, looking surprised but happy.

"Benjamin!"

"Who's here?" Ben growled, feeling like an over-possessive husband.

"Just someone from school," Tim said.

Ben pushed past him and stepped over Chinchilla, whose whole butt wagged in greeting. He stomped into the living room to discover a mousey girl poring over spiral notebooks.

"Is that your car outside?" Ben asked, suddenly feeling stupid.

"Huh?" the girl replied, finally noticing him. "Yeah. Do I need to move it?"

"No. Sorry."

"Actually," Tim said, entering the room, "we're going to have to do this tomorrow. Something's come up."

"There's only two days left!" the girl complained.

"I know," Tim said. "We'll really nail it tomorrow, promise."

The girl didn't look convinced, but she gathered up her things and left.

Ben sat on the couch, head spinning. Chinchilla yapped at his feet before piddling in excitement. Tim was there almost instantly with paper towels. He eyed Ben with concern as he cleaned up the mess.

"You didn't leave a note on Jace's door, did you?" Ben asked. "Or have someone else do it?"

"No. Why? What happened?"

Ben started to explain, getting worked up again in the process. Tim interrupted him to run to the kitchen. He came back with two bottles of beer. After a long swig, Ben's words poured out, some angry and others confused. Tim didn't offer any advice. He only made sympathetic noises and occasionally asked a question.

Once Ben's demons were expelled, another round of beers was fetched and they began talking about their end-of-studies stress. Both of them were under pressure, but Tim was taking it much easier than Ben. Considering that he was already independently wealthy, he had little need for a degree.

"Why are you even bothering?" Ben asked him. "I'd drop it all in a second if I were in your shoes."

"I promised Eric."

They heated up a couple of frozen pizzas and downed them with another round of beers. The light had left the day now, along with Ben's sobriety. He rarely drank, so three beers was his version of a binge. When their buzzes began to wear off, leaving them tired, Ben followed Tim upstairs and made a clumsy pass at him. Tim gently pushed him away and redirected him to one of the guest rooms. If Ben needed proof that Tim was innocent, this was more than enough.

Ben slogged through the next two days of classes with his brain to the grindstone—not the traditional saying, but exactly how he felt. For once Tim wasn't on his mind. Ben was too upset about the rift between him and Jace. This drove him to distraction until he finally gave in and called.

"Where are you?"

"Chicago."

"Are you flying back tonight?"

"No. Not for a couple of days."

"Oh."

"Look, Ben, I think we both said things we didn't mean, but I think we should take a break."

Ben couldn't respond.

"You have a lot going on right now with school," Jace continued. "I understand how much pressure you're under. I remember. Focus on your finals and your thesis and make sure you graduate. Once that is out of the way, then we can talk, okay?"

"I guess."

"Good. I love you."

"I love you too."

Ben hung up the phone, feeling empty inside. Jace's suggestion was perfectly reasonable. Unfortunately, it was opposite of what Ben needed. He had expected Jace to say that being apart was too hard, that he was sorry for their argument. Instead he seemed to have flipped his emotional switch to off. Ben couldn't do that. As he curled up on the bed and cried, he wished more than anything that he could.

CHAPTER 25

Three days later and finals were out of the way. The last thing Ben had to worry about now was his thesis. He didn't understand why they had to be so damn long. The topic he had chosen was how pronunciation and intonation had subtly changed over the centuries. This theme had seemed a good way of combining his major in English Literature with his love of singing, and while the topic interested him, he was tired of trying to track down the source of every fact. He was tempted to write "the internet" under his references and leave it at that.

Saturday was a real scorcher, the heat making work on his thesis twice as grueling as usual. As if reading his mind, Tim called him on the cell phone.

"Two words," he began. "Swimming pool."

He could have said "free ice cubes" and Ben would have come running.

The pool behind the house had an elegant winding shape, the edges lined with stained wood, the walls covered in decorative tile. Tim, wearing the same tight swim trunks and a plain grey tank top. Balanced in one hand was a serving tray loaded with a pitcher and glasses. Chinchilla was busy dragging towels around the edge of the pool, growling as if she'd just vanquished a deadly foe. Ben sighed, unable to picture a more inviting scene.

"Monsieur," Tim said as he poured a glass of Kool-Aid.

Ben took a sip and tried not to wince. The drink mix contained too much sugar, but at least it was cold. Ben downed the rest before stripping down to his trunks and jumping in the water, Tim cannonballing after him.

"This is really nice," Ben said, treading water after submerging a couple of times.

"It's not bad," Tim said. "Too small to do any laps though, making it a glorified bathtub."

"Whatever you say. Pools are meant for relaxing, not working out."

"Working out *is* relaxing."

"Whatever, muscle boy," Ben teased.

"I don't remember you ever complaining." Tim dove

underwater, performing an underwater handstand before surfacing again. "Finals out of the way?"

"Yeah," Ben nodded.

"And Jace? You two patch things up yet?"

Ben turned in the water, not wanting Tim to see the unhappy expression on his face. "Kind of the opposite. We're taking a break."

"Wow," Tim said after a moment of silence. "Benjamin Bentley is back on the market."

"Not exactly."

"No?"

"I don't know."

Ben let the topic drop. He didn't want to think about it right now. Instead they started splashing Chinchilla, who ran around the edge of the pool, barking. She would dodge the water before running back to drink from the puddles they left behind. Soaking her would have been easy, but they made sure to miss on purpose. Eventually they tired of the pool, so they retreated to the deck chairs.

"Put some oil on my back?" Tim asked.

Ben snorted. "Could you think of a more clichéd line?"

"Tried and true," Tim replied shamelessly. "It's withstood the test of time for a reason."

"Fair enough." Ben sat on the edge of Tim's deck chair. He was about to squeeze some of the oil onto his back when Tim rolled over.

"Think my front needs some, actually."

Ben waited for a laugh, but Tim's face had grown serious. The bottle of oil shook in his hands as the oil dribbled onto Tim's chest. As he rubbed it into the dark brown skin, Ben struggled with guilt. Did he have any right to enjoy this? He and Jace were taking a break. Worse than that, Ben felt like Jace had abandoned him at the worst possible time. Those were all excuses though. Justifications. Ben wanted this. The feelings he had for Tim came unbidden, and he was tired of trying to resist them. His uncertainty turned to lust when Ben re-experienced just how good Tim's body felt. He rubbed his pecs, feeling the nipples harden beneath his hand. Then he moved down to the six-pack.

Tim was transparently hard by this point, but then, so was Ben. Thoughts faded into the background as instinct took over.

Tim grabbed Ben by the arms, pulling him down for a kiss. Lips and tongues danced as Tim's hands pulled and yanked at their swimsuits. Ben worked with him, squirming until his trunks were low enough to be kicked off. He glanced down at Tim's dick, which looked even bigger than when they were a teenagers. Or maybe it was just swollen from the heat of the moment.

Their kisses intensified while they rubbed against each other. Ben was about to go down on him when Tim grabbed the oil. He squeezed some onto both of their cocks, grinding them together and then pulling Ben upward so that he could get between his legs. Before Ben could protest, Tim took him by the wrists. With his hands pinned behind his back, Ben was forced to lay all of his weight on Tim. He gasped in pain and then pleasure as Tim entered him.

"Wait," Ben hissed.

"All I've done is wait for you," Tim said, his movements slow. "I don't think I can any longer."

Ben couldn't either. Too much of him wanted this. Tim built up speed until he was like a piston in one of those sports cars he loved so much.

Ben squirmed and writhed, eager to reach down and play with himself but unable to with his hands restrained. His cock rubbed against Tim's stomach, sending waves of pleasure through him that threatened to drive him mad if he didn't find release soon, but Tim didn't relent. They continued in this manner for what felt like an eternity, both of their bodies slick with oil and sweat, until Tim's thrusting shifted to a higher gear. The friction was enough to send Ben over the edge at the same time that Tim grunted into his ear that he was ready. They moaned loud enough for the entire neighborhood to hear before collapsing in an exhausted heap.

Tim released Ben's wrists and wrapped him tightly in his arms instead. "Welcome back," he murmured.

Allison pinched the bridge of her nose and sighed. Then she dropped her hand and shook her head while giving him a "Mm, mm, mm, mm." Ben hated when she got so dramatic, but he probably deserved it.

"I knew it," she said, picking up her fork and poking at the leftover crème brulée. "As soon as you offered to take me out to dinner, I knew you had done something stupid."

"Stupid might be putting it strongly," Ben said in defense.

Her response was one word. "Jace."

The name hit him like a punch in the gut.

"You're right," Ben sighed, "but I don't even know where things stand with him."

"Do you still love him?"

"Yes."

"Then what are you doing?" Allison's expressive eyes pleaded with him to start making sense. "I know we're both shocked to learn that Jace isn't perfect, but how many times has he forgiven you? Patch things up with him and put as much distance as you can between you and your past."

Ben shook his head. "Tim isn't my past. Not anymore. He's just as much a part of my life now as Jace is. Was. I know you've never forgiven Tim for hurting me, but I love him. It's inexplicable and probably stupid, but I do."

"You can't have both of them," Allison said. "There's a reason you never see three old people walking through a park and holding hands. It just doesn't happen."

Ben wasn't sure about that. The world was a big place, but it was a moot point since Jace wouldn't tolerate such an arrangement. As possessive as Tim could be, he probably wouldn't either.

"Tim was your first in a lot of ways," Allison pressed. She pointed through a waiter to the entrance. "If Ronnie Adams walked through that door right now, I'm sure my heart would skip a beat, but we had our chance and it didn't work out. We've both moved on, and that's for the best. You moved on too, but Tim never did. Now he's dragged you right back to where you left off."

She had a point. Regardless of the years that had passed, he and Tim had picked up again as if nothing had happened. But she was wrong about them having had their chance. His relationship with Tim had been cut short, ended by Tim's fear of what society and his parents would think. Now he was old enough to live his life without fear. Allison and Ronnie's relationship had played out naturally, but his romance with Tim never had that chance.

"Earth to Ben."

"Sorry. You've just given me a lot to think about."

"Let me ask you this," Allison said. "What is it you see in Tim? He's gorgeous, yes, and I understand the whole high school sweetheart thing, but is there really more to it? Anything of substance?"

Ben had never found this easy to explain. There was so much more to Tim beneath the surface. The vulnerability on his face when he'd given Ben the painting as a birthday present was a good example. Everyone figured that Tim's good looks made him self-assured, and sometimes he was, but more often his lonely upbringing made him insecure. Ben's parents had taught him to believe in himself, and that was worth so much more than a handsome face or a showy car. Tim could be vulnerable, and needy, and giving.

These emotions had been easier to see since their reunion. The sentimental way Tim spoke of Eric and how naturally he'd taken to caring for Chinchilla. Then of course, there was the way Ben felt wanted—Tim's desire for him almost overwhelming at times. None of this was obvious to anyone but Ben.

"I know this is going to sound lame," he said at last, "but when he and I are alone together, he's different. He needs me. Sometimes I look at him and all I see is that hurt teenager whose parents never treated him like they should. I see that, and I want to help him. Jace is the opposite since he has it so together. I know he loves me, but he was fine before we met and will be now that it's over."

"Don't you see?" Allison said. "The way you feel about Tim needing you, that's how it is for Jace. He's always been there to support and guide you, and I bet that makes him feel complete. There's no way he can just shrug that off. If you can't say goodbye to Tim so easily, then don't think Jace cares so little about his role in your life."

Ben's mind was abuzz with this new perspective. "God you're awesome."

"I know." Allison smiled before getting back to business. "You can reward my excellence by promising me something."

"What?"

"Go see Jace tomorrow. Don't call him, just go over there, look him in the eye, and talk. That's all."

Ben nodded.

The next day he began the drive to Jace's apartment, but

then he imagined confessing that he had slept with Tim. Jace would probably admit his own infidelities then, which would hurt almost as bad. The entire scenario sounded heart-wrenching. Ben simply couldn't face it. Allison would want a full report if he returned to their duplex, so instead he drove to Tim's house.

No one was home, but Ben found the sliding door in the back unlocked. He let Chinchilla out to potty first. Entering the silent home felt like unearthing a tomb that had been sealed for centuries, one full of potential treasures and traps. As much as Ben felt he understood Tim, he'd always had the nagging sensation that there were details he didn't know, too many thoughts kept hidden. As Ben explored the house, he searched for those answers.

One detail stood out. Despite the house being full of art, none of it was Tim's. Even in their youth, Tim had hung a painting on his bedroom wall. Maybe this was a hobby he didn't pursue anymore, but Ben found that hard to believe. Surely he had a studio hidden away somewhere.

Ben walked from room to room and turned up nothing. While looking out a staircase window he spotted the garage. Tim never parked his car inside, even though he still fawned over his vehicle like a beloved pet. Ben tried the door on the side of the boxy building, but it was locked. This led to another search. Finally he found a set of keys in a kitchen drawer. One turned in the lock with a satisfying click.

The garage was flooded by natural light from a skylight. Except for a clear area in the center where a lone easel stood, the rest of the room was lined with paintings, stacked three or four deep. Tim was a busy boy!

Ben began looking through his work. Some pieces he recognized from the past; others were new. Tim's painting had become much more expressive. Some were wild and daring, with shocks of thick paint dominating the canvas. Others were dark, small, and claustrophobic. Is that how Tim felt when he hid from the world? Or were they from his time alone after Eric had died?

Then there was a third style found in only a handful of paintings. These contained elements of realism, usually an object in the center that was surrounded by small wisps of color, making it glow with an ethereal light. Ben had never seen anything like it before.

The painting on the easel was done in such style. It featured an older man who looked sickly and tired. This was no doubt Eric, but bathed in the radiance of Tim's new technique, he looked more like an angel than a dying man.

The sound of Tim's car pulling into the driveway snapped Ben out of his thoughts. He hurried out the door, which was thankfully on the opposite side of the building, just before he was spotted.

Tim grinned at him. "Wow! Think hard enough about something and it'll come true."

"What do you mean?"

Tim took him upstairs to the bedroom and showed him.

Afterwards, Ben rested his head on Tim's chest, idly tracing with a finger the lines and contours that shaped his body. "What are we?" he asked.

"After that? Exhausted."

"Seriously."

"Well," Tim replied, "I'd like to think that you're my boyfriend."

An unspoken question hung in the air. What about Jace?

Rather than answer this, Ben changed topics. "Are you staying in Austin after you graduate?"

"I guess so. I don't really want to go back to Houston. Do you?"

"No. Do you ever visit?"

Tim shifted underneath him. "For the holidays, yeah."

"Your parents will be surprised to see me in your life again."

Tim didn't say anything. His silence spoke volumes.

"They don't know you're gay, do they?" Ben prompted.

"Why bother telling them?" Tim said. "They're hardly a part of my life."

Ben propped himself up on an elbow so he could better scrutinize his would-be boyfriend. "You said you came out!"

"I did! To friends and lots of other people. I don't tell my family anything about me."

"But what if they found out?" Ben said. "Last time that almost happened you ditched me rather than be discovered."

"I'll tell them if you want," Tim grumped. "Am I supposed to call them right now, or can we relax?"

Ben wanted to retort with something smart, or ask why

all of Tim's paintings were hidden away in the garage, but he didn't want to ruin the afternoon. Instead he offered to make something to eat, the cooking time buying him solitude to think before he served the meal. Ben debated whether or not it mattered that Tim's parents didn't know. Now that Tim was no longer dependent on them, they had no say in his life. Ben could imagine that they weren't close to their son. Still, it hurt him that the one secret that had ruined their relationship the first time was still being kept. If Tim wanted Ben to be a part of his life, that would have to change.

Whenever Ben thought of defending his thesis, he often imagined a trial—judges sitting high above him in a cold and stony courtroom, scrutinizing his every word and demanding answers to questions he had never thought of. As he discovered Monday morning, the process was much more relaxed. He faced one of his professors and two other faculty members who were politely bored throughout his presentation. They asked a few token questions before informing him that he had passed. Ben was glad a graduation ceremony was still to come. Otherwise his academic career would have ended with a yawn rather than a bang.

Ben had plans to meet Tim in the cafeteria for lunch. Now that he had finished earlier than expected, and had a good idea where Tim's current class was, Ben decided to meet him there instead. The halls began to fill with other students as he found the right area. Finally he spotted Tim. He raised a hand and was about to call out when he saw who Tim was talking to.

The other person had primped hair and clothes that were a bit too flashy for someone not on stage. Ben stared, not believing his own eyes. How could this person be here instead of Boston? And yet, there Aaron was, school books in hand as he chatted casually with Tim. Ben practically gave a battle cry as he ran toward them. Aaron was turning away by the time he reached them, but Ben grabbed him by the shoulder to spin him around.

"You go to school here?" Ben snarled.

"What the hell?" Aaron said irritably, but then his face registered recognition. "Oh god! Leave me alone!"

He tried to pull away, but Ben grabbed him with his other hand and tightened his grip.

234

"I thought you were from out of town. You're a student here, aren't you?"

"Ask Tim!" Aaron squealed. "Leave me out of your little love triangle."

Ben let him go, having heard enough. He barely spared Tim a glance as he turned to leave, but now it was his turn to be restrained.

"Benjamin, wait," Tim said. "Let me explain."

"You lied! And I was stupid enough to believe you. And now Jace—" He choked on the name, tears welling up. He wasn't the only one. Tim was clenching his jaw, fighting back tears of his own, but a few had already escaped.

"I would do anything to be with you," Tim said, voice strained. "Yeah, I lied, but I don't regret it. If that's what it took to get you back, then it was worth it."

Ben barely heard his words. He kept thinking of the pain he had put Jace through, and how much worse it would be when Jace learned that he had been with Tim.

Tim tried pulling him close, but Ben put all his strength into pushing away. He ran to the parking lot, Tim trailing behind and saying anything he could to get him to stay. His words fell on deaf ears until Ben was unlocking his car door.

"You wanted to believe the lie."

Ben dropped his keys.

"You wanted an excuse to come running to me. You wanted your relationship with Jace to fall apart just as much as I did."

Ben turned and leaned against his car for support. Tim reached out and caught him by both shoulders. He was right. If Ben was completely honest with himself, he knew Jace would never cheat. Especially with someone as superficial and tasteless as Aaron. Ben had shut away all rational thought when arguing with Jace. He did it to be free. Free to love Tim again. But why? Jace was everything he had always wanted. Why throw that away for a little excitement?

"What is it with us?" Ben asked. "Our lives are always so fucked up when we're together. Is that what makes us attracted to each other? What happens when the danger dies down, when our love is no longer forbidden or a secret? What's left between us then?"

"A lot," Tim said. "I promise."

"How can I even trust you anymore? You lie about coming out, you hide your paintings… Is there anything real about you? Do I even know you?"

"Don't say that," Tim pleaded. "You know me. You might be the only one, but you know me."

"Well, maybe I don't want to anymore."

Tim let go of him. Ben slipped into his car and roared out of the parking lot, but he couldn't escape the guilt that filled his stomach.

Ben was done. Done with love, done with drama, and done beating himself up for his own mistakes. He threw away the cell phone from Tim and the keys to Jace's apartment. Ben would rather say goodbye than break Jace's heart with the truth. Allison, his forever friend, agreed to screen his calls. Tim called every day, and with graduation looming, Jace started to also.

Ben made sure to be away from home as much as possible, which was wise, because he found a note from Tim taped to his window and a rose from Jace on his doorstep. Ben decided to go to Houston for the summer and figure out what to do with the rest of his life from there.

First he had to get through the graduation ceremony. Allison agreed to leave after both their names were called. Wyman would thankfully be one of the last, so Tim couldn't follow them out if he wanted to stay for his diploma. His calls were coming less frequently, so maybe he had taken the hint.

Ben's dour mood faded during the ceremony. The stadium overflowed with the energy of new graduates who were both eager and reluctant to start new chapters of their lives. Ben was nervous when his name was called, proud when he took the diploma, and nostalgic on his way down the steps. He cheered when he heard Allison's name, and as soon as she received her diploma and left the stage, together they ran for the parking lot. His happy heart took a plunge when he saw Jace there, but the exit was far enough away that they could escape without him noticing.

"Jace!" Allison shouted.

Ben's mouth fell open in disbelief at her betrayal.

"It's for your own good," she said. "I'm going back to party."

She left him there as Jace strolled over, looking sharp in his well-cut suit and holding a bouquet of roses. Ben wanted to say something meaningful—to apologize or simply speak his name—but instead he started to cry.

Jace kissed him, and Ben reciprocated, even though he knew he had no right. He blubbered embarrassingly until he finally managed to ask Jace to bring him home.

"I thought I'd take you out to eat?" Jace suggested.

Ben shook his head as another wave of tears hit him. "I want to go home," he said.

Jace made small talk in the car. Ben did his best to respond, but it was hard. He wanted to be selfish and pretend that he hadn't done what he had, but he couldn't. Jace deserved to know the truth, even though it would mean the end.

"I meant my home," Ben said as they pulled into Jace's apartment complex.

"I know what you meant," Jace replied gently.

Ben felt as if he was saying goodbye to everything as he entered the apartment. He knew when he stroked Samson that it would be for the last time, and he couldn't bear to think of all the other things he was about to lose. He had to tell Jace now while he still had the courage.

"I was with Tim. We slept together."

Jace's face was strained. "I figured. Got it all out of your system now?"

Ben nodded.

"Good." Jace slipped out of his shoes and started working on his tie. Wasn't he going to take Ben home? Or maybe he was expected to walk back.

"Don't you want to get out of that doofy robe?" Jace asked.

"I don't understand."

Jace sighed. "My love for you doesn't stop just because you made a stupid mistake. An extremely stupid mistake, I might add. I love you, and if you promise to trust my word in the future, then I'll trust you again too."

A strange combination of laughter and tears of relief overwhelmed Ben. Jace helped him out of his robe, took off his own jacket, and led them to the bedroom. Ben crawled into bed and Jace got in behind him, spooning himself against Ben's back. They lay there for hours, taking turns holding each other while Samson purred contentedly at their feet.

PART THREE

AUSTIN, TEXAS
2003

CHAPTER 26

Falling in love is a subtle process, a connection sparked by attraction, tested by compatibility, and forged by memory. In this same manner, Austin had become a part of Ben and Jace's life. They had dined in its restaurants, danced in its clubs, and lazed away more than one afternoon in its parks. Austin had everything they needed, and moving would mean leaving behind the backdrop to both good and bad times. Ben and Jace had fallen in love with Austin and found, quite by surprise, that they were already home.

Allison was staying too. She plunged into her career, not even taking a summer break. She got a job at a local shelter for teenage runaways, apprenticing at a psychiatric hospital in her spare time. There she met the man she would marry. Brian was a struggling alcoholic and—proving how strange love could be—Allison found everything she was looking for in him.

Ben didn't share her instant success. He took most of the summer off, travelling occasionally with Jace and seeing brief glimpses of the country. He spent a month at his parents' house, the first proper visit with his family since he left for college. When he returned to Austin, he worked as a temp for a year, still uncertain of what he wanted to do.

Allison suggested a position at the hospital where she now worked. A part-time job as a speech therapist had opened there. Allison had enough influence that he didn't even need to interview. Ben took the position to get away from menial temp work, and almost instantly found the job rewarding.

His clients were varied, to say the least. Some were accident victims who had lost their ability to speak due to physical or mental traumas. Others were stroke survivors, and occasionally he worked with children born with speech impediments. Ben enjoyed breaking the words apart to reshape and customize for each individual to say. For the first time in his life, he felt like he was doing something worthwhile.

Never one to leave things half-done, Allison found him another job to occupy the rest of his time. Brian, who by now had been sober for almost two years, was also part-owner of a dinner theater. There, a play featuring a few musical numbers was scheduled. Unlike speech therapy, Ben did not easily warm to this idea. He had no theatrical training and little urge to perform for an audience he imagined as a sea of bald and blue-haired heads.

He intended to turn down the opportunity, but then Jace switched to the international routes he had always wanted. Ben was happy for him but knew this meant even more time spent apart. Deciding it would help keep him occupied, Ben accepted a small role at the dinner theater. His first part—a poor street urchin who loses his life to the cold harsh winter—only had a few speaking lines and one song.

Everything changed the first night he stepped out onto stage. The magic of theater turned him into that urchin as Ben sang with his entire soul. He received a standing ovation, and continued to with every performance. He never would have thought it possible, but he had fallen in love with the stage and eagerly took on larger roles.

In what would have been spring break if he was still in college, four years after they had met, Ben and Jace went to Paris. They both knew what this meant. The air was thick with anticipation as they both waited for the big moment. It came when Jace proposed to Ben during a breakfast in bed. He had hidden the ring in a French croissant, which made Ben laugh so hard that he almost couldn't say yes.

Now their wedding day had arrived, and so far it was nothing like Ben had pictured. Movies were full of grooms with cold feet, but Ben couldn't be more ready. Choosing to spend the rest of his life with Jace was the easy part. Getting the wedding party organized while juggling the needs of their guests wasn't. Right now Ben was most worried about the tablecloths. Wind was picking up across the lake and threatening to send everything flying through the park.

"I think we're going to need some rocks," Ben said.

"I know the caterers are late," Allison said drolly, "but I don't think that's a good solution."

"Ugh, don't remind me. Do you think I should run to the grocery store and pick up some veggie platters? Or a bag of fun-sized Snickers at least?"

"Everyone is fine," Allison said. "The food isn't supposed to be served until after the ceremony anyway. If they're still not here by then, we'll order pizza."

Ben looked to the gazebo they had reserved, which had enough Asian influences that he called it the pagoda. White roses covered every inch of the wooden surface that wasn't already awash in ribbons and balloons. Against the odds, he and Allison had managed to bring a garish amount of decorations together into a beautiful display. The thought of what was about to take place there distracted Ben momentarily from all that still needed to be done.

He scanned the crowd until he found the only person dressed in a white tuxedo. More handsome than ever, Jace was surrounded by a gaggle of aunts and cousins, nodding pleasantly and smiling since they wouldn't let him get a word in. He caught Ben staring and gave a helpless little shake of his head. Ben would have to extract him from his family or they would never get started.

"There's the catering van," Allison said. "No, you stay here. Brian!"

As usual, whenever Allison called, Brian responded. She may have found someone even more patient than Jace, because Brian seemed to be always running an errand for her or performing some task. The poor man was run ragged, his reddish-brown hair steadily thinning, his skin pale from working too many hours indoors, but Brian had nothing but love in his eyes for Allison.

The DJ's speakers rumbled into life. Ben's eyes widened when he recognized the song. "That's our wedding march! The idiot is playing it early!"

The next thing Ben knew, Jace was at his side and guiding him to the pagoda. The guests were scrambling for their seats, while Ben kept trying to protest that this was all in conflict with the schedule.

Then they were standing in front of everyone. Neither Ben nor Jace were particularly religious, so they had chosen to be married at a lakeside park rather than a church. The idea of having any sort of priest presiding over their ceremony didn't suit them either, at least not at the time. Ben now wished more than ever that someone was there to guide their actions.

The song came to an end, and Jace began his speech. Ben only heard some of it, words like commitment and laughter, and something about growing old together, but the word that stood out the most was forever. No more uncertainty or wavering, no more lonely nights or pain. Just forever, with Jace.

At that moment Ben wanted nothing more. He had written a speech, and it was a good one too, but he didn't have the patience for it now. Ben grabbed the rings set on a pedestal before them, shoved one into Jace's hand, and kissed him.

After a surprised silence, the guests broke into applause and the DJ cued the next song. Ben had no idea what to do next, since he hadn't planned this part, but Jace took him in his arms and began to sway to the music.

"So we're married?" Ben asked, still not believing it.

"Yup," Jace said.

"Simple as that?"

Jace laughed. "Simple as that. Just a promise and nothing more. Hard to believe that anyone makes a big deal out of it."

"It is a big deal!" Ben protested, but this only made Jace laugh more.

As they danced, food was unloaded from vans, corks popped out of champagne bottles, and music was played, but it was some time before the newly married couple ended their embrace and walked hand in hand into a crowd of people who loved them.

The summer sky was clear, a gentle breeze keeping the temperature mild. On nights like these the theater was never filled to capacity. Ticket sales didn't go down, but attendance did since not as many people showed up. Ben imagined the audience becoming distracted on their way to the theater, lured away by parks and riverside strolls.

Ben wanted to escape back into that summer night as well. He had already performed all but his final scene. He was playing the suitor of a powerful older woman. His character intended to marry the woman for her money but had inadvertently fallen in love with her, evidence of his once-greedy intentions coming to light just before the wedding. Ben's last appearance in the play was a song to his lover, begging her forgiveness.

The usual terror and excitement stole over him as he returned to the stage. He pleaded through song for his fiancée to forgive him, but she rejected his apology as she did every performance, leaving him alone. Ben turned to the audience, the remaining lyrics those of remorse.

"Had I but known you when you were poor, had you but known me when I was pure."

He swept his eyes over the audience, barely seeing them through his musical trance, but something pulled him back. A gaze more intense than others. Had the eyes been silver?

"If I could pull this love from my chest, leave you standing with all the rest."

Tim. Ben was sure he was out there. Seeing the audience from the stage was never easy, but the shape of his face, the glint of those eyes. It had to be him. Ben wanted to step forward, out of the blinding spotlight, but he wouldn't allow his voice to waver.

"And now there's nothing left inside of me, just broken pieces no one can see."

The lights faded, the entire theater in shadow. The applause made Ben flinch before a harsh whisper reminded him to return backstage. He waited in the wings as the rest of the play went on, squinting into the darkness at the figure he had seen, convinced at times that he had been mistaken. Then came the curtain call. Ben joined his fellow actors in their bows, impatient for the lights to turn on so the audience could leave. By the time they did, the table was empty.

The next night was much the same. From his first line Ben's attention was on the audience more than the play. The figure sat at a different table this time, but there he was, a solitary silhouette who never took his eyes off Ben, even when the lines weren't his. Ben could see him a bit better at this new table, nursing a beer. Was that a cocky smile between swigs?

"Isn't that right, Jacob?"

Ben's imaginary fiancée put a meaningful hand on his shoulder.

"Y-Yes!" He scrambled for his line. "Yes, my dear, that is precisely what we shall do. Run away together and prove the naysayers wrong!"

He turned his full attention back to his acting, not looking at the audience again until his final song. He put all of himself into his voice, singing only to the table he could no longer see. *I know you're there,* he wanted to communicate. *I don't know what you want, but please don't run away.*

When the lights turned on at the end of the show, a bottle and empty glass were the only evidence that the table had been occupied.

— — —

"There's someone waiting for you," Brian said as Ben scrubbed the makeup from his face. "In reception."

"Jace?" Ben asked, already knowing otherwise.

"No, but maybe I should give him a heads up," Brian said, raising an eyebrow. "Whoever your mystery man is, he's smoking hot."

"Allison's going to be sad when she finds out you're crossing over," Ben joked.

Ben didn't hear Brian's snappy comeback. His chest felt tight and his breath short as he hurried to make himself presentable. Was he excited? Nervous? Did he have any right to be either or was that the beginning of infidelity?

Steadying himself, he walked to the reception area, resisting the urge to run. Only one person waited there, and he was indeed breathtakingly beautiful. Silky blond hair framed his young face. His complexion was perfect, his mouth delicate and pink. His blue eyes looked Ben over before settling into a scowl. The anger only accentuated his handsomeness.

"You're Benjamin?" the boy asked.

"Ben," he corrected, having already put the pieces together. This wasn't good.

"So much for the legend." The beauty faded momentarily, overshadowed by hate.

"And you are?"

"Ryan, Tim's boyfriend." He waited for a reaction, disgusted when none came. "What, he never told you about me?"

"I haven't spoken to Tim in years."

Emotions played across Ryan's face—doubt, suspicion, sorrow. How young was he? Still a teenager, that was certain. Ben suddenly felt old. He thought back to his emotionally tumultuous adolescent years. What would he have wanted to hear if he were Ryan?

"You've got nothing to worry about," he said. "I'm happily married. I'm not interested in Tim anymore."

Ryan's handsome visage returned to anger. "That doesn't mean he's not interested in you! I know he's been coming here, so you can stop with the lies."

Ben sighed. He wouldn't be able to defuse this situation. Better to retreat and let them sort it out at home. "I have to go, but I hope you two work things out." He turned to leave but stopped when he saw Brian standing in the doorway.

"Another one for you," he said, looking concerned.

Tim stepped out from behind him. The last few years hadn't been kind. He had circles under his eyes and stubble covered his cheeks. Even his once-invincible physique had grown paunchy. He appeared vulnerable and uncertain until he spotted Ryan. Then his face became a mask of fury that Ben hadn't seen since they parted ways as teenagers.

Oblivious of their surroundings, Tim and Ryan began shouting at each other. Ben stared in shock before shooing Brian away, promising to lock up. By the time he returned his attention to the conflict, Tim had grabbed Ryan's arms and was shaking him while yelling. Ryan was alternating between crying and shouting back.

"Let go of him!" Ben growled, adrenaline taking over. "I said let go!" When neither man paid any attention, he pulled on Tim's shoulder. Tim rounded on him, eyes blazing before his face crumpled.

"That's right, show him how you treat me," Ryan yelled, lifting the sleeves of his black concert T-shirt. His arms were bright red where Tim had gripped him, but there were also bruises. "Did he do this to you too?" Ryan demanded. "Is that why you left him?"

Ben turned to Tim, jaw clenching, but his former boyfriend couldn't meet his gaze.

"I'm going to kill myself," Ryan bawled, heading for the door. "I'm going to kill myself and leave a note blaming it on you!"

The door slammed, the glass shaking in its frame. The silence that followed was filled only with Tim's heavy breathing. Ben could smell alcohol on his breath, much more than the theater would serve.

"I guess I should go after him," Tim said.

"I guess you should."

Tim turned when reaching the door.

"La Maisonette, tomorrow. Seven o'clock?"

Ben hesitated.

"Please?"

"All right."

Tim slunk into the night wearing a burden of shame. Ben was tempted to lock the door after him, but he didn't. He still trusted

Tim, still knew him. There had to be a reason for everything he'd seen tonight, and he wouldn't be able to rest until he found out why.

Tim was already at the restaurant, seated at a table and waiting. His appearance was better than it had been the day before, face clean shaven and hair freshly cut. He still didn't look as though he'd slept recently. Ben sat, not knowing what to expect and warily noting the half-empty bottle of wine on the table.

"I'm sorry about yesterday," Tim said, lifting the bottle. "Drink?"

Ben nodded. He didn't plan to partake but he figured it was one less glass for Tim.

"Is your boyfriend okay?"

"Ryan? Yeah, he says stuff like that all the time."

"And do you react like that all the time?"

Tim's expression was miserable. "No! I never hit him. We had a fight last week, and I grabbed him. I don't know my own strength sometimes, and he really knows how to push my buttons. Those were the only two times, but I'm afraid of what might happen if things don't change."

Ben didn't know what to say. He didn't know Ryan or his history with Tim, and part of him was unwilling to ask. If Ryan caught them here things would only get worse. Jace wasn't thrilled with Ben being here either, but at least he hadn't kept it a secret. What could he do, walk away? Let his last memory of Tim be of the broken man before him?

"Okay," Ben said. "Tell me everything."

Tim had met Ryan at a bar a year ago and they had everything in common. Both came from well-to-do families with distant parents. Ryan's family had turned their backs on him when he came out, eventually cutting him off from his college tuition. Tim had supported him but eventually learned that Ryan never attended the expensive classes he was paying for. Ryan had little interest in anything other than partying, and Tim had indulged him, joining in and feeling like a teenager again.

"For a while things were good," Tim said. "Well, maybe not good, but entertaining. Then the lies started. First my wallet was stolen. I didn't care about the cash, but the credit cards were a hassle. Part of me suspected, so I didn't cancel them right away.

Sure enough, they were used at Ryan's favorite clothing store. The brat even showed up in a new outfit the next day. It's not like he has a job or any other source of income besides me, so it couldn't have been more obvious.

"Then a friend of his turned out to be much more. I put an end to that, but it wasn't pretty. I suppose it was karma for what I put you and Jace through. Every time I try to rein him in makes him act out that much more, usually by partying. Last week Ryan ended up in the ER to have his stomach pumped. All he cares about anymore is drinking and drugs."

"Looks like you've been indulging a bit yourself," Ben said.

Tim moved his hand away from his glass and nodded. "Ryan is your opposite. You always brought out the good in me, changed me for the better. With Ryan, I just don't know. I used to see myself in him. His parents are just as cold as mine, and I saw the pain hidden behind that pretty face of his, but he has a mean streak. Ryan turns his hurt back on the world, and I don't know what I can do to make him better. Sometimes I think he's who I would have become if I had never met you."

Ben listened, mentally searching for an answer to Tim's problems. Tim had tried to do right by Ryan, but the anger Ben had seen last night still concerned him. If the situation didn't change, Tim might do something he would regret. In any case, Ben didn't like to see him suffer like this.

They soon asked for the check. Neither had touched the appetizers, and Tim had already finished the wine. Ben insisted on driving him home, pretending for the briefest of moments that the man next to him was a teenager with an injured ankle.

"This isn't how it was supposed to be." Tim grimaced. "How I wanted us to meet again, I mean. I had this dream about you being on stage. Isn't that crazy? I had no idea you did theater, but I dreamt it anyway."

Ben glanced over at him. "And that's how you found me?"

"Well, that and some Google-powered stalking."

Tim still lived in the same architectural mess as before, but the driveway was overflowing with cars. None of them were sporty enough to belong to Tim. Heavy bass pounded from the house, accompanied by a babble of voices. A forlorn howl occasionally cried out above the din.

"I told him not to leave her out back," Tim complained as

they got out of the car. "She hates being alone at night."

"Chinchilla?"

"Yeah." Tim smiled. "Come on. She'll be glad to see you."

Ben didn't expect Chinchilla to remember him, but her whole butt wagged at turbo speed when she saw him. The puppy Ben had once known was gone, replaced by a stout dog who was all grins as Tim kissed and pet her. Her leash was tangled around a tree, Tim casting angry glances toward the house as he unclipped the line from her collar.

"This happens almost nightly," he muttered.

"I don't mean to state the obvious," Ben said, "but why don't you just break up with him? I know, I know, you said the sex is really great, but things are only going to get worse."

"You're right, but I don't know how. You heard him last night. He always threatens to kill himself. The night he overdosed was because I suggested taking a break."

Ben thought about this while squatting next to Chinchilla and rubbing her belly. "Here's what we'll do. You send Ryan on a trip, a long one, somewhere in Europe. Tell him it's your way of apologizing. While he's gone you sell the house and move somewhere new. When he comes back you never contact him and he won't be able to find you."

"Think so?"

"Yeah. You guys will get some distance between you and things will cool off. Not only that, but wherever you send him, make sure it's a gay resort." Ben chuckled. "Or hire an escort to pick him up from the airport. He's young and hot. I'm sure someone will snatch him up soon. Then he'll be somebody else's problem instead of yours."

Tim laughed. "You know, that's just crazy enough that it might work."

Ben laughed too, but he knew that this wasn't the solution. Tim had put up with Ryan for so long because of more than just his suicidal threats. Emotion was there, no matter how unhealthy it might be.

Glass shattered inside the house. Judging from the way the music grew louder, most likely a window had been broken. There was a brief chorus of laughter before the party continued raging.

"All right," Ben sighed as he stood. "Time for me to make everything better. Come on."

If Ben had felt old when meeting Ryan, he felt positively ancient as he navigated a sea of intoxicated teenagers. With Tim in tow, he felt like they were a pair of angry parents who had come home early from their vacation. A few recognized Tim, but their expressions were amused rather than ashamed, even those who were still laughing over the broken window and the potted plant that had been thrown through it. They had no respect for Tim, and that made Ben all the more incensed.

Once he had battled his way to the living room, stepping over a pile of puke on the way, Ben ripped the heart of the party out by unplugging the stereo. A number of complaints followed, one louder than the others.

"What the hell is he doing here?"

The crowd parted for Ryan, whose skin was pale and sweaty. From the way his pupils were dilated, it was safe to assume he was on something.

"I'm here with my boyfriend," Ben said, reaching over to take Tim's hand.

Ryan bared his teeth like an animal. Ben had never seen anyone actually do that, but Ryan's fury was so intense he was shaking. He shouted something unintelligible that might have been "I'll kill you!" before charging toward them. Tim tensed up, ready to defend Ben, which would only escalate into violence. Ben didn't want that, so he placed a hand on Tim's face and turned it toward him.

And then Ben kissed him.

His newly discovered acting skills weren't needed for this. As it had always been, the emotions he felt for Tim weren't far beneath the surface. From the way Tim reacted, he felt the same way. The room went silent as every person there witnessed a kiss worthy of the big screen. The silence was broken when Ryan began sobbing.

Ben pulled away from Tim and saw the pain on Ryan's face. The kiss had convinced him that they were in love, and the kid was too young and stupid to realize that Tim loved him too, that emotions like these never went away completely. Ben felt sorry for Ryan, but he didn't dare show that now.

"I'm moving in," Ben said. "Tim asked me to. You're leaving and never coming back. All of you," he said loud enough to be heard.

Nobody moved.

"I called the cops."

People began to stir.

"And they're bringing drug dogs."

That did it. The partygoers fled, and within minutes, everyone was gone except Ryan, who was beginning to tremble with anger again.

"I'll kill myself," he said. "I swear to god I will."

Ben opened his mouth to retort, but it was Tim who spoke.

"No you won't. I know you won't, because you're too much of a coward. You've been running away since the day I met you, away from your family's disapproval, away from the one person who loves you, but most of all you've been trying to escape from yourself. I was once that cowardly, and you still are."

"I overdosed!" Ryan reminded him.

"And I was there holding your hand in the hospital as they pumped your stomach. When I told you that you almost died, you cried. I thought there was still hope for you then, but I've seen you almost overdose every night since. I don't know how to fix you, Ryan, I wish I did, but it's not going to be my money that helps destroy you. Not anymore."

Ryan tried to argue further, but Tim wouldn't have it. Ben stepped back and let him deal with everything as Ryan unwillingly packed his bags. Tim called a taxi to take him home, and Ryan began to beg, but Tim stood strong. Only after the taxi turned down the street did Tim's shoulders slump.

"You okay?"

"Yeah," Tim answered, throwing his full weight into a hug that almost knocked Ben off his feet. "You always know how to make things right," he murmured into Ben's neck. "I'm a mess without you."

"I'm awesome, I know," Ben said, detangling himself. "I'm also in trouble. Jace is going to give me hell when he finds out I kissed you, no matter what the reason. You *are* going to make all my suffering worth it by never seeing Ryan again, aren't you?"

Tim nodded. "Since you're going to be in trouble anyway—"

He stepped close, but Ben pushed him away and they both began laughing. Face lit up with a smile, Tim looked more like his old self again.

— — —

What should have followed, Ben felt, was a long-lasting relationship that finally allowed them to be friends. This utopia did exist briefly. They saw each other regularly, Jace often joining them, and things were simple. But then the feelings between them began to stir. They both felt it. Sometimes their gazes locked for too long. Other times they found excuses to be closer to each other than necessary. Hugs became too intimate, Ben breathing in his scent or Tim rubbing his nose lovingly against his neck.

The decision was hard to make, but it had to be done. Ben showed up at his door in the middle of the night. Tim was sitting on the front steps, as if he had been expecting him.

"You're either here to do something that you really shouldn't," Tim said, "or you came to say goodbye."

"I'm sorry," Ben said. "I wish we could just be friends."

"No you don't." Tim smiled sadly. "That's the problem, isn't it?"

"Yeah." Ben wanted to reach out to him, to hug him at least, but he didn't even trust himself to do that anymore.

Tim took a deep breath. "You think we would have made it? Say we never had the cops chasing us that night, that we kept on going. Do you think we'd still be together today?"

Ben thought about it, but it was hard to imagine his life without Jace anymore and impossible to transpose Tim into all the memories he and Jace had made together. But for a moment, he could picture more nights of sneaking into Tim's bedroom, the relief they would have felt when they moved away to college, and how those liberal years would have finally allowed them to be everything that he had once dreamt of.

Ben swallowed. "I have to go."

"I don't know what I'll do without you, Benjamin. I don't have anything left."

"You do too."

"Did I tell you that I came out to my parents?"

"No." The lump wouldn't leave Ben's throat. Little by little, Tim had always tried to please him.

"Yeah. They weren't thrilled. If they were distant before—" Tim shook his head.

"They'll get over it," Ben said. "And if they don't, then they can go fuck themselves."

Tim smiled.

"Don't go back to Ryan. You don't need him. Or me. Or anyone else for that matter."

Tim's expression was pained. "I've always needed you."

"You might want us, but you don't need us. You said I bring out the best in you, but all those wonderful things were already there, even before I came along. Live for yourself, Tim. Decorate the house with your paintings. Don't hide them away. Don't hide yourself away either. There's a whole world out there waiting to see you. The real you. You're so beautiful, and I don't just mean your face or your body."

"Don't go," Tim pleaded.

Ben could only shake his head. If he said any more it would be too late for both of them. He turned and walked slowly to his car, grateful for and despairing every second that passed without Tim trying to stop him. Ben opened his car door and looked back to where Tim stood.

"Until next time?" Ben said.

Tim laughed. "Until next time."

CHAPTER 27

Jace padded into the kitchen, naked except for a pair of flannel boxers. He poured his ritual cup of coffee and walked to the bay windows as he had every morning since they bought their new house. Ben admired his body, affection welling up as he eyed Jace's bed-head—hair sticking up in every direction. Four years of dating and two years of marriage, and Ben found him just as attractive as when they first met. He didn't think that would ever fade, no matter how many decades went by.

Jace turned to him with a knowing expression. "I thought I wore you out last night?"

Ben smirked. "I slept well."

Jace tried to grin in response but winced instead.

"Are you all right?"

"My head is killing me," Jace said.

"You didn't drink anything last night."

"No, but I'm beginning to wish I had, especially if I'm going to have the hangover anyway." He sat at the kitchen table and rubbed his temples. "Grab me a couple aspirin, would you?"

"Sure."

His face was pale and drawn when Ben returned. "Maybe it was something you ate? Is your stomach okay? You could be coming down with a bug."

Jace shook his head and tossed the aspirin into his mouth, chasing them down with a swig of coffee. The cup shook as he tried to return it to the table before his hand spasmed. The cup shattered on the linoleum, hot coffee splattering across the floor like blood at a crime scene.

"So clumsy," Jace said, standing to fetch a towel. His legs buckled beneath him and he crumpled to the floor, the fear reflected in his eyes fading to emptiness.

Ben was at his side instantly, holding his head off the floor and launching a barrage of questions that went unanswered. He felt helpless, touching Jace's face, feeling for fever, trying to find some way to help him. Jace remained unresponsive.

Ben called 911 and in his panic gave the operator their old address. He called back when he realized his mistake, fearing they would think him a prank caller and never come. Then he waited, switching between checking on Jace and running to the front door. What was taking so long? Didn't they understand how serious this was? Couldn't they get here sooner?

He ran to the driveway when he heard the sirens, his words rambling and confused, but he managed to point the paramedics in the right direction. Jace was unmoving when they collected him off the floor.

"Is he dead? Is he dead?" he chanted, but all the paramedics said was to stand back.

He barely had the presence of mind to shut the door behind him as they left, praying Samson hadn't escaped. Ben clambered into the ambulance, watching as they put a device over Jace's mouth, a bag that the paramedic squeezed to keep him breathing. That was good. That meant he was alive.

"Aneurysm."

The doctor had said much more than that, but this was the word Ben fixated on. He struggled to remember what it meant, something to do with the brain. A tumor? Or just a blip of electricity in the wrong place?

"His grandmother died from one," Ben remembered. "Oh god, is he going to—"

"That he made it here alive is a promising sign," the doctor assured him. "Jace has a five-hour surgery ahead of him. If he can pull through that, he has a good chance. I must warn you though, there could be complications. Are you family?"

"Yes."

Every potential complication was described on a piece of paper Ben was asked to sign. He barely scanned the list of nightmare possibilities. This was a choice between life and death. If Jace survived, they could deal with whatever came next.

Jace's family arrived while he was still in surgery, which was a great relief to Ben. Finally he was with people who understood that the world was coming undone at the seams. That calm unshakable Jace had fallen was impossible.

A nurse informed his family that Jace had suffered a class four cerebral aneurysm. They were able to explain to Ben what this meant. An aneurysm was a ballooned portion of blood vessel filled with blood. If left undetected it could rupture, causing bleeding in the brain. Once that happened there was only a fifty percent chance of survival.

Waiting for the results of the surgery was pure agony. Ben tried to imagine his life without Jace and couldn't. He had been the center of Ben's world for too many years now. Going on without him was unthinkable. Ben would rather also die. How could anyone expect him to do otherwise?

Redemption came in the form of a very tired surgeon. He gave them a weary smile and the news that the surgery had been a success. Now it was up to Jace to recover.

The next four days were crucial, the high risk of fatality still looming over them. Ben maintained a constant vigil as Jace flitted in and out of consciousness. At times he didn't know who Ben was, or he would say strange things, worrying once that Samson was going to be late to work. Their laughter at such times was frantic and short-lived. What if this is how he would behave from now on? What if Ben remained forgotten?

Equally worrying was the lack of movement on Jace's left side. Among the constant warnings from doctors and nurses was the possibility of permanent paralysis. When Jace began clapping on the fifth day, for reasons known only to him, the entire family cried with relief.

By the end of the week Jace had returned to them. He knew who they were and remembered what had happened. He also complained of pain and how loud everything was. Another side effect. They had to whisper when around him, otherwise they sounded like they were shouting.

"I'm sorry about all of this."

This was the first coherent sentence Jace said to him. Ben responded by weeping while covering his face in kisses.

"Welcome home!"

Ben wanted to shout this gleefully, and he nearly did before remembering how sensitive Jace was to noise. That was a new development. One of many, but today they were focusing on the positive. After nearly ten days in the hospital, Jace was finally home again. Ben held open the front door and turned, still expecting to find the confident man with a warm smile on his face and a gleam of good-natured humor in his eyes.

Jace was still there. Just a slightly different version. He

grimaced more than he smiled, and the dark circles under his eyes made him seem perpetually tired. He still had his hair at least, thanks to coil embolization. That meant the surgeons didn't need to go through Jace's skull to get at his brain. Rather they went through one of his arteries, starting at his groin, which seemed crazy because it was so far from his head. Ben still found it confusing despite hours and hours of online research. He had even asked his mother to bring the old family medical guide—the same one he had once used to diagnose a third-degree sprain. Ben had once looked to the book for morbid entertainment. Now he looked to it for hope, and what better sign of that could there be than Jace's homecoming?

"I love what you've done with the place," Jace said, entering their house at a cautious pace. "Especially the balloons."

Ben might have gone overboard. The living room resembled a child's birthday party due to the many streamers and balloons. A large bowl on the table was filled with fortune cookies. He had even bought party hats and cut the tip off of one, so it would fit Samson. Trying to put it on the cat had been a grave mistake. Quite a few treats were given in apology before Samson forgave him. And speaking of the little furball, that's who came rushing into the room.

"There's my special guy!" Jace said, picking up speed to reach him.

"Hold up!" Ben said. "I don't want you bending over."

"I'm fine."

"I know, you're doing great, but you're still healing. Here. Have a seat. He'll like that better anyway. Lap time!"

Jace went to the couch and slowly lowered himself. Samson didn't waste any time. He hopped right into Jace's lap, kneading his paws and purring loudly.

"I missed you," Jace said. Then his chin started to tremble. "I wasn't sure I would see him again."

That set Ben off too. He didn't bother trying to hide his tears. He had cried so much in the past week that he no longer found it embarrassing.

Jace made more of an effort to appear courageous. "Could I get a glass of water?"

"Sure."

Ben took his time in the kitchen, giving Jace the privacy

needed to work through his feelings. Much like Ben, he probably felt an overwhelming cocktail of emotions. For him personally, happiness was chief among them, because Jace was home again! Ben savored those words. It had been a close call, but things were slowly returning to how they were meant to be, and how he prayed they would always stay.

Loving someone meant caring for them. Ben had learned that early on in his romantic life. And later too, when one of them got the flu, or simply had a bad day and needed pampering. Jace's condition was completely different. His body had a lot to recover from, and not just physically. The emotional trauma was rough. They might need Allison's counselling skills to help deal with it. Nearly losing each other had been terrifying, but it also was a blessing. You didn't know what you had until it was gone. Ben now had the benefit of knowing without losing. That made it easier to overcome the rest.

The physical side effects bothered him the least. Jace was always tired. He would often sleep through breakfast and have to be woken for lunch. Rare was the night that he wasn't asleep again before nine. The sensitivity to sound and light was an ongoing issue, but from what he understood, this was fairly common. It still caused some stress though, like the time Ben was feeling happy and singing, and Jace had responded by glaring openly.

That just left the personality differences. Jace wasn't quite the same person. That was proven the first week in, when Ben had decided to prepare a special treat. Jace was on the couch, surrounded by pillows and blankets. Samson was always on his lap or sitting nearby, having concluded that one nurse wasn't enough.

"Your mom told me about her tomato soup," Ben said, standing not far away and drying a bowl with a dishrag.

"The homemade kind?" Jace asked, a longing in his voice.

Ben nodded. "Yup! She would only make it when you were sick, right?"

"Or if I had a rough day at school." Jace grinned. "Don't tell her this, but I once faked a fight, just so she would make her soup for me."

"How do you fake something like that?"

"By asking your sister to give you a black eye." Jace shook his head at the memory. "Anyone who says 'you hit like a girl' as an insult hasn't actually been hit by a girl. It hurt! Totally worth it though."

Ben thought about Karen hitting him and was certain he would've hit back. "I bet you could use some of that soup now."

Jace laughed. "I see where you're going with this. I don't know the recipe. No one does. She refuses to share it with anyone."

Ben looked smug. "Anyone but me."

"No!"

"Oh yes! Hungry?"

"I am now!"

"Then I'll get started." He returned to the kitchen with a spring in his step. Lately he felt desperate to show his affection to Jace by any means possible. Ben owed Mrs. Holden a lot of gratitude for giving him a new way of doing so. He just hoped his cooking skills didn't fail him. Again.

The process involved pan roasting onions, garlic, and bell peppers. Fresh produce only. Even the tomatoes. The recipe included some surprising components like mango and goat cheese. All of this, when ready, went into the blender in portions so the texture would be smooth. And maybe to hide the ingredients from prying eyes. Ben was blending the first batch when Jace stormed into the room.

"Turn that off!" he shouted, his face twisted up with rage.

Ben moved his finger away, but didn't think to hit the off button. He was too confused—and shocked—by Jace's demeanor.

"I said off!" Jace yelled, rushing forward to do it himself.

Ben stepped back and watched as Jace grabbed the pitcher off the blender with his left hand, but of course this didn't stop it. The motor kept whirring. Loudly. He was having his sound sensitivity issue again, but it must have been really bad for it to bother him from a different room. Jace jabbed ineffectively at the blender with his free hand. Then it got really bad. Frustrated with his lack of success, Jace tried to set the pitcher on the counter but his fingers didn't unclench. Another side effect they were still working on. Unfortunately this meant—when he pulled his hand away, expecting it to be empty—that the pitcher tilted dangerously. The lid came off and hot soup sloshed everywhere.

Jace growled in frustration and ripped the electrical cord from the wall.

The room was silent except for the drip drip drip of soup hitting the floor. Jace turned to him, grimacing in pain. Or in regret. "I'm sorry," he began.

Ben didn't let him get any further than that. "It's fine! Really." He hurried forward to help free the pitcher from Jace's fingers. "Breathe deep, like they taught you. Try to relax."

"I ruined everything," Jace said.

"Breathe deep," Ben repeated. "Are you okay? Did you burn yourself?"

"I'm fine," Jace said, his hand unclenching at last. He brought it to his mouth to lick off soup. "It's tastes amazing," he said despondently. "It was perfect and I screwed it up."

"No you didn't," Ben said. "That was just the first batch. There's still more."

"I'll help clean up and—"

"Why don't you go lay down? I'll take care of the rest. Please. I insist."

After a little more coaxing, he finally got Jace to leave the kitchen. Ben turned to face the mess, took a deep breath, and exhaled. Did he even know the man he was married to? He bit his bottom lip. Then he stood up straight and squared his jaw. Hell yes, he did! He might be seeing a side that Jace had previously kept under control, but it was still part of him and didn't change Ben's feelings one bit. He grabbed the paper towels and went to work. When he was ready to blend again, he took it outside and used one of the electrical outlets there. If that was still an issue, he would start going over to the neighbor's place whenever he needed to do loud things.

Twenty minutes later and he had two steaming bowls of soup on a serving tray along with buttered toast. He brought these to the living room where Jace still looked miserable, a question on his lips.

"I didn't hurt you?" he asked. "You didn't get burnt?"

"I'm fine!" Ben said with a smile. "I can't wait to eat this soup. After tasting it, I think it's worth two black eyes!"

This seemed to make Jace feel a little better. His expression was one of pure ecstasy during his first few bites. Toward the end of the meal is when he got morose again.

"I was thinking we should hire someone to help," Jace said. "I'm useless right now, and I can't expect you to do everything."

"I don't mind," Ben assured him. "At all." They couldn't afford a nurse anyway. Banking was another responsibility that Ben had taken over. They were always tight on money, but the hospital bills they faced were especially intimidating. With Jace not working at all and Ben taking so much time off... They would make it work somehow.

"I don't want this to be your life," Jace said. "I'm going to get better. It's just harder than I thought it would be. I promise I won't always be this way."

"I don't care if you are!" Ben said. "Are you kidding me? After everything I've put you through? All my juvenile temper tantrums when I didn't get to see you enough, all the times I came crying to you because I was sick of studying and clueless about what I wanted to do with my future. Or how about a certain ex-boyfriend. What was his name again?"

"No idea," Jace said, a little humor returning to his voice. "I think the aneurysm wiped that part from my memory."

"Well lucky you, because I made some really stupid mistakes. All of them were my fault. What happened to you isn't your doing, so don't feel bad." Ben set his bowl on the coffee table and leaned over, snuggling up to one of Jace's arms. "All you've done since we've met is guide and take care of me. It's about time I gave a little back. I hope for your sake that all these side effects go away, but if they don't, I'll still be here." He fought down tears so he could continue speaking. "Getting to be your husband is a privilege. Do you know that? I still feel like the luckiest guy in the world."

Jace reached over to place a hand on his cheek. Despite all they had been through, it still felt just as reassuring as it always had.

"Mr. Holden!" the surgeon said as he entered the examination room. "You must have really enjoyed our hospitality or you wouldn't be back so soon!"

Jace smiled. "Believe it or not, I only came back for a nap. The bed was surprisingly comfortable."

Dr. Nichols looked up from his clipboard "Really? You might want to get a new mattress at home, because you're the first person to ever say that. Next you'll be telling me the food was good too."

Jace looked to Ben and pressed his lips together, as if holding back. Ben thwacked him playfully and didn't take it personally. He was too pleased that Jace was doing so well. He was no longer confined to the house. Jace now insisted on tagging along on trips to the grocery store, or just the other day, he had mowed the lawn by himself. That nearly gave Ben a heart attack, but Jace managed fine. Ben had even returned to working his usual hours, and not once had he come home to a disaster. Things were looking up, and this follow-up appointment would hopefully give them more good news. Then, later in the week, it was off to the Ozarks to celebrate. Ben's parents had bought them flights and paid for a cabin, so they could unwind together and visit Jace's family, who lived in Missouri.

"Let's take a look," Dr. Nichols said, going to the computer in one corner and clicking to bring up a scan of Jace's brain. "I lost a pair of scissors around the time of your operation. They're either floating around inside of you or the woman who has an appointment tomorrow morning. Anyone want to place a bet?"

They laughed and waited. And waited. The doctor wasn't cracking jokes anymore as he scrolled through image after image of Jace's brain. This seemed to go on forever as he zoomed in and out, taking notes. Then he finally turned around in his chair.

"Let's start with the good news. I'm really pleased with how the first aneurysm is healing. Especially in such a short amount of—"

"First aneurysm?" Jace asked.

Dr. Nichols sighed. "My wife diagnosed me with foot-in-mouth syndrome. I think she's right. Listen, before you panic, I want you to know that this isn't an emergency. The contrast picked up two other aneurysms we didn't see before, but they aren't as large, nor do they seem ready to rupture. This isn't unusual. Your family history includes aneurysms, so the likeliness of reoccurrence is higher, and in a non-emergency situation, easier to deal with. We'll need to schedule an appointment to have them coiled—"

"We can do it today," Ben said. He looked to Jace with an apologetic expression, since this was his decision, and said, "Sooner the better, right?"

Jace nodded. "Right."

"Soon," the doctor assured them. "I still see signs of trauma that I would like you to recover from first. You're continuing to have short-term memory issues?"

Jace nodded, for once managing to stay calm as they went over the difficulties he struggled with. Ben was barely able to make it through this without interrupting. Finally he had his chance to speak again.

"I know there might be complications, and that he needs to heal, but isn't his life at risk? Isn't that more important?"

"When operating on an unruptured aneurysm, the mortality rate is less than one percent. Let's go over your concerns one by one and address them."

The doctor did a great job of answering their questions, but those concerns were logical. What remained unsatisfied were Ben's emotions. He had already experienced what it was like to nearly lose the love of his life. He didn't want to do so again, but he supposed this was the price he paid. Jace had become the most important person in his world. Ben would always fear losing him, if not to a medical condition then a freak accident, or violence, or any other nightmare scenario. Now he understood why Rapunzel had been locked in a tower. Someone must have loved her with all their heart.

The ducks snapped up the bread greedily, occasionally bickering with each other and trying to steal more than their share. For Ben and Jace this was a game as they tried to ensure that every duck received its fair portion. Sitting cross-legged on the dock, they were benevolent judges, casting torn bread to the meeker ducks in the back and refusing those who behaved too aggressively.

The lakeside cabin had been intended as a gift from Ben's parents to celebrate Jace's graduation from six weeks of physical therapy. At the time, no one had realized that he and Jace would have other matters they needed to escape from. The unruptured aneurysms had caused a lot of tension between them, especially since Jace's self-assured calmness had all but disappeared. In the past, when Ben's emotions got the better of him, Jace was the one who kept his cool and de-escalated the situation. Ben found himself having to play the reverse role lately, since Jace was now the one to snap and snarl. They were only human. On bad days they got into shouting matches, but the serene environment surrounding this trip had helped.

"I'd like to go back to work again," Jace said, tossing a chunk of bread to a duck brave enough to come onto the dock.

"You will eventually."

"Not if I can't remember safety procedures, or what drink someone ordered." Jace frowned. "And not before the next surgery."

"I'm just glad to finally have you home so often," Ben said, placing a hand over his. "If that means I'm married to an invalid—well, I'm willing to pay that price."

Jace smiled and pulled him closer. "I'm not an invalid, you brat! Maybe I can get a job at one of the check-in counters. Lifting luggage would be good physical therapy and the computer wouldn't share my memory problems. Unless it's low on RAM."

"Stop talking about work, you jerk! I'm trying to have a romantic moment here."

"And I'm dreaming of a better future," Jace said. "For both of us. It'll be some time before I'm able to go on international routes again. Or domestic. So even when I do go back to work, I'll still be home more often than I used to."

"Good," Ben said. "I'll take any silver linings I can get."

"We should talk," Jace said, his tone serious. "Just in case."

"Nope," Ben said, shaking his head and reaching for another slice of bread. "I'm not interested in worst-case scenarios. Nothing you can say could prepare me for that, or make me feel better."

Jace exhaled. "Okay. We don't have to take it that far, but assuming the surgery is a success and the aneurysms are no longer an issue, I might not be the same person. I'm already different."

Ben tore up the bread as fast as possible and tossed it into the lake. Then he grabbed Jace's hand and turned it over to examine the palm. "Let's see... The fingerprints look the same. It might surprise you to learn than I have them memorized. That's just how obsessed I am with you. Oh! And look! There's the wedding ring belonging to my husband. I've never seen anyone else wear it, so you must be the same guy."

Jace smiled at him warmly and gave him a peck on the lips. "Seriously. The issues I have might become worse. The anger—"

"Is kind of hot," Ben interrupted. "Truth be told, the memory problems are pretty funny at times too. I hate that you struggle with sound and light, but only because I don't want you to be in pain. From what I've read, most people lose those symptoms after a while. So I'm not worried about who you'll be."

"Okay," Jace said. "Just be prepared. All right? Be prepared, even for the worst."

Ben shook his head. "I don't have to, because I wouldn't live through that."

"You would," Jace said. "You have a brave heart. You always have. You can handle this."

Ben clenched his jaw, refusing to even entertain the thought. Instead he reached into the bag of bread for two more slices. "And you can handle this. We've got hungry customers to feed."

They doled out bread to the audience of ducks. What a simple joy this was! The perfect kind that truly didn't come at a price. Just a couple of bucks at the grocery store. Few things in life were so pure and mutually beneficial. Ben could only think of one other.

Loving Jace.

"Come here."

Ben looked up from his script. Jace was standing there, a hand held out to him.

"Come to bed with me."

"We just got up," Ben said, checking his watch.

"Come."

Ben took his hand and followed. He understood what this was about. The next surgery was only a few days away. They were both tense. Jace had lost his temper a few times just the other day. Nothing major, but even after all he had been through, he still treated the smallest amount of anger like an unpardonable transgression.

"We're okay," Ben assured him as he sat on the bed. Samson blinked at them sleepily before continuing his nap.

"No, we're not," Jace said. He wouldn't let go of Ben's hand. Instead he pulled him down, wrapping Ben's arm tightly around himself so they were pressed together. That was unusual. Normally it was Jace who held him.

"What's going on?" Ben asked. He could feel a heart thudding against his arm.

"My head hurts." Jace swallowed back tears. "Just like last time."

Ben tried to get up but Jace wouldn't release him.

"Just stay with me," Jace pleaded. "It was a miracle I made it last time. I'm not going to again."

"You don't know that!" Ben argued.

"You know the statistics as well as I do."

Only fifty percent of people survive a ruptured aneurysm. Of those only another fifty percent survive the emergency surgery, and the chance of making a full recovery without complications was even slimmer. Ben had repeated those facts in his head over and over again. He could only imagine how often Jace had too.

"Please," Jace said, his voice raspy. "I don't want us to argue, not now, and I don't want to die in a hospital."

"Jace."

"Please do this for me. I love you, Ben."

He couldn't. Nothing in the world was powerful enough to force him to. He would rather burn the world to the ground than let that happen. Even if Jace ended up hating him, it was better than letting him fade away.

"Please," Jace said again, the word a gentle whisper. And with that Ben was proven wrong. He could do this out of love, even though he knew it would destroy him in the process. He didn't care. Without his soulmate, there wouldn't be anything worth living for.

"Are you sure?"

"Thank you," Jace said, clutching his arm closer. "This is all I've ever wanted, being with you."

"I never deserved you," Ben said, body shaking with tears, but he forced himself to calm down. For Jace. He wanted this moment to be perfect for him. "I love you anyway. More than I've ever loved anyone. You know that? No one ever came close to how I feel about you."

Ben held him and kissed him, and told him a hundred times how much he was loved. He didn't stop, even when Jace's breath became ragged. He held him until his body ached with discomfort and his stomach grumbled with hunger, long after

Jace had stopped breathing. When the last of the light had left the room, Ben took Samson and shut the door behind him.

That the sun still rose the next morning was incredibly unjust. Someone good had died. People still woke up, had breakfast, went to work, and it was wrong. Flower petals still opened in the sun's early light, and animals still grazed the day away, their minds untroubled. Someone good had died and the world had the audacity to move on.

Ben refused to. He no longer ate, and when he drank it wasn't to give his body nutrition. He didn't read, he didn't watch TV, he didn't entertain himself. He didn't work, shower, or clean the house. The only task he allowed himself was making the necessary arrangements for Jace's body, and even that was quickly taken over by Allison when she discovered the state he was in.

Ben knew he would die of a broken heart long before the funeral. If he didn't, he would find another way to be with Jace again, no matter how extreme. Ben had never given much thought to the afterlife, but now it was his obsession. If he could get there, they could be reunited.

Three days after Jace's death, Ben realized he hadn't fed Samson. Everything had been forgotten in his grief, but the cat's yowling could no longer be ignored. Ben wavered uncertainly before opening the can of cat food. What was to become of Samson? Who would take care of him after Ben was gone? Someone would, surely, but what if he was unwanted or mistreated? Jace had loved Samson more than anything and wouldn't want to see him with strangers. What was Ben going to do, kill the cat before he killed himself?

Samson began meowing desperately as Ben tried to make up his mind. The cat had been aloof and unhappy the last couple of days, but obviously he still wanted to eat. Ben opened the can, his mouth watering at the smell. Hunger hit him hard, causing his stomach to cramp and his head to swim. He scooped the food out onto a plate on the floor before opening the cupboard and grabbing a loaf of white bread.

Ben shoved a piece into his mouth. The flavor was exquisite. After seventy-two hours of not eating, the spongy slice was a meal fit for a king. Ben didn't think about what he had done until he swallowed. He, like the rest of the world, had decided to go on, and the thought made him cry.

He promised himself to never stop hurting, to never let the pain leave him. Ben would ache inside and out, just as much as he did today, never letting it fade. He would never allow anyone to believe he was okay. Time would never heal his wounds. More than anything, Ben promised himself he would never love again.

PART FOUR

AUSTIN, TEXAS
2008

EPILOGUE

The doorbell rang again, sounding more mechanically grumpy than it had the first two times.

"I'm coming, I'm coming!"

Ben stumbled for the door, kicking off the shoe that he had been putting on. He expected a late-night package delivery or someone handing out religious pamphlets as he opened the door. Instead he found an elegant woman wearing a black sequined dress and a hairstyle complex enough to puzzle M.C. Escher.

"How do I look?" Allison said, gesturing over her body like a showroom girl selling herself.

"Fabulous, but since when do you ring the doorbell?" Ben asked. "The door wasn't locked and you have a key anyway."

"We have to conduct ourselves properly," Allison said in her best British accent as she glided into the house. "We *are* on a date, you know."

"I still need to get my shoes on and check my hair." Ben found one shoe in the hall before searching the living room for the other. "Jesus you look good," he said, eyeing Allison as he tied his laces. "I think I might be underdressed."

"Hmm," Allison considered him over eyelashes that were longer than they had been the day before. "Do you still have that grey sports jacket?"

"I think it's clean, yeah. But grey with a pink dress shirt? Isn't that kind of eighties?"

"You can pull it off, and there will be more colorfully dressed people where we're going."

"I wish you would tell me where that is," Ben complained.

"But that would ruin our secret romantic mystery date!"

"Stop calling it that," Ben scolded.

"I need this date!" Allison pouted. "They never seem to happen when you're married."

"Take that up with Brian," Ben said as he ducked into the bedroom to find his jacket.

"You could use a date too, you know," Allison said when he returned. "It's been two years," she added as delicately as possible.

Ben shrugged on his jacket, trying to make it sit right on his shoulders. He stopped suddenly and fixed Allison with a stare. "That's not what you're doing, is it?"

"What?" Allison asked a bit too casually.

"No," Ben said, beginning to take the jacket off. "Forget it then."

Allison rolled her eyes. "I'm not fixing you up with anyone."

"No blind date?"

"Not blind, deaf, amputated, or anything else. It's just me and you going out for a night on the town. Promise."

Ben eyed her a moment longer before feeling satisfied. He glanced over at the framed photo of Jace on the end table. The full-length shot showed Jace sharply dressed in his flight attendant uniform, every detail immaculate from the white starched collar down to his pointed shoes.

Ben smiled. He had grown tired of Jace's name being synonymous with sorrow. No longer would he tarnish his memory. Jace had gone out of his way to make him happy and it wouldn't please him to see Ben moping around. The memories they had made together were all that was left, and these days Ben tried his best to find joy in them.

"Ready?" Allison prompted.

"Yup."

The roles were a bit reversed for a traditional date. Not only was Allison driving, but she was also paying. Ben had been happy to oblige since he was perpetually strapped for cash these days. A meal out anywhere was appreciated, but he was nevertheless taken aback by her choice of dining establishment.

The restaurant was supposed to be Cajun, but how Mexican food and karaoke factored into that was beyond comprehension. Ben and Allison were severely overdressed considering the rowdy vibe of the dining room, but he was at least glad not to see any romantic hopefuls waiting at their table. Knowing Allison, she had only chosen this dive so they could sing together, which was fine by him. They picked over their greasy meals before abandoning them for the stage, where they crooned a number of their favorite songs together.

They continued singing in the car on the way to their next destination. Ben suspected they were going to hit a few clubs, but Allison drove them downtown to Second Street. She found a free parking spot, acting as if she had just won the lottery. Ben had to chuckle, envying her enthusiasm. They walked together for a few blocks until they approached an art gallery where people wandered in and out.

"This is why we needed the fancy duds?" Ben asked.

"Mm-hm." Allison nodded. "Piece of gum?"

Ben accepted it from her with suspicion. "No blind dates?" he asked again.

Allison smiled broadly, and Ben knew it was too late. He took the gum anyway. Ben scanned the people standing outside the gallery, looking for someone who seemed particularly expectant or nervous. He didn't spot anyone.

"We're here to look at the art," Allison said innocently.

Ben glanced through the nearest window and away again before doing a double take. The painting on the nearest wall was of a bulldog, bounding through a canvas glowing with iridescent colors. Emotion raced through his system, centered in his chest and nestled there comfortably, glad to be home again after so many years.

"Want to go inside?" Allison asked gently.

"I don't know if I can handle this," Ben confessed.

"I'll sort of make you anyway," Allison whispered.

"Okay." Ben laughed nervously. "Is he— No, don't tell me. Let's just look at the art."

They browsed the gallery, Ben trying to focus on only the paintings, but his head whipped around every few seconds in an attempt to spot the artist. He recognized some of the paintings from their younger days. Others he had never seen before, pieces from a life that he hadn't been a part of. One was beyond simple, a finger-painted frog on a box of some sort, that caused Ben to laugh despite his nervousness. And then there was the portrait of Eric, completed now and glorious in its beauty. A small crowd of admirers surrounded it.

The teeth-grinding sound of microphone reverb cut through the gallery. "Is this thing on? Whoa! Too loud. Sorry."

Ben practically ran toward the sound of that voice. The rest of the gallery moved with him, clogging halls and frustrating his attempts to get there first. By the time he reached the main room, it was already half-full. Ben stood on his toes, straining to see past the people in front of him. The old man just ahead moved to join his wife before a portly lady scooted to the side, perhaps sensing the laser beams shooting from Ben's eyes.

And there he was. Tim Wyman. He looked fantastic. The pudginess was gone from his belly, the tight dress shirt revealing the all-too-perfect physique that Tim had before meeting Ryan. His jet black hair had grown out some and was styled messily around silver eyes that no longer looked tired. Instead they shone with a light that Ben had only seen in their most private of moments. Those eyes were searching the crowd, but before they found Ben, the portly woman had shifted back, obscuring him from view.

"Uh, I'm really glad you all decided to be here," Tim began. "I'm not really good at speeches, so bear with me."

The audience laughed. Ben began working around to the side of the crowd, hunting for a way through to the front.

"The art you see here is about twenty years in the making. I'm sure most of you have seen my crowning achievement, 'Frog Goes Sailing on Boat'?"

The audience laughed again.

"That's from when I was eight and is the first painting I ever did."

Ben had finally broken through to the front, but was so far to the side that he was beyond Tim's peripheral vision. At least he could see him now, nervously shifting from foot to foot while mumbling into the microphone.

"I owe this art to a lot of people. The subjects in each piece, of course. My dog Chinchilla, or Eric, who was a father, a hero, and much more to me. Even strangers, like the old woman I saw lying in the grass at the park, staring up at the clouds and giggling like a little girl at what she saw there." Tim paused, searching the crowd again. "So many people have inspired me, but only one gave me the courage to show what I had painted to other people. I hope he's here somewhere tonight, and as I finish this clumsy speech, I'd like you all to clap for him, not for me. Thank you, most of all, to Benjamin Bentley."

The audience burst into applause. Ben blushed, even though he was effectively incognito. Tim turned off the mic and gave a little bow. People slowly began to disperse. Some remained behind to talk to the artist. Ben watched them with envy—how easily they could walk up to Tim without being overwhelmed by a decade's worth of feelings.

Tim chatted politely, shook hands, listened, nodded, and all the other gestures a gracious host was supposed to make. Occasionally he would risk glancing away to search the room, looking slightly more disappointed with each failure. Nerves buzzing, Ben walked to the center of the room where he could easily be seen.

Tim nodded, said goodbye to an elderly gentleman, and tried again. This time he found Ben, and without the slightest reservation, ran to him and scooped him up into his arms.

"I'm so glad you're here!" Tim said, spinning Ben around a few times before setting him down again. "And even more glad that you're late! I just gave the most embarrassing speech!"

"I thought it was really good," Ben said, grinning when Tim turned bright red.

"I thought for a second that Allison had changed her mind."

"Where is she anyway?" Ben asked.

"Running an errand for me," Tim said enigmatically. "Hey, have you seen much of the paintings?"

"A little," Ben replied, "but a tour from the artist himself would be appreciated."

Tim guided him around the gallery, zigzagging from room to room and moving in a counterintuitive fashion. One painting would remind him of another, causing him to drag Ben off in a completely different direction.

Seeing Tim so enthusiastic about his work was amazing. He wasn't shy at all in front of the large number of people examining his art and listening in on his explanations. Occasionally a bystander would ask a question, which Tim would answer with gusto. This was a stark contrast to the self-deprecating artist who had once kept his paintings locked away in a garage.

"There's one more piece I'd like to show you," Tim said. "Something really special to me."

Ben was led through the gallery to a room not intended for the public and out a door to the parking lot. Spotting which car belonged to Tim was easy enough. It was the newest shiniest one.

"Have any idea what sort of car this is?" Tim asked as he opened a door for Ben.

"Nope."

"Care to know?"

"Not really."

Tim chuckled. "It's a Bentley. I figured it was the next best thing to the real deal."

Ben tried to roll his eyes but ended up smiling instead.

As they began to drive, Ben started to feel concerned. As happy as he was to see Tim again and as irrefutable as his feelings for him were, Ben was still married, even if only to a ghost in his heart. Going home with Tim tonight didn't feel right. It was all too soon, if there would ever be a right time at all. He was about to ask to be taken back to the gallery when the car turned into Ben's subdivision.

"Don't tell me you bought a house next to mine too."

"Now there's an idea," Tim said, parking in the driveway. "Wish I would have thought of that myself."

"Then what are we doing here?"

"I wanted to show you a special painting of mine."

"You mean the one you gave me for my birthday," Ben said, catching on. He couldn't help but swoon a little at the romantic notion. "You can't have it back you know," he said in mock seriousness.

Tim merely smiled and stepped out of the car. "After you."

Ben led the way to the living room and turned on the light. Samson woke up from his favorite place on the couch and blinked at them. He was getting on in years and was a bit raggedy, but he still had a lot of spunk. Ben felt a momentary surge of guilt and looked over at Jace's photo in its frame. Perhaps this was a bad idea after all.

"Jace—" Ben began.

"—was a good man," Tim continued for him. "The best, in fact. I would never dishonor his memory and I will never *ever* be able to replace him. No one could."

Samson meowed, jumped off the couch, and went straight to Tim. He rubbed up against him affectionately before doing the same to Ben. He looked at the pair of them, purred, and hopped back on the couch to continue his nap.

Maybe it would be okay.

Ben turned to point out the painting, but it wasn't there.

Something new hung in its place. In a way, it was the very same piece of art that Tim had given him all those years ago but realized in his new style. Instead of two hearts, there were now two hands clutching at each other. One was strong with thick fingers, the digits of the other thin and fair. Ben raised his own hand in amazement. Tim had captured its likeness perfectly.

The hands were bathed in radiant light, incorporating the same colors of the old painting. This was a message perfected, an expression of what Tim felt for Ben, but this time unhindered by fear and free of uncertainty. Ben stared at it, feeling as though he had finally heard the words from Tim that he had so longed for.

Tim reached over and took Ben's hand, positioning it in his own so that they matched the painting. "I love you, Benjamin Bentley," he said. "I should have told you that twelve years ago. I've always loved you."

All his doubts, every fear, even the smallest insecurity inside of Ben gave way to the unstoppable, immutable, uncompromising force that is love.

"What now?" Ben asked.

"Now we start over."

Tim leaned forward for a kiss, eyes dancing with hope and affection. Ben regarded him for a moment, seeing only the cocky teenager he had once dared to love, even though it had always been against the odds. Then Ben closed his eyes and leaned forward.

And so they began again.

AUTHOR'S NOTE

Dear Reader,

You are powerful! Reviews and word-of-mouth are what truly make a book successful, and I need your help more than ever. I'm an independent author, which means I don't have the backing of a publisher. That's by choice. My stories are unabashedly queer. I don't want to compromise my vision in the name of marketability. Providing you with an authentic experience is too important to me, especially as a gay man who writes from the heart. So if you enjoyed spending time with Ben, Tim, and Jace, please consider writing a review, sharing a link to the book on social media, or contacting a friend to express your excitement. You can also become a patron to the arts by joining me on Patreon where I offer exclusive content. Thank you for the support (and exceptional good taste) you've already shown by purchasing this book!

With love,

-Jay Bell

FOREWORD FOR SOMETHING LIKE MARRIAGE

You're about to read an incredibly short story that might seem a little random, so please allow me to explain. Some time back, I was on the verge on mailing out the Kickstarter rewards for the second volume of *Something Like Summer* comics. Not everyone who reads the comic is familiar with the books, so I thought it would be clever to send them a little sample. A short story that didn't require much knowledge of the sprawling continuity of the series. Returning to Ben and Tim's teenage years seemed the safest bet. The biggest challenge was to write a story that would fit on both sides of a single piece of printer paper. The end result is brief, and I'm not sure how it will feel as a follow-up to the actual novel. Maybe it's a perfect fit, since it allows us to see Ben and Tim loving each other with the same dizzying intensity that they always used to. We can only hope more of that is in store for them both. Anyway, I thought the hardcover edition of this book was a good place for *Something Like Marriage* to take its place amongst the rest of the series. I hope you enjoy this little trip back in time!

-Jay Bell

SOMETHING LIKE MARRIAGE

BY JAY BELL

THE WOODLANDS, TEXAS
1997

Ben was already grinning as he threw open the front door. His smile widened when he saw his boyfriend standing there, casually looking over his shoulder as if he didn't really care whether or not anyone answered. So cool! Or more accurately, super paranoid, since Tim was probably worried about someone from high school seeing him here. Forget all that real-life stuff though. Ben had already decided that this weekend was about making his wildest dreams come true.

"I have a surprise for you," Ben said after ushering his boyfriend inside and closing the door, sealing them off from the rest of the world. "My parents are out of town."

Tim glanced around. "Really?"

"Yeah! Exciting isn't it?"

"It's great," Tim said after a smooch, "but nothing new. My parents leave town all the time."

"Well sure," Ben said. "But that's *your* house. It doesn't feel like home. Not to me."

"Me neither," Tim guffawed. "So what's the deal? We're playing house?"

"Exactly!"

"In that case," Tim murmured as he moved closer. "I've got a surprise for you too. Wanna guess how big it is?"

"I don't need to," Ben replied. "You made me measure it last week."

"Only because you said that we're the same length. And what were the results?"

"We're *almost* the same length," Ben said through gritted teeth.

"That's right. And I'm pretty sure I've grown since then. Where's the ruler?"

Ben rolled his eyes. "We'll take care of that later. And we won't even have to worry about my parents overhearing us. Speaking of which, come upstairs to my room."

"So much for later," Tim said. The cocky grin slid off his face when they entered the bedroom. Books and other random stuff covered the mattress, which had already been stripped of its sheets. There wasn't enough free space left for them to have any fun. "Uhh…"

"I need your help." Ben put on his best doe eyes. "I want to rearrange my room."

"Really? Your parents are out of town and that's your masterplan?" Tim shook his head. "It amazes me that you aren't more popular."

"Blame yourself. The headboard keeps hitting the wall, as you know, so I thought we'd move the bed over there, and the shelves over here…"

Ben described what needed to happen, and before long, Tim was lugging stacks of books to the other side of the room, his muscles already bulging, and when it came time to move the actual furniture, it resulted in half an hour of nonstop flexing.

"Whew!" Tim said, shaking his arms loose when they were finished. "Not a bad workout. Now how about you put some sheets on the bed? Or not. I don't really care."

"One more favor," Ben said, batting his eyelashes. "I promised my parents I would mow the lawn. Would you mind doing it for me? I'll get everything set up here in the meantime."

"Can't it wait?"

"They come home tomorrow and I don't want to worry about it anymore."

"All right," Tim said as he stretched. "Let's do this."

Ben hurriedly made the bed and then went downstairs to peer out the window. Tim was jogging back and forth across the yard while pushing the lawn mower, trying to get the job done as quickly as possible. That was fine with Ben. Twenty minutes later, Tim walked through the door that led out to the garage, accompanied by the scent of freshly cut grass.

"What the hell?" he complained. "Is the air conditioner broken?"

"Maybe I switched it off by accident," Ben said innocently. "Did you work up an appetite?"

"Well yeah," Tim said, strutting over to him.

Ben pressed his hand against a damp T-shirt to stop him. "That's not what I meant. I'm going to make potato salad and corn on the cob. All you need to do is grill the steaks I bought."

"Steaks?"

"Yup!" Ben opened the refrigerator to show him, Tim looking as if he wanted to crawl into the cool interior. "Do you mind? The charcoal and everything else you'll need is out back."

Tim sighed and shook his head. "The things I do for you. And uh… the things you do for me. Right? There's going to be payoff for all this?"

"Later," Ben promised.

He waited until Tim was outside before taking out the potato salad he prepared earlier. Then he snuck over to the windows and watched as Tim stood in front of the grill while poking at hot charcoal. He kept wiping the sweat off his forehead and glaring up at the sun. By the time Ben brought him the steaks, Tim had stripped off his shirt, his brown muscles glistening.

"Please tell me you turned the air on again," he said.

"Yes," Ben confirmed on his way back inside. "Hurry up. I can't wait much longer."

He didn't mean the food. As soon as Tim returned indoors with a tray of sizzling meat, Ben took the steaks from him and set them on the counter. He watched as his boyfriend plopped down in one of the dining room chairs, his arms hanging loose and his legs spread wide in an effort to cool off. He certainly looked hot! His tanned chest was covered with a sheen of perspiration, and as Ben neared, a musky scent filled his nose that drove him wild. He sat down on Tim's lap while facing him and began kissing his lips ravenously.

"Where's dinner?" Tim asked when pulling away.

"I thought we'd start with dessert," Ben said, going in for more.

Tim reciprocated. Briefly. "Shouldn't I take a shower first?"

"No! I mean… You don't need to. I don't mind."

Tim dodged a kiss so he could study Ben's expression. "Oh,

I see. You *like* me this way, don't you? Mowing the lawn got me all sweaty, and the grill got me to take my shirt off."

"I don't have a clue as to what you're talking about."

"Uh-huh. And what was the real reason for moving your furniture around?"

"So my parents wouldn't hear us anymore. And um... Maybe because of these." Ben slid a palm down Tim's arm to squeeze the bicep.

"You wanted to get me all pumped up?" Tim grinned before flexing both arms for him. Then he flexed something else. "Mission successful. Although next time, we can do it twice in a row instead. That'll have the same effect."

"Sure, but then I wouldn't get to see my future husband in action."

Tim's eyes went wide. "You mean me?"

Ben shrugged, as if it didn't matter. "Or someone like you. This is just a test run, don't worry."

"I am worried," Tim said, wrapping his arms around him. "If some other guy is destined to take my place, I'm going to give him some serious competition. Did you make the bed?"

"Yes I did," Ben said before biting his bottom lip.

"What a waste of time." Tim tightened his grip and stood, lifting Ben up with him. "My future wife likes it right on the dining room table. Mind giving *that* a test run?"

"I'll see what I can do," Ben said breathlessly.

Soon he was clinging to Tim's torso, convinced that he was a natural homemaker, because if his future was anything like this, he'd be a very happy boy indeed.

———————

The story continues—

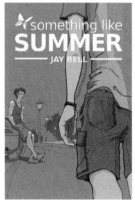 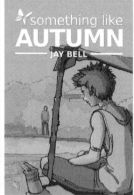 

—in the *Something Like…* series, each book written from a different character's perspective, the plots intertwining at key points while also venturing off in new directions. The quest for love takes many different forms, changing like the seasons. Which is your favorite?

Current books in the series:

#1: *Something Like Summer*
#2: *Something Like Autumn*
#3: *Something Like Winter*
#4: *Something Like Spring*
#5: *Something Like Lightning*
#6: *Something Like Thunder*
#7: *Something Like Stories – Volume One*
#8: *Something Like Hail*
#9: *Something Like Rain*
#10: *Something Like Stories – Volume Two*
#11 *Something Like Forever*
#12 *Something Like Stories – Volume Three*

Learn who each book is about and where to buy at:
www.somethinglikeseries.com

Also by Jay Bell
Something Like Autumn

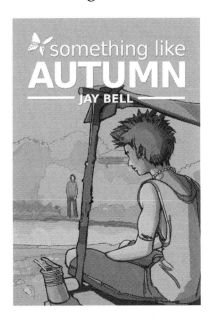

For some, a romantic relationship seems like an impossible dream.

Growing up as a gay teenager in small-town Missouri, Jace Holden is convinced he'll die single and alone. When he meets Victor—a wild spirit and fellow outsider—his chances of finding love go from hopeless to a very uncertain maybe. Bracing his heart, Jace chases after his desire anyway, all in the hope of making his biggest dream come true.

Something Like Autumn reveals the story of Jace's life before the events of Something Like Summer while also revisiting his endearing relationship with Benjamin Bentley.

For more information, please visit:
www.jaybellbooks.com

Also by Jay Bell
Something Like Winter

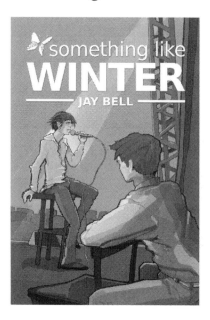

There are two sides to every story. When you're still in the closet, sometimes there are three.

Tim Wyman hoped moving to Texas would mean a new beginning, but he soon finds himself falling into the same old patterns. Until he meets recklessly brave Benjamin Bentley, who brings love and compassion to his world. Certain that society won't understand what he and Ben have together, Tim is determined to protect their relationship, even if it means twisting the truth. Buried beneath his own deceptions, Tim must claw his way to the surface in the hope of learning to fly.

Something Like Winter retells the story of *Something Like Summer* from Tim's perspective, offering previously unrevealed moments and personal journeys as he strives to become worthy of Ben's love.

For more information, please see:
www.jaybellbooks.com

Also by Jay Bell
Kamikaze Boys

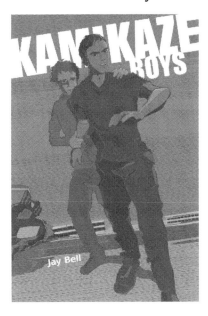

True love is worth fighting for.

Everyone at school says that Connor Williams is a dangerous psychopath, but when he rescues David Henry from the clutches of bullies, the two outsiders form an uneasy alliance that soon blossoms into more. The world isn't done messing with them though. David and Connor will have to fight to keep their love safe if they ever want to reach their happily-ever-after.

Kamikaze Boys, a Lambda Literary award-winning novel, is a sweet and emotional coming-of-age story about two young men who walk a perilous path in the hopes of saving each other.

Also by Jay Bell:
Straight Boy

From the author of
Something Like Summer

JAY BELL

STRAIGHT

BOY

I love him. And I'm pretty sure he loves me back... even though he's straight.

When I first met Carter King, I knew he was something special. I imagined us being together, and we are, but only as friends. Best friends! I'm trying to be cool with that, even though I know he has secrets, and there have definitely been mixed signals. I don't want a crush to ruin what we already have. Then again, if there's any chance that we can be together, it's worth the risk, because Carter could be the love of my life. Or he might be the boy who breaks my heart.

Straight Boy is Jay Bell's emotional successor to his critically acclaimed *Something Like...* series. This full-length novel tells a story of friendship and love while exploring the blurry line that often divides the two.

Hear the story in their own words!

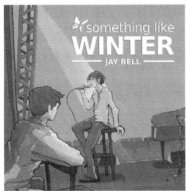

All of the *Something Like...* books are available on audio too! Listen to Tim's tale while you jog with him, or ignore your fellow airline passengers while experiencing Jace's story. Find out which books are available and listen to free chapters at the link below:

www.jaybellbooks.com

Who the hell is Jay Bell?

Jay Bell is a proud gay man and the award-winning author behind dozens of emotional and yet hopelessly optimistic stories. His best-selling book, *Something Like Summer*, spawned a series of heart-wrenching novels, a musically driven movie, and a lovingly drawn comic. When not crafting imaginary worlds, he occupies his free time with animals, art, action figures, and—most passionately—his husband Andreas. Jay is always dreaming up new stories about boys in love. If that sounds like your cup of tea, you can get the kettle boiling by visiting www.jaybellbooks.com.

Printed in Poland
by Amazon Fulfillment
Poland Sp. z o.o., Wrocław
16 July 2023

c82be2d2-9422-4a9e-89c2-ce8310402815R01